# THE
# COUNTDOWN
# CLUB

## Lucienne Diver

BellaRosaBooks

THE COUNTDOWN CLUB
ISBN 978-1-62268-145-7

First Printed: December 2018

Library of Congress Control Number: 2018964826

Also available as e-book: ISBN 978-1-62268-146-4

Book design by Bella Rosa Books

Printed in the United States of America on acid-free paper.

BellaRosaBooks and logo are trademarks of Bella Rosa Books

10    9    8    7    6    5    4    3    2    1

# Acknowledgements

When you kill off a computer between drafts and certain files (like the list of people you want to thank in your acknowledgements) don't survive, you live in terror that you'll forget someone who went out of their way to help you. I'm hoping and praying that I've caught everyone, but if not, please feel free to boot me in the behind the next time we see each other. You've earned it.

First, I need to thank my family, Peter and Abby Wheeler, because without them leaving me the heck alone when I need to write, this would never have been completed. Pete is an amazing sounding board, whose advice I seek out on a regular basis . . . and then promptly ignore to go off in another direction, because I'm ornery like that. And yet, our marriage survives. Abby puts up with endless questions about school and such and even, occasionally, will agree to read sections to make sure I've gotten things right.

Next, I want to thank Kevan Lyon for her awesome support and my critique partner Amy Christine Parker for her wonderful insights. Thanks to Debra Sandstrom Fleming and Kathleen Hennessy for listening to me blather on and then reading my books to boot! Huge shout out to Sarah Troiano for all of her support and for reading and commenting and always making my day. Also to my cousins Heather Ackerman and Angela Diver Clark, who I haven't seen in far too long, but who I appreciate so much.

And a big THANK YOU to Jana Oliver, Alyssa Breck, and Tina Bausinger for reading a tricky scene and helping me out with whether or not Jack was coming across as intended. (I hope so, because I came to love him so much it's ridiculous!)

Finally, a shout out to the YA Chicks who rock my world – Vivi Barnes, Christina Farley, Racquel Henry, Lynn Matson, and Amy Christine Parker. You go, girls!

# CHAPTER 1

RAYNA

*Six Days To Die.*

The note was handwritten in bold, angry lettering, the pen nearly slicing through the page and the "i" in Die dripping blood-red ink. It stared up at Rayna from just inside her backpack. Her breath caught, and she whipped her head around to catch anyone watching or aiming their phone to record the moment their sick joke hit home. Because it *had* to be a joke, right? Anyone who could get close enough to slip a note into her backpack without her noticing could surely have done worse.

But no one was looking or laughing.

She wanted to shrug it off. She wasn't the kind of girl who made waves. Or enemies. But the news was full of people bullied or beaten just for existing. Being different. Saying *no*.

*Six Days to Die.*

A chill ran straight up her spine, raising the hairs on the nape of her neck beneath her Kool-Aid blue ponytail. Her heart was pounding. Her breath was coming way too fast, and yet didn't seem to be bringing any oxygen with it. If she kept up like this, she was going to pass out. She needed to calm down.

Now that she thought about it, she'd left her backpack unattended at lunch while she ducked out to the ladies' room. Well, not *unattended* exactly. She'd asked Evan to keep an eye on it, but he wouldn't have taken that too seriously. Why would he? He could have gotten distracted talking or even . . . Evan was always pulling pranks. He could even have done this himself. If so, she was going to kill him. Literally. Today. Screw the six-day waiting period.

But her breathing didn't slow. There was no relief at a mystery solved. She knew in her heart Evan wouldn't do this. It was too mean-spirited. And on top of that, there was no pay-off. They didn't have fifth period together, so he'd never get to see her reaction.

But *no one* was paying any attention. Or if they were, they were damn good at hiding it. Just in case, maybe she should tear up the note to show how little it meant to her. To prove that she wasn't freaking out.

As soon as she could bring herself to touch it.

The bell rang and Ms. Ibrahim told them all to take out their textbooks and turn to chapter twelve. Still Rayna stared at the note. It was just a piece of paper. Probably harmless, but what if the note itself was the threat? It could be laced with poison or powder or something that would mess her up on contact. It would have to be a slow-acting poison to make her suffer for nearly a week. But wouldn't that be too unpredictable? How could the killer know it would take six days, no more, no less? And why give a warning so she could get a head start on a cure rather than wait, thinking she had the flu or something?

Unless there *was* no cure.

"Vanessa?" Ms. Ibrahim said sharply. "Something wrong?"

The other students all had their books out and were now staring at her. So much for playing it cool and unaffected.

"Uh, yeah. I mean no," Rayna said brilliantly. "Give me a second."

She took a deep breath, brushed the note aside with the tips of her fingers and grabbed her textbook, letting the breath out when nothing happened. She put the book on her desk, opened to the right chapter and stared down at it like she could focus on a single word. At least Ms. Ibrahim wasn't tormenting them with the rumored pop quiz. All Rayna could think about was the note and monitoring herself to make sure touching it hadn't been a fatal mistake. Was her breathing harder? Was her head starting to hurt? Was that fear or reality?

It took the whole period to assure herself that she was all right.


In the hallway between classes, Rayna felt eyes on her, but that could have been her imagination. It didn't have to be that she was caught in someone's crosshairs. It could be that she was visibly shaken enough to draw attention. Or just that there were so many kids crowding the halls that attention was unavoidable.

She jumped out of her skin when a hand landed on her shoulder. She whirled, hands up and fisted, ready to block a blow or throw one herself. She came face to face with Evan, who took a step back and threw his own arms up in defense.

"Hey, hey, it's just me! I give!"

She looked at her fisted hands and decided not to let them go to waste. She punched him in the shoulder a bit more than playfully. "That's for scaring me."

It felt so good, she did it again. Other shoulder this time.

"What was that one for?"

"You know," she said, glaring.

There were curses as people had to shove around them. They were stopping traffic, and there wasn't a lot of room for passing. Evan grabbed Rayna by the strap of her backpack and pulled her off to the side, up against a set of lockers.

"What the hell?" he asked. "What did I do?"

She could only see one of his eyes now—his ever-wild hair had fallen over the other—but there was confusion in it.

"The note," she said pointedly, forgetting she'd decided that it couldn't be him. It felt so good to have a target, an outlet for her fear.

"What note?"

Crap. It really wasn't him. He had no idea at all what she was talking about.

Silently, Rayna shrugged her backpack off one shoulder, unzipped it and reached for the note, still hating to touch it. She pulled it out with the barest touch of her fingertips and offered it to Evan, hoping she was right that it wasn't tainted.

He took the note gingerly and unfolded it along the single crease. The message hadn't changed.

*Six Days to Die.*

He stared blankly for a moment, then turned it over to see what, if anything, was on the other side. There was nothing.

He glanced back at Rayna, trying to get a grin going for her benefit, but she could see it was a struggle. "A death threat? Well, damn, girl, aren't you hot stuff? I thought if anyone was going to piss off someone to the point of violence, it would be me."

"The day's still young," she said, trying to match his cool. "You think it's for real then?"

Evan looked as serious as Rayna had ever seen him, and they'd been friends for a *long* time. He shook his hair out of his face; his crazy golden-green eyes blazed with an intensity that always sent a jolt through her.

"There's one way to find out," he said. "You know that group I'm part of? The one I told you about?"

"That forensics club?"

He nodded. "This is right up our alley. Let me take the note to them and see . . . well, whatever we can see."

He hadn't said she was overreacting.

She nodded, and Evan refolded the note carefully along the crease, not touching it any more than he had to, either to preserve prints or out of his own sense of caution. Then he slipped it into his own backpack.

"What do you think you and your friends can get from the note?" she asked, the knife edge of panic abating now that Evan shared her burden.

"You'd be amazed," he said, his eyes glinting.

Almost like he was enjoying this.

Then again, it *was* Evan. Brimming with character, too smart for school, with so few challenges that he jumped on anything to beat back the boredom. Mostly it was pranks or puzzles, but . . . That twinge of doubt sparked again. He wouldn't manufacture something like this to stir things up, would he?

No, she knew him too well for that. Not her Evan. Well, not *hers* exactly . . .

It could be one of her fellow art geeks, building toward some special project, a photo-collage of the Faces of Fear. Or it could be the teaser for some twisted performance piece. But in that case, she'd expect the presentation to be more dramatic or artistic, maybe. The stark threat and angry, uneven lettering spoke more of passion than presentation.

"See you later?" Evan asked, breaking across her thoughts.

"Later," she said, sounding more casual than she felt.

She jumped when the bell rang for the next period, and then Evan was off like a shot—too cool to run, but not for his long legs to eat up the distance anyway.

She tried to send her worries away with him.


JACK

*Shit, shit, shit.* He was going to be late. Again. He didn't give two craps about that, but if the school called home to report him as tardy or a skip, his father would use it as yet another excuse for a beating. Not that Dad ever needed an excuse.

But every beating got Jack closer to using the bug-out bag he'd been stuffing for the last nine months—stealing change left on the counter, hoping it wouldn't be missed, shaking down kids here and there for their lunch money, once even grabbing a twenty sitting out in the open on a teacher's desk. That had been risky, but the risk had paid off, and he'd certainly needed it more than Mr. Jorgenson.

He'd have bugged out already if it weren't for his little brother. Jack knew he'd do okay on the street by himself. He was tough and good-looking. Women wanted him. Not arrogance, just fact. Whether they thought he was older or just didn't care, he'd had enough eyelashes batted and phone numbers slipped to him that he had no delusions there. He was sure he could find a soft heart out there somewhere. Women loved a bad boy. But Eric . . . he couldn't leave him behind undefended, and he couldn't bring him along. His brother wouldn't do well out in the world. He needed medical treatment and health insurance and all kinds of things Jack couldn't give him.

So he stayed. And rushed to school, almost sure he could charm his homeroom teacher into not reporting him late. He wouldn't even have to make anything up, just tell her about caring for his sick brother. She'd eat it up.

He slowed to a fast walk in front of the school. Once in, he skipped his locker and went straight for homeroom, winking at Maria Sanchez as he slipped into his seat. As usual, she blushed and glanced away, gripping a book to her chest.

When Mrs. Plante called him to her desk, Jack gave a world-weary sigh and got ready to spin a tale about his tardiness. He knew he couldn't really tell her the truth about Eric. He couldn't risk anyone taking an interest in his home life. It was far too volatile.

Avoiding the tardy was pretty much the high point of his day. By the end of fifth period he was ready to cut and head home, check in on Eric and see how his treatment had gone, but he couldn't afford the skip, and anyway, Eric would be sleeping and Mom probably passed out in a drunken stupor by now, so it wouldn't do any good.

But maybe the day was looking up. Unless his eyes were playing tricks on him, that was Maria waiting at his locker. Or maybe she was waiting at her locker, which was right next to his, but she watched him as he approached. He had no idea why. Maria always treated him like the big bad wolf, though all he'd ever done was wink at her and offer a smile. He'd never huffed *or* puffed.

But the closer he got, the more clearly he could see her expression, and it wasn't welcoming.

"Hey," he said casually, like her stopping by was no big thing. Like he'd suspected it was only a matter of time before his charm brought her around.

"Did you do it?" she asked, arms crossed over her chest.

The accusation took him aback. "*It?*"

"The note I found last period," she prompted, body language protective, hugging herself, but braving it out, staring him in the face for answers. Whatever she was talking about had to be important to her.

"I don't know what you're talking about, but if it's from a secret admirer, I can do better." Damn, he hadn't meant to say that. He gave a smirk along with it, so she'd know it was just his usual flirting.

Her mouth twisted as if she tasted something bad.

"Nevermind," she said, and started to brush past him on her way out.

He grabbed her arm to halt her. She flinched and he eased up, even though he hadn't been rough in the first place. "Wait, what's going on?" he asked. "You're acting all . . . I don't know, weird."

"You don't know me," she said, shaking her arm out of his hold.

She was gone before he could say anything else stupid, like about how he'd like to know her.

He stared after Maria, thinking of all the ways things could have gone better. Then he shrugged it off. She wasn't for him anyway. Maria was a good girl. Quiet. Serious. Going places. Jack not so much. So he didn't understand why it hurt so much that she'd accuse him of . . . whatever it was she was all worked up about. A note? What was the big deal?

*Screw it.*

He changed out his books and got to sixth period with thirty seconds to spare, but then stopped cold at the sight of his desk. Sitting right there, dead center, was a piece of paper, folded in two. A note, clearly. A coincidence or had Maria left it?

One way to find out.

Jack plunked down in his seat, dropped his backpack to the floor and picked up the note, flicking it open.

*Twelve Days To Die.*

He glanced around to see whether anyone was watching and

caught Chase Benson's eyes. "Love note?" Chase asked, like he'd been waiting on the chance. Sure, he'd have seen the note when he came into class. He must have wondered.

"I wish," Jack answered.

Then he crumpled the note up in his fist. If someone had left it hoping to rattle him, he wasn't going to give them the satisfaction. He tossed it at the garbage can in the corner of the room, but missed so that it disappeared between the basket and the wall. Out of sight, out of mind. He hoped.

But his brain ticked away. Was *this* the kind of note Maria had gotten? If so, it was no wonder she was freaked.

Someone threatening him he could understand. Jack had made enemies. But *Maria* . . . what could she have done? He couldn't imagine a single thing, which meant some sicko was probably getting his kicks scaring people. He couldn't take it seriously. Anyway, he could handle anything some anonymous loser could dish out. Anyone too afraid to confront him in person didn't seem worth worrying about. For himself. For Maria . . .

No, she'd made it pretty clear she wasn't his problem. He had enough actual problems that he didn't need to go looking for more. He put the note out of his head.


INTERLUDE


*He watched from across the hall as Grace opened her locker. She turned at a friend's greeting as she swung the door open, so she didn't see his little love note right away. The second she did, she let out a squeak, her head whipping around like an owl's. She surveyed the hallway, searching for the culprit.*

*It was gratifying. Her dark eyes were wide, her pixie face drained of color. The fear looked good on her.*

*Rayna's reaction had been more subtle. Disappointing, almost. She hadn't taken him seriously enough. But she would learn, even if she wouldn't have long to appreciate the lesson.*

*He had his phone out, and glanced down as if reading a text, though really he was watching Grace from beneath his lashes as she looked around the hall. Her gaze, as usual, swept right over him. Discounting him as she did others, as just part of the herd. That was the problem, wasn't it, everyone so damned bleating and oblivious.*

*Well, not for much longer. This was their wake-up call. Right before the big sleep.*

# CHAPTER 2

RAYNA

Rayna was in the main office to see whether anyone had turned in the sketchbook she'd left in the lunchroom the day before when Liam came in, white as a sheet, hand clutching a note. It was on unlined printer paper, folded into quarters, and her mind went instantly to the note she'd found in her backpack. She was next at the counter, but as anxious as she was over the sketchbook, she let Liam go first so she could listen in.

He barely acknowledged the courtesy, but she didn't take it personally. Liam spent a lot of time in his head, solving quadratic equations or world hunger or who knew what. She didn't know him well, but she couldn't remember ever seeing him rattled. Now, the dark eyes behind the darker-framed glasses were shell-shocked, and the hand holding the note shook slightly.

Mrs. Marshall peered up at him as the previous student finished her business, and said, "Yes?"

Liam held out the note. Mrs. Marshall took it, mild confusion on her face at his silence. She glanced down and immediately back up again, eyes narrowing.

"What's this?" she demanded. "A threat?"

Liam squirmed and started to stammer. "I-it was in my locker. R-right on top of my books. I wasn't sure what to do. Or who left it."

"Hold on just a minute," she said, rising from her seat. That was practically unprecedented. There was no point in Mrs. Marshall delivering messages in person when she had her intercom.

But she left, taking the note with her.

Rayna stood for a second undecided. Should she say something or keep her silence? She didn't actually have anything to show for herself. Evan had taken her note. Would Liam think she was just vying for attention? Did it matter? If she could learn something . . .

Before she knew she'd decided, Rayna leaned forward. "What did yours say?" she asked.

Liam jerked as if he'd forgotten or never realized she was there. He swiveled like a desk chair, his eyes anime-wide. "You got one too?"

She didn't want to talk about her note, but she couldn't see any way around it. "*Six days to die*, it said. I . . . I was hoping it was a joke."

Liam's big brown eyes were nearly swallowed up by his irises, making them a little spooky. "I wanted to think that, but if my friends were making a joke, they would have said something like *Welcome to the Rapture* or *Beware the Flood*. Video game references," he tacked on, in response to her blank look. "But *Two Days to Die* . . . I don't know what that is."

Rayna shuddered for him. Two days. *Two*. How was he not freaking out?

"So you don't know who—"

Mrs. Marshall came back then, already talking and unaware she was interrupting. "Principal Grayson wants to see you," she told Liam. "Do you know your way back?"

"Rayna got one too," he said quickly, as though he didn't want to be alone.

Rayna shot him a betrayed look. Just because she'd told him didn't mean he had to blab it.

"Well then, both of you go on back."

Rayna followed Liam down the hallway, worrying the whole way. What if she was wrong, and it *was* Evan? Or what if it was some kind of prank and she and Liam were playing into it by tattling and setting off a school-wide panic?

*But what if it was real?*

The hallway wasn't long enough for all her doubts. Liam was

already pushing open the office door, and Principal Grayson was looking at them expectantly, his face jowly like that of a basset hound or pictures she'd seen of President Nixon.

"Take a seat," he said, indicating the two chairs in front of his desk. His gaze took in Liam, moved on to Rayna. "Ms. Butler, may I have your note?"

Of course he knew her name. It wasn't that big a school, and she was the only blue-haired girl in it. This week.

Rayna gazed down at her hands, picking at a broken nail. "I don't have it. I thought maybe a friend was playing a trick and I showed it to him. He was going to show it to someone else."

"And that friend would be?"

She glanced up at him and said firmly, "He didn't do it, so there's no point in bringing him into this."

He stared at Rayna a moment longer before turning to Liam. "And you? Do you have any suspicions about who would have put this in your locker? Is there anyone you're having trouble with?"

Before he could answer, there was a knock at the door, which opened instantly thereafter, as though the person on the other side had been signaling intent rather than asking permission to enter. *Ready or not, here I come.*

In walked a man in uniform with an impressive mane of hair that was more salt than pepper. His facial hair was a lot darker in contrast and defied definition as either stubble or beard, landing somewhere in between. Their school safety officer could have been anywhere from forty to sixty, and kids sometimes placed bets on the subject, but as he'd yet to confirm or deny anything, no one had been able to collect. The one unmistakable thing about him was his air of readiness. He was always watching, ready to spring into action at any sign of trouble. Once upon a time, maybe, guarding a school had been a softball assignment, light duty. No more.

"I asked Officer Fontanez to join us," Principal Grayson said unnecessarily. "To help us evaluate the threat."

They all nodded at each other in acknowledgment, and the

Principal handed the officer Liam's note, filling him in on things so far. He finished with, "Liam was about to tell us about who might want to hurt him."

Liam looked like a deer in the headlights. "That's just it, there's no one! I mean, Amal and I get into it sometimes, like now for example, but it's never turned physical. And there's this kid on my bus who's kind of a bully, but I don't have any *enemies*. No one who'd want to hurt me."

Officer Fontanez read the note he'd been handed, flipped it over and back as though there might be something more to see. He glanced back up to Principal Grayson, "I don't think we can take this lightly." He speared Liam and Rayna with his gaze. "I'm going to call this in and see if we can get any prints off the note. We'll start an investigation. For now, I want you two to be extra careful. Make sure you're never alone, especially not after dark. Let me know if you need a walk to your car or your bus. Be aware of those around you. Good advice at any time." He watched to make sure they weren't just tuning him out. "And I don't want you protecting anyone's feelings. No being too nice. If you suspect someone—anyone—I want you to tell me or Principal Grayson. We're not going to go off half-cocked, but we will investigate."

It felt like the last word on the subject, but Principal Grayson wasn't finished. "Policy is to make calls to all the families to let them know that threats have been made and that we have things in hand. Otherwise, rumors will start and blow things way out of proportion."

"We don't know what the proportionate response is yet," Officer Fontanez said seriously. "Don't make them *too* comfortable. We want everyone watchful."

"That's always the trick, isn't it?" Principal Grayson asked. "To inspire awareness without outright panic."

Rayna was hovering between the two. She'd have felt a helluva lot better if Officer Fontanez had dismissed the notes out of hand as the prank she hoped they were. Time would tell, but she wasn't sure she'd like what it had to say.

JACK

Jack stopped back at his locker at the end of the day to grab his books for math and science, the two subjects he actually liked. Words were unreliable, manipulative. You had to interpret and guess at meanings. They could get twisty and turn on you. But math and science had actual problems with actual solutions, even if some of those solutions ended up in imaginary numbers. Answers gave him a strange sense of satisfaction. Accomplishment. For a little while, the world made sense. It only went to hell when people got involved.

Like Maria Sanchez. She was at her locker now, probably still thinking he was the bad boy he seemed or worse. Usually her attitude amused him. Today, knowing she thought him capable of threatening her made him feel a bit like a monster. Like his father.

It was unlikely anything he said would convince her otherwise. But now that he knew what her note was likely about, he couldn't let things go. He was worried for her and it pissed him off.

Jack grabbed his books quickly and closed his locker, appearing at Maria's side before she could run away. "Maria," he said, as non-threateningly as he knew how. "Hold up a second. That note you got earlier. What did it say?"

She jerked, as if startled, and when she popped her head out of her locker it was to give him a dark look. "What do you care?"

He hadn't really thought this through. Now he glanced around to see if anyone was paying attention. He didn't want whoever had left the note to think he was spooked. He didn't want anyone else to get the wrong idea either. But no one was paying any attention.

"I got one too. It was on my desk in sixth period," he said, meeting her eyes again. "A threat, right? How many days?"

Now she was more than suspicious. She looked frightened. "I'll show you mine if you show me yours," she challenged.

*That's what she said*, he thought instantly, but he didn't say it. He had that much self-control. "I, uh, can't."

"Because you don't have one. Because *you're* the one writing them," she said. She held a book against her chest protectively, but she was facing him down. There was fire in her eyes.

"No, I—" He stopped; she wasn't going to believe him. Given his reputation, one he'd earned, he probably wouldn't believe him either. "I threw it away. I didn't want whoever sent it to think I took it seriously. Look, I don't care if you believe me. I was just concerned is all."

He turned to go, and something—no, some*one* slammed into his shoulder, knocking him against the row of lockers, slamming Maria's shut. She just barely got her fingers out of the way in time. They both glared after the retreating figure.

*Dalton.*

"You want a piece of me?" Jack yelled after him.

Dalton whirled around like he'd only been waiting on the reaction. Other kids got out of his way. His shoulders were each easily bigger than his head, which despite housing what Jack figured to be a pea brain, was of pretty impressive size. His hair was cut military short, either because of ROTC rules or because he liked to remind everyone that he was a toy soldier.

Jack was nearly his height, but wiry and about forty pounds lighter. He wasn't sure he could take Dalton, but he was willing to try.

"Any time, any place, tough guy," Dalton sneered. "But I'd rather have a piece of *her*." He made smoochy faces at Maria, who shot him a look that could kill.

Jack took a step forward, his fists clenched. "You want to get to her, you're going to have to go through me."

"Seriously, would you idiots grow up?" Maria huffed.

Dalton's laugh echoed down the hallway, but he spun around and kept going.

Jack turned on Maria. "What did I do?"

She gave Jack a you're-shitting-me look, only she probably wouldn't have used the s-word. "Winking, leering, generally treating me like a piece of meat. Any of this ringing a bell? How is that different than Dalton's stupid kissy faces? And you were ready to *fight* him over me. For all I know, you made up the threat to get my attention. Maybe I'm supposed to turn to you for protection or swoon into your arms?"

He stared back at her, dumbfounded. "Forget that. I've got my own stuff going on. You want to handle things on your own, go for it."

"Good, go do your *stuff*. I can take care of myself," she fired back.

It felt like Maria had slapped him. Jack watched her walk away, pretending that he wasn't doing any such thing when she glanced back over her shoulder. She could take care of herself. *Fine*. Great. He had enough to deal with already. He tucked the hurt deep down where his scars were starting to accumulate.

# CHAPTER 3

Rayna didn't see Liam at school the next day. She made a point of looking for him to be sure he was okay, even though there was still one day left before his supposed date with death. *Two days to die.* She could only imagine. With any luck, tomorrow would pass quietly and they'd find it was all a hoax. She tried to hold onto that thought, but the sickness in her stomach let her know how unsuccessful she was.

All while she was searching for and not finding Liam, she was studying everyone she *did* see, wondering who had it out for her. Even if the death threat wasn't real, someone wanted to scare her. And others. It was ugly, and it cast a cloud over everything. She didn't want to look at the world and see shadows. She wanted to focus on the light, like she did with her artwork, trying to draw out everything's inner beauty. But there was something to be said for art as truth as well, and the truth wasn't always pretty. *People* weren't always pretty. She knew that; she just didn't want to internalize it.

But by lunchtime her stomach had tied itself into knots. She couldn't wait to get to the cafeteria. Not to eat—she couldn't imagine holding anything down—but to see what Evan and his friends had discovered about the note.

She didn't find him at their usual table, but all the way in the back of the lunchroom sitting with two kids—a guy and a girl. The girl she recognized—Grace . . . Something. They had world history together, and it would have been impossible to miss her there, since she had all the answers. And since she always dressed like she'd lost a battle with a painter's palette. Today she wore a cotton candy pink sweatshirt with *Aeropostale* splashed across it in taffy blue, a burgundy skirt and lime green stockings. Her hair, in contrast, was nearly colorless—so blonde it was almost white.

She didn't notice Rayna's arrival at first, too busy pushing around the anemic offering the school called salad.

The boy, however, watched Rayna's approach intently. She'd seen him around, she thought, but couldn't come up with a name and wouldn't have been able to pick him out of a line-up. He was stocky with close-cropped hair and more than a smattering of freckles across his face. He wore blending-in clothes—a plain navy blue T-shirt, baggy dark-wash jeans. She bet that if she checked under the table for his sneakers, she'd find them unremarkable too. He was like the anti-Grace.

As soon as Rayna hit the table, Evan started in on introductions. "Rayna, meet Charlie. He's one of the friends I was telling you about. And this is Grace. She—"

"We know each other," Grace cut in. "Sort of, anyway. World history, right?"

Rayna nodded. "You sit in the front and . . ." *know everything,* she'd been about to say, only she wasn't sure it would come across like a compliment, even if she was almost sure she meant it that way.

Grace offered a twisted smile.

"Sorry about that," she said, as if she knew what Rayna left unspoken. "I have kind of a photographic memory. You tell me something and it'll go in one ear and out the other, but if I read it, it's locked in here forever." Grace tapped her head.

"That sounds awesome," Rayna said. "No studying. You must save a ton of time."

"Yeah, great," Grace said without enthusiasm. "Or it would be if I had a filter. I really mean it about things getting locked in. Once I know something, I can't *un*know it."

"Like what?" Rayna asked.

"*Seventeen days to die.*" Grace pushed her salad away. "That's what my note said."

"*Six* for me," Rayna said. "Not that it's any kind of a competition."

"I'm so sorry." And she looked it. Grace's face was as expressive as her clothing.

Rayna shrugged. "Me too. But we're getting ahead of ourselves. I mean, this has to be a bad joke, right?"

The others exchanged a glance. All part of the club. All in the know . . . leaving Rayna feeling like an outsider.

Grace began fidgeting with the cords of her hoodie, but wouldn't meet Rayna's eyes.

"That's what I thought at first," she said. "I figured it was one of the Meddlers playing some kind of game. Leaving a clue to a puzzle they wanted me to solve."

"Meddlers?" Rayna asked, turning to Evan for an answer.

"That's what we call ourselves," he said. "It's from *Scooby Doo*. You know, 'We would have gotten away with it too, if it weren't for you meddling kids'."

Grace was nodding.

"Um, okay," Rayna answered.

"That's why the club was formed," Grace said. "Reggie Driskoll brought us together because of this old case—"

"His *uncle's* case," Charlie put in.

Grace gave him a glare at the interruption. "I was getting to that." She turned back to Rayna. "Reggie's uncle was convicted of a murder Reggie's sure he didn't commit. Things weren't what they seemed, just like the hauntings in Scooby Doo, but the police think they've got their guy—"

"And so we're meddling," Charlie finished, earning an elbow in the ribs from Grace.

*Murder? Evan was tied up with murder?* The knot in her stomach tightened.

"That's terrible!" Rayna said. "But how did you all get involved?"

"We're all geeks of one kind or another," Grace answered. "Puzzle geeks, forensics fans. Reggie sort of collected us. We've got a club now so we can bring in speakers, learn stuff. And, of course, we each take a part of the field to research, do presentations for the rest . . ."

"And have you learned anything from the notes?" Rayna asked.

"I've got this," Charlie said before Grace could respond.

He pushed his tray away, wiped his hands on his pants legs, even though there was a perfectly good napkin on his tray, and reached for his backpack. He pulled out a black folder covered in bold yellow hazmat symbols. He made sure the table in front of him was clean and relatively free of crumbs before setting the folder down.

"So I've been studying the notes," he said, glancing at them each in turn, but not yet opening the folder, like he was building dramatic tension. "I can't tell you for sure how serious this guy is about carrying out the threats, but I can tell you that the notes were written in a state of high emotion."

He snapped open the folder, drawing out two plastic sleeves, each protecting a sheet of printer paper. He laid the sheets down side by side. Parallel, to make comparison easier. The pages looked the same, the all-caps lettering in big, bold slashes, but while Rayna's note was still pristine, the other—Grace's note— was smudged and stained.

"You said you can't tell about 'the guy' carrying out the threats. Do you mean you can tell the author is male just from the letters?" Rayna asked.

"Oh, sorry, that's my own bias. Odds favor it being a male."

"Remember, women are fifty-one percent of the population," Grace said, "so let's not play the odds. I know one woman right here who'll gladly wring your neck if you don't get on with things."

"Are they like this all the time?" Rayna asked Evan.

"Pretty much."

Charlie huffed in exasperation. "Look, here's what I can tell you—Handwriting 101, okay?" he said, getting nods all around the table, even from Grace. "There are a bunch of different factors here, but I'll skip straight to the most telling. See how the writer has done big block letters and used multiple strokes on each one to make them stand out, all aggressive and slashy, nearly tearing through the paper? That indicates a state of agitation, with conflict and frustration spilling onto the page."

Rayna leaned over so she could see better. She could tell that the writer had used multiple strokes to make the letters stand out. That was all.

Still she nodded so he would continue. He waited for the others to do the same.

"Okay, now see the way the letters slant to the left?" They all nodded again. "Here's the thing—upright letters show a sense of balance, living in the now. It's all good, right? Slanting to the right is looking to the future, not really rocking the boat in terms of getting there. But to the left—that's living in the past, rebelling against the present and future."

"What else?" Rayna asked, intrigued. She felt like when she was a rookie art student, learning to focus past the big picture to the brush strokes. She wondered if art appreciation could be applied to investigation . . .

As though he sensed her little thrill of interest, Evan gave her a shoulder nudge, and she nudged back. Evan was enjoying this. It made her queasy.

"Now notice the spacing between words," Charlie continued, oblivious. "See how they're set well apart? It could indicate someone who distances himself from others, someone who feels isolated."

"And the blood imagery?" Rayna asked.

"Driving the point home. The handwriting might show passion, but the placement of the notes, the spreading of fear, it shows planning. Intent."

"In other words, the danger is real," Evan said, going serious.

"I can only say that the handwriting analysis is consistent with someone who *might* carry out a threat—an antisocial personality, someone who's not feeling the love."

Grace rolled her eyes. "Woo-woo science," she said. "Evan, I can't believe you're listening to all this. Handwriting analysis is no better than phrenology—that's when shrinks used to read the bumps on people's heads," she said as an aside to Rayna. "It's all guesswork."

"Is psychology woo-woo science too?" Evan asked, his eyes glittering, still green, but now like the wild wetness of a rainforest after a storm. She'd love to sketch him that way. Dark. Intense. She blushed and looked away.

"It's a soft science," Grace answered, refusing to back down, though her tone wasn't nearly as argumentative as it had been with Charlie. Those two seemed like fire and kerosene. "You know what doesn't leave room for interpretation? Forensics. Evidence. Cold, hard facts."

"Fine," Charlie cut in, waving the smudged and stained sheet at Grace. "What did you turn up in *your* examination?"

Grace peered down at the chewed ends of her sweatshirt cords, and Charlie sat back in his seat, crossing his arms over his chest. From the smug look on his face, he already knew the answer.

"Nothing," she admitted. "No prints. Written on regular computer paper. Eighty percent brightness, which is pretty standard. Standard weight. No watermark. Nothing at all to distinguish it. Permanent ink, like from any black Sharpie in existence."

"So the person knew how not to leave a trace," Evan said.

"Not necessarily. I mean, anybody with a brain knows to wear gloves, and there was no envelope to lick, so . . ."

Silence swallowed the table once again, until Charlie couldn't take it anymore and exploded, "Take the BTK letters. Look at how much they revealed about Dennis Rader and—"

Charlie yelped suddenly, half jumping out of his seat as Evan or someone kicked him under the table. She could see it dawn on Charlie that maybe he'd gone too far in bringing up a serial killer in the context of the notes. He might want to defend his handwriting analysis, but talking about the BTK killer (which even Rayna knew stood for the Bind, Torture, Kill) was just disturbing.

Rayna had no idea what kind of expression she wore, but she imagined horror was a good part of it. And fear. Her stomach clenched so hard she was glad she hadn't tried to put anything on top of it.

"Uh, nevermind," he finished off. "Evan could tell you a lot more about that anyway."

Rayna glanced at Evan, as though seeing him anew. He could? *Evan?* She knew he was interested in mysteries and puzzles, mind benders and games, but serial killers?

"It's kind of my thing," he said, defensively. "You know that. I want to go into psychology."

"But serial killers?"

"*Forensic* psychology," he said.

"*Anyway,*" Grace said, trying to get things back on track, "we meet on Thursdays. You should come this week. Bring anyone you know who's gotten one of these notes. I'm sure if we all put our heads together, we can figure out what we all have in common . . . or who. Come up with a list of suspects, backtrack their movements."

Rayna's heart squeezed. "Thursday is two days away. Liam doesn't have that kind of time. Shouldn't you turn all this over to the police?"

As if that was a cue, a tray suddenly struck the cafeteria floor, making a huge racket. The whole place went silent as everyone looked for the source. And there was Liam, staring down at the splattered mess of his tray with Dalton hulking behind him.

"Whoops!" Dalton said, in a way meant to carry across the lunchroom.

The whole place erupted in hoots and hollers, jeers and cheers. Liam's face flamed and his fists clenched. Rayna's heart went out to him. She'd dropped a tray once and thought she'd die of embarrassment.

But this didn't look like an accident. Liam glanced from his tray up at Dalton with his face so red Rayna thought he might pop a blood vessel. His fists were clenched, and as Rayna watched, one of them rose up like Liam might actually take a swing at Dalton.

"Better clean that up," Dalton said, turning on his heel and walking away, a huge grin on his face. He accepted high fives and fist bumps as his due and reveled in the averted eyes of the kids silently thankful they weren't today's target.

Rayna nearly went after Dalton herself. If someone had threatened *his* life, Rayna would understand entirely. But Liam . . .

She rose to help, but before she could get there, Liam had picked up his tray and thrown the whole thing in the garbage, leaving the mess behind on the floor. Even the lunch monitors left him alone as he stalked out.

Rayna hadn't even realized she and Liam shared a lunch period. Now she'd never forget.

## JACK

Jack arrived home to an eerily quiet house. He immediately went to check on his brother Eric, who he found sleeping in his room, his laptop shoved up against the wall and ready to slide down between it and the bed.

Jack rescued the laptop, moved it to Eric's rarely-used desk, and went back to his brother. His breathing was even, but his lips were chapped and cracked, his skin dry as a desert, and his sparse hair brittle.

The big water bottle Jack had left on his side table that morning was empty. Crumbs from the ginger crackers Eric kept by his bed were caught up in his blankets, but Jack didn't see evidence of any other food for the day.

His anger started to rise, raging through him. He pushed it down, as always. He wanted to find his mother and kick the snot out of her for leaving his brother in this condition. She was home all day. She was supposed to take care of him. But more often than not, she slept until noon, then drank herself senseless at some point not long after. On her good days, she took care of Eric between times. Today was apparently not one of those.

But he knew no good would come of confronting his mother, even if he could rouse her enough to do it. She had no shame and no end of excuses. She couldn't face Eric's illness, she always said. It was too hard. This was her way of coping.

*Too hard.* As if she got to just tap out.

But pushing it meant that when his father came home and found out he dared take her on, there'd be hell to pay. Definitely yelling and other stresses Eric didn't need. Almost certainly more.

He debated waking Eric. He needed to drink more water, eat something, keep up his strength. But did he need the sleep more? How much had he slept today already? Was he weak from hunger, the illness or the treatment for it, which seemed almost as bad?

Jack was too worried to let him sleep. He put a hand to his brother's shoulder. "Eric? Buddy? I'm home."

Eric made a noise that sounded something like speech and rolled over, crumbs cascading from the blanket as he did.

"Buddy?" he tried again. "It's Jack. Do you need anything? Food? Juice? Did Mom bring you lunch today? I can make you some soup."

Eric's eyelids flickered and closed, flickered again.

"Buddy?" Jack said again, trying to keep down the panic. What if he couldn't wake Eric? What if he needed to take him to the hospital? His parents had never gotten around to taking Jack for his driver's license. He could call an ambulance, but . . . the mounting medical bills were already killing them. Dad would probably take the cost out of his hide. Not that he couldn't handle it, but . . . he'd call that a last resort.

Eric's eyelids fluttered again, then stayed open at half-mast. "Jack?" he said, voice groggy, dry and rough.

"It's me. How about I make you some soup?"

"Not 'ungry," he slurred.

Eric always said that. The treatment made him feel sick all the time. It was nearly worse than the leukemia.

"I'll make you some anyway. Have you been to the bathroom? Do you need help?"

Mom was supposed to take care of that too. Sometimes Eric was too weak to make it on his own.

Eric shook his head, and Jack retreated to the kitchen to open a can of chicken noodle soup. He grabbed a pot out of the cabinet next to the stove, poured the soup in and turned the heat up to medium. It would take a few minutes, long enough to use the bathroom himself and then make sure his mother hadn't drunk herself to death.

School seemed pointless in the face of all of this. Maybe he should drop out. He'd be doing that soon enough anyway, once Eric was better and he could get them both out of there . . . He supposed that until then he should stick it out. If it took him up through graduation, well, maybe the diploma would make it easier to get a job to build a life for them both.

He just hoped they'd last that long.

# CHAPTER 4

JACK

Jack bolted awake when he heard the sirens. His first thought was *Eric!* But as quickly as the thought came, he realized from the sound that the sirens were already past, headed away. The relief dropped him back down onto his pillow.

His heart didn't relax as easily. It still pounded about twice as fast as normal, and he felt out of breath, like he'd run a marathon.

He lay there for a minute, listening to the sound of the dopplering siren, wondering where it would stop, thinking of Mrs. McGillis down the street, who was ninety-something and had already gone off in an ambulance once this year. Hoping it wasn't her. Or anyone else's wife or brother or . . . No matter what, it was a sucky night for someone.

There was no way Jack was getting back to sleep. He rolled over to check his bedside clock and found it to be after 1 a.m. He groaned and got out of bed. Maybe if he looked in on Eric and saw that everything was okay he'd be able to get back to sleep . . . eventually.

He opened his door cautiously, not wanting to meet his father in the hallway. There was little chance of meeting his mother. Down the hall, light from the television flickered. The sound of his father's snores rose above the voices of the characters. The coast seemed clear.

Jack slipped out of his room and into the one next door.

"Jack?" Eric said groggily.

"It's me, Bud."

"I heard sirens."

Jack approached his bed and stared down at his brother, waiting for his eyes to adjust until he could actually *see* him.

"Me too. Woke me up. You need anything?"

Jack wouldn't say the sirens made him think of Eric, but his brother wasn't stupid.

"Water?" he asked.

"You got it. Be right back."

He took his brother's water bottle to the kitchen and refilled it from the tap, adding just a bit of ice. He brought it back to Eric and helped his brother sit up for a sip.

"Thank you," Eric whispered, sounding halfway to sleep again already.

"Welcome," Jack answered, laying him back down.

He left the room not feeling much better, but at least his brother was hanging in there.

Jack didn't find out until morning who the ambulance had come for . . . and that it had arrived too late.


RAYNA

Rayna did her best to ignore the news—her mother's choice of morning programming, not hers. It was always so depressing. Gloom and doom, horrors and politics. A down way to start the day. She felt guilty at the thought, knowing she should be more aware of everything, but feeling it like a burden.

She ate her cereal, doodled between bites and tried to tune out the voices . . . until one story caught her attention.

> *House fire. Two bodies discovered—mother and son. Cause of the fire is still being investigated, but sources say foul play is suspected. Names are being withheld until next of kin can be reached.*

Names withheld. And yet, the news station showed the smoldering home, firefighters and police among the wreckage.

A female news anchor in a navy suit with a stark white shirt was giving a recap—what time the fire had been called in, word on the firefighter who'd been rushed to the hospital for the treatment of injuries from a beam that had fallen when he'd gone back to search for survivors . . . of which there were none.

Rayna dropped the spoonful she'd been holding, and her mother looked away from the tiny kitchen television at the clatter.

But Rayna was off and running to her room for her laptop before her mother could say a word. She stayed there rather than bring it back to the table. Mom would ask a lot of questions that would slow her down. She wasn't ready to talk. Not until she knew. But she had a really horrible feeling about at least one of the dead.

"*Comeon-comeon-comeon,*" she chanted as the laptop took its time booting up. Even before all the icons appeared on the screen, she was tapping at her browser, trying to speed it along. That was when she realized she didn't know Liam's last name.

She threw her laptop temporarily to the side, grabbed her cell phone off the charger and called Evan.

"'Ello," he answered, voice rough from sleep.

"Evan, quick—you know Liam? The kid from the cafeteria yesterday, the one I told you got one of the notes?"

"What about him?"

"I . . . don't know his last name." She was embarrassed to admit it. "Do you?"

There was silence for a second, and then. "Hinkle? Something like that."

"Thanks." Rayna hung up and grabbed again for her laptop, typing furiously, glad her father had forced her to take the typing class she'd thought pointless, since she never planned to work in an office.

She called up a local directory, typed in their zip code and *Hinkle.* Two listings came up: Theodore Hinkle and A. Hinkle. She assumed it was "A," since the other address was outside their school zone. She copied the address that came up and then called up Google Earth.

The phone rang as a pop-up screen appeared, wanting her to

download stuff and offering her more options than she knew what to do with. Frustrated, she answered the phone, knowing it would be Evan after she hung up on him so abruptly.

"What?" she snapped.

"Hello to you too, sunshine. What's going on?" Evan asked.

"Have you seen the news?"

"The *news?*"

"Yeah, you know, that thing that tells you what's going on in the world. Turn it on."

"Can you give me a hint about what I'm looking for?"

"House fire. Two dead. A mother and son."

"O-kay," he said, clearly not making the connection.

Google Earth was still in mid-download, and Rayna growled at the pace. She wasn't even sure . . . of anything, really. Whether she had the right address. Whether she'd actually be able to zero in on Liam's house. Whether images were updated frequently enough so that she could tell if that particular house had burned down or was still standing. There had to be a better way.

"Have you left for school yet?" she asked. It was a silly question. Evan barely sounded conscious.

"What, and be early?"

"Good, come pick me up."

"Any time, but why today?"

"We're going to drive past that arson scene to see . . . whatever we can see."

There was dead silence on the other end of the phone.

"Give me a minute to run through the shower," he said finally. "I'll be there in ten."

There was a knock at Rayna's door, which she hadn't taken the time to fully close behind her. Her mother loomed in the entrance. "Everything okay?" she asked.

Principal Grayson had called her parents about the note, and Mom had been especially attentive ever since. Worried. Hovering. There was no reason to upset her any further until she knew the fire was connected. She might stop Rayna from going off with Evan. She might try to keep Rayna safe at home. But the sick feeling in her stomach said that being at home hadn't protected Liam and that it wouldn't do a thing for her. She had to get to school, talk to Grace and Charlie. Maybe they could call an emergency meeting of the Meddlers. They had to do something proactive. They couldn't just wait for death to come for them.

"Fine," Rayna lied and hoped she was convincing despite her lack of practice. "I just remembered a project. I have to get to school early. And I may have to stay late. I'll let you know?"

"How are you getting in early? I don't have time to drive you and Dad got in late last night. I know the principal talked to you about not being alone—"

"I won't be alone," she cut in. "Evan is going to drive me. But I have to hurry. He'll be here in ten."

"Are you sure you don't want to stay home today? Maybe I can call in sick?"

She'd do it, but it would cost her. Mom hated lying, hated missing work, would practically have to be on her death bed to stay home. And it wasn't like they could do it indefinitely. Besides, this wasn't Rayna's day to die. Not according to the note.

"I'm sure. Safety in numbers, right?"

Her mother sighed and cupped her cheek and chin in one hand. "Just promise me you'll be cautious. That you're taking this all seriously. And keep your phone on you at all times. I don't care about school policy. I don't want you going anywhere without it, in case . . ."

She didn't finish the thought, but then, she didn't need to. The morning's news footage was enough to bring the possibilities to vivid life.

She took her mother's hand from her face and held it in hers as she said, "I swear I won't let anything happen to me." She just hoped she could keep that promise. Reluctantly, she pulled away, adding, "For now, I have to shower."

Mom let her go, but not happily. Rayna was downstairs eleven minutes later with her hair still wet and minimal make-up on her pale face. Just enough concealer to hide the bags under her eyes and a little liner and gloss. She didn't have time for anything else, and she couldn't really care.

Evan was there a minute later. His hair was less wild than usual this morning, still laying the way he'd blown it dry. For a change, she could see both eyes at once, and they were . . . She wasn't getting hung up on his eyes. It was just annoying that he was totally put together, like he'd been up for hours, despite how groggy he'd sounded on the phone. Her state reflected her feelings—disheveled, chaotic, out of control.

"Drive," she ordered as she got into his car.

"Wearing your cranky pants I see," he said, throwing a look her way.

She was, in fact, wearing ripped jeans with just enough fabric still holding them together to get by the school sensors, a babydoll T-shirt that read "You can't have E*art*h without art" and multi-colored Converse sneakers she'd decorated herself. Her hair was yanked back into an elastic band to get it out of the way.

There was no point in a glare. Evan knew very well why she was in a rush. He was just trying, as always, to lighten things up. It wasn't his fault that now was not the time. She was definitely wearing her cranky pants.

He started the car, waved to her mother, who watched from the window, and pulled out of their driveway.

Rayna noticed two insulated coffee cups in his center console. "Is one of those for me?" she asked.

"No."

She gave him an exasperated look he couldn't see because he was focused on the road, but he seemed to feel it. "Oh, okay, have the one in back. But you reach for mine, you'll pull back a bloody stump."

Rayna froze with her hand on the coffee mug.

"Gah," Evan said almost instantly. "I'm sorry. It's just a figure of speech, you know that. I was just trying . . . nevermind. Drink it. Pour it in my lap. Whatever floats your boat. Um, that's another figure of speech. It means—"

"I know what it means," Rayna said, surprised at the flipflop of emotions this morning. She almost smiled at the thought of how shocked Evan would be if she took him up on the whole coffee-in-the-lap thing. Then she thought about them running off the road. "Anyway, thanks."

She took her coffee and sipped it. He'd said they were both for him, but she knew he was kidding . . . unless he'd suddenly decided to start taking his light and sweet.

The coffee gave her something to focus on as the roads sped by. Marsden wasn't a huge town and didn't have traffic jams to speak of unless there was an accident on the road. One side of town to the other was barely twenty minutes. They were to the turn onto Liam's street in half that time, but a Detour sign and bright orange cones kept them from it. The Detour took them around and finally onto Liam's street a couple of blocks down from the emergency vehicles and crime scene tape, which they could see in the rearview mirror. Rayna wondered what happened if someone lived within the cordoned off zone. Surely they let residents in and out.

Evan pulled into a driveway up ahead and made a K-turn back toward the barricades.

"What are you doing?" Rayna asked.

"All part of the plan. When a cop tries to turn us away, I can ask questions."

He pulled up to the orange cones and stopped. Sure enough, one of the uniformed officers walked over to tell him to move along, but Evan ignored that to ask, "What's going on?"

Ahead on the right a fire marshal's truck and several police units nearly cut off the sight of a burned out husk of a house. All Rayna could see was the second floor. She didn't know what color the house had been originally, but now it was char and ash, windows blown out and blackened, half the roof collapsed.

In addition to the police keeping people back and the fire marshal's people investigating, neighbors were out in force. Some stood or sat on porches, watching, holding coffee or unread newspapers in their hands. A few were clumped together talking, one with a babe in arms and a toddler clinging to the tail of her oversized shirt, probably her husband's. One guy, his car door hanging open, was arguing with another uniformed officer about something, maybe neighborhood access.

"Police investigation," said the cop who'd stopped them, as if they couldn't see that for themselves. "You'll have to move on."

"Is this the fire we heard about on the news? Is everyone okay?" Evan asked.

He knew very well they weren't.

The cop's eyes went from all-business to suddenly sad before he answered. "If you've seen the news, I'm sure you know—"

"It's not Liam, is it?" Rayna gasped, as if she'd just realized whose house they were seeing.

She must not have been completely convincing. The cop lowered himself to peek through the window for a better look at her. "And you are?" he asked, turning his head to include Evan in the question.

"Classmates," she said. "Please, tell me it's not him." Her voice broke. There were tears in her eyes she didn't have to fake. She hadn't known Liam well, but still . . . She felt his death. She couldn't imagine the terror he must have felt. Had he known death was coming? Tried to choke down suddenly toxic air? Wrestled with a doorknob that was locked or too hot to touch? It was terrible that the best case scenario was that he'd been dead already when the fire started.

Rayna's breath felt short, like she was suffering in sympathy, and a huge weight seemed to crush her chest.

The officer straightened again, releasing his over-intense scrutiny. "I can't confirm or deny," he said, sounding regretful about it. "I'm sorry, you're going to have to move along."

The man in the car behind the barricades had stopped arguing with the other officer and gone back to his car. His door slammed, and his motor revved.

"Wait a minute," Evan said to the officer at his window.

He started to open his door, and the officer immediately went on alert, hand going toward his holster. Evan didn't seem to notice, but stood with one foot in and one out of the car to wave. "Reggie!" he called.

A kid their age had come out of one of the houses on the block, and Evan was flagging him down.

"We're just here to pick up our friend," he told the officer.

That was news to Rayna, but Reggie veered in their direction as if in confirmation of Evan's story.

"Hurry it up," the officer said, stepping back to remove the cones for the man in the red car.

Rayna presumed this was the same Reggie who'd brought the Meddlers together. She recognized him from around school, but didn't really know him. She thought he was on the accelerated track, which would explain why they weren't in any classes together. He was at least six feet tall, but the weight of his backpack seemed to drag his shoulders down. It certainly was bursting at the seams, the top zipper only three-fourths closed, which made Rayna think he was one of those kids who didn't bother with a locker, but carried his world on his back. He was stick-thin, like he'd gained his height all at once and hadn't yet filled out. His skin was dark and his eyes were long-lashed behind hipster black glasses.

"Hey," he said when he reached them, bumping the fist Evan held out to him. "What's up?"

It seemed such a normal greeting for a day that was anything but.

"Want a ride to school?" Evan asked.

Reggie stooped down to peer inside the car and gave Rayna a nod. She gave him one back. To Evan he said, "What's the deal?"

"You're alibiing us. We told the cop we're here to pick you up."

"And you're really—"

"Here to see what's going on," he said gravely, nodding toward the still-smoking scene.

Reggie's lips compressed down to nothing for a moment, "Yeah, that."

There was sorrow on his face, and a sort of resignation she didn't understand, echoed in those two simple words. She had a feeling there was an entire iceberg of meaning beneath it all, and they were just seeing the tip.

Reggie opened the back door, groaned as he removed the backpack and swung it onto the back seat. He followed after it, folding himself inside the car.

Evan got moving as soon as the door closed.

"Reggie, meet Rayna. Rayna, Reggie, founding member of the Meddlers."

Rayna turned in her seat and gave him a small wave.

"Rayna," he said, testing it out. "You're one of the people who got a note?" His voice was nearly as deep as he was tall, like he dredged it up from his toes.

She nodded, and the tears she'd shed threatened to spill over. She quickly wiped them away.

Intensity was coming off Reggie in waves. "You're in terrible danger," he said.

As if she didn't already know.

# CHAPTER 5

RAYNA

By fifth period the news was all around school. The police had finally released the names of those killed in the house fire. As suspected, they were Liam Hinkle and his mother. Rumor had it they were dead before the fire began. Murdered. The police weren't yet releasing details, like *how* they'd been killed. That probably had to wait for the autopsies. The thought of Liam being cut open, his organs being removed, weighed, all that stuff she'd seen in cop shows . . . Rayna shuddered, closed her eyes and tried to fight down nausea.

The Meddlers had called an emergency meeting. They sat now in a coffee shop near the school since they weren't allowed to meet on the grounds without a faculty advisor, which they couldn't line up on such short notice. Rayna wasn't sure they'd actually tried. Something like this—no teacher was going to want them messing around.

She and Evan were the last to arrive. He'd waited while she got cleaned up from last period art class and then walked her over. They now stood impatiently at the counter while the girl behind it took forever with their orders. More coffee. Twice what she normally drank in a day.

As they walked up to the table the others had grabbed, Reggie moved over one chair so that Rayna and Evan could sit together, as if they were a couple. Beside Reggie sat a goth girl with an open laptop in front of her, pounding away at the keyboard and paying them no attention at all. Next was Grace, who today wore an eye-searing sweater in a confusion of colors that slouched off one shoulder to reveal the hot pink tank underneath, and Maria Sanchez, who Rayna had a class or two with every year. Beside Maria was an angry-looking boy she knew only by reputation. Jack Harkness. Rayna had never been shaken down by him personally, but he had that kind of reputation. Word was, if Jack brushed by you in the hallway, you checked for your wallet and watch. She could guess that Jack was there because he'd received a threat, but Maria . . . Surely Maria had never done anything to offend anyone. Maybe she was one of the Meddlers?

Reggie nodded to them as they sat, then tapped the goth girl on the arm to let her know things were about to start. She glanced up, studying Rayna with heavily kohl-lined eyes. Rayna studied her back—the multiple piercings, the black and red flannel men's shirt over a basic black tee, her hair an ombré cascade of brunette into burgundy. It was an effective look. The girl popped out one earbud so that she could hear the conversation around her.

"Kali," she said with a nod toward Rayna, who nodded back and gave her own name.

It seemed all that was required. Kali immediately went back to her computer, though she left out the earbud.

It was good enough for Reggie, who kicked things off with, "What do we have so far?"

Jack sneered at that. "We have a dead fuckin' kid, that's what we have."

Maria's eyes widened at Jack's outburst . . . or maybe at his language. She hesitantly put a hand to his arm as if to sooth him. "Calm yourself. It's not their fault. They want to help."

Jack looked like a man on the edge, but he seemed to step away from it at Maria's touch. Rayna immediately thought of *Beauty and the Beast* and then felt terrible for her fleeting smile.

"I'm just glad you figured out *I'm* not the bad guy," Jack said to her.

Clearly there was history here.

Maria glanced away. "I was emotional before. You're no angel, but I don't think you could kill someone. I can't imagine anybody . . ."

"But somebody did," Evan said, as gently as he could while still cutting to the chase, his usual prankster self nowhere in evidence. "I know it's a terrible thing, but if we give ourselves time to wallow, the next deadline will be up before we know it and we'll be too late to stop another death."

He shot Rayna a sidelong glance, and she thought *he's talking about me. My death.*

Six days to die. Four now. Four days to catch a killer.

"Sure," Jack said. "We'll just turn off our emotions." He air-flipped an imaginary switch. "There, all done."

Evan eyed him sourly. "Why is *he* here?" he asked Reggie.

Reggie didn't look any happier about it. "Maria brought him. She got a note. She says he got one too."

Everyone turned to Jack. He shrugged, like it was no big deal, but he wasn't selling it. His whole body was tense, as if ready for the threat, prepared for action. Even sitting, he was a coiled spring.

It was Kali who stopped clicking away at her computer long enough to jumpstart the discussion. "What we *have*," she began, echoing Jack's words, "is two dead, threatening notes we'll eventually have to turn over to the police, and one poorly protected e-mail account." She turned her laptop around to show us that she'd logged into Liam's school-provided e-mail.

"You hacked into Liam's account?" Maria asked, horrified.

Kali just quirked an eyebrow in response. With the piercing and her kohl-lined eyes, it made quite a statement.

"It's not like he's using it," she said defensively.

"Anything interesting?" Reggie asked, getting up out of his chair to peer over her shoulder.

Kali bristled at his looming and growled out two words, "Personal space."

Reggie backed off a step, and Kali rewarded him by angling the screen his way.

"Nothing so far," she answered. "School stuff, some plans for gaming, a flame war with Amal—"

Rayna stared at Kali, "Liam mentioned to the principal that

he was having trouble with a kid named Amal."

Kali glared her down. "Amal didn't do this."

"How can you know that?" Rayna asked. "Isn't that what people always say—'but he was such a quiet boy; we had no idea'?"

Oh, if looks could kill . . . "We're friends," Kali snapped, like that was the end of story. "He's a gamer boy. And completely non-confrontational. He gets all his aggressions out in the games. He doesn't have any reason to go around threatening people."

Rayna was about to suggest there were two sides to every flame war, calling into question the 'non-confrontational' thing, when Grace chimed in, "Plus, I can't see what he'd have against me. And it sounds like you don't even know him."

"He never made it to school today," Evan said, not accusingly. Just an observation. "At least, I don't think so. He wasn't in math class. Or science."

"I didn't see him at lunch," Maria said quietly. "Not that I'd necessarily notice."

"Doesn't mean anything," Kali snapped. "Evan, you all know the psych. You're practically an expert. If one of us killed someone, we'd do exactly what we'd normally do. We wouldn't break our routine. We wouldn't miss school. Anyone sending out death threats is hoping for a reaction. They want to see the fear they've caused, watch the monkeys dance to their tune. Revel in their power. If all you care about is the killing, you just kill."

"But that's the whole thing," Grace said. "Whoever did this *did* send threats. And not just the normal way. They're playing at something."

"There's a *normal* way to send threats?" Jack cut in.

Kali and Grace both gave him a *look*.

"I mean," Grace said, voice quietly serious, "Why risk breaking into backpacks and lockers? Why not just send an e-mail? Everyone in school has the same format to their e-mails. You don't need to know anyone's specific address, just the spelling of their last name and the year they graduate."

"More dramatic?" Reggie suggested. "Flame wars happen all

the time. No one takes that stuff seriously anymore. But a note in a backpack or a classroom says, 'I can get to you'."

"Or," Maria suggested quietly, "Maybe he didn't send it via e-mail because he knows about you guys. He might suspect Kali could hack in and trace a message back to the source."

"Well," Grace said, clearly uncomfortable, "Amal *did* come to a few meetings when his dad made him join a club so that he wasn't spending all his time in front of a computer. It didn't last. Even Liam came to a meeting or two. I think Amal brought him . . . or maybe it was the other way around. They were friends before they were enemies."

"But if arguments were motives for murder," Reggie broke in, "no one would get out of high school alive."

"All the same," Evan said, "maybe someone should call Amal. Just to make sure he's all right," he added. "For all we know, he got a note too, and we just haven't heard about it."

Rayna was watching Evan—this new Evan she didn't know a thing about. He wasn't bored, wasn't goofing around to entertain himself or others. He was . . . focused, intent. More real than she'd ever seen him. Kali had said he knew his psychology. *Criminal psychology.* Rayna felt her world shift around her. Like she was climbing a familiar rock wall but about to fall because someone had moved all the handholds.

She'd known Evan since way back in the seventh grade when he'd intercepted her note to Sierra and sent it back to her with a sketch of their history teacher as a baboon flinging erasers like feces. She'd had to hide her laughter behind a sudden coughing fit. She told him after class that he showed real promise as a cartoonist. Sierra agreed. They'd all been friends ever since.

How was it Evan kept such an important piece of himself to himself? Or, she guessed, shared it, but not with her?

Kali didn't look any happier than she felt. "I'll call Amal," she said, pulling her cell phone from her backpack and calling up Facetime, tilting the screen just enough so that Grace and those closest could lean in to see.

The phone made a repetitive *bloop-bleep* sound like the ring of a phone, only completely different. It went on and on.

The call went unanswered.

Everyone looked at each other. "It doesn't mean anything," Reggie said. "He could be away from his phone. His battery could have died."

*Or he could be dead himself.* But no one voiced that thought.

Keeping things bottled up meant Rayna couldn't release the pressure of her fear. Amal and Liam had known each other. Maybe the killer had lumped them together, hit them both on the same night. Maybe there was another body yet to be found.

She couldn't think that way. Right now all they had was a missed call. It didn't mean anything. Amal could be home and not taking calls because he was in mourning for his friend . . . or feeling horribly guilty over how they'd left things. Charlie wasn't here either, for that matter . . . Where—?

"Amal lives in my neighborhood," Jack said suddenly into the silence. "Maria and I can swing by his place on the way home and make sure everything's okay."

Maria shot him a surprised look. So did everyone else.

"What?" he asked, voice going hard. "You think I live in a trailer park and couldn't possibly go home to a nice neighborhood like the rest of you?"

"Just wondering how you know where Amal lives," Reggie said.

"*I'm* wondering when you and Maria became besties," Kali remarked.

Maria made a squawk of protest, and Jack talked over it, glaring at Reggie. "Amal and I ride the same bus—one I missed today to come here." He turned the glare on Kali. "And before you ask, Maria only invited me because she found out I'd gotten a note when she accused me of writing them. She offered me a ride home today so I could make this stupid meeting. That's it. End of story."

"And did you?" Reggie asked, studying him.

"Did I what?" Jack bristled, seeming to grow right before them, almost like Dr. Jekyll turning into Mr. Hyde.

"Write the note," Reggie answered evenly. Without his backpack dragging him down, he was sitting tall, showing his true height. Jack didn't look intimidated.

Jack snarled and stood. "That's it, meeting adjourned. I'm out of here. If you treat all of your visitors this way, it's no wonder Amal and Liam didn't stay."

Kali glared. "You can't adjourn the meeting. For one, it's not up to you and for another, we haven't accomplished anything yet."

"Fine, you sit around talking. I'm taking action. Maria, are you coming?"

Rayna didn't know how Jack planned to get home if she said 'no', but it didn't look like he cared at that moment. She could practically see steam coming off him in waves. She wondered what kind of rage simmered beneath his surface. She remembered something else Liam had said in the principal's office the other day—"There's a kid on my bus who's kind of a bully." What were the odds it was Jack?

Maria glanced around, like she didn't know what to do, but then she rose. Jack was already to the door.

"I'm sorry," she said, "but—"

She didn't finish the sentence, instead taking off after Jack. Rayna and the others heard them arguing as she caught up.

"You don't get to boss me around like that," Maria said, her usually quiet voice going sharp.

"What bossing? I asked you a question. How you answered was up to you. Don't try to say I *made* you do anything."

Jack yanked the door open and stormed through. They didn't hear Maria's response as she followed.

# CHAPTER 6

JACK

They walked in silence all the way to Maria's car, a dinged-up white sedan. Not the kind of car any teenager would pick. Parental hand-me-down, Jack guessed. He wondered what it would be like to get something other than a fist in the face from his parents.

He stopped with his hand on the car door. "I'm sorry," he said, not looking at Maria. It cost him, but he didn't want to be his dad, taking something out on her that wasn't her fault. "Maybe I overreacted in there."

"Get in," Maria said, opening her door.

He did and she did, and they both sat there in her cozy interior, tension buzzing between them. Finally, she glanced over at Jack. "It wasn't the trailer park thing, you know."

"Huh?" Jack studied her face. It was so full of something like sympathy that he had to look away. He didn't want her sympathy. She didn't know anything. Not . . . anything.

"They were just shocked you volunteered to help."

Jack didn't glance away, and tried not to let his lips twist or bitterness show on his face. "You all think you know me."

"Jack, no one knows you, that's the thing. We don't know, so we have to guess. And what we guess depends on how you present yourself to the world."

"So how do I present?" he asked, crossing his arms over his chest, challenging.

"Like trouble. Like someone who'd fight you soon as look at you. Like someone who maybe could have written those notes."

Jack was livid, his hand on the car door, ready to jump out

and get back to going it alone, when Maria put a hand on his arm . . . again. She was getting bold. "I don't think you're really like that, though," she said quietly.

"Oh?" he asked. "Based on what? All the quality time we've spent together?" He realized the words were wrong as soon as he said them, but he didn't like the hope that she might actually *want* to know him. Or at least give him a chance. Better to crush it before he got crushed.

Maria's lips pressed thin, and she drew her hand back, but not her gaze. "You don't realize you give yourself away. It's your eyes. Sometimes they're . . ." she seemed to debate finishing her sentence. "Vulnerable," she said finally. "You don't want to be, and so you act tough."

"Sounds like psychobabble to me. Maybe you should get back in there with the others where you belong. Or are you one of those girls who thinks, 'I can save him'? That I'm just misunderstood? Sorry, but you had me pegged. Trouble. Not homicidal, maybe, but not warm and fuzzy either, so you'd better get those thoughts right out of your head."

Her expression didn't change. Jack had the impression that his words weren't getting through. It should have pissed him off.

"Whatever," she said calmly. "You'll have to guide me to Amal's house. I've never been."

Jack gave directions and otherwise they sat in silence for the ride.

"Here it is," Jack said, as they drove up on a yellow split-level house with brown trim and pansies of all colors spilling out of the flower beds, making the place appear cheerful and cared for. He only knew they were pansies because his house used to have them too. Now they had weeds. And ferns high enough to qualify as trees.

"How do you know which one it is?" Maria asked.

"Are you going to start too?" he asked, trying not to lose it.

He didn't want to admit that he and Amal had once been

friends. That he'd been a geek and a gamer and a normal kid a lifetime ago. Before Eric got sick and before Jack reserved all his game time for his brother. He didn't want Maria's pity. Or her disbelief that someone as smart and stable as the class valedictorian or salutatorian or whatever Amal was this week would be friends with such a lowlife. He knew what she thought of him. Hell, he'd fostered it.

She took her hands off the wheel in a no-harm-no-foul gesture, and Jack subsided. Still, he was out of the car the second it stopped moving. All he wanted was to get this over with and get back to Eric.

Amal would be okay, he was sure of it, and no one would have any reason to concern themselves with how Jack knew where he lived or anything else. Amal would be fine. Maybe just in mourning for his former friend and baffled by their concern.

Jack stormed up Amal's porch, leaving Maria in his wake. He heard her car door slam as he rang the bell. The inner door was already wide open with just the screen door in place, and he heard Amal's mother before he saw her. She yelled, "Amal?" and flew to the door, yanking it open as though ready to throw herself into his arms. She stopped short when she saw Jack.

"You're not . . ." She trailed off, studying him. "*Jackie?* What are you doing here? We haven't seen you in so long. Do you know where Amal is? Is he hurt? Is he with you?"

Her words came out all in a rush, and she craned her neck to see behind him, spotted Maria and looked back at Jack, expression vacillating between hope and terror awaiting his response.

Jack hoped Maria hadn't heard his childhood nickname, but there were bigger things to think about.

Amal wasn't here.

His mother was worried.

Things were not all right.

"I—we—" Jack started awkwardly, "Maria and I came looking for him."

Mrs. Mehta's face fell instantly. Her lips quivered. Tears started to form. "So he's not been with you?" she asked, just to be sure.

The tears leaked out. Jack wanted to back away. Wanted to tell her Amal was staying late at school or . . . anything but the truth. But it was too late, and lies wouldn't do anybody any good.

"Have you called the police?" Jack asked instead. "When was the last time you saw him?"

"Come in," Amal's mom said, opening the door wider and grabbing him by the wrist so he couldn't get away. "Tell me everything you know. Maybe we can make a list of his friends. Make a phone tree. Start a search grid. Something. I've already called the police and all the hospitals."

Her voice broke on the last sentence, and Jack felt like his heart was going to break with it. He could only imagine if something happened to Eric. Or if he came home one day and his mother wouldn't wake up from her stupor. It was a fear he pretended he didn't live with, because he didn't know why he should still care. His father . . . he didn't know how he felt about his father never coming home. He just knew how he was *supposed* to feel.

The house opened onto a foyer with two sets of stairs, one up and one down. Mrs. Mehta led them upward, toward the kitchen, and once there stood in the center of it, as though she'd forgotten what should come next.

"Can I get you anything?" she asked, probably out of habit. "Iced tea? Water?"

Maria gave Jack a stern look, as though he needed a warning to be on his best behavior, and went to pull out a chair at the table for Mrs. Mehta. "Sit," she said. "We're fine. Can we get *you* anything?"

Mrs. Mehta shook her head and then put it in her hands, elbows resting on the table to hold it up. "He was gone this morning when I went to get him for school." She brushed away at the tears spilling down her face. "Sometimes he's up late playing games or working on a paper. It's not always easy to wake him in the mornings, but when he didn't come out, I went in and . . . he was gone. He's never just gone. I searched for a note. I called his cell phone, but . . . nothing. I phoned the school, in case he went in early, but they had to wait for attendance. When he wasn't there I called the hospitals. I called the police to find out about accidents and how soon I could report him missing. They wouldn't take me seriously. They thought he was just playing hooky. Or skipping classes. They don't know him like we do," she said, as if Jack hadn't been out of their lives for too long to make that claim. "They took the report, but . . . Please, help me."

*Breathe*, Jack thought. He wasn't sure she'd taken a breath during that whole speech.

Maria sat down in the chair nearest Mrs. Mehta and reached over to grab her hand. She squeezed, and Amal's mom blinked up at her with tears stuck in her lashes. "Amal's father is on his way home from a business trip. I have to go pick him up from the airport. What am I going to tell him?"

They didn't have any answers. Jack had to focus on the only thing they did have. It wasn't going to be a comfort.

"We can give you a list of his friends," Jack said. "The ones we know, anyway, but they haven't seen him. That's part of why we came."

He didn't mention Liam. Mrs. Mehta was already beside herself.

If she didn't know about Liam already, she'd find out soon enough. There was no reason to connect his death with Amal's disappearance. They didn't know for a fact the two things were related. It was only a horrible feeling in the pit of Jack's stomach. He tried not to think about the old times, gorging on Cheese Doodles and soda, blowing away zombies for hours on end.

There was a notepad by the phone, and Jack went to get it while Maria comforted Mrs. Mehta. It gave him time to collect himself.

When he came back, he set to filling it with names, asking Maria for last names where he had none. They did what they could.

"Are you sure you're okay to drive," Maria asked. "I can take you to the airport to pick up Mr. Mehta."

Mrs. Mehta's eyes shown glassy and bright with tears as she patted Maria's hand. "Thank you, but . . . I need to tell him, and it's not a conversation I want to have in front of others."

Jack cringed, already imagining how the conversation would go. The accusations, the shouting, car probably veering into traffic when things got physical. That's how it would go in his house. And no, they wouldn't want any witnesses.

"You should stay here and wait for Amal," Jack said quickly. "We should go."

Mrs. Mehta offered him a smile that collapsed in on itself. "No, it's something I have to do. Thank you. I'll leave a note and . . . can I give you both my cell phone number? Will you call me if you hear from him? Or better yet, tell him to call?"

"Of course," Maria answered for them.

They took her number and left her at the kitchen table, showing themselves out.

"What now?" Maria asked as they stood on Amal's doorstep.

Jack's mind was racing through a million different scenarios, desperately trying to come up with one he believed that had Amal safe and sound. But a more urgent thought kept intruding. "I have to get home," he said.

"Curfew?" Maria asked. "Ankle bracelet?" But she said it with a smile to let him know she was teasing. It came across tinged with sadness, though. After the scene inside Amal's house, humor was more than either could manage.

"Ha ha," he said anyway. "Responsibilities. Hard to believe, I know."

But he was torn. Part of him wanted to canvas the town for Amal. The other part of him *had* to get home. Had to make sure everyone there was alright.

He didn't say any more, and she didn't ask. He didn't invite her in when they got to his place. He pretended to himself that he didn't care that the mailbox hung open, the yard cried out for mowing and the flowerbeds needed to be plowed under entirely.

Anyway, he was too worried about Eric. He'd been gone too long.

"Thanks," he said, getting out of the car quickly, ready to bolt for the door.

"Jack," Maria said, her voice somehow holding him there.

"Yeah?"

"We'll find him."

He looked at her quickly through the open window and tried to think of what to say to that. He didn't want to dash her hopes, but neither could he believe, as much as he wanted to.

He'd made the mistake of letting Maria drop him off in front of his house.

His father was waiting for him at the door.

# CHAPTER 7

RAYNA

Rayna held Evan back as the meeting wrapped and everyone else collected their things to go. "Not you," she said, feeling for a minute like a teacher keeping him after class, which was silly. He hadn't done anything wrong. She didn't even know why she felt so . . . unsettled about everything. "We need to talk. It's like you've kept this honkin' huge part of yourself from me. Like I don't even know you."

Evan raised an eyebrow and cocked his head at her dubiously, then flashed one of his grins. Mischievous. Devilish, even. "The 'We have to talk' speech, really? You know, you can't break up with me. We'd have to go out first." He waggled those expressive brows at her.

*Wait, what?* She'd just begun and already things weren't going the way she intended.

"Do you want another drink?" Evan asked, suddenly out of his seat.

He was putting her off-kilter, and she felt unsteady enough as it was. "I don't want another drink," she snapped. "Any more coffee and I'll be shaking like a Chihuahua. Will you just sit?"

Evan's smile subsided as he sank back into the chair, as if he knew things were about to get serious.

"You never told me about this," Rayna began. "*Any* of it."

He met her gaze steadily. "I told you about the club. Aside from that—" He shrugged. "You never asked." He said it matter-of-factly, but she felt it like a barb.

"I— You—" Rayna had no idea what she wanted to say.

"Was I supposed to?" she asked.

"Friends do, you know. I figured not asking meant you didn't want to know."

"But—" She didn't really have a defense. She *had* asked what it was they did in the club, and he'd said they worked on mind-benders and mysteries, including a real life case, but beyond that . . . She really hadn't asked. She guessed it was like the news—she expected the details to be harsh and so she turned away.

"Am I really like that?" she asked instead of whatever she'd meant to say.

Evan had gone serious, and she was suddenly the focus of all that intensity. It sent a jolt of electricity through her—scary and a little exciting all at the same time.

"Like what?" he asked, looking deeply into her eyes for an answer.

She almost forgot the question.

But he was waiting on her response. Watching her. Psychology guy. Rayna wondered what he could read in her eyes and what he'd known about her all along. It left her feeling exposed.

When she didn't answer right away, he let her off the hook. "A little naive?" he asked. "Living life in your own sort of bubble? Yeah, you're a bit like that."

"Shallow," she said, voicing her fear.

He reached out and took her hand, and she was reminded of Maria reaching out to Jack, getting him to stand down. Except, Rayna wasn't on the edge, was she?

"Never," he said. "No one who knows you would think that. You care," he said. "That's kind of your problem, I think. You're afraid that if you pay too much attention, the bad will crush you or the darkness will take over. You're afraid to care *too* much."

Rayna dropped her gaze and saw their linked hands. She started to pull away and then stopped. Evan said she was afraid. This just illustrated it. Why was she pulling her hand back? Because she wanted to? No. Because she was afraid that letting it sit there would reveal something to him, like the feelings she buried because she didn't want to risk herself. Or their friendship.

"You make me sound awful," she said, still not looking up.

He squeezed her hand, rubbing his thumb over it. Rayna wasn't sure she even breathed for fear—there it was again, fear—that her breath might give something away.

"I don't mean it like that." He said. He sounded so sincere. "I mean I understand why you didn't ask. I don't hold it against you. But that's why I didn't tell you more."

Evan took his hand back finally, and she felt loss and relief almost equally. He tried to take a sip of his coffee, but the cup was empty. She could tell from the tilt of the cup and the way he stared into it afterward, as though checking to be sure.

He set it down on the table and gave his attention back to her instead.

"Okay, so enough about you," Evan said, bringing back his smile, dimple forming on his cheek, making him look more like the Evan she knew. "You want to know how I can be fascinated by these things that horrify you."

Rayna nodded. *This* was where she'd been trying to steer things all along. She hadn't planned on the detour down self-discovery lane. She still felt shaken. Evan didn't hold things against her, but maybe she held things against herself. She felt like a terrible friend. And she wasn't sure she was ready to let Evan off the hook either.

"I don't know how to explain it, exactly," Evan said. "Let's try this. You know how various people can study a piece of artwork and see different things. One person might view a painting of a boy in the forest and see quiet contemplation. Another might see despair, hopelessness, a little boy lost. You'd probably look at the painting to form your own opinion. *I'd* be watching the watcher. Art, literature, the threatening notes . . . they're all like a Rorschach test. The way people respond tells you something about them."

"Okay, I get that." Rayna said. Really, it was sweet that he was putting things into art terms for her, as if to reconcile their worlds.

"The thing is," he continued, "I love puzzles, but they've already been solved. There's always an answer key. But the mind is the ultimate mystery. There's so much still unknown. Until we solve it, it's like we all live in the same world, the same painting, but it's near-dark and we're not seeing each other clearly. Or ourselves. We can get lost. We can miss each other entirely or bumble around crashing into each other, causing harm. But if we can shine a light—" he stopped suddenly, blushing. "Nevermind, it sounds silly."

This was his passion, she could tell. And yet he seemed nervous about sharing it with her. She didn't think she'd ever seen Evan unsure. Or anything less than cocky and completely confident.

"Not silly at all," she said, and meant it. What he'd said sounded deep. Noble.

All of her own self-doubt came rushing back.

"What does my art say about me?" she asked. It just popped out and she instantly wanted to take it back. This wasn't about her. It was about Evan and his world. But she hadn't been able to help herself. She had to know.

He gave her a smile. "It says you look on the bright side. You see beauty in the world around you and you want to show it to others. You want to bring us all into the light."

That didn't sound so bad.

"You . . . like my stuff?" she asked, and then bit her lip to keep from saying anything else. She sounded so needy.

"I do," he answered. He seemed to be saying a lot more, his gaze locked on hers, but she was afraid to find out what.

There was that word again. *Afraid*. She needed to find a way to banish it from her vocabulary.

There was a police car waiting in Rayna's driveway when she got home, backed in, nose out in case they had to take off in a hurry.

"Whoa, what did you do?" Evan asked, pulling up one house away as if he didn't want to be seen and associated with her.

Rayna slapped his arm, which she did all the time playfully. It didn't seem so playful this time. She knew she hadn't done anything. Probably the police were just there to question her about the threatening note and her connection to Liam, since Officer Fontanez would have passed along her information. It didn't stop the feeling of dread in the pit of her stomach. Liam was dead. *Dead.* She still couldn't process. She'd seen him just the other day.

"You know I didn't do anything," she said.

Evan reached over and put his hand on her arm where it rested in her lap. His hand was warm, almost hot, as he gave her a squeeze. "I know," he said. "Want me to come in with you?"

He tried for neutral with the question and did a darned good job with it. Rayna couldn't tell whether he wanted to come in to protect her or whether he was hoping she'd let him off the hook. The distance he'd stopped from her house seemed to suggest the latter.

"I'm fine. You go."

"Call me later?" he asked. "Let me know how it went. Anything you find out."

"Will do."

"I'll pick you up again tomorrow. Until further notice, I'm your ride. You're not going anywhere without me. Well, maybe to the bathroom," he said, making an exaggerated face of horror.

Rayna swatted him again, less seriously this time. She was touched that Evan was so concerned, but she was more worried about what was happening inside. The cops weren't sitting in their vehicle waiting for her. Which meant that either Mom or Dad was home and had let them in. She couldn't tell whose car might be pulled into the garage, but usually it was Dad's, his convertible being more susceptible to the elements. That meant he would *know*, really know, exactly how much danger she was in. And curtail her freedom accordingly.

She couldn't blame him. Maybe she even wanted it. Just for the short term. Just until they caught . . .

The Killer.

She had trouble even thinking it. But when she did, the word was definitely capped. In some kind of gothic horror script. Blackened and dripping blood.

She got out before Evan could ask if she was okay. She wasn't okay. But she was better than poor Liam.

She could feel Evan watching her all the way to her door and heard him drive off just as she unlocked it. He didn't wait on her wave.

"Hello," she called tentatively into the house as soon as the door was cracked.

"Rayna, back here," her father called. "In the kitchen."

He met her in the hallway, grabbing her for a huge hug. His cologne was all woodsy, though she couldn't remember the last time he'd even entered the woods. She hugged him back, hard, so glad to have him. Thinking about Liam's mom. About Liam.

Tears wet his shirt where her face smashed against it at shoulder level. Rayna was tall-ish—five foot seven. Dad was just shy of six feet, hair sandy instead of blue. Rayna'd gotten her naturally dark hair from her mother, which meant she always had to strip her hair with bleach before dying.

When Dad pulled back, he kept one arm around Rayna while he released the other. She could see the police officer behind him, watching the whole thing.

"Hi, Rayna," the policewoman said. "I'm Officer Myra Stiles."

In contrast to Rayna and her father, the officer was short, maybe all of five-three or four. Her hair was tightly pulled back into a small ponytail. Her mahogany skin was flawless. She wore the unflattering brown uniform like she was made for it. Or like it was made for her. Maybe she'd added an extra dart or two somewhere. Maybe the force had finally gotten around to his and hers styles. But Officer Stiles's eyes—those were her real strong point. They were dark and beautiful. Almost a perfect almond shape. Rayna thought that she'd love to draw her. Probably an inappropriate thought, under the circumstances, but she couldn't help it. She itched for a charcoal pencil.

"You're here about the threats?" Rayna asked, cutting right to the chase.

"I am. Can we talk?"

Rayna nodded, and her father led her into the kitchen where

he and Officer Stiles had already chosen seats, as she could tell by the coffee cups in front of each one. Rayna went to the refrigerator for a store-bought yogurt shake before sitting down in one of the free chairs. She hadn't eaten anything at lunch . . . again . . . and felt faint. All coffee and no food was starting to give her the shakes.

"I guess you've heard about Liam Hinkle," Officer Stiles began.

Rayna's father glanced at her sharply, making Rayna wonder what he and the officer had talked about before she got home if not this.

"The boy who was killed?" her father asked sharply. "What does that have to do with Rayna. I thought you were here about that note she received in school."

So many things shot through Rayna's mind at once. First, that the police had released Liam's name to the press. Her father must have heard about it, but the name wouldn't have meant anything to him . . . unless the school had called home, as they were known to do with student deaths so that parents were informed there'd be grief counselors available to the students. It was clear, though, that if the school had called, they hadn't connected Liam's death to the notes. But her father was making the connection now. She watched the horror dawn across his face, and the look he turned on her was pure terror.

Officer Stiles saw the same thing, and her voice was heavy as she confirmed his worst fear. "The boy who died received a note as well. We're concerned about Rayna." She turned on Rayna as she said her name. "We need to know everything you can tell us about the note. Anyone you're having trouble with at school. Who you think might have written it. If you know of any other students who've received notes. Any connection you have to Liam or the other students . . ."

Rayna's father cut in. "No offence, officer, but if this is a murder investigation, why aren't we talking to detectives."

"This is an initial canvas," Officer Stiles said. "Right now the detectives are focused on the crime scene and on the deceased. I'll pass along to them the information I gather, they'll cross-check against what they have, follow leads and be back in touch. I know they'll want to talk to Rayna themselves. But there's a lot of evidence that needs to be gathered in a very short time. The first forty-eight hours are crucial. Everyone in the department is on board."

Her father relaxed a bit at that. "Sorry, I'm just . . . I can't believe Rayna's in danger. I can't imagine anyone wanting to hurt her. She's so *good*."

Rayna looked at her father and found him staring back. He didn't often express himself—except when she forgot to put her dishes in the sink or when she left her art stuff around the house or lost track of time. Then she got an earful.

"A killer's motives rarely make much sense to those outside his mind," Officer Stiles said. "Detective shows always make motives appear simple and concrete—money or revenge or custody issues. But . . ." she shot a glance at Rayna as if just realizing that maybe this wasn't the time or place for the discussion, as if she was used to dealing with adults.

"But school shooters and such are different," she continued, apparently feeling she'd gone too far to turn back. "It's usually a build up over time until the person lashes out. Rejection, small slights, not achieving the recognition they think they deserve, feeling the world or someone in particular is out to get them. Often there's a problem at home, coupled with a personality disorder . . . I don't say this to scare you." She was watching Rayna closely for her reaction. "I say it so that you won't leave anything out. Don't decide that something is too small to mention or not worthy of violence. It may be a small thing to you, but exaggerated in the mind of the killer. It might be something you saw—the wrong place at the wrong time. Something you did or failed to do."

It was too much. All of it.

Rayna racked her brain for anything . . . *anything* . . . that she could tell Officer Stiles, but, as with Principal Grayson, she came up empty. If she'd done something to someone, she had no idea what it was.

## JACK

The front door opened as Jack approached. His father loomed there, all six foot two inches of him, arms held loosely, at the ready, as though the beating might start before Jack even got inside. He knew it would be bad. The death glare on his father's face gave it away. And the fact that he was home in the middle of the day. If everything was all right, he'd be at one of his construction sites. If it wasn't, well, he'd need to take it out on someone . . .

Jack forced himself not to run, but walked steadily toward the house, hoping not to give his dad any reason to engage.

"Get in here," he growled.

Jack heard wheels on the sidewalk behind him and turned to see Mrs. Delany pushing her two-year-old down the street in a stroller. She avoided looking at them and sped up at the sound of his father's voice. Jack wouldn't get any help there. Or from anywhere else. He never did. He wondered if the neighbors really didn't know what went on in his house or if they just didn't care. Didn't feel it was their place to get involved. Gave his father a pass because of what was going on with his son, ignoring the fact that he had two, one often seen with bruises and the other rarely seen at all.

He tried not to hate Mrs. Delany and the others. After all, he'd never *asked* for help, probably wouldn't have welcomed it. Not when the police or child services or whoever might try to take him away, separate him and Eric.

He didn't ask now either. Instead, he did what his father ordered. He went inside. He knew from experience there was no chance of stopping what was ahead, but he could never buck the stupid hope that if he did everything right he could lighten the blows.

His father grabbed him by the scruff of the neck as he got close, propelling him into the house and straight up against the foyer wall, kicking the door shut behind him. Jack's back slammed into the wall, aggravating barely-healed bruises, but he refused to wince. He looked his father right in the eyes now, knowing it would go worse if he didn't, if his father thought he wasn't properly attentive.

"What the hell were you thinking leaving your brother alone?" his father growled right up in his face, ignoring the fact that Jack's mother, *his own wife*, was supposed to be there for Eric. "Was *a girl* more important than your brother? Were you too distracted to let anyone know where you were or when you'd be home?"

"There's no girl, and I left a voicemail for Mom," Jack said, even though he knew it wouldn't do him any good.

His father hauled off and hit him close-fisted upside the head. Something sharp caught on Jack's ear—the buckle on his father's watch?—and the pain ripped through him. He felt the blood start to flow down the side of his neck.

"*Don't you god-damn lie to me!*" his father roared. He cuffed him again for good measure, right in the same spot. Jack's head rang; it felt as though his brain bounced from one side of his skull to the other. "I *saw* her. She dropped you off right in front of the fucking house. Do you think I'm blind? That I'm an idiot?"

Jack bit his lip on the smart-ass response that rose to his lips.

"You gonna run off with her? Eh?" he asked when Jack didn't answer. "Leave your brother fighting for his life while you screw some whore? Do you even think about anybody but your-self?"

He tried to focus on the physical pain rather than the emotional. His father shouldn't still have the power to hurt him, but the unfairness of it ate at him.

"Guess I'm too much like my old man," Jack answered before sense kicked in to stop him.

"What?" his father spat at him, eyes about bugging out in disbelief.

He pulled at the bloody part of Jack's ear, twisting painfully, upping the throbbing not only in his ear, but in his whole head. It was all he could do not to let the pain buckle him to the ground. "You'll notice I'm here and you weren't," his father said.

"Why?" Jack asked, knowing it was stupid, unable to control

his mouth. If he was going to get hit anyway . . . "Shouldn't you be at work? Or getting sloshed somewhere with your drinking buddies?"

Jack knew as soon as the words came out of his mouth that he'd screwed up big time. He wondered if his father's blow had given him a concussion or whether the pain was clouding his judgment. It didn't matter. His father's eyes widened. He pulled his fist back for another swing, and Jack ducked it at the last second.

His father's fist impacted the wall so hard it shook the house. As he recoiled in pain, Jack ducked under his other arm and took off up the stairs to the bedrooms two at a time, in a rush to put a door between himself and his father before he could kill him. From the cursing and the clattering footsteps behind him, he wasn't sure even a door would stop him.

"Jack?" Eric called, sounding scared.

"It's all right, Buddy," he called back.

No way Eric would be fooled, but . . . Jack debated about his room versus Eric's. He didn't want to draw Eric into things, but he was desperate to assure himself that Eric was okay. Or as okay as possible.

The hesitation cost him. He could hear his father, far too close on his heels.

Jack reached Eric's room, dashed inside and slammed the door behind him, just as something slammed into it from the other side. He twisted the lock an instant before the door handle turned in his father's grip. He'd made it just in time. But his father could wait him out. He'd have to leave sooner or later—to use the bathroom or to get something for Eric—and then the beating would be twice as bad for his small victory.

"Jack, what's happening?" Eric asked, his voice quaking.

Jack looked away from the door into Eric's anxious face.

"Nothing, Buddy, everything's fine."

"You're bleeding."

Jack reached up and touched his ear, came away with fingers covered in blood.

"It's nothing."

"He hit you again, didn't he?"

Jack cursed under his breath. Lying to his brother wouldn't do any good, but what truth could he tell? "He's just . . . worried about you and has no idea how to express it."

"I hate him," Eric said quietly. So quietly, Jack wasn't sure was meant to hear.

*Me too.* But he kept the thought to himself.

Then Eric asked, "Where were you?" and Jack's gut twisted up, the pain worse than anything his father could do to him.

If he told Eric about the notes, all he'd do was worry, and he couldn't afford the stress. There was enough in the house already. If he didn't . . . would Eric think like their father, that Jack didn't care about anybody but himself?

"I can't tell you, Eric. I'm sorry."

Eric looked hurt. "Was it a girl?"

So he'd heard that.

"Not the way you think. A girl did drop me off, but we're not . . . It's not about her. We're working on a project together," Jack said. "It's really important. Like life or death."

Eric eyed him doubtfully.

"Cross my heart," Jack said, suiting words to actions. "I wouldn't have stayed late if it wasn't deathly important. And I *did* call Mom."

He should have called and called until she answered. *Made sure* she was awake to take care of Eric.

His father was railing outside the door. They both ignored him.

"She did bring me lunch today. A peanut butter and jelly sandwich. Only she forgot the peanut butter."

It wasn't funny, but they smiled at each other, united against their parents. "When Dad falls asleep or whatever, I'll sneak out and make you a proper sandwich."

"Okay."

They fell silent for a second, and then Jack asked, "Why's Dad home in the middle of the day?"

He was afraid of the answer.

# CHAPTER 8

RAYNA

*Six days to die.* Three down, three to go. Three days to find a killer and save herself.

Rayna was so upset after the questioning that she nearly shut the door on Sasha when she closed herself in her room. But the cat managed to just clear the door, yanking her tail up out of the way and fixing Rayna with a reproachful look.

When Rayna flopped down on her bed, back to the wall, legs out in front of her, Sasha jumped into her lap and kneaded her legs painfully before settling down. If it weren't for her jeans, her legs would have been shredded. She stroked Sasha's silky black fur, trying for calm, counting on kitty therapy.

It failed her.

Liam was dead. It twisted her gut that she thought of him more now than she had when he was alive, but . . . they hadn't really known each other. They hadn't had any connection. Until they both ended up on a killer's hitlist.

Rayna realized her hands were shaking and stilled them before she conveyed her nerves to Sasha.

Had she done the right thing, giving those names to Officer Stiles? She couldn't imagine anyone she knew as a killer. Sure, Mark blamed her for the cracks in his midterm pitcher in pottery—it had been her turn on kiln duty the day the piece was ruined. He'd accused her of leaving it in too long, overfiring it. He'd been spitting mad . . . even angrier when she pointed out that the piece itself had been flawed—the walls not uniformly thick, and so different parts dried at different rates, causing stresses. He'd called her some pretty awful names and told everyone she'd sabotaged his grade.

Some of his friends had even listened.

Then there was Dalton, the weekend warrior, who seemed to think his ROTC stuff made him better than everyone else. He hadn't been at all happy when she'd turned him down for a date. He'd even suggested that she played for the other team, as if she couldn't possibly like guys if she didn't fall for *him*. She'd heard other things about him as well, but . . . those were second hand. Rumors. She wasn't going to pass along rumors to the police. It was bad enough she'd given them his name. If he found out . . .

What? What would he do. Either he was the killer and planning to hurt her anyway or he wasn't.

But if Dalton was going to kill anyone, she was pretty sure guns would be involved. Or maybe knives, commando style or whatever. But maybe she was wrong. His training already gave him the chance to play with weapons. Maybe he wanted something more up close and personal. They didn't yet have any idea how Liam and his mother had died.

A sharp pain bit into her hand and she yelped, half rising from the bed. Sasha was an angry ball of black lightning, hissing and spitting, leaping from her lap and turning on her as if she'd been attacked.

Rayna looked down to see her hand covered in blood. In her tension, she must have squeezed Sasha too hard, and the cat had gone on the offensive.

"I'm sorry," she cooed to the cat, even as she searched for something with which to wrap her hand. She found a sock at the bottom of the bed that had fallen short of the hamper and used it to press against the bleeding. The red immediately started to penetrate and spread.

So stupid. How unsanitary was a dirty sock? Probably as unsanitary as a cat's mouth. She was going to have to clean out the wound and bandage it up. She bit her lip in contemplation of how much it was going to hurt.

As soon as she opened the door into the hallway, Sasha shot

through and didn't look back.

Rayna continued to the bathroom and turned on the water, cool and soothing, hoping that would be okay. She should make it boiling hot to kill any germs, but hydrogen peroxide would have to be good enough for that. She rinsed the bite out with water and a little soap applied very gently, patted it dry with a towel and then poured on the peroxide, hissing as it stung and bubbled. Bandaging was tricky. The wound wasn't in a good place, and she was working one-handed. The bandaging was sure to come off. She did the best she could, then hid the bloody sock at the bottom of the bathroom garbage can. She didn't want her parents to see it and freak. This whole death threat thing had made them paranoid. More hovery than usual. Mom, who hated guns, was talking about them getting one, taking her to the gun range, teaching her how to shoot. She didn't want any part of that.

She heard her phone ringing back in her room and went for it, sure it was Evan wanting to know how the talk went with the police and pretty sure that if she didn't answer, he'd worry. Probably he wouldn't panic and call in the cavalry, not right away, but she didn't want to take any chances. And she *did* want someone to tell her everything was okay, that she wasn't a narc, putting people on some police watch list for no reason at all.

Who killed people over pottery or rejection or . . . anything?

Rayna got to her phone just as it would have gone to voicemail, but the person on the other end was not who she expected. She didn't recognize the voice at all. Male, urgent. "Rayna?" the voice asked, "Rayna Butler?" As if there were two of them. She'd yet to meet another Rayna. Not that they didn't exist.

"Who's this?" she asked instead of answering.

"Oh, sorry, it's Charlie. Evan's friend. From the Meddlers."

"Yeah," she said, still unsure why he was calling. Or how he'd gotten her number.

"I'm sorry I missed the meeting today. Doctor's appointment. But I'm catching up now. Evan said the police were at your house, and I wondered if they'd, you know, said something about the murders that could help us figure things out."

"I thought we were all meeting again tomorrow," she said, feeling on the spot. There was no reason he couldn't know tonight. It was just . . . she was still processing it herself. If it had been Evan on the phone, she might feel differently, but she didn't really know Charlie.

"I thought I could get a jump on things," he said.

*The first forty-eight hours are crucial*, Officer Styles had said. But she didn't think that was it exactly. Not based on the almost breathless anticipation in his voice.

Then she realized what it was. "You want to be the one to solve the mystery," she said, stunned. "This isn't a competition, you know. There's no prize for winning. This is serious."

"No, no," he said quickly, "I know. I get that. It's just . . . time is so short. And anyway, I can't focus on homework or anything else with Liam's death."

She understood that. She couldn't think about anything else either. She hadn't cracked a book since the threat. Hadn't even considered it. Her grades were going to slip. She might not live long enough for it to matter.

A chill hit her as though someone had just walked over her grave.

She realized Charlie had gone on while she'd zoned out. ". . . they ask about anyone in particular? Mention any suspects or cause of death or . . . ?"

It wasn't difficult to catch up. "They asked a lot of questions, but they didn't give anything away. I guess they're good at that."

"Probably waiting for someone to know something they shouldn't. So they didn't say who might have done it?"

There was an extra note of urgency in his voice, which struck her as off.

"Why?" she asked suspiciously. "Who should they have mentioned?"

There was a pause on the other end of the phone. In that moment, she didn't even hear him breathing.

"The police came to my house too," he said finally. "I didn't get a note, so I assume that means someone gave them my name."

No wonder he was extra worried about solving things. "And you assumed it was me? We hardly know each other."

"That's why I called. I knew it couldn't have been you. You wouldn't have any reason to think that I'd . . . Anyway, I don't know what to think. Maybe the police are questioning everybody who knew Liam."

"Did you know him?"

"Not well. Like Grace said the other day, he came to one or two meetings, but he didn't stick around. I knew him a bit from school, but just to say, 'hi', not to hang."

"What did the police ask you?"

"The usual stuff. I mean, I guess. I've never been questioned by the police before. Really it was pretty cool. Now I know what it's like."

*Pretty cool?*

He seemed to realize what he'd said. "I mean, not cool in the sense of what's going on, but it gave me some insight and the chance to ask questions about things we've been talking about in the Meddlers, about interrogations and micro-expressions and all that. They did *not* like me asking questions though."

"Too ghoulish?" she asked.

"Maybe." Charlie was silent for a second. "Sometimes I just get so caught up. I guess it doesn't really matter; they already considered me a suspect."

"You weren't able to eliminate yourself? You don't have an alibi?"

"Home, alone in my room doing homework or asleep, depending on TOD—er, that's time of death. Not much of an alibi."

"I'm sorry," Rayna said.

She still didn't know what to make of the conversation and wondered if Charlie realized he'd given away more than he'd gotten in return . . . not that she had any information to give. But she now knew Charlie didn't have an alibi. He'd known Liam, if not well. The police considered him a suspect.

"Not your fault," he answered. "Well . . . goodnight. I guess I'll see you tomorrow."

"Tomorrow."

Rayna hung up, but still held the phone in her hand, thinking over the strange conversation and the even stranger, more horrific day. She hadn't given the police Charlie's name. It didn't seem like the others had any issues with him either—except maybe Grace, but surely their bickering was more good-natured that murderous.

So who had given the police Charlie's name? Was there another threatening note and another potential victim out there the Meddlers knew nothing about?

Evan had equated crime-solving with working a puzzle, only tougher because there was no picture to guide you. Worse, there were so many pieces missing that it was hard to fit together even those they had. She hoped tomorrow's meeting would bring more answers than new questions.

She texted Evan to let him know everything was okay and to mention that Charlie was odd—like he didn't already know that. Then she put her phone on the charger and laid down on her bed. If she was lucky, she'd wake up and this would all be a bad dream. She didn't seem very lucky lately.

# CHAPTER 9

JACK

The rumors were flying fast and loose around school Friday morning. Jack never paid the rumor mill any attention. Usually, he was more the subject of gossip than the recipient, and it was rare there was even a shred of truth . . . like when Katy Baransky was out for weeks last year for mono and everyone said she was pregnant. Various guys were rumored to be the father, him among them. So stupid.

But when Reggie caught him at his locker with, "Hey, man, did you hear about Amal?" he paid some attention.

"No, what?" he asked, slamming his locker door closed.

Reggie reeled back. "What happened to your ear?"

Damn. Jack shook his head hard to make his hair fall into place, a shaggy mess that concealed his face and ears, covering most bruises. The shaking was a huge mistake. It brought the throbbing back to his head.

"Nothing," he said, shrugging like it was no big deal. "Cut it on something." *Like my dad's watch.* "About Amal?"

Reggie was still staring at Jack's ear, as though he could see through all the hair. "Oh, yeah, Amal. Rumor is the police are searching for him, but not just because he's missing."

"They think he did it? Killed Liam and his mom?"

"I guess they'd say that he's 'wanted for questioning'."

"How do you know?"

"The news this morning. I've been scouring it, television and online. The police spokeswoman didn't mention Amal by name. It was all 'seeking missing teen in connection with the murders of

Alexandra Hinkle and her sixteen-year-old son', but who else could it be?"

Not Amal. Jack himself was a more likely suspect. Or . . . well, anybody. The Amal he'd known was all about winning. He'd been driven, compulsive, completely rule and goal oriented. A-student, teacher's pet. Nothing Jack had seen made him think Amal had changed. Or that he'd stray so far from the rules of society as to commit the ultimate crime—murder.

But what if Amal had seen Liam as a rival? An obstacle that had to be removed to achieve his goals? Or what if he saw this as a game and all of them as merely players? The notes could have been like a call to action or the initial cut scene that sets everything up.

But what would be the prize? If the danger had stopped with Liam it might have been top placement at school. But then surely Amal wouldn't have skipped out, disappeared. It would defeat the whole purpose. Likewise taking himself out of play . . . unless now saw himself as the man behind the curtain. The game-master.

No, Jack had a terrible feeling about Amal. He thought back to Mrs. Mehta's tear-stained face and couldn't stand the idea that she'd seen the same reports Reggie had. Bad enough her son was missing, but to see him practically accused of murder . . .

"It can't be Amal," Jack said definitely.

He must have been more adamant than he'd intended, because Reggie took a step back. "Okay, man, it's not Amal," he said, holding his hands up defensively. "Meeting today after school? Coffee shop again?"

Jack's gaze slid to the side. "Can't," he mumbled. Eric had a treatment today, and even though Mom would have taken him long before Jack got home—she always managed that at least—Jack had to be there when he got back. And anyway, with his father on a rampage, he couldn't risk it.

"But—"

Jack stalked off before Reggie could ask any questions.

"Maybe we can Skype you in, or . . ."

Jack raised a hand in good-bye but didn't look back.

He could practically feel Reggie watching him as he walked away. He wondered whether Reggie could see right through him with all of his investigative techniques. Jack wondered how he felt about that. He hadn't told anybody about his family, too ashamed at the way things had fallen apart, his failure to get himself and his brother out. Ashamed about his mother falling down drunk and his father . . . *everything* about his father. But Reggie was smart. He'd been a friend before Jack had pushed him away. Maybe he could help. It might be a relief not to carry the whole burden.

But no. If anyone found out . . . If Child Services came in, they might take Jack and Eric away, separate them because Eric needed special treatment while Jack could be sent off to a home or a foster family. There was no way he was going to be away from Eric when he needed him. And at least Eric was somewhat protected. He had to go for treatment regularly. He had to be seen by people. Doctors, who would recognize signs of trauma or abuse. Who'd be required to report it. No one laid a hand on Eric.

Or maybe Mom and Dad just loved Eric more, blamed Jack for being the healthy one while the better son was sick.

Jack hated thinking that way. He didn't *want* to be the favored son. He didn't care to be anything to those people. And Eric . . . how could anyone *not* love Eric.


He got home after school to a quiet house. Silent. Eerie.

Just stepping through the door he could tell it was empty of life. There was a stillness, a nothingness that instantly ate at the soul. He should be glad of the quiet time. If he was who everyone thought he was, he'd turn up the music to house-shaking levels, raid his parents' liquor stash for anything Mom might have left, and maybe even invite some hottie over to enjoy it with him. In reality, he hated the emptiness.

And feared it.

What if his dad came home early *today?* Got him all alone while he had another wild hair up his butt. No witnesses, nothing to stop him . . .

Jack could run, he knew that. But eventually, he'd come back. For Eric.

And then it would be worse.

So much worse.

With his rep, Dad could always say Jack got his injuries fighting or that someone caught him stealing or . . .

The ring of the doorbell made him jump about a mile, his tensions were running so high.

He didn't want to answer. Everyone he loved . . . or didn't . . . was gone, out of the house. The only people coming to the door of such a bedraggled house would be Jehovah's Witnesses or maybe lawn service people trying to drum up business.

Or the killer.

The bell rang again, this time with some serious knocking and a voice coming through. "Dude, open up."

Reggie. Man, he was going to kill him for the scare.

The irony of the thought didn't hit him right away.

Jack stomped to the door. Reggie's body and face took up the whole of the narrow, grimy window beside it as he stared in.

He yanked the door open and took a step back with it, shocked to see a whole gaggle of people on his stoop. Evan, Kali, Rayna, Grace . . . and Maria. So, not the killer then. Not unless they were all in it together.

"Surprise," Maria said, watching his face. "We brought the meeting to you."

"You can't be here," Jack said, the words surprised out of him.

And when Maria opened her mouth to protest, he added, "No, I mean you *really* can't."

He craned to see beyond them, to make sure his father wasn't pulling into the driveway or trolling down the street. Jack could see and hear him now, the vein throbbing on Dad's forehead, face red with anger. "Your brother's at the hospital and you have *friends* over? Is his possible death interfering with your social life? Is it? Answer me, boy." The blow would come before he could possibly respond.

Maria glanced over her shoulder as if to see what he was searching for.

"But—" Reggie said.

"No buts. You have to go. And I mean now."

Concern creased Maria's face; Reggie's gaze was riveted on his ear. He could almost see them putting pieces together and wondered what the picture would look like when they were finished with it.

"Jack, man, don't have a cow," Evan said, jostling toward the front. "We were just worried about you. And," he looked back at Rayna and lowered his voice, as though everyone wasn't close enough to hear, "Rayna doesn't have that much time. We need all hands on deck."

He'd seen Rayna's note. *Six days to die.* She'd received it on Monday, and here it was the end of the week. This could be the last weekend of her life. He didn't know what to do.

A neighbor's car did a slow roll by, and he felt like it rolled over his grave. What if someone reported back to his father. What if . . .

"Come in. Quickly. But you can't stay long. I mean that."

He took them straight through the house and out back to the concrete slab that doubled as their patio. There was a glass table and rusting ironwork chairs they used to sit on for outdoor family dinners. Now the table held an accumulation of ash from Mom's cigarettes and an overflowing ashtray. It was still cleaner than the rest of the house, and he refused to worry about it. Much. They'd come unannounced and uninvited. They got what they got.

At least his back yard was private, a six-foot stockade style fence all around.

"Sit," he said. He'd meant it to sound like an offer and it came out like an order. He was completely out of practice at being social. "I'd offer you all something to drink, but, as I said, you can't stay."

"What's going on?" Maria asked. "Why are you acting like you're in witness protection or something?"

Jack eyed her. "That's it, I'm in witness protection. We all are.

Dangerous for you to even associate with me. Best if you leave."

"Seriously, man, what's going on?" Reggie asked.

"You didn't come here to talk about me," Jack reminded him.

Reggie stared, still towering, since he hadn't yet taken a seat. Jack stared back, unimpressed.

There was a hard knock on the front door, followed by a double ringing. Jack eyed the gathering. "You expecting anyone else?"

"Probably Charlie," Grace said. "Late as usual."

Jack went for the door, glaring at everyone left behind. Knowing they'd be talking about him and that there wasn't a thing he could do about it.

"Um, hey," Charlie said, going almost as red as his freckles in response to the scowl on Jack's face. "I'm here for the Meddlers?"

"In the back," Jack growled. "Follow me. Don't touch anything."

They'd taken two steps when the bell rang again and Jack groaned. "Now what? You, stay here. Don't move."

He headed back for the door and opened it with a death glare he hoped would scare anyone away. It was the wrong move.

# CHAPTER 10

RAYNA

Jack came back, head hung like he had the weight of a hangman's noose around his neck. He trailed Charlie, which was expected, and was followed closely by two official-looking people, which was not. Police. Even without the badge one wore around her neck and the other at his hip, Rayna would have recognized them. They reeked of authority and suspicion. Their gazes were like laser-beams.

They didn't look anything like detectives on TV. They weren't glamorous, didn't wear thousand-dollar suits. The guy was balding on top. He was big and bulky, with muscle going to pot and a nose that had been broken a time or two and not professionally reset. His partner was tall and narrow in khakis, a white V-necked shirt, and an oversized jacket that didn't give her any shape at all. Her long, red-blond hair was pulled back into a tight ponytail, and if she wore any make-up, it was subtle. But she was pretty in that way you had to search for. Her features were perfectly even, her nose just a little uptilted and her skin so pale it was almost translucent.

"Everyone, police. Police, everyone," Jack said, crossing his arms over his chest and leaning aggressively against the side of the house.

The officers glanced around the group . . . until the male cop's gaze lit on Evan. He zeroed in like Evan was wearing a target on his shirt.

"Evan," the cop said. "I heard you were part of all this. I thought your father warned you off. Now I catch you here."

Everyone's attention swiveled to Evan. He shook his hair out of his face and fixed the cop with a defiant look.

"My father knows me better than to think I'd listen."

Rayna looked from Evan to the detective. "Evan, who *is* this? Do you know him?" Was he the reason Evan hadn't wanted to face the cop at her place yesterday?

His lips twisted as he turned to her. "This is my Uncle Cal."

There was a gasp, and Rayna's head swiveled, trying to see who it had come from. From the way Grace had her hands pressed over her mouth, she could guess. Reggie, in contrast, didn't look surprised at all.

"Lucky me," said the detective dryly. "We're not done with this," he added to Evan, who shrugged and glanced away.

Meanwhile, "Uncle Cal's" partner had scanned the rest of the group and stopped on Reggie, who was gazing back at her with eyes gone as hard and glittering as glass.

"Reginald," she said with a stiff nod. Her voice was as warm as the polar ice caps.

"Officer Travers," he responded, voice even chillier than that. Like the depths of space. "Officer Kincaid."

*Something was going on here.* Rayna wondered what she was missing.

Had Reggie been the victim of racial profiling at some point? Or . . . Wait, Evan said Reggie had started the Meddlers because of his uncle's murder case. Had Detectives Travers and Kincaid been part of that? If so, was it awkward for Reggie that Evan had joined the Meddlers? Or had he been recruited *because* of his relationship with the police? But that assumed Reggie had known. It wasn't necessarily the kind of thing that would come up in conversation. However it had started, *Uncle Cal* clearly wasn't excited about Evan's involvement now.

"We were hoping to talk to Jack alone," Cal said, glaring meaningfully at Evan. "But since you're all here, maybe you can help us out. I'm *Detective* Kincaid, and this is Detective Travers." It was only then Rayna realized Reggie had demoted them in his greeting. "And you're the Meddlers, am I right?"

No one answered at first, though everyone's attention was riveted. Reactions all over the map. Charlie gawked at them with something approaching awe. Maria with concern, Kali and Grace with studied interest. Reggie with a burning anger. Almost, she'd say, hatred. Evan appeared . . . he'd clamped down on his expression. She really couldn't tell anymore.

Jack looked like he always did—pissed. Ready to take on the world. But behind it all . . . Rayna had seen his reaction when the Meddlers had shown up at his door. He'd been scared. What she couldn't understand was why. Jack didn't seem the type to scare easily, so what on earth could he fear from *them*?

"Don't you need our parents around to question us?" Charlie asked. He seemed to have shaken off his initial awe, and now crossed his arms over his chest as though trying to appear tough.

"We don't *need* your parents," Detective Travers said. "Not unless you're suspects." She fixed him with a stare that said his question had been telling, "Are you?" she asked. "Suspects?"

Charlie looked around for backup, but no one was reaching for their phones. No one else was asking for their parents. He subsided with a surly, "No."

"Good." Detective Kincaid met his partner's gaze. "Then I'm going to go inside and talk to Jack while Detective Travers keeps you company."

He motioned Jack into the house, but Jack didn't move.

"I didn't invite you inside," he said, staring Kincaid down. "I don't see why we can't talk right here."

"You have something to hide? Something you don't want us to see?" the detective asked.

It was the same thing Rayna had wondered, and yet she bristled when the detective said it. Out of the corner of her eye, she could see Maria bristle as well, and lean forward as if she might say something in Jack's defense. But that would be a huge mistake. She didn't think Jack would take well to being defended.

"No," he said for himself. "Is there some reason you want to get me alone?"

She heard Maria suck in a breath. As first impressions went,

Jack was not helping himself. Of course, he was a victim, not a suspect. She didn't know why nobody, herself included, could remember that. Maybe it was his attitude.

"Fine, we can talk here. For now," Detective Kincaid said ominously. "Can you clarify your relationship to Liam Hinkle?"

He shrugged. "We used to be friends."

"And now you're . . ."

"Well, I'm alive and he's dead. I assume that terminates the friendship."

No one cracked a smile. If he was going for humor, it fell flat.

"And before that?" Detective Travers asked, maybe hoping she'd have more luck than her partner.

"We gamed together sometimes and then we didn't."

"Did you have a falling out?" she asked.

Jack eyed her levelly. "No."

"What about Amal Mehta?" she asked, consulting a small notebook she'd taken from a jacket pocket.

"What about him?"

"Were you friends?"

"We were, way back in time. I gamed with him too."

"But now you don't?"

"No," Jack answered.

"Why not?"

"Got busy."

"Doing what?" the detective asked.

Rayna felt like she was watching a tennis match, back and forth. Only no one was scoring.

"Shaking kids down at school?" Detective Kincaid jumped back in. "Petty theft?"

Jack glared around the table as though he suspected one of them had ratted him out. Rayna wouldn't have thought it possible that he could become any more set-apart, any more closed in on himself. She was wrong.

"I plead the fifth," he said, lips barely moving they were pressed so tightly together.

"Wait," Kali cut in. "Is Jack a suspect? You realize he was

one of those threatened, right? And what about Amal? There are rumors flying around school—" She stopped short of sharing those rumors, poking blame at Amal. He and Liam had fought, but that didn't mean anything. Kali had been the first to defend him.

Detective Kincaid glared her down, as though he might intimidate her into continuing.

When she didn't, he said, "As of now, we haven't ruled anyone out. He could have sent himself a note as misdirection. Not that we've actually seen this alleged note. Your friend Jack here had a connection to the victim. He had a connection to the missing boy. According to witnesses, he's been aggressive toward one of the others who received a threat." His gaze flicked to Maria and away. "And now I find him here with all of you, including Ms. Butler, who is next on the killer's list . . ."

The chill of that seeped into Rayna, freezing her to her core. She'd known, or at least suspected, that she was next, but hearing it stated so baldly made it all too real.

"That's ridiculous," she said instantly. "Jack didn't even know me before all this. He'd have no reason to threaten me."

"According to you, *no one* had any real reason to threaten you. And yet here we are."

Both detectives zeroed in on her. It was not a comfortable feeling.

"You didn't answer my question about Amal," Kali said, impatience edging her voice. "Have you found him? Are you looking? Should we be worried?"

"About him or for him?" Detective Travers asked.

"You tell us," Kali challenged.

"We can't comment on an ongoing investigation," Kincaid said.

"I'm not asking for details. I'm asking about potential threats. If we see him, do we 'proceed with caution' and all that."

"You should *always* proceed with caution," the detective told her, including all of them in his gaze.

Evan glared at his uncle. "Yeah, thanks for that. Aren't you going to tell us we have nothing to worry about? That you're here to protect and serve? That you always get your man?"

Evan shot a sidelong glance at Reggie, who looked about to boil over. Reggie didn't notice. He had eyes only for the detectives.

"What about Liam?" Maria cut in quickly, heading off whatever confrontation was about to happen. "Did you find out what killed him? Do you have suspects?"

The detectives exchanged a glance. "You're assuming homicide?" Travers said, as if they'd slipped up in some way.

"Come off it," Jack said, speaking for all of them. "Liam was threatened and now he's dead. You can't think that's a coincidence. Besides, the news said the fire was suspicious. Was it arson? Do you know how it started?"

"Do you?" Detective Travers asked back.

Jack huffed. "This is ridiculous. You're just wasting time with us when the killer is *out there*." He waved his hand vaguely toward the door.

Detective Kincaid ignored the attempt at a send off and fixed them all with a hard look, one after another, lingering on his nephew. "This group you have going, this murder club or whatever you want to call it, is a *bad* idea. You're not equipped to investigate crimes. This is dangerous business, and you need to stay out of it."

Reggie stuck out his chin at that, glaring them down. "Or maybe we're more equipped. We don't have to worry about our clearance rates or a rush to judgment. We don't have any preconceived biases."

Detective Travers bristled. As tall as she was, it was impressive.

But it was Detective Kincaid who spoke up. "Your uncle is *guilty*, Mr. Driskoll. I'm sorry you can't accept that."

There was absolute silence on the patio. It was as if even the crickets held still at the comment.

Everyone watched Reggie, who was staring daggers at Detective Kincaid. "No," Reggie said, "he isn't. And I'm going to prove it."

Rayna thought he was going to launch himself across the patio when Detective Travers snorted. Evan and Kali had to hold him back.

"Now, Mr. Harkness. Jack," Detective Travers said, dismissing Reggie that easily, "why is it you can't produce this note you allegedly received?"

And just like that, Rayna went from relief to concern. The police were looking to point fingers. But were they after the *truth*? Could they be trusted to find it?

# CHAPTER 11

RAYNA

Rayna folded herself into the back of Evan's ten-year-old junker, leaving the shotgun seat to Reggie and his long legs. She barely let the door close before asking Reggie, "What's the deal with you and the cops? What's going on with your uncle's case?"

The words had escaped, as they had a tendency to do. People either found it endearing . . . or they didn't. She wished she had a pause button between thoughts and words. She was absolutely sure there was a better way to ask than just blurting things out.

Reggie and Evan exchanged a significant look. It was interesting that whatever Reggie's trouble with Detective Kincaid, he seemed okay with Evan. More than okay. They were friends. Evan was part of his inner circle. Of course, Evan was friends with *everybody*.

Reggie turned in his seat to meet her gaze as he said, "He's in prison for murder. That's the deal. Case closed, as far as the police are concerned."

Bold-faced, almost thrown at her. She didn't know how to catch. It hung in the air for a moment before dropping to the floor like a lead weight.

"Oh," Rayna said, embarrassed and not sure why. For him? For herself? For his uncle?

"He didn't do it," Reggie added when he was satisfied with whatever he saw in her face. "He couldn't have."

*Why not?* Rayna wanted to ask, but she bit it back this time, afraid it might be taken as a challenge or disbelief rather than a simple request for information. Reggie's whole body was rigid. On edge. At that moment, he reminded her of Jack, waiting for the insult or injury.

"Why do the police think he did . . . what he's accused of?"

*Murder*, he'd said, but whose? And why wasn't it the talk of the school? Old news? Had she really been so caught up in her own little world?

Evan put his hand on Reggie's shoulder, as though to signal that he'd take this one if Reggie'd rather not go over it again. He inclined his head in permission. "His Uncle Jim's girlfriend was killed," Evan said gravely. "You might remember the case from years ago—a woman named Marley Thompson. You'd have been pretty young, though. We all were. Jim didn't have an alibi. His DNA was found at the scene—"

"*Of course*," Reggie jumped back in, "because *they were dating*. He was over at her place all the time."

"They'd had a public fight the night before."

"Over a guy she was seeing on the side," Reggie cut in again. "And who the police never even identified or interviewed."

Evan glanced at his friend, over his shoulder at Rayna and then back to the road. She couldn't read his expression. It was closed off. If his face was a window into his soul, someone had slammed it shut. She didn't know if it was because Reggie had cast doubt on the police investigation and maybe his uncle's part in it or because he felt that Reggie was grasping at straws. Or maybe it was something else entirely.

"Whatever happened . . . They never found the guy," Evan said. "The police claim he never existed except in Jim's mind."

"They think he killed Marley in a jealous rage?" Rayna asked, studying Reggie's profile for clues. He'd turned back around and was now staring fixedly out the front window.

"Strangled her. That's what they said in court," he responded, words tight through his clenched jaw. "Black man. White woman. They didn't look very hard for alternative theories."

Evan didn't add anything to that, and they rode in tense silence for a few miles. Rayna recognized the neighborhood Evan turned off into. Liam's. Reggie's. They were close to his home.

"That's the reason I started the Meddlers," Reggie said finally, realizing time was running out. "I knew I couldn't investigate it alone. I knew Evan. And Grace. She knew other kids who were into the whole detection thing. We're working on Uncle Jim's case, teaching ourselves things we need to know. We want to pull together enough information to convince The Innocence Project to take the case."

"The Innocence Project?"

"It's a group that reviews cases where people have been wrongfully accused. They put pressure on to get the cases re-opened, sometimes get them new trials or . . . Anyway, it's worth a shot. So far, all Uncle Jim's appeals have been denied."

"How long ago was this?"

They pulled up in front of Reggie's house, but he sat there for a second, staring out the front window, not moving to get out. "Five years," he said. "Five years he's sat in prison for something he didn't do, losing hope every year. He can't—" Reggie's voice didn't break. It just stopped.

"He can't take much more," Evan finished. "Reggie's afraid for him."

Rayna didn't ask "afraid of what?" She could guess. She couldn't imagine living the rest of her life in a jail cell. Maybe Reggie's uncle couldn't either.


JACK

Jack stared at the business card in his hand. Detective Kincaid had left it. He suspected that the detective—*Uncle Cal*, as Evan called him—wasn't the type to just wait for a callback. For all Jack knew, he'd already left a message for Jack's mother. Or his father. Or both.

Jack's mother wouldn't have her phone on at the hospital. And his father . . . he wouldn't answer a number he didn't know and risk getting a bill collector or telemarketer or obnoxious au-tomated political call. Not that Jack could exactly blame him about that. Even if the caller ID came up as the police department, he couldn't see his father being all that concerned. He wouldn't worry that Jack might be hurt. Or arrested or found dead in a ditch. He might leave Jack to rot. One less mouth to feed.

He couldn't just sit there staring at the card and worrying about what would happen when his father checked his voicemail. There was no predicting. Jack would love to believe his father would actually care about the threat to his life and the fact that people were dying around him. But he knew better.

Somehow, it would be all Jack's fault. He was pretty sure the first question out of his father's mouth would be, "What did you do?" Assuming whoever had it out for Jack had good reason to want him dead. That he'd invited the violence. That was probably what his father told himself every time he kicked the shit out of his son.

Whatever. He definitely couldn't stay around waiting and worrying. No doubt he should start his homework, but he didn't think he'd be able focus.

Anyway, if he was going to be dead in a week, it wouldn't much matter. *Twelve days to die.* Five down, seven to go. The detective had called them the murder club, but it was more like the countdown club, ticking down to death.

He looked at the clock in the kitchen. He wasn't sure how much longer he had before his mother and Eric got home. It depended on how things went. How much time Eric needed to recuperate enough for the trip home.

He almost certainly didn't have time to start the search for Amal. Not in person, but online . . . Well, he might know a few things the police didn't about how to find him.

He started with the multi-user online gaming servers. He never paid attention anymore to who was online. He'd ignored so many pings that his old friends had stopped sending them, but he could still find *GigaMan* (Amal) or *MechGod209* (Liam) or even *Fractious12* (Reggie) if he wanted. All he had to do was set up an alert that would let him know when they were online. Of course, Liam was dead, and he had no idea where or how Amal could play if he was on the run, either from the police or the killer, but it was a place to start. Unless, of course, he'd changed his username in all this time.

But Jack didn't stop there. There were boards for each of the games he knew Amal liked . . . or used to like . . . and for the new games he suspected Amal would have gotten into as well. Time flew by. Before he knew it an hour had passed while he scrolled through message after message, his vision blurring. The worst thing was, he couldn't even be sure he wasn't missing something. For all he knew, Amal had a gazillion different screen names by now. Or was PM-ing people or sending coded messages or . . . There were ways to search, but only if you knew what keywords to use, and Jack had no idea.

If Amal was anywhere online, Jack couldn't find him. Of course, he was no hacker—not like Kali.

RAYNA

Her friend Sierra was waiting on her porch when she and Evan drove up after dropping Reggie off. Rayna glanced sideways at Evan. "You called her, didn't you?"

Not that she minded. The last thing she wanted was to be alone, and her parents wouldn't be home yet.

"Of course," he said, unabashedly.

He got out of the car, leaving her behind.

"Sie!" he called as he approached the porch. "What movies did you bring?"

Rayna huffed, unbuckled her seatbelt and got out after him, hurrying to catch up.

Sierra popped right off the ground, purple plaid skirt flaring around her black tights as she rose. The plaid of the skirt matched the loose tie around her neck over her black button up shirt, which matched her Mary Janes. Sierra might get her hands dirty, but never anything else. She looked like Emo Barbie. The only way to tell she was an art geek like Rayna was the paint underneath her nails.

Sierra held up a brown plastic bag. "I brought some of every-thing—monster mash-ups, mindless explosions, chick flicks. Even a musical." She glanced past Evan toward Rayna. "I figured we could torture Evan with that if you were in the mood. It's called *Hairspray*. I hear it's got John Travolta in drag."

Rayna ignored the bag and moved in with a hug for her best friend. Well, her *other* best friend. "Hey, girl. I appreciate you guys trying to take my mind off things, but I'm not sure it's going to work."

Sierra pulled back, blew a stubborn lock of her thick chestnut hair off her face and looked Rayna in the eyes. "What'll it take then? Wild party? Something from your bucket list? I'd have said we're too young for a bucket list, but . . ."

Sierra ran out of steam mid-sentence.

"No, it's just . . . these might be my last days," Rayna said, "and I don't want to die—"

"A virgin!" Evan cut in, his eyes alight with mischief. "Totally get it. I volunteer myself. It's a sacrifice, but it's one I'm willing to make. For you." He began to tease up the bottom of his T-shirt. "Take me. All I ask is that you be gentle."

Sierra snorted and Rayna grabbed down the edge of his T-shirt, putting her hands over his and trying to ignore their heat, which matched the heat flooding her face.

She was blushing and laughing all at once. "Cut it out, I'm not going to ravish you."

Evan deflated. "Not even a little? Damn, and I wore deo-dorant today and everything."

"Something we *all* appreciate," Sierra said, putting a hand to her chest to show it was heartfelt.

"I was just saying that I don't want to die. Period. There's got to be something more we can do."

"There is," Evan said. "We haven't mentioned part two of our evil plan."

"Evil plan?" Rayna asked, raising an eyebrow.

"Well, not so much evil as the exact opposite. Good? Beneficent? Noble? Yeah, I like that one. Noble." He puffed his chest out, about-faced and swaggered to his car. His superhero walk? She had no idea, but it put a smile on her face. Again. Here she was days from death, and Evan could still cheer her up.

He popped his trunk and disappeared into it. When he re-emerged, he was weighted down with a bundle of wood—two-by-fours of various sizes. "A little help here?" he asked.

Sierra and Rayna raced to help. There wasn't much left in the trunk, but Rayna grabbed a mallet and a few remaining pieces of wood and Sierra slammed the trunk shut.

"What's all this for?" Rayna asked. "You going to board up my windows?"

Evan waited by the front door for her to let him in, which she did. "No, we're going to fit blocks of wood into all the window tracks and into your sliding door so no one can break in that way."

"They can still break a window," Sierra said.

"Yeah, but that would make noise and give Rayna time to get away or call 9-1-1."

"I like it," Rayna said. It seemed like a good short term solution, and it wasn't irreversible, so she her parents couldn't object.

"Then what?"

"I e-mailed you a list of things I found online. I don't know if your parents have time to get motion sensors or an alarm installed, but there's a ton of other stuff they can do—make sure all the outside lights are on and working, cut back your bushes and trees and stuff to prevent anyone sneaking up on the house without being seen. There's even, get this, a film you can put over the windows to hold shattered glass in place so that burglars *can't* just bust in through them."

Rayna's shoulders untensed a little with every word out of his mouth. Evan went straight through to her kitchen and dumped the wood there.

"So, I have permission to play handyman?" he asked.

There was a tingle in her nose, as if she might cry. Evan had really gone out of his way. "Sure," she said. "I'll just be a minute.

Let me check my e-mail and forward the list to my parents. Maybe they can grab stuff on the way home."

"Gotcha."

"And Evan?"

He looked up from eyeballing the wood and the sliding glass door that led off the dining room onto their deck, "Yeah?"

"Thanks."

He smirked and saluted. "No problem."

Rayna stepped into the hall and blinked back the tears that had started to form so that she could see her phone and do what she'd said she was going to do. Sierra stepped out after her.

"He's pretty great, isn't he?" Sierra said.

Rayna agreed.

"Do you think he'd marry me?" Sierra asked.

Rayna laughed. "Now?"

"I was thinking twenty, thirty years. You know, if the Hemsworth brothers turn me down and all hope is lost."

"Then definitely," she answered, even though that thought gave a little kick to her stomach.

For the next two hours, they secured her doors and windows, watched movies, and gorged themselves on microwave popcorn. Rayna hardly thought about dying at all.

# CHAPTER 12

JACK

Jack had set his alarm for crazy-early Saturday morning. School early. He expected to be the first one up in his house, and he was right.

The first thing he did, after making sure his parents' door was still closed and that his father was snoring like a cartoon bear, was check on Eric. He was sleeping too, but not nearly as deeply. Jack watched him for a minute—saw his eyes shifting crazily beneath his eyelids. REM sleep, Jack knew. Dreaming. But the dreams didn't seem to be happy ones. Not based on the scissoring of his legs, his clenched hands and the "No, no!" coming from his lips.

Jack debated what to do. He knew Eric needed the sleep, but . . . He wasn't sure whether to wake him and end the bad dream or let it go on. Would it really be restful the way things were going or would Eric wear himself out? Wake more tired than when he started?

He couldn't take it any longer. "Eric," he said, starting from a foot away. He really didn't want to startle him awake and add any stress to his system.

Nothing happened.

"Eric," he said, approaching. "Wake up, Buddy. It's just a dream."

His leg kicked out, but pulled up short, twisted in the sheets.

"Hey, Buddy."

He put his hand to Eric's shoulder, and his brother jumped like he'd been tasered. "No!" he shouted, lashing out.

The punch hit Jack in his gut, but he barely even felt it. Eric was too weak, even sleep-fighting.

Jack shook him a little harder, hating it. If Eric didn't wake up this time, he'd figure he was in too deep.

But he did. Eric jolted upright, scanning around the room for trouble, his eyes open, but unseeing. His breath coming fast. Jack was worried about his heart rate.

"Eric, it's me, Jack."

He didn't touch his brother again, but waited for him to calm down and for his eyes to focus.

"Jack?" he asked, his voice muffled, as though his tongue was swollen or his lips were too heavy to move.

"I'm here," he said.

"I had a bad dream," Eric told him, his amber eyes meeting Jack's darker brown.

"I know, Bud."

"You left," Eric added, accusingly. "You went away and left me."

"You know I'd never do that," Jack said, untwisting the sheets from around his brother's legs.

Eric stopped him. The clawlike feel of his hand made Jack look at him. "You should," Eric said, when he had Jack's attention. "You should run."

Jack stared at him in disbelief. His heart gave a leap and then sank to the bottom of his stomach. He knew that wasn't literally possible, but that's what it felt like . . . like it was made out of lead, too heavy and constricted to beat.

"What are you saying?" Jack asked, trying not to get angry at Eric. It wasn't Eric he was mad at. It was himself for that leap of the heart, the split second of hope that there was a way out.

"I'm saying . . ." Eric glanced away, but his gaze snagged on Jack's crusted-over ear. "Dad won't hurt me. At least, not now. I know you want to protect me, but I'm not the one who needs protecting. You are. Please, you have to go. I can't stand to see you hurt any more, so you'd be doing it for me."

Jack's nose tingled like he'd snarfed soda and he felt tears starting. Stupid tears. They were *not* going to fall. Maria was coming for him in half an hour. They'd arranged it last night. He couldn't cry. And he couldn't leave. Not like Eric was suggesting.

"Don't even, bro. I'm not leaving you, and that's that. Someday, when you're better—"

"You can come back for me then," Eric said, his eyes holding an appeal.

"Not going to happen," Jack said firmly.

He couldn't tell Eric that he might go away whether either of them wanted it or not. If he was killed. If he died . . .

He had to solve this mystery. He had to find Amal and . . .

Dammit. He wiped away the tear that actually managed to fall, trying to hide it from Eric, but he knew his brother saw. He saw everything.

"Listen, Bud, I need your help," Jack said. To distract Eric. To give him a purpose. He couldn't let Eric protect him, but he could let him help. "I have something to do this morning. It's really important. Remember Amal, who I used to game with?"

"The kid who's missing?" he asked.

Jack nodded. "His mother asked me to help. I'm going to go searching this morning around town, but you're a computer wiz. I figure that if I give you all his e-mails and screen names that I remember, you can look for him online. I did some poking around yesterday and didn't see anything recent, but . . . like I said, you're the pro. Maybe check any social media you can think of too. Tumblr, Vine." Amal didn't strike him as an Instagram kind of guy.

"I can do that, but—"

"And there's a girl who might be able to help, if you find anything and maybe need to follow a trail. I'll give you her e-mail address." He wished he'd gotten Kali's other contact info. Maybe Maria would have it.

"Oooh, a *girl*," Eric said, his eyes shining almost like his old self.

"Relax, she's a goth girl. Just someone I know from school."

"You say that like goths can't be hot. What's she like?"

"She's two years older than you, that's what she's like."

"I'm okay with older women."

"Whatever," Jack said, but he couldn't hide a grin.

"Sure. Whatever yourself. You just be careful, okay?"

That was something, Eric worrying about him. He rose from the bed and smiled back at his brother. "You know it," he said.

Maria was waiting for him down the block, her car running as if she was his getaway driver. Which in a way, she was. It wasn't that he wasn't allowed out. It was that if caught his father would make it a big deal, like he was deserting the family, leaving a million things undone. At minimum he'd insist on every one of those things being finished before Jack could leave, and he'd never get out. That was how it always felt, like he'd never get out.

But he didn't let any of that show when he slipped into the passenger's seat of Maria's car. He had his mask firmly in place.

"Everything good?" she asked, like she had a sixth sense.

"Yeah, great," he answered.

She didn't look like she believed him. He struggled not to care.

"So, where to?" she asked.

He'd already thought a lot about where to search for Amal, but he didn't want her to feel like just a chauffeur, so he figured on talking it through. "I'm not sure. Maybe you have some ideas. The police have probably already checked out the obvious places —the train station, the shelter, the bus station—but it doesn't hurt to check them ourselves in case they missed him. I was thinking maybe we could hit the shantytown out by old Route 41. A lot of the homeless live there. Runaways too, I'd think."

"We have a shantytown?" she asked, stealing her gaze away from the road to stare at him in disbelief.

"Yeah, haven't you ever seen it? The tents, the lean-tos made out of aluminum and plastic sheeting."

"I guess. I mean, I've seen it, but I just thought it was . . . I don't know what I thought."

Typical, really. People denied what they didn't want to see. Or excused it. He couldn't imagine why else none of his neighbors had ever called the police over the yelling and banging that went on in his house, or over Jack's bruises afterward. They didn't *see* the abuse, so it never happened. Or maybe it just wasn't their business. Allowances could be made for the poor family with the dying kid. A shame the other was such trouble.

Jack didn't say any of that, but it took time for his jaw to unclench. "There are other places too. Not too many deserted houses around here, but there are a few that are bank-owned and empty. Some closed down businesses, like that boarded up old hardware store on Layton."

"How do you know about all the houses and stuff?" she asked, gazing at him out of the corner of her eyes, head still turned toward the road.

"Research."

He left it at that. She didn't need to know *when* this research had taken place. Or why. That shantytown . . . it was a scary place. No way could he take Eric there. Ever. Amal wouldn't last a day, which really worried him. Amal probably wouldn't know that. He might think he was tough. He'd beaten out zombies and alien militia. He'd have no idea about the real world.

"I guess we start with whatever's closer."

"Train station it is."

But Amal wasn't at the train station. Maria had wanted to go up to the ticket counters and ask after a boy her age, a friend she was worried about. But the police would already have checked those leads, maybe even reviewed video camera footage. The ticket sellers might report a curious girl asking after the boy they were looking for. So she grabbed time tables so they could check whether Amal had connections at any of the stops while Jack checked every stall in both the men's rooms. Nothing.

They searched the station itself, but there really weren't any places to hide . . . unless Amal had gotten into the staff area. And there weren't any suspiciously slumped figures—sleeping, homeless or otherwise. By otherwise, Jack was very much afraid he meant dead, but since no one fit the bill, he didn't have to analyze his fear too closely.

After that, they went systematically, peering into alleyways where there was debris that *might* be a sleeping person, checking out closed up shops and other buildings for tampering or other signs of squatting. There was one old bakery that had been broken into, but the man and his dog who called it home did not take *at all* well to their intrusion, and Jack had the torn jeans to prove it. It was his one piece of luck that the dog hadn't broken the skin. He'd have had to go for a rabies shot.

By the time eleven o'clock rolled around, they were both dispirited, ready for an early lunch and to call it quits. But there was still the shantytown. Jack got chills just thinking about it. Some things were worse even than his family. He couldn't imagine being one of the kids who lived there. He'd seen a couple of them—dirty, hollow-eyed, ragged. More like scarecrows than children.

It gave him an idea.

"I think we need to make a stop first," Jack said.

"Where?" she asked.

"Convenience store? Thrift store? Maybe both. The people there . . . they've got nothing. I mean really nothing. I think we'll get a lot farther if we can help out."

Maria turned full-on from the road this time to look at him. "I'm seeing another side of you."

Jack shrugged. "Nah, you're not. Purely self-interest."

"Uh huh. So what are you thinking? Blankets? Granola bars?"

"All that. Maybe bottled water. But, uh, the thing is, I don't have a lot of money." He always carried a twenty on him. Something in case he ever had to get away in a hurry, but not so much that he couldn't afford to lose it from his stash if he was pickpocketed. He was willing to give it up for a good cause. For Amal. Anyway, he wouldn't be able to spend it if he was dead in a few days.

"We'll do what we can," Maria answered.

She pulled into the thrift store lot and they came out later with the only five blankets in the place—at two dollars a pop. Already, half Jack's money was gone and they didn't have a lot to show for it. How many people could they help with twenty bucks? Or even forty, assuming Maria had the same. Was it just enough for people to fight over? Jack hoped they weren't going to make everything worse.

Then Maria took them to a grocery, saying their money would go farther there than at a convenience store. They stocked up on store brand peanut butter and cheese crackers, bottles of water and two-for-one cookie deals. In the end they spent fifty bucks and had three bags full of stuff. It wasn't much, but it was what they had.

The drive out to the shanty town was mostly silent, until Maria spoke up. "So, what should I expect."

"I don't really know how to answer that. Have you ever been to a homeless shelter or, like, a soup kitchen?"

She shot him a glance. "No, have you?"

From her tone, he could tell she'd taken his question as a challenge, like he was implying it was something she should have done, and she was throwing it back at him. He knew she was asking whether he'd *volunteered* at one, not whether he'd gone as someone pretending to consider the shelter for his community service hours and asking too many questions, like about what they had to report to authorities. For example, did they have to inform the police about underage kids arriving without guardians?

He answered her initial question instead. "I won't lie, it's rough. There's no running water. No plumbing, which means . . . well, be prepared for the smell. I think when you live there, you don't notice so much, but it's different coming in from outside. Mostly, it's people on their own. Some have lost everything and don't have any family to take them in, but there are others . . . Let's just say that some are off their meds or self-medicating with booze or worse. Still mostly harmless, but . . . Maybe you should stay in the car."

"Are there . . . kids?"

That had been the worst. Jack watched her to see how she was taking it all. "A few."

He left it at that. They were two blocks away now, and it

might have been his imagination, but he thought he could already smell the place creeping in through the closed windows.

There was a tiny two-pump gas station on the corner with bars on the windows, which were nearly papered over by graying advertisements for beer and cigarettes. He wondered whether it was safer to leave Maria in the car or to take her with him. Would the car still be there when they came back? Was he being unfair, judging the neighborhood by its appearance like people judged him? Or by his father's reference to the gas station/quickie mart as a Stop & Rob?

Maria made the call. "I'm coming with you," she said, parking right in front of the store and looking around. "I'm not staying here."

Jack shrugged, but really, he felt better about that as well. He didn't want to leave Maria alone.

"Okay then, let's go."

Maria took a deep breath, probably the last she'd be taking for a while, and then got out of the car. A young guy with a buzz cut, a camo shirt and pants about to fall off his hips came out of the store and leaned against the entrance to eye them. "Can I help you?" he asked.

Jack hadn't meant to buy anything. He was out of money, but it seemed best to get the guy's good will if they were going to leave the car in his lot. He glanced over at Maria, who said. "I'll just be a minute."

She slid past the guy, who watched her go, checking out her ass as she walked away. Jack clenched his fist.

"She your girl?" the guy asked when Jack cleared his throat meaningfully.

"Yes," he lied. He didn't want the guy getting ideas.

"Niiice."

"Thanks," Jack answered tightly.

"Well, I'd better go check her out," the guy said, reentering the shop.

Jack let out the growl he'd been biting back and followed behind him. No way was he leaving Maria alone. It seemed like his new refrain.

Maria already stood at the counter, a jar of Vicks and a Diet Coke in hand. The clerk took the opportunity to ogle her again, from the back and then from the side as he rounded to a swinging door that led behind the check-out window, made of what Jack presumed to be bulletproof Plexiglas with just a small opening to slide money and cigarettes through. He locked the door behind him.

The clerk looked at the purchases Maria had laid on the narrow counter in front of the window and then at her. "Ah, a do-gooder. Should have known."

She didn't answer, but handed over her money.

"It's the Vicks. You must be new at this. Most people bring it with them." He glanced behind her to Jack. "Guess that makes you the muscle. Be careful out there. It's not what you expect."

"What do I expect?" Jack asked.

The clerk looked stumped. "I don't know, man, but just be prepared."

With that ominous pronouncement, he handed over their change, and Jack and Maria were on their way. Maria took a huge gulp of her Diet Coke, then left it in her cupholder as she opened the Vicks and smeared it liberally under her nose. "For the scent," she said, handing it to Jack.

He wondered if he should resist, if the people there would be offended by the menthol scent, knowing immediately what it was all about, or if their senses of smell would be so deadened by their time in the shanty town that they'd never notice. Well, Maria already smelled like Vicks. The damage was done. He might as well join her.

As soon as he was done, she locked the Vicks in the car along with her soda and they trudged toward the makeshift village, the scent growing stronger with every step. He was glad he'd gone with the Vicks. It was powerful enough to overcome the worst of it.

When they got to the outskirts, a whip-thin dog of indeterminate breed cringed, whimpered and wagged its tail close to its body all at the same time, then edged himself forward, scared but drawn by the smell of food through their bags.

"Hey, boy," Maria said, holding out a hand for him to sniff.

He edged just a little closer, sniffing without touching, but when Maria twitched her fingers as if she might pet his head, he jerked and ran away.

They reached the start of the shanty town, dirty tarps flapping in the wind, strung up with tent poles or PVC and held together with duct tape and fraying rope. The path they walked was gravel so flattened into the dirt it didn't even turn beneath their feet. Makeshift shelters were close on each side, some actual tents, some more tarp constructions, others nothing but lean-tos that appeared to be made from the sides of shipping crates or other scrap metal. The path was quickly choked off by partitions that ran every which way and by refuse that clogged the spaces in between.

Jack could feel all the eyes on them, even those he couldn't see, watching as they stopped just inside the town.

Immediately, a tall older man with hair like steel wool and several weeks worth of beard stepped out of one of the tents to block their way. He wore a military style jacket and held onto a half-carved walking stick large enough to be used as a weapon.

"What're you here for?" he asked, eying their bags.

Jack stepped forward a bit, drawing all the attention. "It's me, Mr. H. Jack."

He'd met Horace—or Mr. H, as he'd been told to call him—the one and only other time he'd been there. It was Mr. H who'd warned him off coming, tried to convince him he was better off at home, even with . . . well, he hadn't gotten into the details, but kids didn't exactly run away when everything was puppies and rainbows.

Mr. H eyed him, then beyond him to Maria. "So it is," he said, without looking back at Jack. "You didn't say anything about a girl. You running away? Your families don't understand you? You got her knocked up? This is no place for a baby."

As if on cue, a small child trundled out of one of the tents, only to be dragged back in by a pair of arms and replaced by suspicious eyes in a ghost-pale face peering out of the depths. Others watched more overtly, coming out of shanties to glare or stare at the sacks he and Maria carried.

"We're not here to stay," Jack said, ignoring the rest. "We just . . . we thought we'd bring some things your way. It seemed like they might be useful."

The watchers started to close in, but Mr. H held up a hand and they stopped. They didn't look happy about it, and Jack didn't think he'd be very popular or much in control if he held them off long.

"Charity?" Mr. H asked. "You didn't seem the missionary type."

Jack's heart raced. He could be imagining it, but there seemed a threatening tone behind the question, like something dire would happen if Mr. H didn't like the answer. Jack figured he was just being careful, protecting his people, but it put him on guard.

"It's not charity," Jack said firmly. "It's payback. You gave me some good advice when I was here. I thought this was the least I could do."

Mr. H didn't make a move, like he knew there was more to the story.

"And I'm searching for someone," Jack admitted. "A friend who's disappeared."

Mr. H studied him, as if he could see into Jack's mind if he looked hard enough. He twitched the fingers he was holding up, and the others closed in, reaching for the bags. Not grabbing them exactly, but not giving Maria the opportunity to snatch them away. They moved off with them down the path.

"Merc, Henny, you divide that up. Make sure it's fair. Trace, Doyle, you see everyone waits their turn."

Others came out now, pouring in from all over the camp and closing around the bags—everyone but Mr. H and two other men . . . teenagers really, not much older than Jack. One held a chain between his hands. Not threateningly, just so they could see it. The other had his hand down along the side of his leg, where Jack thought he probably held a knife.

Once the bags were well away, Mr. H said, "I'm sorry, we can't help you."

He didn't sound sorry.

"But my friend is in trouble. The police are looking for him, and his mother's beside herself. You don't want to bring any trouble on yourselves if they come searching and find him here."

Mr. H's boys bristled. Jack hadn't meant for that to come out sounding like a threat. One of the guys took a step forward, the one with the chain. Mr. H didn't stop him.

"Even if we had any boy such as yourself here," Mr. H said, "we wouldn't give him up. Not our way. People don't come here without good reason or really bad fortune. As you should know."

He felt Maria's eyes on him from behind. He hadn't heard her so much as shift through the whole encounter. He wondered if she was cursing him for bringing her or scared out of her wits or giving them all the glare she'd given Jack when she thought he'd written the threatening note. The girl had courage. No doubt about it.

"Could I leave you with a message?" Jack asked, knowing there was no way he'd get past Mr. H's two bully boys to look around for Amal himself, knowing that if he tried things would get out of hand. Surely, the mention of Amal's mom would have brought him out if he wanted to be found. On the flipside, the stir they'd created in coming would have given him more than enough warning to hide away if he didn't.

"Won't do any good," Mr. H said, grudgingly.

"Just in case—if you see him, tell him Jack wants to talk to him. Tell him . . . tell him I know it's been awhile, but I want to help. And I won't call anybody he doesn't want me to. Okay?"

"And the girl?"

"Maria wants to help too."

"Uh huh. Don't know no boy, but if he shows up, I'll pass it on."

"Thank you. That's all I ask."

"Get now," Mr. H said, "if that's all you came for. You make my people nervous, and Trace here is practically begging to go."

The guy with the chain smiled, showing straight yellow teeth and a big gap between the front two. It was supposed to indicate sensitivity, but in this case, Jack doubted it.

He turned to go, finally getting a look at Maria. She was shaking, but based on the expression on her face before she turned, it wasn't with fear. Maria looked furious. Her fists were clenched like his had been back at the gas station. If anyone had made a move, Jack suspected she'd have chosen fight rather than flight, and he tried to stifle his pride.

She wasn't his, no matter what conclusions Mr. H had jumped to. Best if he remembered that.

Maria was silent all the way back to the car, which was, thankfully, exactly the way they'd found it. The kid who worked in the shop stood outside, leaning up against the building smoking a cigarette, something Jack was pretty sure wasn't recommended around gas pumps, but maybe he was far enough away not to worry.

The guy nodded as they approached, ogled Maria up and down one last time, then threw the cigarette to the concrete, smashed it with his foot and went back inside. Maybe in his own way he'd been watching out for them.

Neither of them spoke until they were back in the car, but as soon as Maria took off, Jack said. "I'm sorry. I shouldn't have brought you."

Maria looked at him, stunned, swerving slightly before she corrected course. "Are you kidding? Yes, you should. There's got to be some way to help them. My church group . . . I'm going to talk to them about it. That food isn't going to last long, and then . . . Well, what then? Did you see that kid? He couldn't have been more than two, three tops. And I heard a baby crying somewhere in the camp."

Jack had been too tense to notice, but he wasn't really surprised, except at Maria. She hadn't been horrified. She hadn't been afraid. She'd been thinking about how to help. He couldn't even speak for a second. In his experience, people only wanted to turn away when confronted with ugliness. They wanted to pretend it didn't exist. They found ways to unsee and unhear. If Maria followed through . . . well, he'd wait and see.

He heard himself say, "If you pull something together, let me know. I'll . . . help."

He didn't know how. He didn't have money to spare, and Eric needed his time, but he'd find a way. If not, he was as bad as everyone else, wasn't he? He already had been. He'd turned away, not coming back with anything until he needed something himself. Mr. H had been right to be suspicious.

Maria gave him another glance, but this time he didn't meet it. He didn't want to see her doubt. They rode the rest of the way caught up in their own thoughts.

Jack instructed Maria to pull up an entire block away from his house this time, and when she started to ask, he told her, "Don't."

"But—"

"Just . . . seriously, don't. I don't want to talk about it and you don't want to get involved."

"But, I could—"

*Help*, she was going to say. He knew it. He cut her off, "You can't help. Trust me on this. You can only hurt."

Her eyes were full of concern and her jaw was set, as though she didn't accept his answer. Not for all time, anyway, but she subsided for now.

He got out of the car and walked the block to his house, slowing with each step at the sight of the unknown car in his driveway. That never happened.

A sense of dread stronger than anything he'd felt back at the shantytown squeezed his heart in an iron grip.

# CHAPTER 13

RAYNA

Rayna woke up in a panic. She couldn't believe she'd let last night get away from her. She'd spent it . . . okay, she'd spent it with friends, which was how she'd want to spend one of her last nights on Earth, but . . . Today she had to do something.

She'd had nightmares last night about burning buildings, screaming, confusion, staircases that collapsed under her as she tried to reach Liam and his mother, splintered wood waiting to catch her as she fell . . . It was horrible. She'd woken up sweaty, shaken and motivated.

She had to see Liam's house. Something in the way the police detectives had looked at each other when the Meddlers had questioned them about Liam's death nagged at her. There was something there. Something strange about the fire or the way he'd died. The police would never share it with them, that was clear. Maybe Kali could hack the records. Maybe. But probably not. Police security was surely air tight and anyway, she couldn't ask Kali to take such a risk.

The crime scene was a risk too. No doubt the tape would still be up. If the other day was any indication, there might be nosy neighbors about. But she told herself that even if the police came, the most they'd do was chase them off. Really, the crime scene had already been investigated. She couldn't see how they'd be accused of tampering, especially if all they did was look. She didn't know whether or not she was delusional, but at that moment she didn't care. She had to do something. She had to see that house. She might not have any idea what she was searching for, but

Grace would know, as a future crime scene tech.

Assuming she could convince Grace to go along. The problem was, she didn't have Grace's number. She could call Evan. Probably *had* to call him to get Grace's contact info, but . . . what if Evan tried to talk her out of it?

"S'up?" he asked when she called.

She fought down a stupid flutter in her stomach and plowed ahead before she could chicken out.

"You do know we could be arrested, right?" he said in answer.

And there it was. She *knew* he would try to talk her out of it.

"Yeah," she answered, drawing the word out while she thought.

"Yee-ha!" he hooted, and she pulled the phone quickly away from her ear, giving it the funny look she wanted to give *him* before slowly easing it back. "Welcome to my world!" he added gleefully.

Rayna's heart thumped. Had she been *hoping* he'd tell her she was crazy? That he'd try to stop her? What did she do now?

"Um, thanks?" she said tentatively. "So, er, I guess if we're going to do this, we need a look-out of some kind, right?"

"Yeah, *me*. And maybe Reggie as your eye in the sky. He can keep a watch from across the street where he can see the big picture. And he can listen in on his police scanner."

"He has a police scanner? Are those legal?"

"Weirdly, yeah. They're kind of like radar detectors. Legal to own, not so much to use . . . at least not in the commission of a crime. Okay, you call Grace. I'll text you her number. I'll call Reggie. Let's do this thing!"

He sounded way too excited. Rayna was already regretting her impulsiveness, but she couldn't turn back now.

Half an hour later, Evan had them parked on a road parallel to Liam's, reachable by tromping through back yards. That way no one connected their car with Liam's place and hopefully no nosy neighbors were noting their license plate and calling police. Nothing in her life had prepared her for any of this. She'd have been fine with that continuing. She supposed that as an artist she needed character-building adversity or whatever, but death threats? Murder? She hadn't even picked up a paintbrush since this all began.

Yet today she had her camera. Not the one on her cell phone, but her good Nikon with its telephoto lens and five pound weight dragging at her neck. At least, that's what it felt like. But it was worth it for the pictures she could take, even at a distance, in case they couldn't get close.

She jumped at the sound of a motorcycle revving right behind her as she got out of Evan's car, and turned to see, of all people, *Grace* driving it, a bit badass in her hot pink helmet with bright orange piping and her denim jacket. She had a passenger in a battered black half helmet clinging to her for dear life.

"You can let go now," Grace said as she removed her helmet and hung it on one of the handlebars.

Her passenger mumbled something and hesitantly eased up on his death grip. It was only when he released his arms and shook them out to get circulation going again that Rayna realized it was Charlie.

Evan gave a low whistle. "When did you get this?" he asked Grace.

Rayna turned and shot a quick pic of him, face alight with appreciation. Men and motor vehicles . . .

Grace's eyes shone. "Last week. Dad upgraded his ride."

"*Nice.*"

Charlie looked at him like he was crazy. "Nice? Sure, *you* weren't nearly killed."

"Oh, suck it up, buttercup. It wasn't that bad." To Evan she added, "Car didn't see us and tried to merge into the space we were still occupying. I got out of the way."

"Meaning she shot forward like a rocket."

"You're welcome," she said wryly. "Maybe you can give Nervous Nellie here a ride home?"

"Yes, please," Charlie said with feeling.

"Um, not to be rude, but what's he doing here anyway?"

Rayna asked. "The more people, the better chance we have of being noticed."

"I had to bring Charlie. He's kind of our arson guy. If anyone can tell us if the place is structurally sound or where the fire started, it's going to be him."

"You have an arson guy?" Rayna asked.

Charlie hiked up his pants, slung his helmet over the other handlebar and then turned to answer for himself. "I like fire, okay?" he said defensively. "It's cool. I build things out in the woods and then let them burn—in a controlled setting, of course. I've filmed the burns or done demonstrations for the group. Sometimes I do computer modeling. There are programs for that. It's not like I'm some kind of firebug."

"Or that he tortures animals and wets the bed," Grace added.

Fire-starting, animal abuse, bedwetting—the serial killer trifecta. Even Rayna knew that. The very thought gave her the chills. Grace had been teasing, but . . . she couldn't know whether Charlie really did any of that. It wasn't like he'd advertise.

"I leave that stuff to you," Charlie said with a death glare. Grace stuck her tongue out at him like a bratty younger sister.

Rayna wondered how seriously to take them. The two fought like siblings, but did Charlie really take all the teasing in stride? Could he be the one threatening Grace? But then what on earth would he have against Rayna? Or Maria? Maybe it was like Officer Stiles had said, and the motive wouldn't even make sense to someone who wasn't unbalanced. It could all be about some slight or rejection that she didn't even remember, had never thought twice about. The idea was chilling.

She tried to shake it off. Sierra and her brother fought like that and worse and no one had ever threatened anyone's life . . . that she was aware of. She wanted to think that if there was a murderer among them, the Meddlers would sense it. On the other hand, where better to revel in everyone's reactions, stoke the paranoia, and follow or guide the progress of the investigation than from within the group?

"So, what's Liam's story?" Rayna asked as they cut across

lawns to get to Liam's back yard, mostly to distract herself, but also because it seemed important to know.

"What do you mean?" Charlie asked, blissfully oblivious to her doubts about him.

"Well, none of the news reports have said anything about his father or next of kin. Is his dad . . . deceased?"

Charlie and Grace exchanged a meaningful look. She was getting so tired of that, always being on the outside.

"He left," Grace said baldly. "Like, what, five years ago? Just disappeared."

"Walked out as in deadbeat dad or *poof*, vanished?" Rayna asked.

"Like that," Grace said.

"I heard he left a note," Charlie added.

Grace snorted. "Too bad it wasn't a bank note."

"Did they suffer?" Rayna realized as the words left her mouth what a stupid question that was. Of *course* they suffered. She'd meant financially, given Grace's comment. But the abandonment alone must have been terrible. Poor Liam. And his poor mother. "Nevermind," she said swiftly.

All talk stopped as they got within view of the ruins of Liam's house. They were no longer smoking, but that was the only change Rayna could see from the other day.

She paused to snap a few photos. The camera had been a combined Christmas/birthday/everything for the whole year present. There was almost no shutter delay. As long as they didn't get caught and the camera confiscated, they should have some great crime scene photos to go over.

Evan held them back while he called Reggie. He reported back to them that the coast was clear. "He says to hurry, though. Weekend buys you a bit more time, but the neighborhood's going to be up and running soon and someone's bound to notice us." He turned to Rayna with a grin that set the butterflies already in her stomach to fluttering. "You ready to break and enter?"

Grace huffed and started forward, not waiting for an answer. She headed straight for the crime scene tape blocking off most of the yard leading toward back of the burned out house.

"No breaking necessary," she said, reaching the tape and sliding under it like it was no big thing. "Just don't get us in any of your pictures. The better for plausible deniability at trial."

"Uh, trial?" Charlie asked.

"You in or out?" Grace challenged.

Evan ducked under the tape, holding it up for Rayna to go through, her camera held protectively against her chest. It left Charlie the odd man out. He stared at them, glanced about furtively, and finally ducked under the tape, grumbling as he went.

The closer they got to the burnt out remains, the stronger the feeling Rayna had of walking over someone's grave. She knew it wasn't so. The bodies were long gone, and while she believed in souls, she didn't think they hung around after death, but still . . . it felt ghoulish to be there, taking pictures. Disrespectful.

She told herself it wasn't just her own morbid curiosity. She wasn't interested in some gothic photo study. She and the others were trying to make sense of Liam's death, make it mean something by uncovering clues that would save others. She thought back to her conversation with Evan about why he did what he did and she started to really understand that his fascination was about making sense out of insanity or order out of chaos. She reordered her world through art; his framework was forensics.

But studying the charred and trashed remains of the house, she also understood how naive she'd been to think there was anything left for them to find.

"What do you think?" Grace asked Charlie as they reached the battered-in back door. It was dark inside, but not so dark they couldn't see blackened debris and the lighter gray of fallen drywall.

"It's a wreck," Charlie said. "Between the fire and water damage, it's not going to be safe, but as long as we don't touch anything that might shift the balance, we should be relatively okay. Oh, and here, you're going to want these."

From his back pocket, he produced a smooshed up bundle of light blue fabric with dangling white strings and set about untangling them.

"Surgical masks?" Rayna asked, taking hers when offered. It was still warm from Charlie's pocket. She wasn't entirely sure she wanted a butt mask. Next to that, stale smoke didn't seem so bad.

"Trust me," Charlie said. "In a fire all kinds of chemicals and stuff get released into the air from varnishes, manmade fabrics, carpeting and all that. There's a reason first responders wear masks. Even so . . ."

He didn't finish the thought, but he didn't have to. Rayna knew many of the rescue workers after 9/11 had continuing problems. She hadn't considered that this would be anything like that.

She and the others tied on their masks. Rayna surprised herself by being the first to step over the charred threshold into the house. Even through the mask, the scent hit like a door slammed in her face. It was toxic. Putrid. Like superheated chemicals and something wet and alive all at the same time. Like a swamp marsh when generations of things had lived and died and were now rotting away, probably from all the water that had been sprayed and left behind, stewing with the chemicals that had liquefied and the ash and soot that had fallen. The inside of her nose burned, and she couldn't take a deep breath.

Grace gave her a firm push between the shoulder blades, and forward she went, breathing as shallowly as she could. She felt at first like she was hyperventilating. Like she couldn't take in enough air, but she raised the camera to her eye and snapped off pictures, trying to distract herself.

She had to step carefully inside. The back door led them into a dining area off the kitchen that was relatively untouched. The table still stood, serving up nothing but fallen drywall. Half of the ceiling had come down, knocking over the chairs and leaving plaster everywhere. It looked like there was some sort of buffet or china cabinet on the far side of the room, but it was beyond what they could reach without shifting debris which would likely bring more down around them. It would be worth the risk if it was likely to turn up evidence, but Rayna had seen the outside of the house and where the damage was most severe. This wasn't the source of the fire. Neither did it seem to be the scene of a murder.

They left the dining room behind for the kitchen, which was off to their left. Here things were even worse. The ceiling hadn't come down, but it was so buckled, it appeared about to crash down at any minute. And a thin sludgy stream of gunk trickled from a crack in the ceiling to pool on the counter. It wasn't a large kitchen, but it must have been overflowing with stuff. There was debris all over the floor—broken glass and ceramics, like from a cookie jar, grocery bags, receipts and mail, coffee grounds, egg-shells and worse from an overturned garbage can, all of it still damp, the ripe scent overpowering.

She snapped more pictures, setting the camera to take mul-tiple photos with every press of the button to be sure she didn't miss anything. Charlie moved out from her side and shifted things around with his foot, maybe to uncover evidence, maybe out of morbid curiosity. She snapped pictures with every shift. Then she saw him reach down to move something aside with his hand. Her stomach lurched at the thought of touching anything in that sick-ening soup, but when she thought she saw him palm something, she almost threw up. Instead, she depressed the button, focusing on the click after click that let her know everything was being immortalized. She had a purpose. She couldn't lose sight of it.

They went out into the hallway and stared at the cracked and blackened banister and charred stairs leading up to the bedrooms. That was where they really wanted to go—where the murders had happened . . . or at least where the bodies had been found. Pre-sumably also where the fire had started. Would the stairs support them? What about the landing? Rayna knew from seeing the scene that part of the second floor had collapsed, as in no walls, ceiling fallen down crushing everything beneath it, putting all the weight on the buckling and broken flooring. But the police and medical examiner must have gotten up there, right? For their investigation. To remove the bodies. Surely they'd reinforced the floors or . . .

Well, she didn't know. Maybe they'd used cranes or cherry pickers or something to get the bodies out.

She turned to ask Charlie when Evan's phone rang suddenly,

a jangling tune issuing from his back pocket.

"Subtle," Grace said, a wicked smile on her face. "Points for stealth."

Evan ignored her to answer the phone, eyes going wide as he listened to whoever was on the other end. "We have to get out of here," he said to them.

"Why? What's up?" Grace asked.

"It's Reggie. There's chatter on the police scanner. Report of a break-in here."

Rayna glanced from them to the stairs and back to them. "You go. I have to get upstairs. This can't all be for nothing."

Grace's eyes bugged out, like she thought Rayna was crazy, but that was just Grace. And anyway, she was feeling crazy.

"Come on," Charlie said, pulling at Grace's sleeve. She didn't look like she needed the encouragement.

"Hurry," she said to Rayna.

Rayna nodded, then put them out of her mind and tried the first step. It bowed under her foot. She decided to keep to the outside of the stairs, where they'd probably be the strongest, anchored to the wall. She couldn't think about anything but putting one foot in front of the other. She didn't reach out a hand to the wall to help support herself, as much as she wanted to. She couldn't bear to touch anything, and anyway she didn't want to leave fingerprints.

The banister disappeared less than halfway up, and when she got there, the top step was gone. Just gone. It had been burnt all the way through. She paused only briefly to snap pictures before she stretched out, ready to overstep the missing stair, testing whether the landing would hold her weight. It was blackened, the carpet that had been there melted to a hard chemical sheen on top of the debris-strewn floor.

Holding her breath, she took the step. It groaned horribly, and she had a moment where she was sure she was going through the floor . . . and then nothing happened. Two more steps were all she could risk. The collapsed section of the upper floor was in front of her, and she took fifty or so pictures in quick succession—through the open doorway into the room to the left. To the right. Straight ahead. Up and down. There was a new scent up here. It wasn't as stifling, with part of the house open to the elements, but it was . . . it was burnt organics this time, overpowering the chemical smell. Hair and flesh and . . . feces. Bowels released in death. The police might have taken the bodies, but something of them remained behind.

Rayna's bile rose, and she had to swallow down acid that burned as it went. Overheated and chilled all at the same time, like she had a bad case of the flu, Rayna turned back for the stairs, but forgot about that top one. She cried out as her foot crashed through, grabbing frantically at the wall but finding no handhold. Her leg sank all the way up to her knee before her foot caught on something. It was the only thing that kept her from pitching down the stairs face first. The camera hit her breast bone with a painful impact, and her leg screamed with pain. Some of the wood fragments she'd fallen through had embedded themselves in her calf, not stopped by her thin jeans. At least her sneakers had protected her feet.

She was struggling to pull herself free when the over-bright beam of a flashlight caught her full in the face. The words, "Stop right there" froze her, as if they had that kind of power.

The police had found her. Rayna panicked, her heart beating triple-time. She flinched away from the light and, thinking fast, used the movement to cover her as she thumbed the memory card out of her camera and closed the chamber. At the policeman's order, she raised her hands over her head, skimming her hair as she did and shoving the memory card into her ponytail. No doubt the police would seize the camera and realize the card was missing, but even if they searched her . . . well, she hoped they'd miss it. She had to get a look at those pictures. Like she'd told the others, it couldn't all be for nothing.

She just hoped they'd gotten away.

# CHAPTER 14

JACK

He approached the door like it was a snake that might bite him. His key was in hand, and he turned it in the lock slowly, hoping it would be quiet enough not to alert anyone. He didn't want to be grabbed inside and slammed up against the wall before he could get a sense of things. Or at all.

He opened the door just as cautiously. It was impossible to be soundless, but it was as quiet as he could make it. Inside he heard voices. Fairly raucous voices, coming from Eric's room. His brother and someone else . . . A girl?

Who on earth?

And where were his parents? His father's car was there. His mother's was probably in the garage, but he didn't hear either of them. Not that they were loud when his father wasn't knocking him around and spoiling for a fight. His mother was likely passed out. It was his father he was worried about. He listened harder and heard the sound of something start up in the garage. A saw? His father working around the house? It couldn't be.

A horrible, horrible thought came to mind—his father finally blowing a gasket, taking things out on Mom when he couldn't find Jack, dismembering her body in the garage like the deer he used to hunt.

He froze. He knew he was keyed up, still on adrenaline overload from earlier. His father had been violent, was growing more so, but Jack couldn't believe he'd actually kill. At least not Mom, who was too passive or passed out to incite him most of the time.

The idea wouldn't leave him, though. He had to check on

her. Before confronting his father in the garage with a weapon and with other potential victims in the house.

Jack closed the door quietly behind him, but not entirely. Latching it would have made noise. He crept up the stairs to the second floor of their split level, avoiding the squeaky step, and started down the hall, past Eric's room with its closed door and the voices behind it to his parents' room. He knocked quietly, just in case, but he didn't wait long before opening the door. He had to know . . .

His mother sat there, propped up in the bed, a sweating drink in her hand as she watched a reality show on the wall-mounted television.

His relief was ridiculous. He wanted to collapse with the release of tension, but he locked his knees and stayed upright.

"Who's here?" he asked when she turned to him, too slowly and somewhat glassy-eyed, but at least present.

"A friend for Eric," she said, not remotely interested, despite the fact that Eric *never* had visitors and that with his compromised immune system probably *shouldn't*.

Not that he said any of that. There was no point.

Now that he knew Mom was safe, his anger was back full force. She couldn't even *pretend* to care. Not about Eric and not about where Jack had been or what he'd been doing. Though for sure his father would ask . . . and wouldn't like the answer he was given.

He went to see the one person who would care. Eric. Anyway, the curiosity was killing him.

He was just outside Eric's door and the voices were now coming in loud and clear. Video game trash talking. There was no mistaking it.

Jack knocked and the voices stopped.

"Come in," Eric said, his voice deadened, like he thought his fun was about to end.

Jack pushed the door open and found—

Pretty much the last person on Earth he expected to see.

Kali sat in the single chair in Eric's room, pushed back so that it was practically in line with his headboard. She had a camo-colored controller in her hand to match the one Eric held, and frozen on the screen before them was the game *Unlife and Limb*. They were hunting zombies. They'd paused the game with one of the ghouls chest shot, blood splattering the screen.

"You didn't tell me you had such a sick brother," Kali said, her kohl-lined eyes glittering.

Jack started to bristle before he replayed the sentence in his head. She probably meant *sick* as cool. It had been so long since he'd thought of it that way.

"Um, yeah, so what are you doing here?" It came out as a challenge when what he should have said was, "Thanks for keeping Eric company."

But, no, what he really meant was *What the HELL are you doing here?* He hadn't invited her into his home. Or any of the others.

"Eric and I got working on the Amal thing, and then we thought it would be easier to work in person, and then we kind of exhausted everything and decided to let off steam while we waited for pingbacks."

Eric was studying Jack, and Jack hated that he looked unsure, as though Jack might fly off the handle like Dad.

"Um, cool," he said, forcing his lips into a smile. His face nearly cracked.

Eric relaxed.

Jack hated to ask, but he had to know. He turned to Eric, hating even more that there was no way for Kali not to overhear and draw conclusions. "Dad thought it was okay?"

"Well, he let her in," Eric answered. His gaze bored into his brother's like he was trying to convey a host of unspoken information.

"O-kay," he said, glancing around for a place to sit, knowing there wasn't anywhere but the foot of Eric's bed, which would put him in the line of fire, between them and the zombies. He gave it up and stayed standing. "So, tell me what you've learned so far."

Kali's phone vibrated then, clattering on the bedside table where she'd laid it. Everyone watched as she picked it up. Her face didn't change expression, but she said abruptly, "I've got to go."

"Quick rundown first? Come on, don't leave me hanging."

She grabbed for her satchel and stuck the phone inside, but she didn't immediately rise to leave. "Okay, quick update: if Amal's gone into hiding, he's gone down some really impressive rabbit hole. We haven't been able find him. Anywhere. We *did* find a huge fight between him and Liam, but you knew that was a thing. Turns out it was over some paper Amal said Liam plagiarized. Liam said it would ruin his life if anyone found out, which it kind of might if it got onto his permanent record and kept him from getting into a good college. He sort of threatened Amal and Amal responded back in kind."

"Speaking of threats," Eric said, leaning forward in excitement, "some kid named Dalton threatened Liam into doing some papers for him and tutoring him in history. He said he'd pound him to dust if he didn't."

Dust. But what about ashes?

"Liam went along with it?"

"Sounds like," Kali said. "But if so I don't know why Dalton messed with him in the lunchroom his last day." Her sharp eyes pierced through Jack. It could be *his* last before too long, and they both knew it.

"Maybe Liam backed out? That would certainly give Dalton a motive."

"Maybe," Kali answered.

"Oh, and there's something else," Eric said eagerly. "Liam was looking for his father. There are these websites where you can post about deadbeat dads and find advice on how to track them and ads for investigators. Liam was all over them."

"How did you find out all this?" Jack asked.

He'd only sent Eric looking for Amal. He knew Kali had hacked Liam's school e-mail, but what else had she hacked? Could it be traced back to Eric?

"Sorry, I really do have to go. You got this, kid?" she asked Eric.

He nodded and hit her with a knuckle bump, which she met with one of her own. Then she rose off the bed, swiped graham cracker crumbs off her black jeans with the ripped-out knees, and swung her backpack over one shoulder.

"Come back soon?" Eric asked. It broke Jack's heart how desperate he sounded. It had to be hard for Eric day in and day out with no one but Jack for company. Maybe he should bring visitors by more often, but . . .

"You know it." She headed for the door. "Oh, and Rayna's been arrested," she tossed over her shoulder.

"What?" he asked, his voice rose dangerously before he could get it under control. He glanced over at Eric to make sure it hadn't alarmed him, but his brother seemed to be eating up the drama with a spoon.

"Uh, maybe we should take this outside," he said, shooting a meaningful glance toward his brother.

"Not on your life!" Eric said. "I know what's going on. Kali filled me in. And even if she didn't, I'd have figured things out. Dad was in a fury when he woke up and found you gone. Almost like he was worried."

But they knew better, didn't they?

And then the words *really* registered. "In a fury?" Jack asked. "Did he . . ."

He couldn't say it. Not with Kali there listening.

"He threw some stuff around and then stalked off to the garage. I don't know what he's doing in there."

At least he hadn't hurt Eric. That was all he cared about.

Into the sudden silence, the sound of a saw wailed again, though it was short-lived. All kinds of things ran through Jack's mind—like his father building a pine box for his remains.

Jack turned to Kali, who was curiously still there. "I'm sorry, you were saying you had to go."

She gave him a shrewd look. "Yeah, I did. Walk me out?"

Jack looked at his brother—at his nearly bald head under the baseball cap he'd probably donned to hide things from Kali, the outline of his bones through his skin, the pallor from the sickness and so long without the sun. He seemed tired now that the adrenaline rush of doing illicit online research and shooting CGI zombies had passed. Another reason to get Kali out the door. Eric needed his rest.

"Sure," Jack answered. "Back in a minute, Bud."

Eric gave him a half wave, and he waited for Kali to proceed him. He walked her all the way to her car, being excessively quiet opening and closing the front door. The saw sound had stopped. He didn't want to risk his father hearing and coming out.

But Kali didn't immediately click open her car. When they got to it, she turned around and eyed Jack, that same all-seeing look in her eyes she'd had back in Eric's room.

"Your brother's really great," she said, as if Jack didn't already know that. "What's his prognosis?"

He stared at her. It was ballsy, coming right out with it. She didn't have the right to ask, but . . . well, anyway, she had. There was no point in pretending Eric's situation was anything but bad. She'd seen for herself. "The doctors give him a thirty percent chance. He's got leukemia. He's been fighting it for a while now. Years on and off. But this time . . . it's aggressive and resistant."

"He's homeschooled?"

"Yeah," Jack answered. In the sense that he took his classes online, not in the sense that his home was any kind of learning institution.

"Must be lonely."

"Yeah," Jack said again. "So, what was in that message? What's the rush about leaving?"

"Changing the subject?" she asked with a smirk. "No, I don't think so. We're talking about you. What's the story here? Your ear and the bruises you're always sporting—they're not from fights at school, are they?"

She wasn't just ballsy, she was out of line. "None of your business."

It wasn't a denial. She seemed to realize that.

"Yeah, I know a little something about that," she added so quietly Jack wasn't even certain at first what she'd said, as if his brain had to fill in the gaps for his hearing.

He stiffened. Was he even meant to hear? Should he ask or let it go? Would it be prying to continue questioning?

She had her car door open and herself locked inside before he could decide what to do. A millisecond later, her car rumbled to life, and he instinctively stepped back. Away. The moment gone as if it had never been.

RAYNA

Rayna felt so many things all at once she thought she might explode. It was like one of those whirly, cyclonic rides at a carnival where the bottom drops out but centrifugal force keeps you pressed up against the walls. Like she couldn't breathe and was terrified, but alive and exhilarated all at the same time.

She'd *done* something. Really done something. Broke into a crime scene, took pictures. *Important* pictures, not just butterflies and bridges and other pretties, but actual life and death. Well, death anyway.

But the feeling didn't last. The reality of sitting in the back of a police car, in handcuffs, headed for the station started to sink in, as did the fact that she was feeling buzzy over taking photos of Liam's final resting place. Morbid. And horrible.

Still, her heart was beating overtime and she didn't feel she could take a full breath. Her chest felt so tight the discomfort of the cuffs barely registered.

She didn't know what to expect when she got to the station, but after a kind of entrance interview, where one of the officers who'd arrested her took all her details and wrote them into a report, she was escorted to a bare-bones room with a scarred table, a few chairs, a viewing window with one-way glass and nothing else. The arresting officer who'd led her there offered her a soft drink or water, and she thought about refusing, having seen enough movies and TV to know they could get prints and DNA from the can, but since they'd already caught her trespassing, and since she was desperately thirsty, she took him up on a Coke.

The soda came before the detectives, and she had a quarter of an hour to sit and think. It was a good strategy. By the time they arrived, she was dying to talk just for something to do. Not that fifteen minutes was so long, unless you were left alone with nothing but your thoughts, a can of cola and whatever designs you could draw in the condensation.

And actually, it was only one detective—Travers. Maybe they thought Rayna would be more susceptible to girl talk. Maybe she was the one who was available. It didn't matter, Travers was the one she got. She remembered Reggie's hostility toward the woman and was instantly on her guard as Detective Travers took a seat across the table from her and opened a file.

That was when it hit Rayna that she'd have a *police record*. Would they charge her? Would that kill her chances of getting into art school? Any sort of college? Would she . . . go to jail?

Travers read something from the file. For show, Rayna was almost certain. She'd have come prepared, wouldn't she?

Then she looked up and met Rayna's gaze. She hoped she was showing no fear, but she had a bad feeling Detective Travers saw all.

"For someone with a spotless record before now, you've certainly jumped right into the deep end. Violating a crime scene. Tampering with evidence. Trespassing."

"Tampering with evidence!" Rayna squeaked. She hadn't done a thing . . . unless they knew Charlie had grabbed something from the crime scene. She was going to kill him. If she ever got out of here, she was going to kill him herself.

The realization of what she was thinking hit her hard, and she let her breath out in a blast as if she'd been gut punched.

Detective Travers watched her with almost a preternatural focus. It was freaky.

"Your camera," the detective said finally. "The memory card is gone. It doesn't take a detective to figure out you didn't go in without a memory card, especially since there aren't any pictures in the camera's limited cache. So, the card held pictures, evidence of the crime. And now it's gone. Where?"

Rayna was afraid to look away for fear the detective would read something into it, so she held her gaze. "Dropped out," she said. "When my foot went through that stair, it startled me. I jerked and must have hit the release button. Have you checked the house?"

Detective Travers eyed her silently for a full minute, during which Rayna distracted herself trying to figure out the color of her eyes. They'd probably be considered hazel, a mix of brown and green fighting for dominance. She wasn't sure which would win and wondered if it depended on the light or what the detective was wearing. The stark black blazer she had on over her boring white shirt didn't help her one way or the other.

"Try again," Travers said when her study was done.

"The officer searched me before he put me in the car. I don't have it."

More silence, and she thought she might scream. She was tempted to say something else into the void, maybe tell Detective Travers that she'd swallowed the card. But that was likely what she wanted, Rayna the noob to blurt out something incriminating. Swallowing the card *would* be tampering with evidence—or concealing it, anyway. They might even keep her in custody waiting for it to pass through her system.

She wondered if she needed a lawyer, but knew her parents couldn't afford one.

*Her parents!* Oh, they were going to kill her.

There was that word again—*kill*. She wondered how many times a day she used it not even thinking.

"Tell me who does have it and you're free to go."

Rayna stared. Did she really think Rayna was *that* stupid? Even if she had handed off the card to someone, she wouldn't just give them up.

Rayna crossed her arms and sat back in her chair. "Am I under arrest? Aren't you supposed to Mirandize me or something?"

Detective Travers mimicked her motion. "When you're officially under arrest, you'll know it and you'll be Mirandized. Is that what you want?"

As if they'd take what she wanted into consideration.

"Look," she said, leaning forward, her face softening as she caught Rayna's eye, like she was changing tactics, "you and your friends are treating this like a school project. Running around, getting underfoot, endangering yourselves. You need to let us handle this."

Rayna was certain her disbelief showed on her face. "You think we're not taking this seriously? Hello, Liam's *dead*. It's my turn next . . . or didn't you get that memo? You want me to sit back and wait for the killer to come? Maybe get my affairs in order? Lock me away if you want to. Maybe I'll be safest that way—" She slapped her hands over her mouth, wishing she could recapture the words. "I don't mean that."

For some reason, the idea of a night in prison scared her worse than potential death. One was real. Immediate. The other—as terrifying as it was, she couldn't wrap her brain around it. Couldn't believe it. Didn't want to.

"I know," Detective Travers said. Her voice matched her softening approach. "Don't worry. When we send you home—*if* we send you home—it'll be with protection. You won't be alone."

"What will it take to get back home?" Rayna asked.

"Cooperation."

It was going to be a *long* day.

But it wasn't, really. After what felt like several hours later but was probably only one there was a hard knock on the door. Without waiting for a response, it opened. Another man, fit, bald-headed, plain-clothed like Detective Travers, came in holding a file with X-rays or film or something overflowing the boundaries. Detective Travers met him halfway across the room—two, three steps, max—and he opened the folder to show her what was inside. She glanced over at Rayna, then back at the folder, and motioned the other detective out into the hall.

"Your parents should be on the way," she threw back over her shoulder as she followed him. "Wait here."

Rayna watched her go, wondering desperately what was in

that folder. Well, there was one way to find out. She was already in trouble.

Rayna crept to the door and pressed her ear to it. She couldn't hear much through it, probably by design.

So she tested the knob. It turned in her hand, and she felt a moment of thrill. It was hard to turn it as slowly as she knew she had to not to be noticed. Or to edge the door open centimeter by centimeter until she could press an eye to the slight gap. Sounds rushed in now. And scents—stale coffee, overripe bodies, bleach —sharper but not much different than in the interview room itself.

But she was solely focused on the figures in front of her. Detective Travers was so intent on the detective she faced that she never noticed. "What do you mean 'It isn't him.' His bed, his house, his mother dead."

She could only see the back of the other detective's head, but he was holding out two films, which he gave a shake. "I don't know what to tell you. The dental records don't lie. Whoever the kid was, it wasn't Liam Hinkle."

Rayna gasped and backed away from the door. The gasp felt like her last breath. She couldn't seem to take another one. In case the detectives had heard her, she hurried back to her chair and collapsed into it. She tried to look innocent, but shell-shocked was about all she could manage.

Someone else had died in Liam's place?

# CHAPTER 15

RAYNA

Her mother cried.

Her father ranted on and on while she sat in the back of the car on the way home, still trying to process what she'd heard.

*Not Liam.*

Did that mean he was still alive or that there was another body out there somewhere, waiting to be found? And if not him, then who? The only other missing boy she knew of was Amal.

Horror clenched her heart all over again. Had they gained Liam but lost Amal? Had they gained Liam at all?

"I asked you a question," her father said, his voice raised. If she were to paint him right now, he would be angry slashes of red across vivid, half-hidden patches of yellow for the fear he was trying to mask.

"What?" Rayna asked, knowing it wouldn't calm him that she hadn't been listening.

"I asked what you were thinking—breaking the law, breaking into a crime scene. Jeopardizing your future."

He took his gaze off the road to study her in the rearview mirror.

"I was thinking I had to do something or I might not *have* a future."

One day to die. It was all she had left, according to her note. The clock had already started ticking. She didn't know the hour of her death. The note hadn't been that specific, but six days from Monday was tomorrow, which meant that any time after midnight . . .

Her mother suddenly choked on her sobs and whirled in her seat. "Don't say that. Don't you dare say that. We have a police escort. You've got surveillance until the killer is found. And when you're not at school, you're on house arrest, got that. I'm not even sure about school."

The anguish on her mom's face nearly killed Rayna right there.

"Mom—"

"Don't 'Mom' me. We can't lose you. We just can't. Okay? Promise me."

As if Rayna could promise. As if the universe would hold her to it. But she couldn't and it wouldn't, and Mom seemed to know that. She turned back around in her seat without Rayna's answer.

"You know we love you, right?" her father asked, his anger apparently spent.

"I know," Rayna said, fighting her own tears now. "I love you too."

They reached their house and her father clicked the garage door open so they could slide right inside. Officer Stiles pulled in behind them. She was going to be staying for a while, at least until her relief arrived. Rayna wondered if they'd have surveillance outside the house as well, but if so, no one had shared those plans with her.

They hadn't even gotten out of the car when her father's cell phone rang. Rayna heard the officer's voice coming through when he picked up. "Teenager approaching. I recognize him from the office files—Evan Nunez. Should I send him on his way?"

"No!" Rayna practically yelled. She grabbed her father's shoulder. "Dad, I know you're mad, but please don't make me sit home all alone. I'll go crazy."

"Alone?" he said, face twisting. "I'm glad your mother and I count for something."

"You know what I mean," she said, not sure how to explain. "Please?"

"He put you up to this, didn't he?" he asked. "That boy has always been trouble."

"No!" she said. "I promise. Look, Mom, Dad, we won't go anywhere. We'll be right here. Safety in numbers, right?"

Her mother and father exchanged a glance. She had no idea what it said.

Finally, her mother said, "Oh, John, let the boy come. It'll keep her mind off things." She turned in her seat. "But you're still grounded, young lady. You only use your phone as a phone. No going online and no using your laptop except for homework. I don't want you broadcasting on social media where you are and what you're doing, making it easier for . . . people to find you."

Rayna opened her mouth to protest about the laptop. She needed it to view those pictures. Without it . . .

"Okay?" her mother asked, making it clear her agreement was the only thing that would get her what she wanted.

She huffed and flopped back into her seat. "Fine. House arrest. You going to put me on bread and water too?"

"Would it help?" her father asked.

It sounded like a feeble joke, but the look on his face was indescribably sad.

"No," she said. "But pizza might."

"I'll take that under advisement."

Her father gave Officer Stiles the go-ahead, and she gave the order to let Evan through. But they were all to stay put—in the garage, out of sight of the street—while she checked out the house. No one was going inside until she gave the all-clear.

She started with Evan as he walked up, frisking him to make sure he wasn't carrying any weapons. She confiscated his pocket-knife, telling him he'd get it back when he left. Then she pulled her service weapon, held it close to her leg so as not to freak the neighbors and went to search their house.

Rayna held her breath. Evan reached out and took her hand, squeezing it. "I waited for you to come home," he said.

She squeezed back. "Thanks."

Evan's hand felt overheated . . . or maybe it was the heat of her father's gaze on their joined hands. He hadn't missed it and he wasn't happy about it. But she and Evan had been friends forever.

Her father should know better.

When Officer Stiles waved them in, she and Evan went right to her room. "Door open!" her father called.

Rayna rolled her eyes, but she kept the door cracked the slightest bit. How the hell was she going to get a peek at those photos?

Evan moved them away from the door with a hand on her arm. "Did you get the pictures?" he asked quietly.

Rayna looked toward the door to make sure it wasn't edging open, then reached up into her ponytail. She had to root around. It seemed easier just to let her hair down. She pulled the band out and finger combed her way through her hair until she found the memory card. Evan watched her the whole time.

"What?" she asked, catching him with an odd expression on his face.

"Nothing, it's just . . ."

"Just what?"

"I hardly ever see you with your hair down. It's pretty."

"Oh." Suddenly, Rayna had no idea where to look, so she focused on the tiny card in her hand. "Here." She held it out to him. "They're all on here, but I'm grounded from the computer."

"You have a card reader?"

"Yeah, but how will that—" She slapped herself in the forehead. "You can plug it into your phone."

She went for the top drawer of her dresser, where she kept her cords and other electronics and came up with the card reader, handing it over to Evan.

"Will your dad freak if I sit on your bed?" Evan asked.

Rayna blushed. "Sorry, I don't know what that was about."

"I do," Evan mumbled. But he didn't say anything more. He plugged the card reader into his phone and fiddled with settings. "I have to download and install the program for it, so give me a minute."

Rayna didn't know what to do with herself. Normally she would have sat down next to Evan and looked over his shoulder, but now she felt . . . fidgety. Something was changing. Whether it was Sierra's comment about him the other day or Evan's reaction to her letting her hair down, suddenly the idea of sitting on the bed with him had implications. And she wasn't ready to deal with them. For one thing, her life was in danger. For another, he was her best friend. She didn't know what she wanted, but she knew what she didn't want, which was to screw up their friendship if she was reading the signals wrong.

So she paced, so on edge she nearly jumped out of her skin when the doorbell rang.

"Who is it *now*?" she asked, as though Evan would know.

To her surprise, he had a guilty expression on his face. "I, uh, might have told the others you were home safe."

A moment later, Rayna's father pushed the door open, and she was doubly glad she hadn't sat down next to Evan. He took a quick look around, noted the distance between them with grim approval and announced, "More guests," before stepping aside to reveal Grace and Charlie.

Rayna wondered whether he'd have let them in or turned them away if he wasn't worried about Evan and Rayna being alone together.

He hadn't told Grace and Charlie to leave the door open, so the first thing Grace did when he left was close it.

"So, what've we got?" she asked instantly.

"Working on it," Evan replied, intent on his phone.

"Well, I've got something," Rayna said.

Evan glanced up from his phone. The others looked to her as well, and she felt the full weight of what she was about to say. Suddenly her mouth felt unbearably dry.

"The guy who was killed in that fire in Liam's house . . . it wasn't him," she said. "The dental records don't match."

There was a second of stunned silence before Grace asked, "How do you know?"

"I overheard it at the station."

"Does that mean Liam's . . . alive?" Charlie asked.

"Maybe. And that someone else is dead."

She eyed him. One hand lay protectively over the pocket of

his pants, the same one she'd seen him tuck something into back at the crime scene.

"Why don't you show us what you picked up at the house?" Rayna said, staring pointedly at the pocket he was protecting. "Maybe it will break the case wide open."

Charlie looked pole-axed. "W-what?"

"Come on, Charlie, I *saw* you. What did you grab in Liam's kitchen?"

Now he had everyone's attention. Grace's, in particular. She was staring at that hand as if she thought she could see right through it. "Give it up," she ordered. "I'd go in that pocket and get it myself, but . . . I'm not going in that pocket."

"It isn't anything," Charlie insisted, but he did reach in and pull something out, small enough that it sat inside his closed fist. "Just . . . a memento."

Reluctantly, he opened his fingers, and resting on his palm was a little soot-stained bird. Silver . . . or silver-toned, anyway. Rayna wondered what it had been doing in the kitchen until she saw the little holes in the top of its head, like for salt or pepper.

"So," Evan said, drawing it out, considering his next words, "you took a souvenir. From a murder scene."

Charlie refused to take his eyes off the little bird to meet his gaze, but Grace wasn't letting him off that easily. "You do know that's, like, one of the signs of a serial killer, right? Taking trophies."

"What?" Charlie squawked. His fist closed around the little bird, his eyes wide and wild as he responded. "You think *I* did this?"

"Did you?" Grace asked.

"What? No!" he said as soon as he could force words out. His eyes were the size of cereal bowls. "If I had done it, I'd have taken something then rather than wait until I had witnesses. And it wouldn't have been a silver damned bird."

"So you've given this some thought?" Evan said casually. Rayna spotted his dimple and thought he was just teasing, but she couldn't be sure.

"Had to ask," Grace said with a shrug.

Both of Charlie's fists were balled now, as though he might throw a punch. Then she saw him take a deep breath and force himself to relax. She could almost hear the countdown in his head.

"No, you didn't," he said. "Maybe that's why you were targeted, Grace. You poke people. You're always poking."

Grace narrowed her eyes at him. "What's that?"

"You," Charlie said, more distinctly now, "are always poking. Prodding. Sniping. Maybe someone couldn't take it anymore. Maybe you poked the wrong person."

"You almost sound like you approve," she said dangerously.

"If someone decided to take you on, face to face. Yeah, I might approve. But this way . . . there's nothing to admire."

"Yet you took a souvenir."

"Come off it—"

"Okay, children," Evan said, oddly the voice of reason, "if you're finished sniping at each other, I've got something here. The photos are up."

Evan stood so that everyone could crowd around, but four people around one phone . . . the visibility wasn't great. And the small screen sucked for detail. Still, he flipped through the photos. The only sound in the room was of everybody breathing.

"It's no good. I'm going to have to get these home to study on the big screen."

"We can't we do that here?" Grace asked.

"Not with a police officer in the house and this as contraband. Also, I'm grounded from the computer," Rayna admitted.

"Then we've got to go."

"My house is closest," Evan said.

"Yeah, but *I've* got all the cool software," Grace said. "At least when it comes to the crime scene stuff. We'll want to call Kali as well. I never know *what* she has access to."

Evan shot Rayna an apologetic look, knowing she was getting left behind. Knowing she'd hate it. "Fine," he said. "Go for it."

Grace got out her phone, and Evan moved Rayna off to the side. There wasn't far to go. The room wasn't that big. He turned her to face him, a hand on each of her shoulders, and looked deeply into her eyes. "I'm sorry about this," he said. "Especially after you got arrested and everything to get the photos, but I promise, I'll keep you in the loop. You've still got your phone, right?"

Rayna nodded.

"I'll call or text you the second we come up with anything. And if your parents don't shoot me on sight, I'll stop back later, okay?"

She nodded again, too emotional to say a word. They were leaving her alone. Well, not alone, she knew that. She'd have her parents and Officer Stiles. But still, it felt like desertion.

"I promise," he said again.

But this time, he followed it up with a quick, hard kiss. Rayna was so shocked she didn't even react.

Evan was gone before she had to, out the door with his phone and her memory card. Grace shot a wink over her shoulder as she followed him out, and Charlie didn't look at her at all.

She was left staring after them.

# CHAPTER 16

JACK

After Kali left Jack went back to check on Eric and found him fast asleep, game controller in his hand curled against his chest like a teddy bear. He turned off the game system and the television and quietly closed Eric's door on his way out.

His father emerged from the garage as he exited, glowered his way and then went about wedging pieces of wood into the track of the sliding glass doors and into the upper parts of windows so that they couldn't be opened. Jack knew he should disappear into his room—out of sight, out of mind—but he stopped to watch.

Had the police talked to his father? Was he taking their warnings to heart? Was he actually . . . protecting Jack? As in, "I'm the only one who gets to beat my son?" It didn't make any sense to him, and he didn't like it. Probably his father was baring doors and windows from outside threats. But how was that going to help against those on the inside? All it did was slow Jack's less obvious escape routes.

His father sensed him standing there, though, and he turned from the window in the kitchen where he'd just finished wedging a dowel to glare in Jack's direction. "I'll be sleeping with my gun," he said, staring into Jack's eyes. "If anyone tries to break in—"

Jack shuddered. His father sleeping with a gun. He wondered how his mother felt about that. He knew how he felt. He'd rather take his chances with the killer.

When Maria called two hours later, he was about ready to climb the walls. He'd gone to his room and done his homework like there was nothing going on . . . and checked his phone about six million times, as though he wouldn't have noticed a call or text coming in.

"We're meeting at Grace's," she said. "Want me to pick you up?"

"You my designated driver?" he asked.

"I guess so. You in or out?"

It was a good question. He'd stayed in his room since the gun comment, not giving himself any chance to set his father off. But he was going stir crazy. He had to get out. And if the others had found something . . .

"In," he said, ignoring the burning sensation that started in the pit of his stomach over the confrontation that was already happening in his head. "Would you pick me up at the end of the block?"

"Um . . . sure. Which end?"

He told her and hung up. Ten minutes, she'd said. He had ten minutes to get out of the house to meet her.

He peeked out into the hallway, hating that it made him feel timid. Hating that he had no idea what he'd encounter.

His father was sitting on the couch in the living room, raising a beer to his mouth. He paused before it hit, as if he could sense Jack from down the hallway.

There was nothing he could do but advance or retreat.

Jack went forward, headed toward the front door.

"Going out," he said, as neutrally as possible.

His father didn't turn around. "With that girl?" he asked.

He weighed his answer. Would he get in more or less trouble if he said yes?

"Going to meet friends. We're . . . trying to figure things out."

"The police told me about that," he said. "They said it's dangerous."

"Someone threatened me and others. He's already killed. I think waiting for him to make his next move is more dangerous."

His father took that aborted swig of beer. There were three empties already on the table next to him. "So you're taking initiative." He said. Hard to tell how he felt about that.

Jack nodded, then worried he'd get in trouble for not answering aloud, unsure his father could see his response in the darkness of the hallway. "Yeah," he added.

"I want you home by dark."

It was on the tip of Jack's tongue to ask what he wanted him for, but he didn't dare. "It's four o'clock already," he said.

"Uh huh," his father said, taking another swig of beer. "Figure you've got about two hours, give or take. Better not waste 'em arguing."

Jack got out before his father changed his mind. He knew what came next.

Maria was waiting for him at the corner, just as she promised, but Reggie was sitting shotgun, and he was forced to get in the back. They were locked in a discussion of some new show he'd never seen, and he had to be content to watch the houses go by as they drove.

Grace's place wasn't far away, a white, box-like one story house with concrete stairs and a low concrete stoop in lieu of a porch. But it was pretty. A wrought-iron railing marched up the stairs and kept people from falling off the stoop, capped at the top by more wrought-iron trellis work shaped like vines and roses. Someone had painted the roses red—the only bit of color in the black, white and concrete color scheme.

Inside, as they found when Charlie came to let them in, the house was bigger than it looked like from the outside, deeper than it was long. Charlie led them past a neat living room with slate gray walls and white furniture, past a kitchen and small dining room of light wood furniture and white accents, and back toward what had to be the bedrooms, though each of the doors (white, of course) was closed except the one at the end of the hall from which voices emerged. It was no wonder Grace rebelled by wearing all the colors of the rainbow.

Jack was the last to the door, and there wasn't really room for him to go much beyond it, which was kind of okay, because after the sparse tidiness of the rest of the house, Grace's decor was a little combative. There was color everywhere, as if her wardrobe had exploded. There were clothes all over her bed, clothes on her floor, jeans and socks overflowing a white wicker hamper. A floor to ceiling bookshelf took up one wall, filled to bursting with a riot of books shoved every which way and two or three deep. He wondered how she ever found anything she was looking for.

Everyone was clustered around her small desk, which faced her window, blinds currently closed to cut down the glare. He couldn't see through the others, but he'd bet the desk was a disaster as well. He wondered if it was a riot of paper or troll dolls or . . . he couldn't even imagine.

"There. Right there," Kali said as they entered. "Enlarge that."

He pushed in a bit, shoving Reggie to the side so that he could see. Reggie was like the Jolly Brown Giant. There was no way to see past him.

Reggie did his best to move, got his feet tangled in something, and started to timber. Jack caught him with a hand to his back and one to his arm.

"Thanks," Reggie said, fixing his glasses, which had slipped askew.

"No problem."

Reggie ended up turning his body, so that he was edge on to the desk rather than facing it, and Jack wedged in uncomfortably beside him to view the computer screen.

On it, Grace—who was the only one sitting, since she had the sole chair—played with an image, grabbing a section, cropping it, enlarging. Enlarging again, choosing some kind of option to up the sharpness and contrast. Jack couldn't tell at first what they were looking at as the filter slid across the image, doing its work section by section. When it finished, he leaned in close, despite the fact that he was about to enter Maria's personal space.

"Is that an earring?" he asked. "What's the big deal?"

Reggie gasped, and when Jack contorted to look at him, he'd

swear all the blood had rushed from Reggie's face.

Kali glanced from the monitor to Reggie and back again, leaning in a little closer. "Is that—"

She didn't finish.

Jack nudged Reggie in the ribs with his elbow. "What's the matter, man? Is it yours?"

He was joking, but Reggie didn't smile. He looked like he'd seen a ghost.

It was Kali who answered. "It's the missing earring from his uncle's crime scene."

Grace enlarged it one more time and then turned wide eyes on Reggie. "Oh my god!"

"It's not *my uncle's* crime scene," he said through clenched teeth, "but how did it get *there?*"

Maria turned and laid a hand on his arm. Jack tried not to let it bother him. "What's going on?" she asked.

Reggie looked down at her as if she was the first thing he'd truly seen since that earring had resolved. "You know how I told you my uncle was put away for a crime he didn't commit—for killing his girlfriend?"

"Yes," Maria prompted.

"The one thing the police never found was Marley's other earring. She was only wearing one when they found her." He was having trouble talking. The words were coming slowly, reluctantly, as if he wasn't just speaking them, he was reliving the whole thing. "They searched my uncle's truck and his house, hoping to find it, thinking it would be the smoking gun. They never did."

"So what's it doing in Liam's house?" Grace asked, as if Reggie would have the answer.

"I don't know."

"It doesn't make any sense," Kali said. "The police would have bagged and tagged jewelry and other valuables at the Hinkle place, wouldn't they? To take an inventory, see if anything had been stolen and all that. How did they miss the earring?"

"They didn't," Evan said, leaning in as close as he could get and pointing. "Someone must have placed it among the debris.

Check it out—there's no ash or soot dulling it. The pearl is still shiny enough that Kali noticed it in a photo of the room at large."

Everyone looked at him.

"But why would anyone do that?" Kali asked. "And who? This was a closed scene."

Grace turned in her chair. "There were footprints in the ash in the pictures Rayna took."

"We figured they were the crime scene techs or the rescue workers," Evan said.

"Maybe not." Kali said. "You all got in. Someone else could have done the same."

"But *why*?" Grace asked. "Why plant evidence *after* the police had come and gone."

"Maybe it wasn't for them." Charlie dropped the comment like a bomb, and it had the same concussive effect.

"It was for *me*," Reggie said into the sudden silence. "Or for us. Whoever did this knows something about Marley's murder. Maybe even murdered her themselves."

"But—" Jack started to say, but it wasn't anything that hadn't been said already. *Why?* Why revisit this old murder, especially if someone else had already gone down for it? What could it possibly have to do with Liam and his mother . . . or whoever had died in Liam's place? And why plant evidence for the Meddlers? How could anyone know it would be found? Unless . . .

He shot a sidelong glance at Reggie, stunned at the direction of his thoughts. The only person he could think of with a reason to bring up new evidence on the old case was the person trying to prove the police had gotten it wrong. And, of course, Reggie wouldn't give the evidence to the detectives, who'd have every reason to play it off and defend their conviction. He'd arrange for it to be found by those who *would* investigate. But why that way, planting it at the scene of the murder?

Going to the Hinkle crime scene hadn't been Reggie's idea, but he'd known about it. They all had. But Reggie lived right across the way. He had the best access and would have had enough time to plant evidence before they all arrived.

But was that all he'd done? He had trouble believing Reggie would hurt anyone outside of self-defense. Surely, he wouldn't kill and commit arson just to plant evidence to convince people that his uncle was innocent. And if he did, he'd do it brilliantly enough that they'd never figure it out, wouldn't he?

Jack must have had a really odd look on his face, because Reggie asked him, "What?"

"Nothing, just . . . you live right across the street. I wondered if you'd seen anything."

Jack couldn't tell about anyone else, but Kali glanced at him sharply when he mentioned Reggie living right across the street from Liam, as if she realized the implications. Her lips pursed, and she glanced from him to Reggie for an answer.

"If I saw something, I'd have said something," he said, staring back at the screen again, at the earring that had no place being in Liam's house. Jack couldn't even imagine what was going through his head.

"What do we do now?" Charlie asked. "Turn this over to the police?"

"No!" Reggie said. When everyone looked at him, he added, "The police will think *I* planted it. Hell, Jack does. Don't you, Jack?"

He didn't glare, but Kali took care of that for him, giving Jack a poisonous look before she turned to Reggie. "How would you have gotten hold of Marley's missing earring?" she asked. "You'd have been, what, twelve when she was murdered?"

"Eleven. But that's the point. They'll be sure the only way I could have gotten the earring was if my uncle had it all along."

"Well if he didn't, who did?" Grace asked. The question tumbled into a sudden dead silence.

Reggie looked stunned. He backed up into Grace's bed and then collapsed, on top of the clothes and all. Beneath him, something crunched, like a snack chip bag. He didn't seem to notice.

It was Maria's turn to glare, and she spread it around, like an enraged librarian who'd just caught them all running through the aisles. Maybe with scissors.

"We can't start turning on each other," she said. "Pointing fingers doesn't do any good. Maybe we need to go back and re-examine Reggie's case."

Jack couldn't help but wonder if that had been Reggie's plan all along.

But the Meddlers were already going over the case. Would Reggie really threaten everyone, kill Liam and his mother just to take things one step further? It didn't seem as though the discovery of the earring would be enough to get his uncle's case reopened. Unless they were able to trace the earring back to someone else.

It would help to get everyone's alibis for the night of Liam and his mother's murders. Starting with Reggie. Only there was no way to ask without practically accusing him of the crime.

# CHAPTER 17

RAYNA

Rayna spent what might be her last night on Earth sitting between her parents, eating pizza and watching a movie—one of her childhood favorites, which they'd seen at least a dozen times already: *Night at the Museum*. She couldn't really concentrate, not when she was listening harder for any noise from outside than she was to the dialogue. But eventually she found herself smiling, was shocked when she actually laughed as though she wasn't under a death sentence.

Officer Stiles had been switched out for another, who'd introduced himself as Officer Joe Repucci. He was nearly twice Stiles's size, and Rayna expected a voice that rumbled up from his toes. She was surprised when he seemed so soft-spoken. He was also constitutionally unable to sit still, and had patrolled the house and the grounds on an almost constant basis since he'd arrived. It probably should have been a comfort, but instead Rayna found that his perpetual vigilance kept her from relaxing. Which was maybe as it should be. She didn't dare let down her guard.

When the movie ended and her parents got up to empty their bladders and refill their glasses, she jumped at the chance to check her phone, which her parents had insisted she put away during the movie.

There were three texts from Evan.

*Found something in the crime scene photos. A lost piece of evidence from Reggie's uncle's case. Weird, right? I'm sending you the pic.*

The next was a multimedia message, and Rayna had to approve the download. What appeared was the grainy photo of a pearl earring in a silver setting sitting among the fire debris. She hadn't noticed it when she'd been there, but then, she'd been more worried about shooting a bunch of photos before the police arrived, hoping she'd have time to study them later.

The third message was different in tone and time stamped about forty minutes after the first.

*Rayna, did you get my messages? Everything okay? Should I come over?*

She quickly typed back, *All okay. So strange about the earring. What do you think it's doing there?*

She didn't know what to answer about coming over.

*Don't know,* he typed back. *Reggie didn't have his files with him, but we're all getting together to review the evidence tomorrow. Your place? Are you still on house arrest?*

She hoped there would be a tomorrow for her, but she pushed that thought down deep. She had protection. No one could get to her. In theory. It would be crazy for them to even try.

*Yeah, grounded,* she sent back, adding *Come over.*

She didn't know what her parents would say, but she knew she could convince them to let him in. The more people around her, the better.

Evan showed up around nine-thirty, even though he couldn't stay long, since his parents had insisted he be home by eleven. Rayna's parents, usually in bed by ten, had stayed up to wait him out. And then some. Rayna didn't know whether they weren't going to bed until she went or whether they were determined to keep watch all night.

Either way, at midnight she couldn't take it anymore and escaped to her room. Her parents' fear was creating a feedback loop with her own, making her crazier and crazier. As did Officer Repucci's failure to settle. She couldn't imagine anyone getting past him. And their newly shatter-resistant windows . . . and their alarm system. Her parents must have put themselves into debt to protect her.

She felt more than a determination to stay alive. She felt an obligation. It was too much. All of it.

By midnight she was keyed up and exhausted all at the same time. She made her own patrol of her room, bracing herself to pull up her blinds and check outside, sure that some demented face would be staring back at her or that something would come crashing or blasting through the window. One quick, clean shot to the forehead and lights out. Or . . . The possibilities were endless. On a silent count of three, she yanked the cord to her blinds and they rose up unevenly to reveal . . . nothing. A patch of lawn barely illuminated by the outdoor lights, but still clearly deserted.

She dropped the blinds before that could change. She told herself it was caution rather than cowardice. After all, Officer Repucci had warned her to stay away from the windows.

She didn't change into her pajamas, wanting to be dressed in case their alarm went off and they all had to get out or . . . anything. She felt better equipped to face whatever might come clothed.

But she did wash her face and brush her teeth and get ready for bed before sliding between her sheets and laying wide awake, staring at the window.

Her cat, Sasha, who'd mostly hidden out since the officers had invaded their home, clawed at her door and mewed plaintively about being shut out. Rayna rose to let her in.

Sasha pressed herself against Rayna's legs, then jumped up onto the bed, right in the center so that there was no way Rayna herself could fit.

"Oh no," she said, gently lifting Sasha to the side, ignoring the green-eyed glare. "You have to make room."

Sasha accepted her new place only because it came with belly rubs, and eventually Rayna's hand slowed. Her eyes drooped, lulled by the warm kitty and rumbling purrs, and she fell asleep.

A sharp sound jolted her out of sleep at some point later. Sasha yowled and hissed and bolted from the bed. Rayna's heart was instantly pounding hard enough to burst. She looked from Sasha, back arched, hissing and spitting at the window, to the window itself. The blinds were still intact. But . . . the sound had definitely come from that direction.

Her door ripped open before she could go to it, and instantly Officer Repucci was there. Sasha dashed under her bed and he raced toward the window and yanked up the blinds. Her parents crowded in behind him.

There, plastered to the window, was a handwritten note, all in block letters . . . again.

*I see you brought a chaperone for your date with death. Someone else will have to die for your sins.*

Rayna gasped.

"Stay with her," Officer Repucci commanded her parents. He was on the move, all that pent up energy suddenly with somewhere to go. He grabbed the radio from his belt and was already calling it in as he raced out to search for whoever had left the note. The killer.

Rayna's mother rushed to her, smothered her in a hug and pulled her out into the hallway, away from the window. Her father closed in after them, shutting the door, joining the hug as though shielding them with his body.

But Rayna wanted to break away, beg Officer Repucci to stay inside. What if he was the one to pay for her sins? She was too terrified for him to give much thought to what sins she was supposed to have committed. What if he died protecting her? She couldn't live with that.

She tried to tell her parents, but they just hugged her tighter, unwilling to let her go.

They all huddled in the hallway, listening for any sound, any indication of what was going on outside. The time until Officer Repucci returned seemed interminable. Rayna finally had to push back on her parents. She didn't feel like she could take a full breath. When she had a little space, she realized it hadn't been the hug. It had been her. She was hyperventilating.

Off in the distance, they heard sirens, but she wasn't really sure why. Hadn't the killer said he was leaving her alone? Finding another target? Was that just a trick to get their guard down? Or was this the trick? Getting everyone to rush here while the real danger was elsewhere?

She couldn't think. Couldn't breathe. She didn't know whether it was worse to be a killer with twisty, horrible thoughts or to be a policeman and have to think like one. She hated it. She hated it all. She wanted to go back to her pretty pictures and happy normal life and . . .

Spots appeared before her eyes. If she didn't get a real breath soon, she was going to pass out. Her mother felt her wobble and clutched her tighter, realized what was going on and sent her father to the kitchen for a paper bag, but Rayna cried out and grabbed her father before he could leave. What if the killer was waiting to separate them? What if that's what he had done with Liam and his mother . . . or whoever had died in Liam's place?

That's when she realized that the killer had done it before. He'd threatened Liam, but . . . they didn't even know that Liam was dead. The killer wasn't playing by his own rules. At least, not the ones he'd shared. They had no idea who was really safe and who was in the killer's sights.

She had a death grip on her father's sleeve, not letting him go, though he'd be free the moment she passed out, surely any second now. Her vision had narrowed to a pinprick in the center of her father's shirt.

But Officer Repucci swept back into the house, his gun held down by his thigh, not pointed at them, and suddenly she was able to take a breath. Then two.

Tires squealed and at least another car, maybe two, she thought, pulled up outside their house. The sirens died, car doors opened, slammed.

Officer Repucci met the others at the door, directed the newcomers to fan out and search in case there was anything he'd missed, and then came to talk to Rayna and her parents.

"Whoever left the note is long gone," he said, looking her father in the eyes. "He took quite a risk, making noise to draw attention. He could just as easily have crept up, left the note and been gone before anyone even knew he was there."

"He didn't want that," Rayna said, thinking of what she'd learned already from the Meddlers. "He wanted our fear. He wanted to see people scramble."

The notes, the taunting, the weird planted evidence like that earring in Mrs. Hinkle's bedroom . . . it was almost as though this was a game. At the beginning of all this, Grace said she thought one of the Meddlers might be planting clues, creating a puzzle for them to solve. She shuddered at the thought. And then another occurred . . .

"You've got to check on the others!" Rayna said, her chest constricting again. "If he killed the wrong person before, he could do it again. That might have been the plan all along, misdirection. We have only the killer's word about his targets and the timing. The word of a killer . . ."

Officer Repucci's eyes narrowed on her. "Why 'he'? And what do you mean 'killed the wrong person before'?"

"He? She? Does it matter? And the killing—something I heard at the police station," she said, scared enough to be brusque. "Look, you can question me all night. Go for it. I'm not going to sleep anyway. But please, please check on the others."

Because *someone* was going to die. She didn't doubt that. She knew it in her quaking heart. And maybe . . . maybe someone else wasn't where they were supposed to be—at home, asleep.

Officer Repucci got on his radio again, asking for Detectives Travers and Kincaid. He was told they'd already been called, but he insisted they be called again and that dispatch patch him through. Then he moved off to the kitchen to talk.

Rayna's father took her by the shoulders, stared into her eyes. She couldn't look away. The fear and the intensity there was just too real. "What did you mean?" he asked.

Crap. She hadn't told them. She'd figured she was in enough trouble. She didn't want to add eavesdropping to her list of sins. The thought of that note and how close the killer had come to her nearly buckled her knees, but her father held her up, still waiting for his answer.

"The kid who died in that fire . . . it wasn't Liam. The dental records don't match," she said, watching to see how he'd react.

"Wasn't . . ." He couldn't seem to grasp that. "Well then, who was it?"

"I don't think they know. Not yet, anyway."

There was a loud knock at their front door, and Officer Repucci went to answer it. Detective Travers. She should have been off the clock hours ago, Rayna thought . . . unless she'd just come back on. Rayna had no idea what time it was.

Crime scene techs came shortly after, and Repucci directed them around the side of the house. Rayna wanted to watch, but knew there was no way the police would let her outside into someone's potential line of fire.

Anyway, Detective Travers wanted to question her. She chose the kitchen for it, made sure Rayna's father closed the blinds over the single small kitchen window and sat in the very spot Officer Stiles had sat previously. Rayna and her mother took their predictable positions, but her father needed something to do. Or maybe needed to feed his caffeine addiction. He bustled about making coffee.

"Rayna," Detective Travers said, staring intently at her, as though she could see right into Rayna's mind if she looked hard enough. "You have to tell me everything you know."

Rayna stared back, "What do you think I know?"

It was on the tip of her tongue to tell Detective Travers about the earring in the picture from Liam's house, but if asked the only picture she could produce would be the poor-quality one on her phone. If she still had the memory card, she might give it up in a heartbeat, but she didn't. She wasn't worried about implicating herself anymore. She just wanted answers, for all of this to be over. But she didn't want to implicate her friends as accomplices. Maybe she could cut a deal.

"I still don't have any idea who might be doing this, but there's something you should know—"

Rayna's phone vibrated right then, and she pulled it out of her pocket, half-relieved at the interruption . . . until she saw the text.

It was a picture, a close up of Grace's terrified face. Eyes wide, a snot bubble coming from one nostril, face wet with sweat or tears. The caller ID listed the sender as "Restricted", but it came with a message. *Time's running out.*

A sick heat washed over Rayna. Not color-crazy, brutally honest Grace, their burgeoning crime scene tech. Not anyone. She should have been the one in that picture. She should have been the one dying tonight. Instead . . .

Rayna ran for the bathroom, leaving her phone behind for Detective Travers to see. Her father called after her, but she couldn't stop. She was going to be sick.

She didn't even make it to the toilet, but bent over the sink, heaving up an explosive burst of whatever was left in her stomach. Straight-up acid from the way it burned. She was shaking so hard in the aftermath that trying to wipe away the spittle only smeared it all over her face. It took two attempts turn the faucet on so she could splash cold water over her face. Again. And again. It was no use. She couldn't wash away the sight of Grace, scared out of her mind.

There was a knock at the door before she was ready to face anyone, and then Detective Travers voice came through. "Rayna, are you okay?"

She grabbed a towel and roughed it over her face, almost punishingly. "Yes," she lied. *Better than Grace.* It sent pain streaking through her again, and her stomach cramped, though nothing new came up. "That picture," she called through the door. "It means Grace is still alive, right? There's still time to save her."

"We'll do our best," Detective Travers said, but she sounded grim. "I've sent the text and photo to our electronic forensics team. Hopefully, they'll be able to track it back to the source. And we have units already en route to Grace's house."

Rayna opened the door, started out at Detective Travers. "Why are you still here then. You need to be out looking for Grace."

"I'm leaving now."

The detective had a quick talk with Officer Repucci on her way out and then was gone.

Her parents waited for her in the hallway and followed Rayna to the kitchen, watching with worry as she collapsed down at the kitchen table, stunned disbelief, guilt and horror all beating at her. She alternately blamed herself for putting Grace in harm's way and the killer for . . . everything.

Her arms and legs were tingling, numb, weak. Her head felt heavy. She put it down on the table, focusing on each breath. She had a strange feeling that if she stopped concentrating, her heart might stop beating. Her brain would shut down and her body would follow.

Her mother stood behind her, rubbed her back in circles as though she could sooth everything away as she had when Rayna had a nightmare as a child. She couldn't take it, and shrugged her mother off. She didn't want the comfort. She didn't want to feel better. Not when she'd possibly gotten Grace killed.

But her mother didn't give up that easily. She lifted Rayna's head from the table with a gentle hand under her chin. Rayna didn't fight her, but neither did she make it easy. Officer Repucci took that out of both their hands, pushing her mother aside and taking Rayna's head in his much meatier hands with a palm pressed to each cheek. He uptilted Rayna's face and searched her eyes, as though for signs of shock or drugs. Uncomfortable, she yanked her head away. She'd been too tired to hold her head up before, but if the alternative was someone holding it for her, she would manage. She forced her arms to move, propped her elbows on the table, and supported her own damn self.

Repucci, apparently satisfied, took Travers's seat and did a credible imitation of her stare. "Now, you were about to tell Detective Travers everything you know," he stated.

Rayna couldn't see that it mattered now, but if it would help . . . She'd do anything. Tell them anything if only it would bring Grace safely home.

# CHAPTER 18

RAYNA

It was around one in the morning that the note slapped onto her window had jolted Rayna awake, after two that she'd received the awful picture of Grace that had mobilized the police. By four a.m. the police had confirmed that Grace was missing, started a canvas, and gotten hold of her phone records and text messages. They knew the exact moment her cell phone had stopped sending signals, either turned off or destroyed, so they had her last known location—a gas station in a bad part of town, where they subsequently found Grace's motorcycle abandoned. Her phone was nowhere to be seen, and neither was she.

The creepiest thing was the message that had lured her out, sent from an unknown number, probably from a cheap burner phone. Either the killer had used a different number with Grace or different settings, since "Restricted" might have set off warning bells. The message itself was innocuous. Maybe even irresistible for a Meddler.

> *Grace, it's Liam.*
> *You have to help me. I don't know who to turn to. I need money and information. Gas station on Fifth and Carmine, 2 am? Please? Come alone. I don't know who to trust.*

Rayna was stunned when Officer Repucci shared the message. He claimed he wanted to see if Rayna recognized the number, but he'd know better than she would if it was Liam's—not that it would prove *he* was the one sending the message. Whoever had killed his mother and torched his house could easily have stolen his phone. She thought that in truth Repucci wanted to gage her reaction, though she had no idea why. Maybe he was suspicious that the killer had passed her by . . . for now . . . but he couldn't think *she* was a suspect. The police had been there the whole time, including when the message came in. She'd had no time to slip out and kidnap Grace. She was horrified at the very thought.

Maybe he just wanted to shake her up, make sure she took the danger she faced seriously, as if she could do anything else. Grace's face would haunt her forever. No. Hell no. Haunt would mean she was dead, and she wasn't. Not yet. There was still a chance.

By five a.m. search parties were starting to mass. Rayna wanted to go, to do something, but her parents wouldn't hear of it. They weren't letting her out of the house. She wasn't even sure her father had blinked since his rude awakening. Her mother's head kept drooping, and she kept jerking herself awake despite the three cups of coffee her father had made for her.

She couldn't take it anymore, sitting around waiting, wondering . . . fearing the worst.

## JACK

The pounding on the door jarred Jack awake. At first he thought it was the door to his bedroom, and was glad he'd locked it so that his father couldn't get in.

But as he stared at it, waiting for the cheap wood to give along the fracture line already there, he realized the door wasn't moving, wasn't bucking beneath the onslaught. It had to be the *front* door someone was pounding on.

He bolted out of bed and swept out into the hall, but his father was already there ahead of him, thundering down the stairs. He yanked the front door open, ready to give the person on the other side of it a piece of his mind or the full force of his fists.

He stopped dead at the sight of the police officer standing there poised to knock again.

"Mr. Harkness?" the officer asked.

His father looked baffled and no less angry now, though he was doing his best to hide it. "Yes," he said. "What do you mean banging on my door in the middle of the night. Someone in trouble?"

His dad looked back over his shoulder and up the stairs at Jack, leaving no doubt about who he associated with trouble. He must have heard Jack blast down the hall after him.

The officer followed his father's gaze, up the stairs to Jack who waited at the top of them. "No sir. We're checking to see that your son is safe. There's been a new threat."

His father's eyes narrowed on the officer. "Why? What has he told you?"

"Sir?" the officer said, hand loosely at his side. He hadn't moved the hand that Jack had noticed, but suddenly he was focused on it . . . and the gun it rested beside. "What should he have told us?"

His father glared at the officer as if it hadn't been his own damned fault he'd slipped up. Sleep deprivation, Jack thought, rather than a guilty conscience. He didn't think his father *had* a conscience.

"You said you're checking on him," his father answered aggressively, ignoring the officer's question. "You couldn't just call?"

Jack waited with held breath to see if the officer would call him on the evasion, hoping he wouldn't. He wanted to find out what was going on, not watch them circle like Pit Bulls playing king of the heap.

"We did, sir. No one answered," the officer said, straining to stay polite.

"Well of course not," his father thundered. "It's the middle of the night. Everyone was asleep."

The officer quirked a brow but otherwise ignored the gap in his logic. He glanced up at Jack, maybe hoping for more sense there. "Son," he said, "you okay?"

Jack's father was sending him a death glare that the officer couldn't see, but he didn't need it to know the answer he was expected to give.

"Fine," he said. "But what threat? What's happening?"

"I'm not at liberty—"

"Look," Jack cut in, "as soon as you're gone, I'm going to be on my phone calling everyone I know. I'm going to find out what's going on. You might as well just tell me."

"If you're going to find out anyway, then you don't need me," the officer answered.

He focused back on Jack's father. "Mind if I search around the grounds? Make sure you're all clear?"

His father looked about to swallow his own lips, his mouth was pressed so thin. "Knock yourself out," he said with bad grace. "I'm going back to bed."

He practically closed the door in the officer's face and turned toward Jack.

Jack didn't see how his father could blame him for the officer's sudden appearance, but knew he'd find a way. Still, he was safe-ish for the moment. As long as there was police scrutiny on them, his father wouldn't dare start anything.

"You up?" his father asked, like it wasn't self-evident.

"Yeah," he answered cautiously.

"I lied to the cop," his father said. "There's no way I'm getting back to sleep now. Going to make coffee. I can make a full pot if you want some."

Jack didn't know what to say. He settled on, "Thanks." The word practically stuck in his throat.

His father nodded, and Jack backed away from the head of the stairs so that his father could pass without getting too close. Then he went to his room and grabbed his phone off the charger, setting up a group text and risking the wrath of his father at the extra five or ten cents it might cost, but it was the fastest way to reach everyone. He left his door open so that he could hear when his father left the kitchen, so that he could go in for his coffee. He didn't drink it much. There was rarely, if ever, enough left over for him. But the sudden coldness inside called for something to warm him up.

That was how he found out about Rayna's note, and that she was safe . . . for now. It was how he heard shortly thereafter about Grace. The two cups of coffee he'd downed turned to acid in his stomach.

When the search was organized a few wakeful hours later, starting at dawn at the very same gas station he and Maria had stopped at yesterday, he was one of the first to volunteer.

They all volunteered—except for Rayna, whose parents still had her under house arrest, and Maria, whose family had decided after last night's scare to keep her under lock and key. There was even talk of homeschooling her. She sounded . . . Jack wasn't sure how she sounded. Upset, hopeless, scared. He hated it. Hated all this. It had to end.

It was Kali who picked him up, her car already loaded with Reggie and Charlie. Reggie sat in the front, staring out the window as though lost in a nightmare. Charlie sat in the back, his face a mask of pain. He looked as though he was already in mourning. But they didn't know for sure Grace was dead.

They just felt it in their bones.

The mustering point for the searchers was at the small grocery down the road from the gas station where Jack and Maria had stopped when they'd gone to the shantytown. It was now a crime scene. Or, at least, Grace's motorcycle had been found there abandoned, and the police weren't taking the chance that any evidence would be destroyed by dozens of cars and people converging. There was, in fact, a detour set up a street away, and a policewoman to direct people into the grocery store parking lot.

Kali pulled in, and they joined a line of other people in long pants and hiking boots bundled against the early morning chill as they tromped toward the end of the parking lot where search parties were being assigned. Evan and a girl Jack didn't recognize who Evan introduced as Sierra pushed through the crowd to join them.

Jack got stares from a few kids he recognized from school,

probably shocked to see him there helping. He shot them a glare and they glanced instantly away. He felt conspicuous. But at the same time that he was being watched and judged, he was doing it to others, studying the people gathered, wondering if one of them might be the murderer, coming back to the scene of the crime.

He was surprised to see Dalton, until he remembered that Dalton's father was a former army MP turned police officer. Of course he would have recruited Dalton to help. He even chose him as one of the grid leaders, which had Dalton flashing a smug and almost predatory grin at the others, like it made him a big man. If he had one wish, beyond finding Grace alive, it was *not* to be put into Dalton's group.

He got that wish. Kali wasn't so lucky.

She gave a world-weary sigh as she went to join him. All the others were separated too, except for Jack and Reggie, who ended up in the same group with a man built like a Mack truck with more hair on his face than on the top of his head. He introduced himself as Loomis, got them to sign in and asked whether they had any ID. Jack didn't, since he didn't have a license and hadn't considered that he might need identification to search for a missing friend. Reggie had a driver's license he never seemed to use, and showed that. He also vouched for Jack. "We go to school together. I promise, he is who he says he is. No one would want to steal his identity."

He had that right.

Loomis grumbled, but let it go.

Jack wondered whether the police thought as he did—that the killer might come help with the search. If so, it made sense they'd record everyone coming in. He'd bet there was even a camera somewhere.

He didn't know how he'd missed them before—maybe they'd arrived after him—but now that he looked, he spotted news people on the far side of the lot, being kept away from the police and search teams, but with cameras avidly angled their way. Closer, in front of the barriers, was a plainclothes photographer Jack would swear was taking far more official pictures.

The search grid consisted of vacant lots, closed businesses, and the swampy, overgrown patch of land that backed the area. He wondered whether the shantytown was being searched as well. Probably so. Jack hoped it wouldn't go badly for them. It would be too easy for things to escalate. Or the shantytown to get shut down in the interest of "public safety".

Jack's group, of course, got one of the swampy sections. Within minutes, he was a sodden, filthy mess. He didn't have the waterproofed hiking boots some of the other searchers had, just his crappy old sneakers, which would probably have to be thrown out. The water and mud oozed in through the seams, gushing through his socks and between his toes, but he didn't feel like he had any right to be miserable when Grace might be out here somewhere struggling for life or . . . He didn't want to think about the or.

He, Loomis and Reggie spread out, but kept each other in sight, as instructed.

When Loomis's radio flared with a static-y blast, Jack stopped moving and strained to hear. Then he wished he hadn't.

"Girl has been found. Repeat, girl has been found," came an urgent voice through the speakers. "All searchers back to base."

Jack's heart skipped a beat. Grace!

Loomis put the radio to his mouth and spoke into it, "What's the girl's status?" he asked. "Found alive?"

He heard Reggie draw in a deep breath and realized he was holding his as well.

There was no answer for what seemed the longest time, and then. "EMTs have been called . . ."

"But?" Loomis asked, hearing the same thing Jack heard in the cautious response. Or rather, what he didn't hear.

"Back to base," said the voice on the other end.

Reggie let out his breath in a strangled sound of despair that ripped at Jack's heart. Jack was so stunned he felt like the tin woodsman without his oil can, like his arms and legs and entire body were too creaky to move . . . more effort than they were worth. And he'd barely known Grace. He couldn't even imagine what Reggie must be feeling.

Reggie was already moving back toward base, outpacing Loomis and Jack, but Jack made himself catch up.

"EMTs," Jack said, "that means hope."

Reggie shot him a sidelong glance and kept moving. "He didn't answer the question about her being found alive. EMTs— that's a procedure thing, if she's not already cold and . . ." His voice went dead on the last word. "They were there the night Marley was killed too. Didn't make a difference."

"Anyway," Reggie continued, "the officer on the radio wouldn't give anything away with reporters and all listening in, even if it was up to him to pronounce death."

Jack's very faint hope died in the face of Reggie's certainty.

There were crashing sounds off to their left, the ruckus of multiple people headed deeper into the swamp-forest as everyone else was clearing out. Jack couldn't help himself, he turned and headed toward the sounds.

"Back to the grocery store," Loomis's voice rang out, trying to be authoritative but coming out defeated.

Jack waved at him in acknowledgement but kept on going. Reggie was right beside him. He had to see; had to know.

Before them were two figures in EMT jackets. They must have been on call close by to get there so quickly. They had a police escort. The officer bringing up the rear heard and tried to head off Jack and Reggie, but they broke apart and circled around him, one to each side as if they'd choreographed it. Jack veered back almost instantly, and came upon a sectioned off area, strung with crime scene tape. He didn't break the barrier, but pushed in, trying to see past another officer who stood with his back to the tape. He couldn't see a thing until the officer moved aside for the paramedics and then . . .

Oh, holy hell.

Reggie was right. Help was going to be too late.

Grace's skin was gray, her neck purple-black and not at any natural angle. Her eyes were wide open, staring blankly right at Jack. At least she was still clothed, her cheerful pink sweatshirt a painful contrast to the horror of the scene. A dark stain marred her jeans where her bowels had voided at the moment of death. Jack couldn't smell it over the swamp, thank goodness, but . . .

His stomach suddenly wanted to come out his throat, and he staggered a few steps away to vomit all the coffee he'd drunk during the night. It burned its way up until his throat felt as raw as his emotions.

Reggie found him that way. He was clutching his own stomach, his face ashen and his whole body shaking.

"You saw?" he asked.

Jack nodded, spitting out the remains of the bile in his mouth. It didn't do the trick. He could still taste it.

Worse than that, he couldn't unsee what he'd seen. Even as he looked at Reggie, a vision of Grace swam before his eyes like sunspots.

"Just like Marley," Reggie said.

"Huh?" Jack's brain wasn't working well. He felt like it was dumb to everything but the shock of Grace . . . dead.

"My uncle's girlfriend, the one he's accused of killing. She was strangled too, though not the same way. I think I saw ligature marks on Grace's neck."

Jack stared at him, anger stirring. "Your friend is dead and you're analyzing the scene?" he growled.

"I can't help it. It's how I process."

"Well, process this—"

Jack was about to hit him. He didn't even know why except that Grace's death made him so angry, so *uselessly* angry and it would feel good to have a target. Reggie made it easy.

But Loomis came up on them both then and grabbed them by the scruffs of their necks like they were wayward schoolboys. Both shook themselves out of his grip, but when Loomis pushed them back toward the parking lot, they went. Jack felt relieved and cheated, angry and helpless and even more angry all at the same time.

He marched straight ahead almost in a fugue, still spoiling for a fight.

When they hit the parking lot, the first people they saw were Dalton and Kali, pulled off to the side being questioned by police. But it was when he spotted the reporters' big directional mics pointing their way that he knew . . .

Dalton and Kali been the ones to find Grace's body.

Suspicion whispered across his mind. *Knowledge of the dump site or just dumb luck?*

Dalton did have a connection with at least some of the victims. Kali and Eric said Dalton had threatened Liam into doing his work and yet still bullied him in the lunchroom. It was conceivable that things got out of hand, that Dalton might have killed Liam for something. Maybe Liam had turned him in to the Principal or sabotaged the papers he'd been forced to write. Jack already knew Dalton intimidated Maria. He wondered if it was the same with Grace and Rayna. The only problem with all this was that Liam hadn't been the person killed, however it had seemed.

And Kali . . . he didn't know her well enough to say, but *she* had been the one to spot the earring in the pictures Rayna had taken of the Hinkle crime scene, one tiny detail in a very big picture. So tiny Grace had needed to enhance the picture before the others could see it for themselves. Almost as if Kali knew it was there. And now this, finding Grace's body. Everyone assumed the killer was male, but . . . He thought about how Kali had gotten that message earlier and dashed off without telling him what it was about. That was a girl with secrets.

The medical examiner's SUV pulled into the parking lot and officers saw to it that the searchers were backed well out of the way. They ended up clustered with the Meddlers. First to find them were Evan and Sierra, the latter's eyes watery and red, then Charlie.

"Anybody know what's going on?" Charlie asked. "Our section leader said they found her, but—"

"Dead," Reggie pronounced, his voice itself lifeless, uninflected. "Grace was strangled."

The words hung there in the air like the morning mist, wrapping them in cold and creep.

Kali was released then by the officer she'd been talking to and joined the group, instantly taking charge. "Dalton rode here with his father, but his dad has to stay to work the scene. I've offered him a ride home. He's pretty shaken up. Plus, it'll give us the chance to question him on the way."

They all gazed over at where Dalton was being interviewed by the police, but it was no longer an officer he was talking to. It was a reporter. There was a camera focused on him and a microphone held in front of him. His shoulders were thrown back, his chest was out. He was, Jack thought, trying to look as heroic as possible, like he'd saved Grace rather than found her broken.

Jack wondered where *Dalton* had been when Grace went missing. He certainly seemed ready to capitalize on her death.

It was no longer Reggie he wanted to hit.

"I don't know," Charlie said, echoing Jack's thoughts. "Dalton looks pretty comfortable here. Maybe we should just leave him."

"Well, it's my car, so I guess you're outvoted. Be right back."

She walked over, careful to keep behind the camera, behind the mic so that the reporter wouldn't spot her and try to suck her in as well. She mimed to Dalton that she was going to drive off. It took him a second to notice her pantomiming off-camera, but when he did, a look of irritation crossed his face. It didn't go well with the one of mourning he was trying for.

Moments later, he was clear of the interview. Kali was already walking away, and he caught up to her.

"Hey, what was all that about?" he asked, reaching for her shoulder and stopping short of actually grabbing it.

"Your ride is leaving," Kali shot at him. "And I couldn't keep watching you pretend to care."

Dalton's face set into hard lines like poured concrete.

Before they reached everyone else, Evan said, "Good luck with Dalton. I'm getting on the phone to Rayna. She needs to know what's going on. Why don't we clean up and regroup at her place? You can tell us what you learned from Dalton, and Reggie can bring everything he's got on his uncle's case. I don't know what it has to do with Grace's death, but that earring, and the fact that she was working on the pictures . . ."

"But we *all* saw them," Charlie protested. "And Rayna's the one who took them. Shouldn't she be—"

"What, dead?" Evan asked dangerously. Jack could see the same rage he felt simmering in Evan's eyes, the same need he felt to lash out.

And he wondered about Evan for just a moment. Evan, everybody's friend, but especially Rayna's. Rayna, who'd survived her threat. When all this began, Maria had accused him of sending her the threat so that he could become her protector. Could that be true of Evan and Rayna? Was that why Grace had been taken instead?

Suddenly, everyone seemed a suspect. No one was safe.

Kali gave him a strange look as she walked up, and he realized he was still staring fixedly after Evan and Sierra.

# CHAPTER 19

JACK

"Shotgun," Dalton called as they approached the car.

Everyone's heads swiveled toward him in shock. Of all the things to be thinking about right now . . .

"Screw that," Jack said. "Reggie's already got shotgun. You can sit in the back with the rest of us."

Three to a seat—him, Charlie and Dalton. Uncomfortable wouldn't begin to cover it. He should have kept his mouth shut.

Surprisingly, Dalton didn't argue, though he also didn't volunteer to take the center. With his size, it wouldn't have made any sense. That fell to Charlie. Poor Charlie. A sheep between two wolves.

"So, you found her," Jack said, as soon as they were on the road and Dalton couldn't just get out if he didn't like the questioning.

"Yeah," Dalton said, subdued, staring out the window.

"Did you do CPR?" he asked.

Dalton whipped around in the seat, glaring right past Charlie at Jack. "Why does everyone keep asking me that? She was dead, okay? Like *dead* dead. Blue-gray. Cold. I know, because I felt for her pulse. I checked to see if she was breathing, but there was nothing. Yeah, I could have done CPR, but it would have been pointless and might have messed up evidence. Chest compressions could have cracked a rib. And . . ."

"And?" Kali asked quietly, not taking her eyes off the road.

Dalton took a shaky breath. "And I couldn't do it," he said, looking away. "I couldn't press my lips up against her cold, dead

. . . I couldn't do it. It would have been like kissing a corpse."

The horror of that sank through to them. Unfortunately, it came with a vivid picture, at least for Jack, but with himself trying to breathe the life back into the body. Into *Grace*. He could feel the chill of her lips, feel it seeping into him, like the deadness could spread along with the cold. He felt like he'd never be warm and never get rid of the sensation. Like he might carry it around forever.

Still, with all Dalton's posturing for the cameras, it was hard to believe he hadn't at least *tried*. Would have made for great fodder for television interviews. Could he have known Grace was beyond help because he was the one who'd made certain of it?

"I'm sorry about Liam," Kali said suddenly, maybe to catch him off-guard.

"Huh?" Dalton asked.

"The fact that he's missing," she said, taking her gaze off the road to study him in the rearview mirror, which she seemed to have angled for that purpose. "I know he was tutoring you. I hope your grades aren't suffering."

Dalton glared back wordlessly, neither confirming nor denying. Finally, he said, "I know what you're doing. My dad's a cop. I've been questioned by the best of them." He didn't make any comment about them calling Liam missing rather than dead. Maybe his father had already let that slip. Or maybe . . .

"Questioned about what?" Charlie asked innocently enough. It was the thing Jack wanted to ask next, but with him it would have come out sounding like a challenge.

"Homework, grades, where I've been. Dad stuff," he said. "As if it's any of your business."

He went back to staring out the window as though finished with the conversation, but Reggie wasn't ready to let him off the hook.

"How were the grid lots assigned?" Reggie asked, speaking up for the first time. "How did you find the body?"

Dalton shot him a venomous look, and Jack felt the menace rolling off him in waves. It was as if all his tension radiated outward, poisoning the air.

"Let me out here," Dalton said suddenly.

When Kali didn't immediately pull over, he roared it. "*Let me out!* I'll walk home."

His hand was on the door handle. Jack was afraid that if Kali didn't pull over Dalton would fling himself from the moving vehicle.

But she did pull over. Dalton wrenched the door open before she came to a full stop, keeping hold of the handle after he was out and glaring back in at them all.

"My father's right. You're playing a dangerous game. You keep poking at people and more of you are going to end up like Grace."

He slammed the door and started down the road the way they'd been going. Jack noticed for the first time that he had a bit of a limp. Had he twisted his ankle walking through the swamp or gotten hurt when Grace fought for her life?

"Was that a threat?" Charlie asked into the silence Dalton left behind.

"Maybe," Kali said. "Or a prediction."


RAYNA

Rayna was ready to scream.

Evan texted her when Grace's body was found. Then again when they knew more. Like how she'd died.

Then . . . nothing. She knew everyone was going home to scrub off the stench of death and swamp and that they'd meet at her place later, but it wasn't enough.

She wanted to be doing something. Now. Something *other* than what her parents had her doing—sitting at the kitchen table pretending to focus on homework while her father pretended to read the paper and her mother played at a crossword puzzle. She was so exhausted her eyes could barely focus, and yet she was far too keyed up to sleep. She didn't think she'd ever sleep again . . .

not until the killer was caught. Then she'd probably collapse and sleep for a week.

But when the doorbell rang two hours later, she jerked awake and had to brush away drool that had gathered at the corner of her mouth and pooled on the table, just missing her math worksheet, which had slid off to the side.

The voice responding to Officer Stiles at the door was better than a sugar overload for getting her back in gear.

It was Reggie, who would have all the evidence he'd collected on his uncle's case and a first-hand account of what had happened with the search for Grace.

She no sooner thought it than guilt overwhelmed her again. It should have been her. She'd been the one with only six days to live. Or *Six days to die*, as her note had said. She hadn't been ready. She hadn't wanted to die. But that Grace should die in her place . . .

She didn't know what expression she wore when Reggie stepped into the kitchen, Evan and Sierra behind him, but immediately, Reggie opened his arms and she rose from the table and moved in for the hug. She didn't know him that well, but she felt as if she did. Shared pain and all of that. He smelled clean and spicy, probably something about his body wash. He was so tall that with his arms wrapped around her, she felt like she was in a fortress. If something . . . someone . . . wanted to get at her while Reggie held her, well, it would be quite the challenge. Even the thought of him taking a hit for her made her step back after what had happened to Grace.

She lifted a tortured smile to him and said, "Thanks. You okay?"

She looked to Evan and Sierra to include them in the question and couldn't decipher the expression on Evan's face.

He wasn't happy. Because of the whole situation? Because she'd been hugging Reggie? Was he jealous? She had so many emotions already vying for her attention she couldn't even process that thought.

Reggie looked around her small eat-in kitchen with only the four chairs. "Should we set up here?" he asked dubiously.

She didn't think it was just about the seating. He flashed a glance back toward the kitchen entrance, where Officer Stiles stood watching them. She'd taken over for Repucci at some point.

Rayna didn't know where her parents were, only that they weren't there when she woke up. Their room, probably, sleeping or showering. Neither one would have gone out and left her behind, even with police protection.

"This way," she said, feeling self-conscious. She was leading them toward what used to be her playroom when she was a kid. It now acted as her art studio and her father's puzzle room . . . and the storage facility for all of her mother's abandoned hobbies. She was always picking up and abandoning things—scrapbooking, beading, crocheting, knitting. They could practically open a craft store with all of her unused supplies. Every once in a while, Rayna found a way to work some of them into her multi-media art projects.

She was going to proceed them in, to make sure that none of her half-finished or more embarrassing pieces was showing, but Officer Stiles cleared her throat from behind them and insisted on checking out the room first.

Rayna peeked behind her to see that the blinds on the door leading to the back yard were wide open and light was streaming into the room, catching dust motes in the air. She hadn't been in the room in a week . . . since that note had shown up in her backpack. She'd lost her passion for the project she'd started, a crazy-optimistic take on life.

As soon as Stiles had the blinds closed, she rushed in to turn the easel around, but Sierra gasped behind her and with her longer legs, beat her to the canvas.

"Rayna, it's beautiful!"

It wasn't. Rayna studied it now and it felt . . . false. It was a huge canvas, the size for hanging over a fireplace mantel. She'd used actual dirt and pebbles mixed with paint for the ground. A mixture of paint and embroidery thread created the texture and gnarls in the roots and the trunk of the tree growing up out of the center of the picture, and pieces of smooth blue and green sea glass interspersed with photos cut into leaf shapes to create the canopy. Small tufts of her mother's green thread poked out of the ground below, little pockets of grass surviving the shade of the tree.

The photos were her take on life—budding plants, children playing, mother cats nursing their kittens, a boy and his dog, a mother with an infant . . . It seemed so naive. Beautiful, but . . . She realized, looking at it now, that there were no shadows. Despite the texture and the raised relief, it was one dimensional. There was no darkness to contrast the light, no death to contrast the living. It was . . .

Evan and Reggie moved up beside Sierra to study it, and Rayna couldn't face their response.

"Never mind that," she said. "We can use this table to spread out on."

At the moment it held all of the pictures she'd sorted and considered for the project along with the detritus from those she'd already cut, but she swept them all up in her arms, mixing them together. She held them against her chest as she searched for a place to put them, losing pieces here and there as they slipped from her grasp. It felt metaphoric. She felt like she was missing pieces of herself already—like Liam and Amal and Grace were pieces she didn't even know were part of the picture, until . . .

Sierra followed behind her, gathering up the falling photos. Rayna carried her pictures to one of the shelves lining the far side of the room and shoved them on top of one of the plastic tubs holding scrapbooking paper in a confusion of colors and patterns.

"What are you doing?" Sierra asked, as though she understood the significance of Rayna sweeping away her mess so casually.

"Don't," Rayna said. It came out almost desperately. "I can't, okay? That picture, it's . . . juvenile. It's done. I'm done with it."

Sierra studied her quietly, sadly. "You'll get over it, Rayna. I know it doesn't feel like that now, but . . ."

"I don't want to get over it," Rayna said, turning back toward the others. "It feels wrong, all puppies and rainbows. I might as well draw LOLcats and be done with it."

"So you're going to wallow?"

Rayna felt as though she'd been slapped. She stared at Sierra, stunned. Didn't she understand death? Loss?

But that was unfair. Sierra understood better than anyone. She'd lost her mother two years ago to pancreatic cancer with no time at all to prepare. Four weeks from diagnosis to death. Horrible. Had Rayna understood then? *Really* understood?

"No," Rayna answered. "I'm going to fight."

"Good," Sierra said.

Only it would be so much easier if she knew *who* to fight.

Reggie set his things on the table Rayna had cleared and opened the box he'd brought, laying out pictures and reports, a manila folder full of clippings.

"And finally, the piece de resistance," Reggie said. "The court transcript." He lifted out a thick, bound manuscript.

"How did you get that?" Sierra asked.

"Freedom of Information Act. It's public record. You just have to apply."

Rayna's eyes had instantly been drawn to the photos. "These too?"

Reggie nodded.

"I'll get us chairs," Rayna said, fleeing to the garage. The top photo in Reggie's pile was a close-up on the face of a beautiful woman with long dark hair half across her face. Her eyes were red, as though blood vessels had burst.

Rayna couldn't look at it without seeing Grace's face superimposed. She had to compose herself before she'd be any good to anyone.

On her way, the doorbell rang again, but she knew she wouldn't be allowed anywhere near the door, so she kept on going.

They had a couple of card tables with folding chairs up against the wall of the garage for when her father got working on an especially big puzzle or her mom wanted to craft with a friend or two. She grabbed two of the chairs and nearly bumped into

Evan as she turned. He'd come in behind her to help and she hadn't even noticed. If he'd been the killer . . .

Rayna jumped, and Evan immediately apologized, even though he hadn't done anything wrong.

Rayna apologized right back, and awkwardly she handed him the chairs and turned for more.

When she got back to the room, everyone was gathered around the table. Evan had grabbed the transcript and was reading through while Kali flipped through the pictures like they were nothing. In her defense, she'd seen them before. Reggie said he'd gotten the Meddlers together partially to work on his uncle's case.

Rayna retreated back to the garage for one more set of chairs, this time lagging behind Evan. They passed clumsily in the hallway.

Then there was no excuse. When Kali put the photos down, Rayna grabbed them up, forcing herself to study them, to notice details as though committing them to memory. She started with the top. The woman, Marley, had had incredible cheekbones . . . or they'd sunken in death. She looked narrow, sleek, like a greyhound. She was facing away from the camera in this picture, dark hair with honey-toned highlights obscuring her face, one hank brushing against her open mouth, as if she'd died gasping for air. The bottom lobe of her left ear could be seen, bruised and bloodied, as though something had been torn from it. There was no earring.

But what really drew the eye was the bruising around the neck, livid spots that made it clear why she'd been gasping for breath. Someone had choked it out of her. Using their bare hands.

The next picture wasn't as close up. It showed a full body shot. She'd fallen like a ragdoll, arms and legs out at odd angles. Her white button-up blouse was still mostly closed. Her skirt was rucked up, but not indecently so. It was as though it had been disordered while she fought for her life, but not as if it had been pulled up by the perp. Rayna was no expert, and she presumed the casefile would say for sure, but it didn't seem as though Marley had been violated . . . at least not in that way. Murder was violation enough.

In another photograph, someone had turned Marley's face to the other side. The bruises were even more wretched from that angle, and among all that dark hair the pearl earring, pair to the one they'd found in Liam's burned out house, was hard to miss.

There was a close-up of her one hand, still holding the broken handle of a ceramic mug, although the shards of it weren't close by, as though maybe she'd shattered the mug on her assailant's head rather than when she hit the floor.

The sadness that swamped Rayna at seeing Marley and the way she must have fought was like a creeping chill, threatening to seize her heart. It felt too frozen to beat, her veins too icy to do more than turn her blood to slush.

The odd thought occurred to her that maybe it wasn't her artwork that was wrong. Not by itself. It just needed a companion piece, a winter tree, barren of all life and hope, snow on the ground marred by only a few late-falling leaves, curling and dead, lost dreams, stolen potential.

Her head hung, the crime scene photos forgotten in her hand. Someone took them from her gently, and when she made herself look, she came face to face with Evan, hair pushed back behind his ears, for once not falling half across his face.

"It's a lot, isn't it?" he asked. "If you weren't affected, you'd be a sociopath."

Rayna blinked at him, the question that rose to mind not at all polite, but it crossed her lips anyway. "How do you do it? All of you?"

She didn't glance around. She'd effectively asked whether *they* were sociopaths. But . . . she didn't really mean it, did she?

Evan didn't appear offended. "We're affected, it just hits us in different ways. Me, I'm goal oriented. I can't change what is, so I work on what will be. I want the answers, the solution. Reggie, he's torn up about the whole thing. Word is Jack threw up at the search site. Kali—well, okay, she might be a sociopath—"

Kali shot him the middle-finger without even glancing up from the file she was browsing.

"But sociopath doesn't mean psychopath. People get that wrong all the time."

Charlie came up and grabbed the picture file from Evan, who barely seemed to notice, he was so intent on Rayna. She didn't look his way either, caught up in the intensity of Evan's gaze.

"What does it mean then?" she asked.

He'd squatted to be at eye-level with her, but now he hooked his abandoned chair with his foot and brought it close. She took a deep breath in the moment he turned away to position it, and then he was back with all his intensity.

"Sociopaths lack empathy and connection. There are various tests, but they never do it on teens or younger, because kids are essentially sociopaths. They're still developing empathy and all that good stuff. But sociopaths never develop it. They'll experience anger, especially if their will is thwarted, but they won't get love, sympathy, guilt. They'll have poor impulse control, because they won't think or care about the way their actions affect others. Consequences aren't a big thing. I could go on and on. Whole books have been written about it. But most sociopaths still live within normal bounds, more or less. They'll get into trouble and make bad decisions, maybe even kill, but if so it's likely a spur of the moment thing, that poor impulse control coming into play."

He paused to see how she was taking it, and Rayna nodded for him to go on.

"A psychopath, though . . . well, there have been studies that their brains are just different, like there's something missing or atrophied. They're the really dangerous ones, because they're usually highly manipulative. They analyze the angles, they like to play people. They've learned to blend, to mimic normal responses, say all the right words, but there's nothing behind them. Psychopath doesn't necessarily mean killer. It might be the girl who gets ahead at work by any means necessary or the con artist who steals peoples' life savings. Your neighbor could be a sociopath and you'd never know it, because he or she has figured out all the socially acceptable responses. But your crazy killers, those who get away with it for a while, leading seemingly normal lives—Ted

Bundy, John Wayne Gacy, BTK—they're all psychopaths. Cult leaders too—David Koresh, Jim Jones, Charles Manson."

"Soulless," Maria said, and then crossed herself.

"The best argument for the existence of a soul I've ever heard," Evan agreed, "is that some people are clearly born without one."

"But that would assume God makes mistakes. I didn't think that was allowed for in your religion," Kali said to Maria.

Maria glared, but didn't have a response to that. At least not on the tip of her tongue.

Evan glanced at her sympathetically. "Philosophers have argued the existence of a soul for eons. I doubt we're going to solve it today."

Charlie gasped, and immediately everyone's attention riveted on him, arguments forgotten. He looked up, feeling the weight of everyone's stares and reached for the picture he'd been studying, his hand shaking like crazy as he held it up. It was too shaky for anyone to see what had captured his attention.

Reggie lunged out of his seat and grabbed the photo out of Charlie's hand, turning it toward himself so that he could see.

But his brow wrinkled, and he quickly glanced up at Charlie, baffled.

"Check out the counter behind the body, upper right corner of the photo."

Reggie studied the picture. "What am I looking for?"

"Little silver birds."

A chill went up Rayna's spine, and she rose to grab the picture from Reggie, doing what he'd done, turning it so that she could see, but then she angled it out for everyone else.

On the counter, behind Marley's body were two little silver birds sitting side by side. Salt and pepper shakers. Twins to the one Charlie had swiped from Liam's kitchen.

"But what does it mean?" Evan asked. "Marley's not missing one from her set. It could just be coincidence. They're probably mass produced."

"Or the same person could have given them to both women,

Marley and Liam's mom," Evan said. "Or he could have seen one woman with them and bought the set for the other, a visual kick for him, linking the two."

"You're saying Liam's father was the other man," Reggie said. He wasn't asking really, only stating the logical conclusion.

"It makes sense," Evan confirmed. "His father disappeared shortly after Marley's murder. Plus, your family lived just across the street. Mr. Hinkle could have met Marley when she was visiting with your uncle or, hell, it's not that big a town. She could have known him some other way."

"There's one way to find out," said a different voice, coming from the doorway.

They'd been so absorbed, they'd practically forgotten about Officer Stiles. Rayna had, anyway.

"Trace the birds," Reggie said.

"Exactly," she answered. "Can I have that picture?" When no one immediately moved to give it to her, she let out her breath in a gush of frustration. "I promise I'll give it back. The picture will have an evidence number attached to it. I'll need that."

Rayna started to hand over the picture, but Reggie put a hand to her wrist to stop her. "Will the police investigate?" he asked, fixing Officer Stiles with a hard look. "It's a closed case. Will they reopen it?"

"I can't make any promises."

"Tell her about the earring," Kali put in.

Guilty silence reigned, until Stiles asked, "The earring?"

Kali huffed and called up the pic on her phone, then grabbed the pile of pictures that were still in Charlie's hand and sorted out Marley's close up, the one with her head turned. She held them both out to show Officer Stiles, but kept control of them the whole time. "Marley's missing earring," she announced. "Found at the Hinkle crime scene."

Officer Stiles looked from the pictures to Kali's face to each of the Meddlers in turn, and pulled at her sparse ponytail, which seemed to be a tell for her frustration.

"I think you'd better tell me everything," she said.

# CHAPTER 20

JACK

Jack thought hard while Kali talked—or rather, negotiated a trade of what they knew and the pictures Rayna had taken in exchange for the agreement not to prosecute them for trespassing or anything else.

He might not be a burgeoning criminal psychologist or profiler like Evan or Reggie or any of the rest, but he did know math, and he couldn't see how things were adding up. It all seemed so crazy. Sending threats. Killing people. Planting evidence.

Who would implicate Liam's family in Marley's killing. Reggie? He and his family had the most to gain if someone else was found guilty of the crime his uncle had been accused of, but why target Liam? Or, presumably his father, who had disappeared around the time Reggie's uncle had been arrested. Maybe it was easiest to blame someone who wasn't around to defend himself? Or maybe the evidence had already been there and the killer was making sure it wasn't missed. But why?

Could Reggie and the others have sparked things off by investigating his uncle's case? If Reggie was right and his uncle was innocent, maybe whoever had done the original frame-up was afraid the Meddlers would expose it and had shifted to a Plan B.

But if that was the case, why plant evidence for the Meddlers and then kill them off? Just to add credence to the idea that they were on the right track? And if that *was* the case, why threaten non-Meddlers at all?

Every scenario he could imagine seemed far-fetched. But then, he wasn't a killer. His mind didn't work that way.

But two things argued against them dealing with Marley's murderer. First, the threats had come to them at school, implying a student or *maybe* a teacher. But something about the threats, written in Sharpie on printer paper, said it was a student. Second, the two different murder methods—then and now—argued for different killers. Marley had been strangled with someone's bare hands. Grace had been throttled with some kind of strap or belt or something, according to Kali. The police still hadn't told them how Liam's mom and whoever had died with her had been killed. Maybe the new killer wasn't as strong as the first, requiring the leverage of a strap.

Also, Marley's murderer had never left any kind of note. He'd never targeted anyone at the school. In fact, he'd been dormant for years. Marley's killing seemed more like a crime of passion.

As soon as Officer Stiles went out into the hallway to make calls without being overheard, Jack brought up the questions plaguing him.

Kali gave him a raised and pierced brow when he finished, "You're assuming facts not in evidence. First, that the two cases are truly linked."

Reggie and Charlie both started to protest, but Kali cut them off.

"Hear me out," she said. "We've all gone through Reggie's files multiple times. I hate to think that it might be one of us, but it's possible. Any of us could have noticed the earring, the salt and pepper shakers. Any of us could be playing a game here."

"Murder isn't a game," Maria said solemnly.

Kali rolled her eyes. With the kohl-lined emphasis, it was especially effective. "Not for us. But for the killer? Who's to say."

"So you're saying the killer could have, what? Duplicated the evidence?" Reggie asked with scorn worthy of Kali herself. "*Real* pearl? *Real* silver? I don't know about you, but even if I could track down duplicates, I don't have that kind of money lying around."

"We don't know the earring was real. We have only the picture to show for it. And the bird could be plated."

They all looked to Charlie, who held his hand tightly to his pocket. "I'm not bringing it out *here*. Anyway, not until that cop agrees to immunity. Plus, I just want to point out that if someone left this as a clue, I screwed it up for him. If Rayna hadn't seen me grab it, it would have been gone. You all would never have known it existed."

"Unless you planned for her to catch you in the act," Evan said ominously. "Unless you took it specifically to draw attention. You couldn't just say, 'Hey look, the very bird in Reggie's crime scene photos, isn't that a funny thing?'"

"Why not?" he asked indignantly.

Evan and Kali exchanged a glance and she delivered the blow. "Because you're not that observant. I'm sorry, but you're not," she said at the crushed look on his face. "If it weren't for the fire, I'd say you were the least likely suspect among us."

His gaze shot daggers her way. "Gee, thanks."

"But your prints are all over the bird now," Reggie said. "And even if they weren't, even if the killer was dumb enough to leave his own prints, chain of custody has been blown all to hell. The police can't use it to get the real killer."

"Maybe they couldn't bring the bird as evidence at trial," Charlie challenged, "but if they can track who bought it, it could lead them to whoever's doing all this."

Silence fell as Officer Stiles reentered the room.

"Are Kincaid and Travers on their way?" Reggie asked eagerly. "Are they reopening the case?"

"*Detective* Kincaid and *Detective* Travers are not coming off a new murder to investigate an old case," she said with the voice of officialdom.

"But if the cases are linked!" Charlie protested.

Stiles fixed him with a look, but it wasn't unsympathetic. "I never said you were being ignored. Or that I wouldn't do some poking around." But when she glanced at Reggie, her expression grew a lot sterner. "You sure you want to go down this route? Anything you want to get off your chest right now, before this goes any further?"

So she'd also considered that Reggie might have a motive. But Jack still had trouble seeing Reggie as a killer. If Reggie had found the planted evidence, he'd know his uncle was guilty and wouldn't have any reason to keep pursuing the case. If he'd bought it to implicate someone else, he surely wouldn't go so far as murder to call attention . . .

But Officer Stiles didn't know him.

Jack wondered how well any of them really knew each other. He clearly wasn't the only one with secrets, and if any of the others were psychopaths, like Evan described, they'd be very good at keeping theirs.

"Nothing," Reggie said through clenched teeth. "Well, maybe 'I told you so'."

Jack watched Officer Stiles's face. That didn't sit well.

"Evan," Jack said, turning to him, "you've got to talk to your uncle. Convince him to let us access the old files. If there was another man, someone must have known about him."

Evan looked around at all the others watching him expectantly. "He'll never go for it. I'm not even sure it's ethical for him."

"But if there was another man, why didn't it come up at trial?" Kali asked.

It didn't sound like a new question, but Reggie's eyes flashed fire just the same. "Because nobody bothered to find him. My uncle's lawyers couldn't and the police didn't even try. Since they couldn't produce the other man as an alternate suspect, his defense attorneys never brought him up, afraid that it would sound like unfounded jealousy and go to motive."

"So how do we know for sure there was another guy?" Kali asked.

"There was," Reggie insisted.

"But how do we *know*?"

"If the police won't talk to us," Jack jumped in again, "we've got to do our own legwork. We need to talk to your uncle. We need to interview Marley's old neighbors."

"No," Officer Stiles said with the tone of finality. "If there was another man, he could *be* one of Marley's former neighbors.

It's too dangerous."

"You can't stop us," Kali challenged.

"I can arrest you for obstruction. The information you've already withheld should be enough for that."

"But you won't," Kali said.

"Oh no?" Stiles asked.

"You're too ethical," Evan answered. "It's written all over your face. You're a protector, but even you won't lock us up for our own good."

"Not to mention it wouldn't help," Kali said. "The second we make bail . . ."

She left the rest to the imagination.

Stiles gave her a hard look. "Would you all at least promise to see what I can do first. If I can get the case reopened . . ."

"No promises," Reggie said. "You do what you can, and we'll see where we are. At the very least, I think a visit to my uncle is in order. He should know what's going on, in case it affects his appeal."

"You mean in case he can shed some light, right?" Rayna asked. "In case he can give us a lead to stop what's going on right now—people dying, being killed . . . This is not just about an appeal."

She was watching intently for his answer. Her words seemed to strike Reggie like a slap to the face. "Of course that," he said quickly. "That's the first thing I thought of, I promise. It's just, I've been focused on the case for so long . . . Anyway, we need to see him. But there's a problem—only two visitors are allowed at a time, and we're under age, so an adult would have to come be responsible for us. Plus, we have to give twenty-four hours notice."

"I'll go," Rayna said immediately. "If my parents will let me. I doubt they're sending me to school tomorrow anyway."

Everyone but Jack and Maria protested. Everyone wanted to go to the jail and see it all for themselves, meet a convicted felon, even one who might be innocent. But Jack couldn't leave Eric any more than he already had. He didn't know Maria's reasons. Probably she knew her parents wouldn't let her go.

But Reggie nodded at Rayna. "If your parents say it's okay. Let me know and I'll make the arrangements."

"I should go too," Evan said. "I can judge the nuances, catch all the little things."

"What?" Reggie asked, his voice rising. "After all this, you still think he's lying? You think he has any reason now to keep secrets? Or that I wouldn't catch on?"

"I think you're biased," Evan said, as gently as he could, which considering the words didn't help much.

"And I think you're an ass," Reggie responded.

Evan shrugged. "Could be."

"Anyway, did you miss the part about two at a time?" Reggie said, glaring daggers.

"No, but maybe we can trade off or something. I want to be there. For moral support if nothing else."

# CHAPTER 21

RAYNA

Rayna sat in the car with her father in tense silence as they waited for Evan to come out. She'd texted him they were out there. So normal, texting with Evan. Like it was any ordinary day, but she hadn't gotten any response, and so they waited.

And stewed.

She and her father had already said everything there was to say. He wasn't happy that they were going to see a convicted felon. He wasn't happy to learn that one of her friends, a boy he'd let into his house, was the nephew of a murderer. He insisted on using that word, even though she'd explained that Jim Driskoll had always maintained his innocence. She'd explained about the new evidence and the other man. Her father wasn't buying it. He wanted her to let the police do their jobs. They'd fought and, okay, she'd cried. It didn't help that the cops had reeled in Officer Stiles and weren't sending Repucci again now that the immediate threat to Rayna had passed. They'd step up patrols in her neighborhood . . . in the neighborhoods of all the kids threatened, but they couldn't keep an officer 24-7 on Rayna alone when they had no real clue where the killer would strike next. Grace had been on the hitlist too. There was no telling whether they'd swapped places in the timeline or whether all bets were off.

The only reason they were here now, that her father had taken the day off and agreed to drive them an hour and a half there and then back from the prison was that he was afraid she'd sneak out and do it anyway . . . or do something even more stupid. She wasn't proud of herself, but she'd threatened as much. After seventeen years of not rebelling at all, except in small ways like her hair, she was going at it in a big way, and her father didn't have any prior experience to fall back on. An only child raising an only child.

He was scared. Well, they had that in common.

Rayna gave up waiting on Evan. "I'd better go knock and see what's going on."

She could see it in her dad's face. He wanted to protest—his automatic response to everything right now—but leaving her in the car would mean leaving her a sitting duck. He'd rather watch her all the way to the door, keep her in his sights, as if that would prevent a sniper attack . . . Now her imagination was just running away with her. There was no sign this killer even owned a gun and here she was making him into a sharpshooter.

Feeling like there was a target painted on her back regardless, Rayna got out of the car and approached Evan's house. She was on the doorstep when she heard shouting inside.

"I said *no!*" It was a man's voice. Deep, surly, booming. "I won't allow it, and you can't afford to miss school. Get your damned backpack and get in the car."

Reluctantly, Rayna rang the doorbell and jumped out of her skin when it was jerked open almost instantly and a towering man glared down at her. Evan's dad.

"Evan's not coming," he said, preparing to slam the door.

Without thinking, Rayna's foot shot out into the path of it and she braced for the pain. It came, but not as bad as she'd anticipated. He'd seen the move and pulled himself up short.

"Can I at least talk to him?" she asked, staring into his anger-filled eyes. She'd never seen Evan's father angry . . . at least, not like this.

He looked like a larger, darker version of his son. His eyes were no less piercing, but they were a deep brown like burnt sienna where his son's were forest green. His hair and brows were likewise darker—mahogany rather than chestnut. Where Evan's hair flopped in his angular face, his father's was cut to about an inch or so on top, shorter around the ears. A businessman's cut—

or a lawyer's—that revealed a more squared-off, less pointed jaw. Evan must have gotten that from his mother. There was nothing soft in his father's face. No give. It looked like he ate lesser beings for lunch and that right now he was contemplating his next meal.

"There's no time. I need to drive Evan to school. We're already late," he said, kicking her foot out of the way and slamming the door in her face before she could react.

Rayna stood stunned, staring for a minute at the door before her father honked and shook her out of it.

She turned back for the car, afraid her father would use this as an excuse not to take her. Sure enough, he had his window down, the better to hear everything that had gone on, not that there'd been much to hear.

"See, I'm not the only parent who thinks this is a bad idea," he said as she got back into the car.

A text popped up on her phone from Evan.

*Sorry.*

She got into the car, clipped her seatbelt and texted back. *All OK?*

The response came almost instantly. *I'd sneak out & meet U at Reggie's, bt I don't suppose your dad wld take me after all that. Guess he heard?*

She didn't even have to ask; she knew the answer to that one. Her father would never take him without his father's permission. For all she knew, it could be considered kidnapping or something. As angry as Evan's father was, she wasn't sure he wouldn't pursue it.

*No,* she answered reluctantly.

*Bastard,* Evan typed back. She assumed he was talking about his own father and not hers. *He won't even let me drive myself to school —not that I probably could with my arm in a sling. He doesn't trust me not to detour.*

*What happened?* she asked.

There was no response for several long minutes, and when it came, it was no answer at all. *Let me know how things go.* It sounded like a demand. She supposed Evan got that part of his personality from his father.

The scene was a lot different at Reggie's. He was waiting for them on the top step of his porch reading an actual physical book. As they drove up, he pushed his glasses up farther onto his nose and rose to his full imposing height, his jeans crisp enough she could almost hear them crackling as he stood. Had they been *ironed*? *Starched*? His button-up shirt, blue with black and darker blue checks was just as perfect. At least his sneakers were worn in.

Rayna looked down at her own clothes. Reggie had gone over the regulations with her—no skirts above the knees, no tight clothes or tank tops or shirts of any kind without sleeves. She didn't have a lot of baggy clothes. They weren't a good idea around paints and pottery. But she'd ended up with unripped jeans and a teal hoodie that emphasized the bluer blue of her hair. She hadn't planned it that way, but there it was. At least there were no rules about that. She couldn't see that there was anything about her that would set anyone off, which seemed to be the whole purpose behind the rules.

Reggie folded himself into the back seat behind her and she scootched her seat up to give him more room for his long legs. She'd have offered the front passenger's seat if she thought he'd take it.

Rayna held her breath as her father eyed Reggie warily in the rearview mirror. He waited for Reggie to buckle in before pulling out. He didn't say anything until they were moving forward, heading for the prison.

"So, Reggie, tell me everything."

Rayna let out her breath. It could have been worse. At least he didn't say, "Tell me about your killer kin" or anything like that.

Reggie's gaze met Rayna's in the rearview mirror, which was askew. She tried to convey apology, although if she was honest, she really wanted to hear him tell it. She and the others had spent hours poring over the trial transcript and other evidence, but as she now knew, that didn't contain the whole story, at least not as far as he was concerned.

Reggie took a moment to gather himself, moving toward the

center of the car so that his long legs straddled the bump, but also so that he could see Rayna and her father in profile or in reflection in the rearview mirror, so that he could catch their reactions. She twisted in her seat so that she'd be able to see him as well, but she knew she wouldn't be able to keep it up the whole drive. It was just too unnatural a position, at least while she was buckled safely in.

"What do you know already?" Reggie began, turning the question back on her father. "Do you remember the case, almost five years ago?"

"The woman found strangled in her apartment," her father commented back. "Hard to forget. We don't have so many murders that something like that gets buried on the back page."

"What else do you remember?" he asked.

"The boyfriend—your uncle, it sounds like—was a person of interest right away. The woman was last seen with him, out to dinner at what used to be Farfardelle's Restaurant, but is now a pizza place. They left fighting, a couple of hours later a friend went to check on her and found her dead. Your uncle didn't have an alibi."

"Actually, he did."

"Not one that held up in court," her father said.

Reggie sighed. "If you've already convicted him, why are you even letting Rayna come."

"A jury convicted him," her father answered, hands clenched on the steering wheel. "I'm trying to keep an open mind, especially if he knows anything that could help."

Reggie took a deep breath of his own and let it out slowly, as if counting his way toward calm. "The part you know is true as far as it goes. Marley and my uncle Jim were dating. They went out to dinner that night and were supposed to go to my cousin's school play afterward. I don't know if the papers mentioned Jim's seven-year-old daughter, who's had to grow up without her father." He waited in silence for a reaction he didn't get. Either Rayna's dad knew it already or it didn't make any difference in his mind.

"Anyway," Reggie continued, "Marley begged off the show,

which was what started the fight. He'd thought for a few weeks that she was seeing someone else, and the way she was acting, he suspected she wanted to get home for another date. She denied it, but I guess things came to a head. They got into a fight right there in the restaurant and left in a huff. He slammed down payment and witnesses say he was a little rough when he took Marley's arm to help her toward the car."

"A little rough?" her father asked.

Reggie stared at his profile, but tried to keep the hostility at the question under wraps. "Yeah, you know, like when you're irritated with someone and you might grab them a little suddenly or a little too hard? Apparently, Marley'd had a little wine with dinner, and she wasn't all that steady on her feet. He took her by the arm to lead her out when she stumbled over the carpet at the entrance. No one said anything then. No one called the police about their fight or showed concern about her getting into the car with my uncle. But after she'd been found dead and my uncle was declared a person of interest, suddenly it was suspicious. Memories rewrote themselves. He hadn't been helping her out, witnesses said then, they'd been struggling. He'd *caused* her to stumble . . ."

Rayna's father glanced over at her as if to see if she could handle things. He hadn't seen the photos. Would have been furious that she'd seen them. But if she could handle the details in the file, surely she could handle this.

"So your uncle took her home," her father prompted.

"He took her home. He walked her to her door, since she was unsteady, and got her inside. They fought some more, and then he left. Neighbors heard them. He went to his daughter's play. *The Wizard of Oz*, in case you're wondering. She was part of the Lollipop Guild with a song and everything. But he was a little late and sat in the back. The ticket taker saw him, but then she came in to watch the play and so couldn't swear he didn't leave again."

"Wouldn't someone have noticed the auditorium doors opening and closing?" her father asked.

Rayna already knew the answer to that one. It had come up

during the trial and she'd read it in the transcript.

Reggie answered before she could. "It happens all the time—someone going to use the bathrooms or get a drink. One woman took out a crying baby, another man had a coughing fit. Someone else ducked out to take a phone call."

"Your uncle saw them all? Wouldn't that alibi him just as surely? He saw them, even if they didn't see him?"

"That was his defense," Reggie agreed. "But the prosecution said that he could have heard about any of it later. People might not notice a lone man sitting in the back of the theatre. He could slip in or out, but a crying baby, a coughing fit . . . that they'd remember. They might complain. He could have picked up on it at intermission."

"I don't suppose he recorded the performance or . . ."

"Not from the back of the theatre," Reggie said before he could finish. "Anyway, that's not really his thing. He knew his ex-wife would be recording it. She's like the ultimate stage mom."

Her father was silent for a minute. Then, "Why do they think your uncle would have gone back again? How do the police know Marley wasn't killed when he dropped her off after dinner?"

Reggie glared. Rayna couldn't exactly blame him.

"Because neighbors heard more fighting some time later. Forty-five minutes. An hour. A knock-down, drag out fight, someone said."

"You think it was the man she was supposed to meet? The one she'd cut short the date with your uncle to see."

"Yes. It was definitely a man. Neighbors heard that much."

"And they couldn't tell it wasn't the same voice?" Rayna asked. Her first question, but it seemed so obvious.

"They couldn't be sure," Reggie said. "They couldn't even really make out what was being said, just that things were heated. Then one of the neighbors hiked up the volume on her television to drown out the fighting and no one could hear anything else."

"What about seeing him leave?"

"No one witnessed the man enter or leave her apartment. An elderly woman, Mrs. Ogilvie, saw a man headed out of the building at about that time. He brushed past her down the stairs, obviously in a hurry, but she was watching her footing, and didn't look up until he was almost on top of her. Tall, she said. Slacks and a button up shirt, like he'd come from an office. Nice shoes. Brown. And he was not at all happy at finding Mrs. Ogilvie in his way."

"It's not much of a description," her father said, but thoughtful now at least.

"If he hadn't been right up on her, we wouldn't have gotten even that much. Mrs. Ogilvie has cataracts."

"Great," her father said.

"Yeah."

"And no video cameras in the building or in the parking lot?"

"No," he said. "It's just a basic apartment building. Nice, but no bells and whistles. No gate, no doorman. They didn't find the guy. I'm not sure how hard they even looked. They had my uncle. They had the witnesses to their fight at the restaurant. They had his fingerprints all over her apartment—of course, because they were dating—"

"What about DNA?" Rayna asked. She knew the answer to this one too, but she asked it for her father's sake. "If she was strangled, she would have fought back. There should be DNA under her fingernails. Wait, was there DNA under Grace's fingernails? Do we know?"

She twisted entirely in her seat to look at Reggie for this one.

"None under Marley's nails," he said. "Medical examiner's testimony was that Marley's killer hit her head against something first, knocking her out or at least insensible. She never had the chance to fight back."

"And Grace?" she asked.

"I don't know. Maybe we can get Officer Stiles to find out for us. But even if they found DNA, it takes weeks for test results to come back, and by that time—"

*Most of us will be dead.* She finished the thought silently, though, as if giving it voice would give it power. Maybe Reggie felt the same.

"Yeah," she said instead.

They'd run out of questions, at least right then. Processing. By the time Rayna thought of more, they'd reached the outskirts of the prison, and the sight shut her up. It was weirdly beautiful, once you got past the electrified fences, one beyond another, topped with razor wire. Past that was a building that looked something like an old fortress with the stone walls weathered gray and green-black where lichen or something had grown. The walls were topped with more wire. Rayna felt as though the metal should catch the light, gleaming in deadly splendor, but instead it was dark—probably the elements, but her brain went first to dried blood or rust, and she wondered if anyone ever escaped the ravages of the wire only to die of tetanus. But this was a maximum security prison. No one should ever have escaped. In theory.

The guard at the gate checked their names against his list and insisted on IDs, shining his flashlight around the interior of the car and into each of their eyes as he compared faces against their pictures. All Rayna had was her school ID, and it was a terrible picture, but it must have been enough. Handing their IDs back, the guard insisted that her father pop his trunk while his partner searched under the car with a wide convex mirror on the end of a long pole.

She didn't know why she was nervous. She knew they didn't have anything weird in the car or anything to hide, but the search made her feel like a criminal somehow. She didn't like it. She couldn't imagine how Reggie's uncle must feel on the inside, especially if he was innocent.

The guard searching the trunk shifted things around, shifted them back and finally slammed the trunk closed. His partner had already finished with his mirror and was watching as the first guard came back toward the shack, giving him a nod.

His partner nodded back and opened the gates for them, instructing them on where to go while they waited for a large enough gap to drive through.

There were signs inside that directed them as well. It wasn't like they could get lost, but it was possible some had tried.

They parked and got out and the butterflies that had started in Rayna's stomach back at the gate were now getting worked up into a frenzy.

"If you've got a pocket knife or a lighter or anything," Reggie said to her father, "you're going to want to ditch it in the car. You can't take it in with you."

"I read the rules," he answered, squaring his shoulders. Rayna wondered if he was nervous as well.

Reggie, the only one who knew what to expect, led the way toward the building. Inside they had to sign in, show IDs again, empty pockets, go through a metal detector, get wanded and generally be declared safe before they were allowed into their appointment. It was why Reggie had insisted they arrive at least half an hour early. Rayna took in everything in silence, noting it for the Meddlers. As weird as it was, she knew they felt like they were missing out. They'd want to know everything.

Some part of her insisted they'd have grilled Reggie on the subject already and wondered if on some level she was really interested for her own sake. She was used to being an observer—through her artist's eye or the lens of the camera. She was comfortable with that role. Finding herself in the center of so much drama, so much that was life and death . . .

It said something about how sidelined she'd been that she was suddenly considering herself in the center of anything. *Reggie* was in the center of things. And Liam, assuming he was still alive. And poor Grace. Of them, Reggie was the last one still standing. Maybe. Probably. But then, *he'd* never been threatened. She'd considered that it might be one of the Meddlers doing all of this, but if Reggie was the guilty one, wouldn't he have threatened himself to throw off suspicion?

She watched him through everything, but she wasn't trained like Evan or like Reggie himself. She didn't know anything about psychology, about tells and microexpressions. If Reggie acted strangely, would she even know?

Finally, they were called.

They all started forward, but the guard stood in their way, staring them down. "I'm sorry," he said, like he was reading from a script and not like he was really sorry at all. "Only two of you allowed."

Rayna eyed her father. They'd discussed this, but still he didn't move.

"Please," she said, face angled up at him. "I have to do this."

His face went through a few expressions she *could* read, knowing him so well—pain, uncertainty. Then he let out all the air in his lungs and took a step back, gesturing them on. Rayna was afraid the guard would protest. Reggie had said that since they were underage, someone had to accompany and be responsible for them. Apparently, taking them this far was far enough. She felt a slight weight drop off her shoulders as she and Reggie followed the guard forward, free of her father's disapproving eye. One less person to watch. She didn't have to concern herself with her father and his reactions. She could focus on Reggie and his uncle and what he could tell them. Her father would want a recap later, she was certain, but that was fine. It might even help her put things into perspective.

The hallway they proceeded down smelled . . . stale. Like old sweat and desperation that someone had tried to beat down with chemicals that weren't up to the task. The scent stung her nose, and she had to breathe out of her mouth temporarily until she could get used to it. By then it was inside her, and she felt as if she'd internalized something that would become part of her. She could never breathe it all out. Some part of this place would stay with her.

The guard led them to a small cubby with two chairs bolted to the floor, two handsets attached by cords to the wall next to a sign reiterating the rules, a window at least an inch thick and nothing else. The window was scratched and smeared. The cubby putty-colored. The handsets stark black antiques. It was as though someone had set a stage for "Abandon All Hope."

Rayna was sad just sitting down. She couldn't even imagine how she'd feel if someone she knew and loved was on the other side of that glass. Or if it was *her* there, seeing that scarred window as a welcome break in routine.

It was a minute before they brought Reggie's uncle in, and then Rayna almost choked on the deep breath she sucked in.

She'd expected a man about her father's age, around all her friend's father's ages. After all, he was Reggie's dad's brother.

But Jim Driskoll appeared about ten years older. His eyes were sunken and yet prominent at the same time, as though the skin around them had retreated, leaving the orbs more or less on their own. That was what made him look older, she realized, as she took in the rest. He was tall—at least as tall as Reggie, but without the stoop or slumping of the shoulders to keep from standing out. He had at least forty pounds on his nephew too, all of it muscle, as far as she could tell through the ugly orange jumpsuit. His close-cropped hair was far more pepper than salt and continued down into a trim beard which skirted a great jawline it seemed a shame to cover up.

Those tired eyes flickered over Reggie, who he gave a nod of acknowledgment, and over to her, resting there. She was instinctively drawn to pretend she hadn't been studying him, but that would have been disingenuous. There was nothing else *to* study. So she met his gaze and tried a smile. One side of his mouth quirked like he might try to give one back, but it didn't quite make it.

The guard who'd brought Jim Driskoll released his prisoner's hands and locked the door behind him, trapping him in the interview room.

Jim picked up the telephone on his side of the window. Reggie and Rayna took the cue to pick up theirs as well.

"Hey, boy," Jim started, drinking Reggie in. "I swear you get bigger every time you I see you. What're you now, six foot? More?"

Reggie gave a bark of a laugh. "And I swear you say the same thing every time I come visit. Six foot one," he answered. "I'm catching up to you."

"You brought company this time," he said, locking eyes on Rayna. "Not that I'm complaining, you understand, but you know there are a lot better places to bring a date."

Rayna's eyes widened, and she glanced at Reggie to see how he was taking it. She couldn't tell if he blushed, but his head did duck down like he was trying harder than ever not to be noticed. "Not a date, Uncle Jim," he said, refusing to meet Rayna's gaze. "You know those friends I was telling you about? The ones helping me work your case? Well, she's one of them."

"Ah," he answered. "Here to grill me. See what my nephew here could have missed? He's pretty thorough. I can't imagine what it might be, but what else do I have to do? Go ahead—shoot."

Rayna had figured Reggie would take the lead, but Jim was looking to her, and she felt like she had to step up. Still, she shot Reggie a sidelong glance, just in case he wanted to take over. Or minded if she did, but if so he wasn't saying.

"Uh, well, I don't know if Reggie's told you, but there've been some developments . . ."

"Developments?" he asked. His gaze sharpened, and he sat a little forward in his seat. "What do you mean developments? New evidence?"

"Murders," Rayna said. She hadn't meant to state it so baldly, but it had just slipped out. "A woman and two kids from our class —or so we think, anyway. One definitely. The other . . . Anyway, Marley's missing earring was found at one of the crime scenes."

"And the bird salt and pepper shakers like she had," Reggie added.

Jim fell back in his seat as though he'd been dealt a physical blow. "They . . . they found her earring? Where? Who had it? Why—"

"Uncle Jim," Reggie cut in, "the police don't have it. Well, they might by now, if it didn't disappear again, but . . . we found it. Rayna did anyway. That's part of why we're here."

Jim's gaze riveted on her. "You found it and you didn't turn it over?" There was accusation in his voice. And disbelief. She couldn't blame him, not if he thought she'd withheld evidence that could exonerate him.

"I didn't know what I'd found until later. I was taking pictures at a crime scene that I'd, uh, snuck into. It wasn't until we enlarged the photos that we noticed the earring, and then the police stopped me for trespassing and I had to hide the evidence—my photos, not the earring—" She was making a horrible mess of it. "Maybe I'd better start over?"

Jim nodded, one hand rubbing at his face while the other held the phone to his ear. She wondered whether it was a sign of stress or if he wanted to hide his reactions. Certainly she couldn't read them while his face was half obscured.

She told him about the threats. And about Liam, who wasn't Liam.

"But you said murders. Plural," he said, taking his hand away from his face finally and staring fixedly at her as she paused.

She'd been about to move on to Grace when a crazy thought occurred to her, all wrapped up in the grief that swamped her whenever she thought about Grace and the fact that she'd been killed in Rayna's place. She wondered whether she should truly be telling Jim any of this. What if the police wanted to question him? Study his reactions first hand? Be sure he didn't know anything he wasn't supposed to. What if she screwed that up?

He couldn't have killed Liam's mom. Or Grace. She knew that. He'd been locked up, as secure as could be. But that didn't mean he couldn't have had it done to implicate someone else, to cast doubt on his case and help with his appeal.

Reggie watched her struggle, as if he could read her mind. She felt like hell. This was his *uncle*. She didn't know whether she was being unfair or if not questioning and taking everything at face value would make her gullible. The old Rayna would have given Jim the benefit of the doubt. It was more romantic, prettier to believe that an innocent man had been sent to prison than that someone she knew, even by relation, could commit murder.

But someone had.

Reggie took up the story, taking the decision out of her hands. "Our friend Grace came next. Someone lured her out with a text, supposedly from Liam, the guy everyone thought had been killed. She was strangled. Just like Marley."

Rayna was about to dispute the "Just like Marley" part. Whoever killed Grace had used a belt or something around her neck. But she stopped herself. That might be something the police would want to hold back.

"Hellfire," Jim said, more to himself than to them. He pinched the bridge of his nose and extended his fingers out from there to rub at his eyes as if he had a headache coming on. "I'm so sorry you kids are dealing with this. No one should have to—" The sob in his voice stopped him. He had to take a second to regroup. "No one should have to lose someone close to them, especially not someone so young."

The rubbing of his eyes turned into wiping away a tear, and Rayna just couldn't bring herself to believe his guilt. If she was being gullible, then so be it.

"You still miss her," she said, talking about Marley.

"Every damned day," he answered. "I know she was . . . not perfect . . . but even imperfect, life was better with her than without. The colors were brighter, you know? Conversation more meaningful."

Rayna nodded, even though she didn't know. Not really. It sounded like love, though. And she knew it could make a person do crazy things.

"I'm sorry to bring this up, Uncle Jim," Reggie said, leaning toward the glass as though he could project his sincerity through it, "but we wanted to talk to you about Marley. About the other man you were sure she was seeing. We thought maybe . . . Well, he seems like a good place to start if we can just figure out who he is."

Jim didn't answer at first. Rayna felt like a Peeping Tom, watching the pain that shot across his face, closing his eyes, hanging his head.

"I never saw him," Jim said without opening his eyes. "But Marley always got a lot of attention. She was so full of life. And she liked the attention, encouraged it. She didn't have a type so much as . . . she always wanted what she was missing. She knew that about herself, how easily her head was turned. Monogamy was . . . hard for her. Something she was trying out like a coat. Because she loved me."

The last line came out breathy, and he took a shuddering inhale before continuing on. "But when she started cutting short dates or texting under the table, I knew. I didn't say anything right away. I didn't want to call her on it, you know? I was afraid that if I made her choose it wouldn't be me. I was lucky to have the part of her I did. But that night it wasn't just about me. It was about Miranda. She couldn't wait for Marley to see her perform and to show off her costume. We were all planning to go for ice cream afterward. I didn't want to disappoint Miranda. And so, I brought it up. Marley denied everything. We fought."

Finally he looked at them again, at Reggie. "You know the rest. It was all there in the trial transcript. Except I didn't manhandle her at the restaurant. I was helping her keep her feet."

Rayna's heart went out to him. Still, they had to ask their questions. "Did you ever suspect who she might be seeing?"

His gaze transferred to her. All she could read from it was pain. "No. I had no idea. The police told me I was wrong. Crazy. The only numbers she called were mine. Her girlfriends. A few exes she still talked to. Her accountant. Her lawyer."

Reggie and Rayna exchanged a glance. "She had a lawyer?"

"Well, not per se. She'd been in a car accident the year before, been sideswiped. Clearly the other guy's fault, but, of course, he was claiming otherwise. Her insurance was dealing with it, and she had a lawyer through them she'd been in touch with a few times. That was all."

"Did he have a name?" Reggie asked.

"I'm sure he did, but I don't think I ever heard it."

"And the accountant?"

"Don't know that either. Just, you know, personal tax stuff."

Reggie turned to Rayna. "Liam's father was a CPA."

He reached as if for his phone, forgetting he'd had to leave it behind. "Damn, I forgot I had to turn my phone in. I wanted to show you a picture of Mr. Hinkle. See if it rang any bells."

"That witness," Rayna said, "did she give a description of the man she saw leaving Marley's apartment?"

"Well, see, that's the thing. She can't actually swear that's where he was coming from. There are a few apartments on that level. The only thing she could say was that he wasn't one of the tenants. Otherwise, details were pretty sketchy. Medium-tall. Dark hair, broad shoulders, dark slacks and a light button up shirt with no jacket or tie. No facial hair. It could have been anybody, really. She couldn't even say about the color of the shirt for sure. Something about cataracts."

Rayna looked to Reggie. "Mr. Hinkle was red-blonde, light colored hair. There's no way it was him."

Jim shrugged. "It's not much to go on. I guess I can't blame the police for not finding the guy."

"I can," Reggie said.

"Now, I've told you before, this has already ruined my life. You can't let it ruin yours too." Jim fixed him with a stern look and Reggie dropped eye contact, not making any promises.

"We'll find him," Rayna said, wishing she was certain.

There was an awkward moment of silence, and then, "I hope so. I truly do," from Jim. He forced a smile. "Any updates on my little Miranda?" he asked Reggie. "Have you seen her?"

Rayna watched as all the starch went out of Reggie and he slumped in his chair even more than usual. "No," he said sadly. "Aunt Laurie still won't bring her around or let us see her." He swallowed hard.

Jim hung his head. "Same old, same old. I hope you find whoever's doing this, hurting those kids. I wish . . . I wish I could protect you. I wish there was anything at all I could do from in here."

He sounded so defeated. Rayna found her hand rising to the glass without even her conscious thought. On the other side, Jim put his palm to hers. If he *was* guilty . . . No, somewhere along the line she'd stopped seriously considering that possibility.

Jim's guard came back into his room at that moment, and such a weight of sadness fell over Rayna that she couldn't imagine how he bore it on his end.

She and Reggie slogged back out to her father. She had a feeling that she'd never be the same again. They had to solve the murders. Lives were at stake in more ways than one.

She didn't talk all the way back. Reggie recapped everything for her father, who kept shooting worried glances her way, but she couldn't internalize anyone else's concern at that moment. She was too full.

It was over an hour until they hit home. She couldn't spend it doing nothing. It felt like every second that passed brought a new disaster closer and that if she wasn't standing in the way of it then she was aiding and abetting. She knew she was just one person, and not even the best equipped, but none of that changed the sense of responsibility and the understanding of what another loss would mean.

Rayna grabbed out her phone and immediately sent off a text to Evan, the only person she felt absolutely sure she could trust.

*U have to interview Marley's neighbors. Esp. Mrs. Ogilvie. Bring pics of everyone associated w/ case. And all dads, etc. Like a photo line-up. Bring backup. Safety in #s.*

She realized as she sent it that school still hadn't even let out. Yet it felt like ages had passed.

# CHAPTER 22

JACK

Jack didn't get out of the car right away when Maria pulled up outside his house. "I might be a few minutes," he said. "Are you sure you don't mind waiting?"

"I could come in. I'm not . . ." she looked up at the sky as if she could see it through her roof, as if she was searching for strength from above. "I'm not too excited about sitting out here on my own. In the open. Not with everything going on."

She hadn't had to bring him at all. Jack could have taken the bus home. With no ride, he'd miss out on interrogating Marley's neighbors—Evan had forwarded Rayna's text to everybody and invited them all along, but . . .

He wished he could clone himself. He didn't want to leave Eric. He'd spent enough time away from him already. Yet he wanted to be part of the investigation and to have Evan's back. He knew *he* hadn't killed anyone. He couldn't speak for the others. What if the only person who showed up was the killer? What if Maria or a witness was endangered because he wasn't there? He couldn't risk it.

As for now, he didn't want to let Maria in. Didn't want her to see his mother potentially passed out somewhere or Eric half dead from dehydration and neglect, but . . . he couldn't leave her out here to fend for himself.

He started to ask himself who the hell had died and left him in charge of caring, but the answers glared him in the face.

"Yeah, come on in," he said reluctantly, "but, um . . ."

Um, what? There were no excuses he could make. No way to

prepare her.

"Nevermind, just come on."

He got out of the car before he could change his mind and walked angrily toward the front door. He didn't know where the anger was coming from. Nothing was her fault. He wasn't even angry at her. It was the situation. And the fact that it was out of his control. Whatever he found inside, she'd see it too.

She'd see where he came from and never look at him the same way again. Hell, she'd never thought he was all that and a bag of chips to begin with. He hoped he wasn't about to confirm her worst suspicions.

But somewhere along the line, he thought she'd stopped seeing him as demon-spawn and started seeing him as a human being. Maybe even one she didn't totally despise. Someone she could get used to having around? That was probably pushing it, but still. He didn't want to go back to the way things were.

No help for it.

Jack opened his front door and paused for a second as he always did, listening. The sound of one of Eric's games blared from his room, so he was awake. He had the strength to be sitting up, killing zombies or fighting aliens or whatever. It was a good sign.

He pushed the door open and held it for Maria to proceed him so that his body would be blocking hers as she stepped inside. He should have thought of that while they were walking up the path to his door. But it wasn't like they were facing a sniper or sharpshooter. Their killer seemed to like being up close and personal.

As soon as he closed the door behind them both and made sure it was locked, he asked her, "Wait here?"

She looked at him questioningly, but didn't ask whatever was on her mind. Jack took the few stairs to the upper floor of the split-level house and went back to check on Eric. He wasn't going to bring Maria if Eric wasn't up to company.

"Hey, Bud," Jack said from the doorway. Eric was so caught up in his game, he jumped at the sound of Jack's voice.

"Hey, yourself," Eric said back, putting his game on pause.

There was a dirty plate on his side-table with the crust of a sandwich, peanut butter and jelly, going stale. So Mom had fed him today. Probably felt all virtuous over it. Celebrated with a shot. Or another glass of whatever had been on sale at the liquor store. There was an empty glass beside it with a trace of red-tinged liquid at the bottom. Kool-Aid instead of plain old water? It was a banner day.

And Eric looked good. Tired, but not as tired as usual. He was wearing a clean black GamerGuild T-shirt, the rest of him disappearing beneath relatively crumb-free sheets.

"You finish your online classes?" Jack asked.

"Yes, Dad," Eric answered with a roll of his eyes. Jack controlled a flinch.

"Can I get you anything?"

"A winning lottery ticket? Genetic enhancements? Skyhook cheat codes?" Eric answered hopefully.

"Sorry, fresh out."

"Damn."

"*Eric.*"

"What? You say it all the time. And worse."

"And you want to be like me? That's so sweet."

He stepped up to ruffle Eric's sparse hair, but his brother threw a hand up to block him. "Ha!" he said as he succeeded. "Denied!"

Jack laughed, and it felt good.

"Boys only or can anyone play?" Maria's voice came from the doorway.

Jack closed his eyes, cursing under his breath so that Eric wouldn't hear and say *I told you so.*

"I thought you promised to wait."

"Oh, did I?"

Jack thought back over it and realized she never had promised. He'd commanded and had expected her to agree. Shades of his father. Only he wasn't tempted to bloody her nose for coming anyway.

Caught out, Jack tried to force a grin. Eric looked *very* interested in the conversation.

"Little brother, this is Maria. Maria, this is Eric."

"Eric," she said, stepping forward. "Pleased to meet you."

She held out a hand and Eric dropped his game controller to shake it.

He slid Jack a sly look. "Damn, bro, how many girls have you got?"

"*Eric,*" Evan said again.

"Fine, *darn* then. Sheesh."

"Girls?" Maria asked, sounding sly as well, like she was enjoying this.

"Kali," he answered. "She was here the other day, searching for Amal online. Eric was helping out. He knows all the gaming boards and stuff Amal would have frequented."

"We didn't find anything," Eric said sadly, "but we did play a killer game of *Unlife and Limb.* You play?"

Maria shook her head and Eric glanced at Jack as though questioning what he saw in her. It brought a smile to his face for the second time in just a few short minutes, but it disappeared as quickly as it came. With everything going on, it felt wrong to smile. On the other hand, he supposed he had to take what pleasure came along. There had been little enough lately.

Then as if he'd cursed himself, he heard his mother come out of her room. He slipped quickly past Maria to meet her in the hall, where she was surreptitiously supporting herself with a hand against the wall.

"I heard voices," she said, her words only slightly slurred. She was always pretty good with that until just before she passed out. "A girl?"

Jack looked back and caught Maria poking her head out of Eric's room. His heart sank to his stomach. There was no help for it now.

"Mom, this is Maria. Maria, this is my mother."

Mom gave a lopsided smile and dragged her hand along the wall as she approached, close enough that she could focus on the girl in front of her with over-bright, glassy eyes. There was no way

Maria wouldn't be able to tell she was drunk. Vodka today, it seemed, since at least she wasn't breathing boozy fumes.

"Pleasure," his mom said, putting her hand out.

Maria took it uncertainly. Yup, she definitely knew. "Uh, pleased to meet you."

"Likewise," his mother said, as if she hadn't started the whole thing.

He had to stop this before it became a disaster.

He took her hand from Maria's and held it, squeezing so that she'd meet his eyes and let Maria go. "Mom, I just stopped in to check on you and Eric, see if you needed anything. He's looking good."

Maybe if he encouraged her, she'd do better more often. He couldn't quite kill the hope.

"Stopped in?" she asked, latching onto that. "You're leaving? Your father won't like that. He'll be home in . . . what time is it?"

Jack closed his eyes, took a breath, opened them again as he let it out. "He won't be home for a few hours. Hopefully I'll be back by then. There's something I have to do."

"Okay then," she said, mercifully not asking what. A good mother would have, but that ship had sailed. "Bring me back cigarettes?"

He hated that Maria was seeing this.

"I'll try," he said.

It was good enough for her. She shuffled past him, on down the hall toward the kitchen. Jack went in and grabbed the glass off Eric's table and followed her into the kitchen to refill it for him. He needed to keep pushing fluids. Maria stayed behind, and when he came back with the glass, she and Eric were laughing about something, but neither would tell him what. He was both irritated and pleased. He really wanted to know, but on the other hand, Eric and Maria were bonding. She had a smile on her face. She couldn't think all bad about him and his family if she was sharing a secret with Eric.

"You ready?" he asked Maria.

"Ready," she said. She put a hand to Eric's shoulder. "Maybe

I'll see you again soon?"

"It's cool," he answered.

Again? She'd be coming back? He didn't want to read anything into it, but that seductress hope just wouldn't leave him alone.


Evan was waiting for them in the parking lot of Marley's apartment complex. Reggie and Rayna were still on the road back from the prison, since her father had insisted on stopping for lunch. Charlie had a doctor's appointment he couldn't get out of and Kali had "something she had to do". She didn't elaborate. That left the three of them, which, honestly, was probably more than enough to descend on strangers asking a lot of questions. And Kali wouldn't have been his first choice for putting anyone at ease.

"How are we going to do this?" Jack asked as he got out of the car.

Evan handed him a couple of full-color pages with pictures arranged like a line-up.

"You two take the first floor, I'll take the second, we'll all meet up on the third, since that's where Mrs. Ogilvie lives and I don't think anyone wants to miss out on that. Marley's apartment was on the fourth floor, the top, so we can split up for the apartments on that level. Anyone who isn't home we can go back to later. Sound like a plan?"

"Are you sure it's a good idea for you to split off on your own?" Maria asked. "What if one of Marley's neighbors is the killer?"

Evan looked at her, then up at the building and back. "Together then?" he asked.

They walked toward the building together. It was nice as apartment buildings went, with a brick facade and wrought iron balconies for each apartment. Through the outer door they could see a tidy foyer with fake potted plants and retro black and white tile flooring in a checkered pattern. A couple of couches flanked a threadbare area rug in front of a full-length window showing a courtyard with a running fountain not much bigger than a bird-bath.

But the locked outer door belied the welcome beyond it. They needed either a key, which they didn't have, or someone to buzz them in. A panel with buttons and labels by apartment numbers rather than names sat to the right of the door, practically flush with the wall.

Which meant that unless the security had been upgraded in the past few years, whoever Mrs. Ogilvie had seen coming from the fourth floor had been let in. Either someone had been careless or the victim herself hadn't seen him as a threat. It was interesting to note.

"When Reggie first brought you all together and opened up his uncle's casefile, did any of you come over here, check it out?" Jack asked.

"I did," Evan said. "I didn't reinterview everyone, but I wanted to see how easy it would have been to get in and out. You've noticed the security?"

Jack nodded.

"The last time it was raining," Evan continued. "Someone saw me poking around, assumed I was waiting for someone and held the door so that I could wait inside where it was dry. Not exactly maximum security."

"Even after the murder?" Maria asked, dumbfounded.

"It was years ago. People forget, drop their guard. Some people live in fear, but most just get on with their lives, assuming it was an isolated incident. They're horrified, of course. They watch the news. They get a secret thrill telling people how close they came, that it was the apartment *right upstairs*. Maybe for a month or so they study faces, but it's hard to keep up that level of concern, especially when the police say they've caught the guy and that it was a love affair gone wrong. Nothing to do with them."

"Cynic," Jack said. But not because he thought Evan was wrong. He'd seen firsthand how people could ignore what they didn't want to face.

"Realist," he answered.

"Come on, kids, let's get this show on the road," Evan said. "You do a good job, I'll take you all out for ice cream."

"How can you joke?" Maria asked.

Evan feigned surprised. "Have you met me? Besides, I never joke about ice cream."

She gave Evan the disapproving look Jack had seen many times before. He took some satisfaction at seeing it turned on someone else.

He wondered what story Maria had given her parents for them to let her out of the house. He was fairly certain she hadn't told them exactly what she'd be doing. Which meant she was being a bit of a bad girl right now, playing on his side of the tracks. But he knew better than to call her on it.

Evan stepped forward and rang all of the buzzers one by one until someone called through the speaker at the top of the panel, "Yes?"

"I'm here to see Mrs. Ogilvie, but she's not answering her buzzer. Can you let me in so I can check on her?"

There was a sigh and then a telling click from the main door. They grabbed it before the lock reengaged and then they were in.

They struck out on the first floor. No one was home at the first two apartments. The door of the third was answered by a timid little girl of maybe five years old who was instantly pulled away by an older woman—a grandmother or a sitter—who appeared utterly exhausted. She eyed them wearily but not unkindly as Jack and Evan let Maria do their spiel, figuring she was the least threatening of the three of them, but the words were barely out before the woman was shaking her head. "You'd want my daughter. She's at work. Do you want to leave me a name and number or something in case she knows anything and wants to call?"

"That's all right, we'll check back," Jack said, guiding Maria away before she could offer up the information.

Like Evan, Jack was a realist. Or a cynic. There was no way the daughter would call. Busy mom, closed case. She'd see no reason to get involved. No reason to tell a bunch of kids anything. Unless she was faced with them in person and they convinced her there was something at stake and that anything she could remember about that night would be a huge help.

The door to the fourth and final apartment on that floor was answered by an elderly man who hadn't been living there at the time of the murder. A total wash out.

On the second floor they found someone who *had* lived in the building when Marley was killed, but she was a bartender and was working that night. She'd missed the whole thing.

Jack realized that he was holding his breath as they reached the third floor and Evan knocked on Mrs. Ogilvie's door. He was putting far too much hope into the coming encounter. That fickle bitch hope. For all they knew, Mrs. Ogilvie had lost more than her sight since the murder. She hadn't been a spring chicken five years ago.

They waited. Nothing happened. Evan knocked again, noticed the bell to the side of the door and pushed that as well.

"All right, all right, I'm coming," came a voice from inside the apartment. She didn't sound at all feeble. Old, yes—there was a crackly, quavery quality to her voice—but still strong. "Give an old lady a chance."

They waited patiently as they heard the plunk-slide of someone approaching the door with assistance. *A cane or a walker?* he wondered. Not that it mattered, except that five years ago she'd hardly have gotten a walker up and down the stairs. The light changed in the peephole and Mrs. Ogilvie's voice came again, "Yes, who is it? I have all the magazine subscriptions I need. I'm diabetic, so I can't have cookies or candy and I've already accepted the Lord as my savior."

Beside him, Maria cracked a smile and then stepped up to the front so she could be seen. Again the lone female in the group, again the least threatening. "Mrs. Ogilvie, we're not here to sell you anything. We were hoping we could talk to you about Marley Thompson. We wouldn't bother you if it wasn't important."

"Marley Thompson? That girl who got murdered? You'd barely have been alive back then."

They all looked at each other. It had only been five years ago.

Maybe she'd gone senile? But she didn't sound senile. She remembered who Marley Thompson was.

The door opened on the end of a chain and Mrs. Ogilvie's clouded eye and an inch or so of her weathered face appeared in the gap created. "What do you want to talk about?"

"Can we come in?" Maria said. "We'd like to ask about the man you saw that night. We have some pictures to show you, but . . . it might be better in good light."

Mrs. Ogilvie squinted from Maria to the boys behind her. Evan's hair was, as always, hanging in his face. If she was one of those older people who thought that made him look like a thug . . . Or if she thought the ever-present glint in his eyes meant mischief . . . Or that Jack's hard edges meant trouble . . . He did his best to relax his body posture, to smile.

She recoiled a bit at the attempt. "You sure about him?" she said to Maria, cocking her head at Jack.

Maria looked at him, amusement on her face. "I wasn't at first, but he grows on you."

Jack's breath caught in his throat. Did she mean that or was it all for the old lady's benefit?

"Huh," Mrs. Ogilvie said.

She shut the door tight, and Jack wondered if it would open again. He was relieved when he heard the chain slide back and he heard the thump slide of her moving aside to swing it inward.

"Well then, come in. But remember, you're vouching for him," she told Maria as the door opened wide. There was a glint in Mrs. Ogilvie's eye, though. Like she was teasing Maria.

Maria nodded and led the way in.

Jack surveyed the apartment as they entered. It opened right onto a small but cozy living room with a worn light blue couch perked up by white throw pillows covered in yellow and brown daisies and a colorful crocheted blanket folded over one arm. There was a matching loveseat and a light wood coffee table between them with a bowl of fake fruit as a centerpiece. Pictures of people lined the walls. Family, Jack presumed. The largest of them caught his eye right away—a big black and white wedding photo with the man standing at military attention in a coat and tails and the woman covered all the way up the neck in an antique-styled dress. She looked like a starlet. He glanced from the picture to Mrs. Ogilvie and back again, trying to determine if there was any way they were the same woman.

She saw it and laughed. "Yes, that's me. About an eon ago. And the man was my husband, George." Her eyes got a bit misty, and Jack didn't ask. The past tense said it all.

"This way," Mrs. Ogilvie said, leading them into her kitchen. "There's more room here for everybody to sit. And anyway, if I settle my old bones into one of those couches, I'm not getting up again any time soon."

There were four chairs around her polished wooden table with two more backed up against the wall out of the way. Jack grabbed one of those and pulled it up to the table.

"Can I get you anything?" Mrs. Ogilvie asked before sitting down. "I'm afraid I don't have any soda, but I could make tea."

"No, that's okay," Maria said. "You sit. We won't take up much of your time."

Mrs. Ogilvie, cane in one hand and tea kettle in the other, ignored that and went to the sink to fill the latter with water.

"Nonsense. Can't have a proper visit without tea."

Maria's smile was back. "Then let me take care of it."

She went to the sink and took the kettle from Mrs. Ogilvie's hand.

"Thank you, dear," she said as she surrendered it. "Don't find manners like yours much anymore."

Mrs. Ogilvie clomped-slid to the table and sighed in relief as she lowered herself into a chair. "There now," she said when she'd settled and leaned the cane against the wall. "You had some questions."

Jack was willing to let someone else take point, since she'd seemed most nervous about him, but it was Jack to whom she directed the question.

"Uh, yeah," he said, caught unprepared. "Uh, the night of Ms. Thompson's death a man bumped into you on the stairs. We know you weren't able to develop a sketch with the police, but we wondered—if we show you some pictures, would you be able to tell us if the man is among them?"

"Maybe," she said slowly, "but it's been a long time. And I didn't see him for very long."

"You may be the only one who saw him at all."

Jack put the pictures on the table, ready for her to say "yes", but first she said, "Why are you so interested? The police certainly weren't. I gave my statement and my description and that was the last I heard about it until that man's lawyer came to talk to me."

"Jim Driskoll's lawyer?" Maria asked, turning from the stove where she'd set the pot to boil.

"I think that was the name. He came to ask me questions, but I'm afraid I wasn't any more helpful to him than I was to the police. Here, show me your pictures."

Jack slid them over, and Mrs. Ogilvie picked them up and held them up to her face. Then closer.

"Dear," she said, turning to Maria, "would you get me my magnifying glass? I think I left it on the counter there somewhere, next to my medications."

Maria hadn't joined them at the table, so she was still right next to the counter. She found the magnifying glass by a pharmacy's worth of medicines and vitamins laid out along the back wall next to an old toaster oven.

She brought it over to Mrs. Ogilvie, who patted her hand when it came into range. "Thank you, dear."

"You're welcome."

Mrs. Ogilvie angled the magnifying glass over the pictures, and then adjusted the position for better focus. Her gaze sharpened, and she suddenly slapped the pictures down on the table, startling them all.

"This one," she said pointing, and they all leaned forward to see her pointing at Detective Kincaid. "I told him at the time that the man looked a lot like him. If they'd just released a photo of him alongside my description, someone would have recognized the man. Someone would have come forward."

They turned to Evan. They all knew what was coming. On the very next page of pictures was Evan's father, who looked enough like his brother, apparently, for Mrs. Ogilvie to have noted the resemblance. No wonder the police hadn't pursued the other man too aggressively, not if Detective Kincaid thought the witness had implicated his brother.

Evan looked sick. Shellshocked. Like he might launch himself across the table and rip the pages away before Mrs. Ogilvie could confirm his worst fears.

Jack watched him closely, ready to stop any such move.

"Evan, maybe you and I should step outside," he said, putting a hand to Evan's arm, "let the ladies talk."

Evan didn't appear to have heard him. But his reaction had been too strong for even half-blind Mrs. Ogilvie to miss. She peered more closely at Evan, leaning forward and squinting through her glasses. Then she shot back in her chair, faster than Jack would have thought she could move. "Glory be. You look like him too. But you're too young," she said. "Far too young."

"Next page," Maria said quietly from her place near the stove. The teapot chose that moment to whistle and she whirled around to stop it, pulling it off the burner without even a potholder and then dropping it like a hot potato and blowing on her fingers.

The tension was such that no one but Jack even glanced up at the clatter.

Evan was staring fixedly at the photos Mrs. Ogilvie had thrown onto the table. "I'm too young," he confirmed, his voice devoid of any inflection at all. "But . . ." He swallowed hard and handed the photos back to her. "Keep going. See if you recognize anyone."

He said it with all the gravity of a judge asking for a verdict. Mrs. Ogilvie peered down at the papers in her hand, exchanged one for another and hit on it immediately. "That one," she said, stabbing the page. Then she looked up at Evan. "He's like enough to be your father."

They didn't stay for tea. Poor Mrs. Ogilvie seemed shaken when they left, but not half as shaken as Evan.

"You didn't know?" Maria asked in her gentle voice.

Evan shook his head, but Jack thought he paused infinitesimally first.

"But you suspected," Jack said, trying and failing to achieve Maria's tone.

Evan surged forward, as though to take Jack on right there in the hallway, but Maria stepped quickly between them. "Evan, stop. *You* gathered the pictures. You knew it was almost guaranteed to be someone's father. It just . . . It sucks that it was yours," she finished lamely. *Suck* didn't even begin to cover it. "But fighting isn't going to make it better."

"And what will?" Evan asked, his eyes blazing, body language still tense, still ready to launch.

"Dealing with it. Facing it head on. You're a smart guy; you've got to have doubts after finding out your father was here the night of the murder and that your uncle kept it quiet. It's not a pretty question Jack's asking, but I think we have to know. Was it a family secret that your father was connected with Marley? How far does it go?"

Jack barely breathed waiting for an answer. If Evan knew, would he have put his father in the line-up? He could hardly have kept him out without them noticing. But if he'd suspected . . . if he'd found evidence, might he have planted it to deflect suspicion away from his father in case Reggie's investigation brought out his involvement? And if he'd done that, what about the murders? The two seemed to go hand in hand.

Still, he'd been genuinely shocked back at Mrs. Ogilvie's place —at least, Jack thought so. Maybe he hadn't known . . . or at least hadn't believed. Or maybe he'd been banking on Mrs. Ogilvie being too blind to pick his father out of a photo line-up after all this time. Maybe he thought Mrs. O would pass his father over and dispel his fears.

"You can tell us," Maria said. "Being in Marley's building that night doesn't make your father guilty of anything but not coming forward. If he's innocent . . ."

"*If?*" Evan asked.

It sounded menacing to Jack, and he bristled. He stepped up beside Maria so that she was no longer between the two of them, in case Jack had to act.

"We need to talk to your father," he said, drawing Evan's anger.

"Or we can start with your uncle," Maria said, "use what we know to get Detective Kincaid to tell us what *he* knows."

Evan glared at them both, "In other words, threaten them with exposure."

Jack glared back. "What else did you have in mind? Become part of the cover-up? I think Reggie and his uncle deserve the truth."

"Go screw yourself," he said.

Evan stalked off to the end of the hallway and then down the stairs. They followed him, watched him take the first set of stairs at full tilt. And the second. Slowing when he reached the bottom to pull his phone from his pocket. He swiped at it, found what he was searching for and stopped just outside the doors of the apartment building to lift the phone to his ear.

Jack and Maria stopped beside him, not sure what to do or whether to listen in. Once they heard the greeting, there was no longer any question.

"Uncle Cal," Evan said into the phone, making eye contact challengingly with them as he talked. "We know about Dad. And Marley. We're coming to the station. You'd better be ready to talk."

Detective Kincaid's protest blasted through the phone, loud enough for them all to hear. "You don't know anything, and I don't have time for this. I'm in the middle of a case. You might remember it."

"You'll find time for this. We think the cases are connected." He held onto Jack's gaze in particular as he said, "And anyway we won't take 'no' for an answer."

"What happened?" Maria asked an instant later, as Evan was putting his phone away.

"He hung up on me. I don't know that he'll talk to us."

"Oh, he'll talk," Jack said, and Maria shot him a sidelong glance as though she expected him to be rubbing his hands together like a cartoon villain. "We'll go down there and wait him out. We'll make such a fuss it'll be less grief for him to give in."

"Is that what you do at school?" Evan asked, a barely-leashed snarl in his voice, "Give kids so much grief it's just easier for them to hand over their lunch money? Did you do that with Liam or Amal? Maybe you're the murderer, huh? Anybody think of that?"

Jack was so stunned he didn't have an immediate comeback. He noticed Maria didn't make any sound of protest when it came to an accusation leveled *his* way. Maybe he'd earned it, but it felt like ages since he'd been that person. It hadn't been that long. He knew that. But back then he hadn't cared what people thought. It would have tickled him that someone thought he was so bad-ass. It bothered him now more than he wanted to admit.

"Yes," he answered simply. What else was there to say? "That's exactly what I did. I hassled people. You've got to play to your strengths. But as for killing—where's the fun in that?"

Neither one answered him.

# CHAPTER 23

JACK

They were turning into the parking lot of the police station when Maria's phone went off. She pulled into a spot father away from the entrance than she probably would have otherwise so that she could get to it in time.

She drew the phone out of her purse on the fourth ring, checked the readout and answered it right away.

The voice on the other end of the line didn't even give her the chance to speak, but launched into something rapid-fire and authoritative. Jack could hear the tone, even if he couldn't make out the words.

Maria looked over at Jack and mouthed *My father.*

"But—" she began.

Her father talked right over her.

"But, Papi—" She turned away from Jack and launched into a response that was equally rapid-fire, but in Spanish. Jack had taken Spanish for two years. He recognized about one word in ten, and those went by too quickly to grab the others in context. All he knew was that whatever her father had said, she wasn't happy about. The frown on her face would have given that away, even if he hadn't caught "no" several times over.

Then both of them were talking at once. Finally, he heard her say that they'd discuss things later. That she was in the car. True enough, but the implication was that she was driving and had to run off for safety reasons.

There was a new barrage of language on the other end of the phone and then a quick sign off.

Maria sighed and threw the phone down into the cup holder at her side. Jack watched her expectantly, waiting for her to tell them what was all about, but she avoided his gaze.

"What?" he said, when it was clear she wasn't going to volunteer anything.

"Dad wants to take me out of town. Me, Mama, Miguel. He's already arranged things at work."

Jack stared at her, a torrent of feelings whipping through him. He should have felt relief. If she was away from here, she'd be safe. But his first instinct was to protest. She couldn't go. They were just starting to . . . what? Circumstances had thrust them together. That was all. They weren't dating. She hadn't even defended him to Evan. Their new partnership probably wouldn't last beyond them catching the killer. But somehow he felt like if she left . . . Crap, he wasn't even going to think the rest. It was too sappy to be believed. Light going out of his world and all that shit. The stuff of chick flicks.

"You should go," he said. "He wants to protect you."

Maria had been staring out the window, continuing to avoid him, but she looked at him quickly now and then away. "I can't go and leave the rest of you with this. I can't be safe if you're not. If anyone else dies and I'm not here trying to stop it, I don't know how I'll live with that."

Jack's heart leapt. He was an idiot.

"I get it, but—"

"Don't," she said harshly. "I already have Papi telling me what to do. I don't need you too."

It shut him up. Jack pushed his way out of the car and started walking for the police station. He didn't really have an answer and she didn't want one.

They met Evan coming across the parking lot, and they all walked in together. Maria didn't say anything about her phone call, and neither did he.

Inside, they told the officer behind the desk who they were there to see, and he practically rolled his eyes at them. "Oh yeah, I was told to expect you. He's busy."

"We're not going home until we see him," Jack said defiantly.

"Yeah," the officer answered, his voice as bristly as his half-grown beard. "He said you might say that. Could be forever. You know he's in the middle of a murder investigation."

"Really? We hadn't heard," Evan said wryly.

"He'll get to you when he gets to you. Meanwhile, cool your heels."

"Cool our heels?" Jack asked.

"It means take a seat," he signaled with a pen toward a row of bench seats that were already mostly occupied.

They were there for only about a quarter of an hour—just long enough for a little girl waiting with her mother to become enchanted with Maria and for the wary mother to become comfortable with them playing peek-a-boo and boop-the-nose—when the door to the waiting area blasted open and a huge presence filled the frame.

Everyone looked up. The man radiated *I am not pleased* as if it surrounded him like a forcefield. Jack recognized the guy from the photo line-up. When he followed the direction of the man's gaze, he knew he was right. This was Evan's father, and Evan was in for it big time.

"You. Home. Now," the man said, pointing at Evan as though there might be any mistake.

Evan crossed his arms, sat back in his seat and stared at his father. "I'm not going anywhere until I get answers."

His dad looked like he could about shoot lasers out of his eyes. "Your uncle told me you were here. He doesn't have time for this, and neither do I. I left work for this, and make no mistake, you're coming home with me."

The little girl had run to her mother and was doing her best to hide behind her.

Evan glanced pointedly around the waiting area. "What are you going to do? Manhandle me out of here in front of all these witnesses?"

"I'm your father. You'll do what I say."

Jack had to fight the instinct to jump in. Evan wasn't Eric.

Mr. Nunez wasn't Dad. Evan wasn't in any immediate danger.

"Or what?" Evan asked.

Maria sucked in a breath. They all waited for the answer. Tense. The little girl whimpered and hid her face.

"Come home now or don't come home at all," his father said. "Your choice."

There was dead silence in the waiting area.

No one knew what to say to that. Clearly not even Evan. He glared at his father with the heat of a thousand suns. If he was anything like Jack, he was going through a million responses in his head, considering and discarding them one by one.

Finally, Evan rose, that same intensity his father had coming off him in waves. Jack had this crazy sense that when the fields crossed, explosions would ensue.

"Fine," Evan said, "but this isn't over."

Evan didn't look at anyone but his father as he went for the door, and his father moved aside to let Evan out first so he could keep an eye on him.

Maria and Jack exchanged glances.

"Does that seem like a family without secrets?" Maria asked quietly.

He didn't answer that.

"What do we do now?" Jack asked instead. "Sit here? Detective Kincaid doesn't seem inclined to talk to us."

"Maybe we can find someone who will," Jack said. "Do you have Officer Stiles's direct line?"

"Rayna would have it, I think," Maria answered.

"Call her."

She gave him an eye roll at the order. She took out her phone and started to dial before excusing herself to take the call outside.

She came back a minute later. "Rayna and Reggie are about five minutes away. She says just hold on. Her father's with them, and he says that if no one will talk to us, he'll make sure we talk to the press." She seemed upset. "Is that fair—talking to the press, outing Evan's father. What if he's innocent? What if he was just in the wrong place at the wrong time?"

Jack had to fight to keep from putting an arm around her for reassurance. "Don't worry. It's just a threat to apply pressure. Someone will talk to us."

When Reggie, Rayna and her father arrived a few minutes later, they could hear Mr. Butler, Rayna's father, at the front desk, railing, demanding to see someone.

The little girl and her mom were called in the midst of it and looked happy to escape.

A minute later Rayna came and signaled them. Ten seconds after that they were being led into the back and shown into one of the interview rooms by an officer they hadn't met before, who left them once again to cool their heels.

But not for long. After ten or so minutes, the door was yanked open and a red-faced Detective Kincaid appeared in the doorway. Jack had a flashback to Evan's father arriving the same way back in the waiting area.

"What the *hell* do you think you're doing disrupting my precinct like this? We have a murder investigation going on. I don't have time to deal with every crackpot theory out there." He focused on Reggie. "*You.* We've been over this. Your uncle is guilty. Period. Convicted by a jury of his peers, who felt there was enough evidence presented to decide beyond a reasonable doubt. I didn't railroad him. I didn't overlook any solid leads. And I am *done* talking about this."

"What about your brother?" Jack asked, stepping into the breach. "Why wasn't he ever a suspect?"

"No criminal record, unreliable witness who can't place him at the scene, only in the building . . . I don't have to justify myself to you."

Reggie was staring daggers at him. "You never said 'no connection to the victim'. I think that's telling."

Kincaid glared back, and he was even better at it. Must be all that experience intimidating suspects.

"What part of 'I'm done speaking about this' did you not get?"

Mr. Butler stepped forward, his gaze steady on the Detective's. "As I told the officer at the desk, you can talk to us or we can talk to the press. You're an officer of the law. You don't get to decide what evidence is relevant."

"As an officer of the law, I decide every day what's relevant —what leads to follow, who's lying and who isn't. There are only so many resources and so many hours in a day."

"What connection did your brother have to the deceased?" Mr. Butler asked, unimpressed by Kincaid's speech.

Kincaid studied him, profiled him, maybe, but he answered. "He was working with her on a claim. He had papers for her to sign."

"The car accident?" Reggie asked. "I didn't know lawyers made house calls. On Friday nights."

Jack tensed up. Reggie had blown it. It was clear from the suddenly shuttered look on Kincaid's face that while he might be coerced into answering to Mr. Butler, he wasn't going to answer to Reggie. Whether it was because of his age or his connection with Jim Driskoll, Jack had no idea.

"Who else?" Mr. Butler asked, jumping back in. "Did you fix-ate on Reggie's uncle from the start or were there other suspects investigated? The fight everyone heard between Marley and Jim was about another man. You're claiming it wasn't your brother. Did you find out who it was?"

Rayna moved closer to Reggie, drawing Jack's eye, so he no-ticed when she grabbed Reggie's hand and squeezed, as if silently telling him to keep quiet. He wasn't sure Reggie even noticed, he was so focused on Detective Kincaid.

"There was an ex-boyfriend with whom she was still in touch. A cop who was on duty at the time. Yes, we checked. Aside from that, there was a man who'd been seen at her place a time or two before who we identified as her accountant."

"Her accountant," Rayna said, "Would that have been Nor-man Hinkle, Liam's father?" Then something seemed to occur to her. "And any chance that cop boyfriend was Dexter Cardiss?"

"Who?" Maria asked.

"Dalton's father," Jack said. It was a guess, but the last name was the same, and he knew Dalton's father was a cop. Dalton made sure everybody knew.

Detective Kincaid fixed Rayna with a hard stare. "You know an awful lot about this case. Maybe too much. Who have you been talking to?"

She didn't answer that. "And what about Liam? Have you found him? Or learned who was killed in his place?"

"No and yes," he said, turning to go. "Now I'd like to get back to my investigation."

"Wait," Jack said, latching onto Detective Kincaid's arm before he even registered what he was about to do. "You can't just leave it like that. You have to tell us."

Kincaid glared down at the hand as though he could wither it with a glance. Jack kept the hand right where it was. He knew Kincaid could shrug him off and that he wouldn't risk assault charges holding on, but he wasn't about to be cowed.

When the look didn't work, Kincaid ripped his arm out of Jack's grasp and stepped away, out of reach. He glanced around the room at all the expectant and angry faces and came to a decision. "His parents have been notified. I'm sure it will make the news soon enough. The body we thought to be Liam's . . . it's Amal Mehta."

Jack felt like someone had kicked him in the chest.

# CHAPTER 24

RAYNA

Rayna was . . . stunned didn't do it justice. They'd suspected that something had happened to Amal, even speculated on the very thing that they'd just learned, but to *know* it . . .

She stared wide-eyed at the others, remembering she was supposed to be suspicious, but all she saw around her was devastation. Maria had her head bent like she was in prayer. Jack looked like he wanted to simultaneously cry and hit something. Like if this had been a historical film, he'd have raged about with a sword, destroying tapestries, overturning tables, spilling flagons of ale and all of that.

As it was, his face closed up the minute he saw that she was watching. All the pain—it didn't dissolve away, but it hardened into a mask, the lines freezing and then smoothing away until he was a stone statue of himself. She wanted to sculpt and comfort him all at the same time. She didn't think he'd welcome either one.

And Reggie . . .

Reggie looked tortured.

"Come on," Rayna's father said into the laden silence. "Let's get you home."

"But we haven't gotten anything figured out," she protested.

"Let the detective get back to work. Let the police do their jobs."

She couldn't tell if he really thought they would or if he was just trying to get her out of there, but she let him usher her out of the interrogation room. Kincaid was clearly finished with them after he dropped his bombshell. It had been his exit line. The others followed them back into the waiting room at the front of the station.

"Text me later," she said to everyone on the way out. "Let me know if anyone hears from Evan."

"You do the same," Reggie said.

"How do you think *that* conversation's going?" Maria asked. "Between Evan and his father."

"I don't know," Reggie said, "I just can't believe it. All this time, and Evan's own father . . ."

Rayna didn't know what to say to that and dropped back next to Jack as they walked out to the cars. He still looked like a still-life of himself.

"Hey," she said, waiting for him to glance at her so she knew he was paying attention. "Amal was dead before we even realized he was in danger. Or missing. There's nothing you could have done."

His face might have been frozen, but his eyes were full of pain. "He was my friend," Jack said. "Maybe we hadn't been close in while, but that was my fault, not his. If I'd been around more, maybe . . ."

Rayna put a hand to his arm and he let it stay. "You're doing what you can now. No one can live with what might have happened. We all have to deal with what actually did."

Some of the earlier anguish seeped back onto his face. "So you don't beat yourself up for what happened to Grace, her dying in your place?"

The barb hit Rayna like an arrow through her heart, and stopped it beating. She fell back, her legs no longer working. Her knees wanted to buckle, but she braced them, forced herself to stay upright.

He'd lashed out. It hadn't been with a sword, but the damage was done just the same.

Maria looked back, saw Rayna standing shell-shocked and glowered at Jack. "What did you say to her?" she asked.

But she didn't wait for an answer. She was already halfway to Rayna, trying to catch her gaze to ask, "Are you okay?"

Maria put an arm around her waist and tried to encourage her to move on, which Rayna did only because she couldn't stay there. And because her father was giving Jack such a look that she figured she'd better prove she was okay. But nothing seemed to matter anymore.

If they'd done anything at all it was make things worse. They'd uncovered pieces of truths, but still didn't know how they all fit together. Time had already run out for some and was quickly running out for others and . . .

*And Grace was dead because of her.*

She was silent on the car ride home. Her father dropped Reggie at his house, watching to be sure he got all the way inside safely with the door closed behind him. Then he took her home, made her some hot chocolate like she was a kid again, and bundled her up on the couch.

"Movie night?" he asked.

She looked up from the hot chocolate to her father. He'd been pretty amazing today. She still felt like hell, but she should acknowledge that.

"Thank you," she said, forcing herself to reach out from under the blanket and take a sip of the cocoa. It started to warm her, which only made her feel guilty. Grace and Amal and Mrs. Hinkle were never going to have hot chocolate again, would never sit on the couch with those they loved and watch a movie, would never . . .

The tears started without warning. She had no idea why everything hit right then, but it did. Everything. The tears started silently and then became deep, racking sobs. Her father retreated for a tissue box, which he handed over and then sat beside her, an arm around her as she leaned into him and cried her eyes out. Every time she thought she was finished, something would strike her anew and the tears would start up again just as hard.

Until they ran out. Half a box of tissues later, her eyes were puffy, her nose was raw from the rubbing, her throat hurt like maybe the sobs had welled up from the depths of her, and she felt . . . wrung out. Empty. She didn't have any more in her. Not for now.

"Movie?" her father said again, rising with a handful of used tissues, ready to throw them away.

That was love—the willingness to hold someone while they cried and then touch their snotty tissues. She expected more tears, but it seemed she'd been drained dry.

Rayna nodded. "You pick."

It didn't really matter what they watched, as long as she didn't have to think or interact or feel for a little while.

She'd left her phone in their foyer, in the string backpack she used as a purse. She'd heard it ding a few times while she'd had her breakdown, but couldn't be motivated to go get it. Now she forced herself to move, trying to leave her own pity party.

It turned out not to be anything. Sierra checking in to see whether she was okay. Reggie mentioning that he'd pinged Evan and not heard back. Kali checking in with a group text to find out what they'd learned that day. She hoped someone else was up to responding.

She heard the mini-explosions of microwave popcorn in the kitchen and took her phone with her to the bathroom to clean up before settling back on the couch and watching a mindless action movie with her father, eating popcorn like it was a normal night.

She must have missed the ping of an incoming text during some of the pyrotechnics. After the movie when she turned her phone over to check it, she found a new text that chilled her to her bones.

*Rayna, it's Liam. You're in danger. I need U to meet me tonight. U, not one of the Meddlers. I don't know who to trust.*

She stared at her screen.

"Everything okay?" her father asked.

She should tell him. She knew that. But what came out was a feeble smile and, "Yeah. Nothing new."

Her mother came through the front door just then, bringing with her the smell of Chinese food. Rayna's text was forgotten. By her father anyway.

Rayna excused herself to go to the bathroom to wash her hands before dinner and her father waved her on, relieved, she thought, to be able to update her mother on the day without her listening in. She was a little curious about how he'd report things, but she was more focused on that message.

Her parents would never let her go if she told them. They'd insist on calling the police and sending them to the meeting. But Liam or whoever it was hadn't said when or where. There was so far no actual meeting to discuss, and once there was . . . she couldn't risk that the police would scare the person off. She had to find out what was going on. To stop this.

But she wasn't stupid enough to think she could stop it on her own.

*How do I know this is Liam?* she typed back.

She set her phone down on the vanity while she ran the water to wash her hands and keep her parents from becoming suspicious. The phone pinged while she was finishing up and she cursed as she reached for a hand towel, hoping her parents hadn't heard it. She turned off the sound on her phone before she checked the message.

*We met up in the principal's office about our threatening notes.*

*Try again,* she typed, *I told the others about that.*

*OK. In fifth grade gym, you hit me in the face with a dodgeball.*

Had she? Rayna thought back. She'd always hated dodgeball. Bullies were the only ones who liked it. Her only hope was to catch the balls aimed at her to get out the kids who chose her as a target. She never really looked when she was throwing the balls back, never actually *aimed* at anybody. And yeah, she remembered causing a mishap once. She'd nearly forgotten the incident. Someone was always getting hurt at dodgeball. As far as she was concerned, it should be banned.

Had it been Liam she'd hurt that day? Rayna thought back, tried to focus in on the kid holding his nose . . . face flushed red . . . Yeah, it was Liam.

*Sorry,* she typed back. *Everyone's looking for U. U ok?*

*2night* he texted back. *10:00. Old hardware store at Wood Glen & Spary Ave. B careful. I'll tell U everything.*

None of this sat right. A text like this one had lured Grace to her death.

*Tell me now*, she typed.

There was no answer.

It was a set up. It had to be. Not that it mattered. She knew she had to go. With backup. Whoever had sent the message, whether it was Liam or the killer or whether they were one and the same, would have answers. It was only a question of whether she'd live through them.

She texted Evan quickly, wanting to call but afraid her parents would hear her voice on the phone. Then she stopped the running water and went out to face dinner with her parents, holding the knowledge that she'd be sneaking out later and that they'd be freaking out if they knew.


It was 9:25. Rayna had pled exhaustion half an hour before and retreated to her room. She'd forgotten about the new alarm system. She couldn't just sneak out her window. If her parents had set it once everyone was home—and she had no doubt that they had—the alarm would go off the instant her window was raised. She was going to have to sneak out, shut it off, reset it and hope it wasn't high tech enough that her parents received an alert to their phones or something every time it went on or off.

She was dressed in black jeans, a tank top and a dark gray, fleece-lined hoodie. She felt like a shadow of herself. She hoped she'd look like a shadow too, and that no one would see her skulking away from the house.

When she poked her head out into the hallway, she was relieved to see that her parents had retreated to their room as well. From the light and the voices, she knew they weren't yet asleep, but maybe their conversation would cover her escape. She slipped down the hall to the alarm panel just inside the front door, turned it off and then reset it to give herself a minute and a half to get free before it went back into effect. As soon as it started the countdown, which she'd set to silent, she rushed to the garage, and slipped out the side door, the exit the farthest from her parents' bedroom. As always since it had been installed, the alarm system beeped quietly to alert that a door was open, but she prayed they wouldn't hear it as she rushed out into the night, closing and locking the door behind her.

She raced around the back of the house, through a neighbor's yard and came out two houses away, where Evan idled in his car, waiting for her. He popped the passenger-side door as she approached and drove off as soon as she was inside.

"You're kidding me, right?" he asked, flashing her a sidelong glance.

"What?"

"A hoodie? Do you not watch the news? Seems as good as a target these days. Neighborhood Watch'll get you if the police don't."

"But my blue hair. I'd be totally conspicuous otherwise."

"Not in the dark. And if you are, well, whoever sent that message is expecting you, right? Best to give him what he expects."

"I'm already kind of blowing that one," Rayna said. "The text didn't actually say to come alone, but it did say no Meddlers. Maybe you'd better stay back."

"To hell with that. I'm not letting you walk into an ambush." She was about to protest, when he kept on going, the reluctance in his voice setting off warning bells. "Rayna . . . I don't want you to get mad at me, but I'm not your only backup."

"What? He said *no Meddlers*. I'm taking a huge chance of scaring him off even bringing you along. If he spots the others . . ."

"No more Meddlers," Evan swore, taking his eyes off the road a little too long so she could see the sincerity there. "But I—uh—called Officer Stiles while I was waiting for you. Too late, I figured, for her to stop us, but not too late to meet us there."

Some of the tension went out of Rayna's shoulders. Whoever texted probably thought "no police" went unsaid, but still, she was relieved that someone would know where she and Evan had gone if anything went wrong.

"What did she say?" Rayna asked.

Evan was watching the road now, but she had a feeling he wouldn't have met her gaze anyway. He looked suddenly uncomfortable. "I got her voicemail. But I'm sure she'll check it."

Rayna's tension ratcheted back up. It didn't seem like Officer Stiles worked nights. Officer Repucci had always taken over for her then . . . which either meant she was available because she wasn't on duty or she was completely unavailable, out with friends or off to a movie . . .

"Do you want me to call Uncle Cal?" he asked, but not like he was excited about the idea.

"You mean because we might be meeting a murderer?"

"Yes."

"No," she said honestly. Of all the things in the world she wanted, Evan's Uncle Cal ripping them to shreds for their stupidity was about dead last. Next to actually being murdered.

He breathed a sigh of relief. "Good."

"How did things go with your father?" Rayna asked.

"I don't want to talk about it."

"Did he—?"

"I said I don't want to talk about it," Evan said, nearly biting her head off.

She was stunned into silence. Evan never snapped. She'd never even seen him angry.

He took a hand off the steering wheel to run roughly through his hair and glanced quickly over at her.

"I'm sorry," he said, going for gentle now. "I'm just . . . I don't know what to think. And he's not talking."

Rayna didn't immediately say a word. She didn't honestly know how she'd feel if she'd found out her father had stepped out on her mother and covered up his involvement with a murdered woman. Lashing out didn't seem an unreasonable response. Besides, she wasn't the only one headed into danger. In fact, Evan's danger wasn't even his own. *He* hadn't been threatened. The killer had left him entirely alone. By asking for his help, she was the one putting him at risk.

Too late, she realized what a horrible, selfish thing that was. If he ended up like Grace . . .

She felt sick. "Oh god, Evan, I just realized . . . You don't have to do this. You can let me out before we get to the old hardware store. You don't have to go in with me. I always call when I need you and you always come running, but this time . . . this time you could be hurt, and . . ."

Evan pulled over to the side of the road, and Rayna's pulse rate went through the roof. She'd said he could let her out, but she didn't really think he'd do it. At least, not so far away.

Evan put the car into park and turned to her.

"Breathe," he said first.

She was, just maybe too fast. Hyperventilating.

He reached over and took her hands, staring into her eyes. "Rayna, I'm coming with you. That's not even in question. Don't you get it yet? Listen, now isn't the time. I keep waiting, but . . . Just know this—where you go, I go, okay? You're my best friend. I'm not losing you to some psycho or anyone else. Got it?"

Rayna stared at him. She didn't understand what he was trying to say. Or maybe on some level she did. But, he was right, now was not the time.

"Evan," she said, meeting his gaze, trying to fight the tears in her eyes at how amazing he really was. "Thank you. I mean, for everything." It wasn't enough, but it was all she could handle with the specter of their meeting hanging over them.

He shrugged. "It's nothing." He put the car back into gear, flipped his turn signal and pulled back onto the dark empty road. "We'd better get moving."

Rayna wiped away her tears and tried to prepare herself.

The old hardware store wasn't far from where Grace had been found, from the shantytown and Marsden's version of the wrong side of the tracks. There were no lights outside of the falling-down old hardware store. It stood on its own, on a small lot next to a strip-mall mostly closed for the night, except for the store selling vapor cigarettes, which seemed to double as a convenience store based on the racks of sunglasses and snacks inside.

They pulled into the empty lot of the closed hardware store, trying to avoid the bowling ball-sized potholes in the asphalt. The place itself was boarded up with graffiti all over the plywood. The stucco of the walls was falling down in patches, gray in others.

Evan grabbed a flashlight out of his glove compartment so they could check it out, since the lights from the strip mall didn't extend as far as the hardware store. He handed it to Rayna.

"I should have thought to grab another from home," he said.

"There's always the light on your phone."

She realized they were whispering and they weren't even out of the car yet. Something about sneaking around in the night had that effect on people. They got out, striving for quiet, but the doors were going to make a certain amount of noise closing no matter what. Whoever waited for them would know they were there.

Instead of reaching for his phone, Evan grabbed a tire iron from the backseat that he must have set there in advance. She should have thought to grab a weapon as well. The flashlight she held was the cheap plastic kind rather than the heavy metal cylinder that could double as a club. At best, maybe she could blind someone momentarily by shining the light directly in their eyes.

There was an iron grate over the front of the store, which was still locked up tight as far as they could tell. Rayna pointed the flashlight around the side of the building, nose wrinkling at dirty lumps of unidentifiable cloth, some of which smelled like they might have been used to wipe . . . no, she wasn't thinking about that. Broken glass crunched under their feet, unbroken bottles were accidentally scuffed and kicked along, rolling noisily before them. They were not stealthy.

"Liam?" Rayna called, but quietly. No louder than the noise they were already making.

In the distance, in the overgrown woods behind the shop and the strip mall, she thought she heard something, but when she strained to listen, it didn't come again. Could have been anything, from animals to her imagination.

It took an effort to turn the beam away from that sound, from the woods, and ahead to the abandoned building, but Rayna made herself do it. They had a meeting to make. And anyway, ambush was as likely to come from ahead as behind. Rayna aimed the beam toward the walls of the hardware store, searching for another entrance, a broken window, anything.

"There," Evan said, pointing at a window at about head height.

It was boarded up like the others, but the board hung at an angle, as though only one nail or screw or whatever was holding it up and it could be pushed out of place. Rayna shone the light as Evan stepped forward to try it. He pushed the board aside and it pivoted out of the way, but the window beneath it was intact and stuck tight, as though seasons of neglect had swelled the wood to lock the window tightly within the frame.

"We could probably break the glass," Evan said.

"How about we call that plan B. We haven't looked all the way around yet."

She moved the light, and they circled around behind the building, where they discovered the back door. Unlike the window, it didn't fit at all in its frame. It stood a bit ajar, an invitation for them to enter.

Rayna didn't have a good feeling about things at all. If Liam was here, why hadn't he answered her call.

She took out her phone, temporarily handing Evan the flashlight, and texted, *We R here. Where R U?*

There was no answer.

"What do you think?" Evan asked.

"We've come this far," she answered.

"I'll go first."

She didn't argue. Front or rear, neither seemed safe. The darkness seemed even darker beyond the beam of her flashlight. Anything could be waiting to grab them. It was a measure of how out of whack her imagination was that she thought of *anything* rather than *anyone*. Logically, she knew that if she was grabbed, it would be by a person, likely the killer, but she'd built up whoever it was as such a monster that she couldn't imagine him any other way. She wouldn't be surprised if Poe's crazed killer from *The Murders in the Rue Morgue* suddenly wrapped its hairy arms around her neck . . .

Speaking of which, every hair there was standing on end.

"You okay?" Evan asked, catching her shiver.

Rayna nodded, aiming the flashlight at the door. "I'll cover you."

Evan's lips twitched upward and suddenly he bent toward her and planted his lips right on top of hers. The shock of it made her jump and her heart thunk against her ribs. Before she could react, it was done.

Rayna looked at Evan like he was crazy. "What was that for?"

"Well, if I'm going to die, I'm going to die happy."

She punched him in the arm. Definitely crazy. On the other hand, the surprise of it seemed to have knocked aside some of her fear. "Go," she said.

"See, telling me what to do, bossing me around. It's like we're already dating."

"*Evan*," she said, full of exasperation.

"Going," he answered.

Evan approached the door like it was a snake that might bite. Rayna got that. She wouldn't have wanted to touch it. Not without a gallon of hand sanitizer. She made a mental note if they survived this to add it to her sneak kit. Right after the note to actually put one together.

Touching the door yielded nothing but a groan of the hinges and the torturous sound of the rusted metal at the bottom of it scraping against the concrete of the stoop. Rayna stepped closer beside Evan, flashing the light inside.

The smell hit them first—ages worth of dust, mold, mildew, rat droppings or worse. Just in front and slightly to the right of the door were two huge empty shelving units that must once have served the shop and now blocked the view of what lay beyond. But on the floor there were footprints and . . . drag marks in the dust.

"Liam?" Rayna called again, her voice less certain than ever.

Evan stepped forward and Rayna moved with him. In a second they were past the shelving units, and as she shined her light beyond them, they spotted exposed pipes which had probably once connected to an old fashioned heating unit. More significantly, they found what looked like a makeshift bed on the floor—a tangle of blankets, some food wrappers and a dark stain.

"Is that—?" Evan asked.

"Blood?" she finished.

He nodded. Silently, they both moved forward to investigate. They were up to the bedding, up to the edge of the dark, gummy substance she feared was congealing blood—it had that coppery scent always talked about in books and movies—when they heard a noise from the doorway.

Rayna's blood ran cold. She wanted to think it was Officer Stiles, but she knew better. Stiles would have announced herself. As one, she and Evan whirled toward the sound. He motioned her to stay put while he sidestepped the shelving to see who'd come in, but to hell with that. She crept up beside him and shined her light toward the door. She caught her breath at the sight of two menacing figures, both taller than she and Evan, one at least twice as bulky. They'd stepped past the shelving units and were staring at them . . . and at the blood on the floor beyond. The frontrunner, the bulkier guy, swung a thick chain carelessly, as though he wasn't even aware he was doing it. But Rayna couldn't focus on anything else.

That bad feeling she'd had turned to bile and burned its way up her throat.

"He said someone was after him," said the second guy.

She heard something snick out and was afraid it was some kind of blade locking into place.

"Who said?" Evan asked, his voice a lot steadier than hers would be.

"What did you do to him?" the guy with the chain asked.

"Nothing!" Rayna said, hoping to draw their steely gazes away from Evan, hoping they'd ease up on the threat, seeing her as just a girl. Harmless. Sexist, but in this case the truth.

She shuddered when their gazes actually hit her, the first one cold, the second calculating. The first didn't believe her and the other didn't care, she thought. He just wanted an excuse to lash out.

Evan tried to step in front of her, and that's when the guy with the chain flew into action, swinging it to gain momentum before bringing it down on Evan. He blocked with the arm holding the tire iron, and the chain wrapped around and around it. The bulky guy yanked the chain back and the tire iron came with it, unfurling from the chain and flying halfway across the room, falling onto the concrete floor with a horrible clatter.

The guy with the knife laughed, seeing Evan disarmed so quickly, and stepped up beside his friend as he swung the end of the chain again. Even a bath towel when snapped could be painful. Rayna couldn't imagine being hit with that chain. She couldn't let Evan take the brunt of it.

Rayna dove out from behind him, hoping to draw the guy's attention, give Evan an opening. For what, she didn't know. He was unarmed, but maybe . . .

The guy with the knife was on her before she was two steps away, grabbing her with one arm and yanking her to him. He brought the knife around to her throat as Rayna heard the crack of the chain and Evan's howl of pain. She whipped her head around, regardless of the threat of the blade, and saw Evan's knees buckle, saw him start to go to the ground and then force his legs to steady.

"We didn't do anything!" Rayna swore, not worrying about whether they sensed her fear, as long as they heard her sincerity. "I swear. Liam was our friend."

The guy with the chain yanked it back, and Evan's arm jerked forward with it, pulling him off-balance and onto the ground at the bulky guy's feet.

"Then where is he?" the guy asked.

"That's what we came to find out," Rayna said. "Look, he texted me. You can see for yourself!"

The guy who held her turned to his friend for a cue as to what he should do. The bulkier boy shrugged. "Take a look at her phone," he said. "It's not like they're getting past us."

Rayna tried to reach for it, and the arm around her gripped harder, the knife pressing into her neck. "I'll get it," he said.

She shuddered as he frisked her with the knifeless hand, going over the pockets of her jacket and finally her jeans, where she had the phone. He did a businesslike job, though. No gross touchy-feely, for which she was glad.

He held the phone out to her so she could press her finger to the scanner to unlock it, then thumbed through her texts, all the while holding the knife rock steady.

"She's not lying. There's a text, but anyone could have sent it."

"Freeze!" came a voice from the doorway. Rayna would have collapsed in relief if it wouldn't send her right into the knife. She thought she recognized that voice. Definitely she recognized the authority behind it. "Police. Drop your weapons."

"Shit, man," said the guy at her throat. "The cops."

His friend shot him a *no-shit-Sherlock*, kind of look and held up his hands, the chain dropping to the floor with a clatter. "We're just protecting the neighborhood," he said, flashing an innocent look over his shoulder that failed miserably. "We caught these two breaking in."

"You can drop that knife now," Officer Stiles said to his friend. She was holding her gun out in front of her, a solid two-handed hold.

Rayna's captor turned with her, still holding the knife to her throat. Now he gave a sheepish grin and held his hands up, knife still in the one with a no-harm-no-foul shrug.

"Throw it away," Stiles insisted.

He glanced at the knife and then at her gun. For a second, Rayna thought he was going to do something stupid. She braced herself for the gunshot.

But then he threw the knife away, over by his buddy's chain.

"Now step away," she told the buddy, gun aimed toward him now that he had two weapons to his friend's zero . . . at least that they could see.

It was a smart move. Rayna couldn't see kicking the chain away having much effect. It was hardly aerodynamic.

"You two," She said, indicating Evan and Rayna with a twitch of her chin. "Go wait by your car. I'll deal with you two in a minute. And don't go anywhere. It seems you've stumbled onto some kind of crime scene, and we're going to need statements."

Rayna and Evan moved away from the other two, going wide around them toward the door. "These guys didn't do it," Rayna felt compelled to say. "In a weird way they seemed to think they were coming to someone's rescue."

Officer Stiles gave her a disbelieving look. Probably the knife and chain had left a bad impression. The way Evan was holding his arm, which was red and already swelling, made her wonder herself whether she was crazy.

"I said *go*," Stiles ordered, cranky now.

They went, out to the car where Evan asked Rayna to pat him down for the keys and open the door so he could sit. He'd blocked with his dominant hand, which was now twice the size it should be. From the tension in his face, the pain was pretty unbearable.

"Should I call 9-1-1?" Rayna asked, after helping him sit, careful not to touch the bad arm.

"Officer Stiles might have done that already. I think we'd better wait to see what she says."

"Do you think it's broken?" she asked, staring at his oversized arm.

"Maybe," he answered, hissing as he shifted into a better position. She had no idea how he could be so calm. She was as shaky as hell.

"I'm so sorry," she said.

"What, that I got to play action hero?" Evan asked, trying for a smile that turned into a grimace. "I'm not. Well, that's not true. I wish I could have made a better showing. Maybe if I'd ripped that chain out of his hand . . . Wouldn't that have been something?"

"Yeah, something," Rayna said faintly.

Evan studied her. "You've got something on your mind.

Come on, share with the class."

"It's just—you could have been killed, and it would have been all my fault. And that chain . . . You don't think *that* could have been what was used to strangle Grace, do you?" It had just occurred to her.

He was shaking his head before the sentence was fully out. "Wrong kind of marks, from what Jack said. A chain would have really torn up her neck. It would have left very distinctive impressions. He said a strap or a belt or something. Anyway, if the chain *did* do it, Officer Stiles ought to be able to figure it out."

Sirens alerted them to the ambulance and the other police units even before they arrived. Pretty soon the place was crawling not only with EMTs and officers, but with a few gawkers who'd come over from the vaping place and were being kept back.

The two guys who'd jumped them in the hardware store were led out in handcuffs, Detectives Travers and Kincaid arrived and questioned them where they sat, each in a separate police cruiser. A paramedic checked over Evan's arm and got his parents on the phone for permission to transport him to the hospital for X-rays. Rayna blew a fit when they wouldn't let her go with him, but an officer took charge of her, and locked her in the back of a police cruiser.

There she waited. One of the paramedics had given her a blanket, and it was a good thing. She was shaking like a leaf in reaction to it all. She twisted the blanket tightly around herself and held it there through hundreds of questions from the detectives. Then through the wait for her parents to arrive. She was grateful for the coverage of the blanket and for the tinted windows on the cruiser. News vans had arrived in full force, and the last thing she wanted to do was face them.

On second thought, if she was honest, the last thing she wanted was face her parents and a lifetime of being imprisoned for her own protection.

And yet, all that blood . . . She hoped it wasn't Liam's.

She wondered what would have happened if she'd come alone.

# CHAPTER 25

RAYNA

It was somewhere around three in the morning when Rayna finally dropped off to sleep. Her father had tried to insist that she sleep with her mother, in their bed. He'd sleep in her room. Or on the couch.

But after Grace had died in her place . . .

There was no way she was letting her father sleep in her room. If the killer came for her and got her father instead she'd never forgive herself.

If they were going to insist on watching out for her, they were going to watch out for each other as well. Rayna let her father drag her mattress into their room and lay it between their dresser and the foot of their bed. Her mother, who slept on the far side of the bed from their bathroom, was going to have to step over or on her if she needed to get up in the middle of the night, but it was the best they could do.

Weirdly, she felt more alone laying at the foot of their bed listening to them breathe and shift and finally, in her father's case, snore, than she ever had in her own room. They had each other. She had no one. Well, she should have had Sasha. Most nights the cat slept at the foot of her bed, occasionally creeping up to her shoulders. Rayna'd even sometimes awoken to find herself wearing the cat like a hat. But Mom and Dad said Sasha had bolted out the door during their rush to get to Rayna, and she hadn't been waiting when they returned.

She'd cuddled her phone like it was the cat until the text came from Evan that he had only a hairline fracture and that he'd be in an elastic bandage and sling but no cast. She wondered how long it had taken him to type that out one-handed. She hoped it was one-handed, anyway. He'd better not be disobeying doctor's orders already, though it would be just like him.

She didn't know what she typed back. Relief washed over her, bringing with it an easing of tensions and suddenly she could feel the exhaustion dragging her down. Her eyelids felt as though they were weighted. Her body grew heavy, like she might sink right through the mattress to the floor. Dad's snoring became a kind of white noise. Comforting, even.

She felt the world start to drop away, and she let it go.

Then a terrible racket bolted her upright. Her father's snore cut off with a snort and her mother jerked awake. They all sat and listened. There was yowling and spitting and shrieking from outside like Sasha had gotten into a catfight. They could hear her thrashing and clawing . . . but there was no answering yowl. No other cat in that fight. Something else had startled her. Or someone.

"Sasha!" Rayna said, rising to go to her, to let her inside where it was safe.

Her father was out of bed before she could get to the door, blocking her way.

"No," he said firmly. "It could be a trick to lure you out."

"It's working!" Rayna answered, frantically trying to get past him.

He reached out and grabbed her, hugged her to him too tightly for her to get away. Still, Rayna kept struggling.

"I'll go," he said when she wouldn't give up.

"No!" she yelled, voice muffled against his chest.

He eased up his grip just a bit. "You won't let me go because you know it's not safe, and you expect me to let you out there?"

He had a point. It didn't make it any easier for Rayna. Everything in her wanted to race to Sasha, to save her cat. It was her fault she was loose. Just like it was her fault Evan had been hurt. This had to stop.

The yowling cut off suddenly with a final shriek. Rayna stood there shaking, waiting for another sound, anything.

There was nothing.

A minute passed. Two. Rayna thought she was going to die. The tears started.

Sasha . . .

There was a scratch from somewhere. The front door, Rayna thought. Her heart gave a great leap and she renewed her efforts to get around her dad. Sasha might be hurt.

"I'll call the police," he said, still standing in her way, now leaning up against the door. "They said they'd have patrols in our area. It shouldn't take someone long to get here."

It made sense. Rayna knew it made sense, but she felt like she was betraying Sasha, who she imagined huddled at the door wondering why no one came to rescue her.

Her father asked if he could trust her to stay, and she nodded. Her mother rose out of bed to enfold her in a hug, as if to take over keeping her back while her father went for the phone.

Five minutes. That was all she was prepared to wait.

It was seven before there was a knock at the front door. She'd given it the extra few minutes because it was the smart thing to do. It didn't feel like the right thing. She only managed to hold back at the thought of what it would do to her parents if something happened to her. She couldn't put them through what she was feeling over Sasha.

Her father went for the door, and despite his warnings to them to stay back, she and her mother went out after him, staying well back from the door. He looked out the peephole, turned off the alarm and opened the door to Officer Repucci, holding a quivering Sasha, red all down the front of her.

"I found her at the door," he said, coming in with the cat right away so that her father could lock the door behind him and reset the alarm. "She's terrified, but she seems to be okay."

"There's blood," Rayna said, rushing out of her mother's arms and reaching for her cat. Sasha leapt to her and clung tightly, her claws scoring Rayna's skin right through her nightshirt.

"She got into it with someone for sure," he said. "Another

cat?"

"We didn't hear one," Rayna said, checking Sasha over as best she could while the cat was clinging to her in terror.

"I can take a sample of the blood off her, I guess," he said. "I'm no crime scene tech, but I don't think we can get them out here for this. They'll still be working the scene at the hardware store."

"I'll get some cotton swabs and a plastic baggy," Rayna's mom said. "Will that be all right?"

Officer Repucci nodded. "That'd do great, thank you."

Her mom went off to the bathroom while Rayna carried Sasha into the kitchen. She tried to set her down on the table, but Sasha just clung harder until Rayna was worried the blood sample they'd get would be her own.

Officer Repucci had to coo at the cat to get near her face, but they seemed to have formed a rapport, and Sasha nuzzled the hand with the cotton swabs, streaking them with the blood from her fur. Officer Repucci tucked the swabs away into the sandwich bag her mother provided and stayed to scratch Sasha behind the ears.

When he was finished, Rayna gently worked Sasha down from her perch so that she could hold her while her mother tried to wipe her down with a damp, soapy washcloth. Sasha didn't like that at all, and dashed from Rayna's lap to hide under the couch. Safe for now.

The humans all glanced at each other. "Well, I guess we should *try* to get back to sleep," her father said finally.

No one jumped on that idea.

"I should get back out on patrol," Officer Repucci said.

"Want some fresh coffee for your Thermos first?" her father offered, but Officer Repucci turned him down and took his leave. Rayna's father followed him to the door to disarm and reset the alarm, leaving her behind with her mother.

"Hot chocolate?" her mother asked.

Rayna nodded. It wasn't like the sugar and caffeine would keep her awake. She had sheer terror for that.

# CHAPTER 26

· JACK

Jack had been up until all hours the night before, following the texts back and forth, quietly sneaking out to the living room to flip through channels to see if there was anything on the news about what had happened. Too soon for it, he supposed. If Evan and Rayna had found an actual body in the abandoned store, the reporters would have rushed to air the story, but blood . . . he supposed that didn't have quite the same flare.

He fell asleep on the couch and woke only when his father started slamming things around in the kitchen, making his morning coffee and cursing the whole way. Jack had no idea what the cursing was about, but he wasn't about to ask. He played dead asleep until his father came and ripped the blanket off him.

"Get up and get out. School," he said, waiting for some sign that Jack was about to snap to, looming in case he didn't move quickly enough.

Jack didn't want to move, but he wanted what would come next even less. If his father was already holding steaming hot coffee, that might come tumbling down—a scalding to get the blood pumping. He wouldn't worry about the mess; it would be all Jack's fault and he'd have to clean it up.

As always, Jack had a fraction of a second to figure out how to play it. Come awake too quickly and his father would know he'd been faking. A sure prelude to trouble. Too slowly and he'd invite the scalding or a boot to the head or something worse to get him moving.

He did his best to go for the middle-ground and was lucky to find his father losing interest even as his eyes opened. A minute later, his father was gone, out through the garage door with his mug in hand. Jack was finally able to breathe.

He walked bleary-eyed into the kitchen, hoping his father had left some of the coffee in the pot, only to discover what he'd been cursing about. There was just the thinnest film of coffee left at the bottom of the carafe and an empty jumbo plastic tub of coffee sitting next to the machine.

It didn't bode well. Coffee was one of their staples. If they had nothing else, they usually had that.

Jack started pulling open cabinets, searching for bread, peanut butter, something he could make himself to take to school for lunch, something his mother would be able to feed Eric later.

There was nothing. Not even the butt end of the bread that half the time got left behind until it grew stale.

If Jack hadn't been so busy running around this weekend, he'd have realized. Now . . . There was no going to school now. At least not on time.

He realized he was cursing like his father, but it felt good, even if it didn't accomplish anything, so he let it go on until he ran out of steam. Then he went back toward his parents' bedroom to rouse his mother.

He tried knocking, but didn't want to be too loud and wake Eric, who needed the sleep. So when that didn't work, he turned the handle and entered, flashing a quick sidelong glance at the bed before looking full on, just to make sure his mother was decent. She was facedown on her pillow, hair obscuring her face, half in and half out of the covers in a green sweat suit that had seen better days. Decent remained to be seen. At least she was dressed.

Jack approached, grabbing her by the shoulder and shaking her. "Mom," he said.

Nothing.

"Mom!" he said louder, shaking harder. "There's no food in the house. We have to go shopping."

Not *you* have to go. He didn't trust her that far.

"Mom!" he said again when he got no response. "I'm not kidding about this. You've got to get up."

This time she cursed and lashed out with her leg, hoping to kick him away. She missed him entirely, but it told him all he needed to know about her state. Still drunk from the night before. No way was she in any condition to drive. The store was too far for him to walk. He was going to have to steal her car keys and her wallet and do the job himself.

Jack let her shoulder go in disgust and searched for her purse, which was turned upside down on her bedside table. She must have been looking for something at some point. He picked up her car keys from where they'd fallen on the floor and grabbed her wallet. There was a dollar and forty-six cents inside. That was all.

Sighing, he grabbed her ATM card. This wasn't the first time he'd had to use it. He knew the PIN number. He worried every time that she'd wake up, find it missing and, forgetting what had happened, call the police. If they caught him without a driver's license and with his mother's "stolen" card, he'd end up in jail.

Back in his own room, he tore paper from a notebook and hastily scribbled a note he left clipped to the refrigerator with a magnet, hoping to head off trouble. Then he got the hell out of there.

He drove to the nearest grocery, careful to obey the speed limits and stop signs. He made it without incident and parked toward the back of the lot—away, he hoped, from surveillance cameras, in case . . . well, just in case.

Once inside, he quickly grabbed what he could—peanut butter, bread, frozen waffles, coffee, soup, milk, bananas, because they were good for Eric and easy on his stomach, flavored rice, pasta and sauce. Things quick and easy. And cheap.

He didn't look at anyone and as far as he could tell, no one was really looking at him. Well, maybe the check-out girl as he got close, but that wasn't in a suspicious kind of way. He gave her one of his smiles, and she smiled back as she checked out the lady in front of him with her twenty-seven coupons.

He was considering a new register without the crazy coupon lady when he saw the man. He glanced right past him at first, knowing he looked familiar, but not making anything of it. And then he realized . . .

He hadn't seen Mr. Hinkle in years except in the photograph they'd put in the line-up for Mrs. Ogilvie. He had less hair on top now and more around his face, as if it had migrated into a beard and mustache, but otherwise, he hadn't changed. And he was checking out of the store two lanes over. *Checking out.*

Finally, coupon lady finished and Jack was up. His leg bounced anxiously, waiting for the check-out girl to scan him through, knowing it was a race. He had to get out of there before he lost Hinkle.

"Hey," the girl said, trying to catch Jack's eye as she rang him up. "I don't think I've seen you in here before."

He flicked her a glance. "Nope, usually I'm in school," he said, figuring maybe she'd be discouraged.

"College?" she asked hopefully.

He shook his head, and she looked disappointed, but not yet ready to give up. "High school then? Senior?"

He held his mother's ATM card, ready to swipe it down the reader the instant the last item was scanned. Two rows away, Mr. Hinkle collected his bags and got ready to leave the store.

"Listen, I hate to be rude, but I'm in a rush," he said, as she took her time weighing the bananas.

"Oh," she said typing in whatever there was to type. "No worries. I'll get you out of here in two shakes of a rattlesnake's tail."

It was a cute saying, and he might have been amused if Mr. Hinkle wasn't getting away.

"There you go, your total is—"

He didn't wait for it, but ran the card down the reader, quickly pressed the button for debit and typed in his mother's code.

*Insufficient funds* popped up on the screen.

No, no, no! He didn't have time for this.

"I'm sorry, sir," the girl said, a little less sunshiny now. "Do you have another card?"

Jack looked at her in horror. There was no time.

"Listen, I'll have to come back later. I'm sorry!"

He left all his groceries just sitting there on the counter with the girl staring after him. He hoped she wouldn't call anyone. After all, he hadn't stolen anything or done anything wrong except leave his stuff behind for someone else to deal with. How could there be insufficient funds? The total had come to less than fifty dollars. But he couldn't worry about that now.

Jack rushed out of the sliding doors as soon as they were open enough, and searched frantically around the parking lot.

There! Mr. Hinkle was halfway across the blacktop, heading near where Jack had parked, the outskirts of the lot. Jack followed him, hardly daring to blink. He couldn't believe that Mr. Hinkle was back after all this time. To collect the death certificate and take charge of the funeral arrangements for his murdered wife? To help in the search for his missing son? To sign paperwork and collect insurance money? He had no idea.

Hinkle glanced around as he approached his car. Out of state license plate, but not a rental, which implied that he'd driven his own vehicle . . . and that he'd been living close enough to see his family any time he wanted. He just hadn't wanted.

Jack didn't duck behind a car or do anything else suspicious as Hinkle glanced his way. After all, the last time Hinkle had seen Jack, he'd been eleven or twelve. And it wasn't like Hinkle had ever paid much attention to them when he and Liam closed themselves off in his room for marathon gaming sessions, hiding out from the adults.

Sure enough, Hinkle's gaze swept right over him and continued on. Just a teenager. Nothing to see here. Jack waited until Hinkle had popped the trunk on his car so he could make absolutely sure it was the one and noted the license plate. JR2 5Y1. It wasn't the most memorable, so he texted it to everyone to be sure he wouldn't forget as he veered away toward his mother's car.

*I'll be there in 5*, Reggie texted back almost immediately.

*But—school?* he texted back.

*5.*

*Take 10. Meet @ my place.*

He still had to get food for Eric. He'd replaced his emergency twenty, but he was concerned about going back into the supermarket and finding a manager or security person waiting for him. With his mother's card and car and no license, he couldn't afford the scrutiny.

Instead he drove to a mom-and-pop type grocery a little farther from his house, obeying all speed limits and traffic signs. The smaller store would be a little pricier, probably, but he couldn't help it. It wasn't the first time he'd had to spend his emergency twenty on enough food to get them through. Bread, peanut butter, soup. His parents were on their own for coffee. It was a risky thing, making that call, but he knew if his father scrounged money together for anything, that would be it. That and beer. He wouldn't give a damn about the rest of them. If need be, they could chow down on the spent coffee grounds, maybe using the filters as some kind of tortilla shell.

Another text came through as he was checking out at the mom-and-pop place and taking his meager change.

The text was from Kali: *Checked on that plate. Car registered 2 Roland Bickram. Check local hotels?*

*U can do that?* he asked. Silly question. She'd never have asked if she couldn't. The real question was whether she could do it *legally*.

*Watch me*, she answered.

Jack got back home without incident. The house was deadly quiet when he arrived, meaning Mom still hadn't gotten out of bed or checked in on Eric. He left the food in the kitchen and went to do it himself.

Eric was still sleeping, and as much as he wanted to let him, Jack had to get him up and get food into him before he left. He couldn't count on his mother.

His brother didn't look so good. Sweat made what remained of his dark hair cling to his head. Jack felt Eric's forehead with the back of his wrist like he'd learned, but he could feel the heat even before he made contact. Eric was hot. A fever would mean a hospital trip they couldn't afford. He knew that more than ever after his trip to the grocery store.

"Eric," he said, firmly, but not too loud, in case he had a headache to go with the fever. "Eric, Buddy, wake up."

"Ungh," Eric said, turning to look at Jack, pulling sweat-dampened covers with him.

"Eric, you need to sit up. You might be feverish. I've got to get you some meds."

Eric shook his head from side to side and refused to open his eyes. Jack's heart kicked into high gear.

"I'm not playing with you. You've got to sit up, Buddy. I'll help you." Jack slid his arm under his brother's head and tried to prop him up, but without any help on his brother's part, it wasn't happening.

"Eric," he snapped, "work with me." He let some of his fear come through, making his voice sharper than it should have been, and Eric's eyes fluttered to half-mast. He started to help, but he was too weak for it to do much good.

Jack did most of the work, getting him sitting, helping him slide back so that the headboard could better support him, slipping pillows behind his back. Finally he had Eric more or less upright. "Don't go back to sleep, Buddy," he warned. "Not yet. I have to get you some Tylenol." He hoped to hell it worked; it was the only thing Eric was allowed.

He rushed off to the kitchen and grabbed a Gatorade from the refrigerator and three Tylenol. He rushed back with them and had to slap at his brother's cheeks to wake him again and make him take the pills. He held the Gatorade for his brother, helping him tilt it to wash the pills down and then setting it aside.

"You okay?" Jack asked. He was full of stupid questions today.

Eric shook his head slightly. "Don't feel well. Want to sleep."

"Let me get you something first. Toast? Soup?"

He shook his head again. "Not hungry. You can bring in the cereal box for later," he said, "'case I get hungry. I know you have to get to school."

"I can stay," Jack said. He didn't mention that he was skipping already.

"No, I'm awright."

From the slurring of his words, Jack didn't think so.

"Be right back with the cereal," he said, hoping he could find a box tucked away somewhere.

But first he stopped by his mother's room, flaming mad, ready to kick her awake and . . . He threw the image out of his head, afraid he was going to be sick. Afraid, not for the first time, that he was going to take after his father. He was so angry. At them, at the situation, at the whole damn universe and whoever might be in charge of it that Eric was sick and their shitty parents weren't taking care of him.

He settled for slamming his mother's door open, not caring about any headache *she* might have. She stirred, opened angry eyes to fix on him where he stood in the doorway.

"Get. Up." He said, biting off each word. "Get the hell up now. Your son needs you. Eric has a fever. I'm supposed to be at school, but I had to take the car and your empty ATM card to save your freakin' ass, to get some food into this house and *where the hell is all the money?*"

She blinked up at him, and he wanted to advance on her, pull her out of bed, throw her into the shower, but he didn't dare. He was afraid of laying a hand on her, of what he might do if she did or said something stupid.

His mother started to sit, mumbling bad things under her breath. Very bad things. She instantly reached for the nearly empty bottle of vodka on her side table, and Jack lost it. He crossed the room in the blink of an eye, hurdling the corner of the bed, and managed to make it to the bottle before she did. He grabbed it by the neck and threw it at the wall, where it smashed into a million pieces of glass and splatter.

She made a sound of protest. *That* got a rise out of her. Not that her son was sick or that her other son was yelling at her for the worthless piece of crap that she was, but that her booze was gone.

Jack stood where he was, close enough to touch, but clench-ing his fists at his sides and glaring her down. "Eric needs you. If I have to call an ambulance, I'm calling the cops too. They'll call child services. They'll crawl all over this place and you'll be charged with neglect at the very least. Maybe taken into custody. Then where will you get your liquor?"

She glared back. "You can't talk to me like that. Your father—"

"What, you'll have him beat me for it? Mom of the year, that's what you are." He grabbed his cell phone out of his pocket and held it up. "Get up. Take care of Eric or I make a call. Dad's already left for work. He can't do a thing to me right now."

She reached for the phone and fell on her face on the bed when he yanked it out of her reach. It was disgusting.

The doorbell rang and Jack cursed. *Not now.* He couldn't af-ford to leave her alone, but he couldn't ignore the door. Not with everything going on.

He glared at his mother to reinforce how serious he was be-fore stomping off to the door, leaving her to gather herself and praying she didn't call his bluff. He didn't want child services. He'd heard horror stories about foster care, and didn't have any idea how Eric would do. They were sure to be separated. If it wasn't for that, he might have called them himself ages ago.

Jack looked through the peephole and found Reggie standing on his doorstep . . . and Kali, which was a surprise. He opened the door just enough so that he could see them but they couldn't see in, in case his mother came stumbling by.

"Situation has changed. I can't come," he said.

"Is it Eric?" Kali gasped, pushing forward.

Jack stood in her way until they were toe to toe.

"Eric?" Reggie asked.

"His brother."

"You have a brother?"

Jack didn't know why that was so shocking. "Yeah, and he's sick. I can't leave him."

His mother chose that moment to shamble out. He could

hear her on the landing behind him. "Who ist," she said, slurring as badly as Eric half-asleep.

"They're just leaving," Jack called back. "You've got to go," he told the others.

He didn't know what his mother was going to drive him to, but he didn't need anyone around to witness it.

His mother made an anguished noise from the kitchen and Jack knew she'd just discovered the empty coffee container.

"Hell with that," Kali said, practically punching him in the chest to push him out of her way. Jack took a step back more out of shock than necessity, and next thing he knew, she was in. "My mother's a nurse," she said. "I've picked up a few things."

"I've already given him Tylenol," Jack called, as she side-swiped him because he didn't move aside quickly enough.

Jack was left with Reggie. "Guess you might as well come in too, see the whole freakshow."

Reggie eyed him with no idea what he was talking about. Jack would love to have kept it that way, but his mother was in the kitchen, continuing with her curses as she ransacked the cabinets as if more coffee might magically have appeared along with the bread and other stuff. If there'd been money in the account, she'd have been right.

"Just . . ." Jack had no idea just what. He couldn't say *make yourself at home*. "Follow me."

He went off to Eric's room, where he stood in the doorway, since there wasn't much room inside, especially not for him *and* Reggie. Kali stood over his brother, who was sleeping again. He'd slid down a bit, but was still more or less in the upright position Jack had put him in.

"Do you have a thermometer?" she asked.

"Somewhere." He went for it and came back with one of the mouth thermometers and the box of plastic covers.

Kali looked it over and figured out how to use it in a second flat—there were only two buttons, after all, it wasn't exactly rocket science. When it beeped, she declared, "100.7. Bad but not critical. How long ago did you give him the Tylenol?"

"Like five minutes."

"Too soon for it to have brought the temp down then. 100.7 is something to watch, but you don't have to worry really until it gets up around 102. I heard your mother in the kitchen. Can she monitor him?"

The look she gave him said she had a pretty fair idea what she was asking.

"Let me talk to her."

Reggie let him pass, and Jack left them behind to talk about him or whatever else while he went to the kitchen to confront his mother. He'd feel better if he stayed to watch Eric, but the mood he was in . . . he wasn't sure that was entirely safe. Maybe if he wasn't there to step up every time his mother fell down, maybe . . . But he didn't really believe she'd suddenly remember how to parent. She'd fallen apart. She was broken. Maybe they all were.

"Where's the coffee?" she asked.

Jack rolled his eyes.

"Did you miss the part where there was no freakin' money in your account? I tried to get some and was hit with insufficient funds."

"I can't face the day without coffee."

She started to reach for a higher shelf, where he knew she kept things a lot stronger than coffee, but there was nothing there either. "Dammit," she said.

"If I get you coffee, will you watch Eric? *Really* watch him? Take his temperature every hour."

"Sure, sure," she said, too determinedly meeting his eyes. Probably she wanted him to believe her sincerity, but it had the very opposite effect. "And a little something more. A little hair of the dog to slip into my coffee, just to keep me going."

Jack stared at her in disbelief. "Mom, I'm seventeen. I can't get you booze."

"I'm sure you have a fake ID or something tucked away." She took a step forward as if to search him, and Jack moved back out of reach.

"I don't," he said, holding a hand out in front of him to keep her from getting close again. "Coffee. That's all."

"Fuckin' useless," she said, turning away from him.

"Maybe we have some cough syrup or something you haven't gone through yet," he said nastily. "Coffee. That's it. Take it or leave it."

"I can go out myself," she said, defiantly.

He didn't point out that she wasn't going anywhere without her car keys, which he still held.

They got her coffee. Jack had just enough change left to get her a jumbo-sized cup at the nearest gas station. He grabbed extra creamers, sugars and straws, since he was certain they were running low on those at home too. Feeling only marginally guilty about it, he grabbed packets of mustard, ketchup, salt and pepper that were on the fixings bar in the middle of the place to take back to the house as well.

He refused to meet Reggie and Kali's glances, and when Kali put a hand to his arm in understanding, he shook it off. At least Maria had missed the whole thing, though she'd probably hear about it at some point.

Back at the house, Reggie and Kali waited in the car while Jack delivered the coffee. His mother met him with a hand behind her back, so he knew she'd found a bottle she'd hidden away somewhere.

He handed her the cup, warned her he'd be back and he'd be checking in. He almost didn't leave again, as much as he wanted to talk to Hinkle and find out what he might know about Marley's death and the other murders. But surely his brother would be okay for a few hours. He'd have to be okay.

Turning back to the car nearly killed him. But if he wanted to be there for his brother long term, he was going to have to solve the mystery and catch the killer before he ended up dead. Time was running out.

"I found him," Kali said as he got into the car, gaze riveted on her smart phone. "Well, I found 'Roland Bickram'."

Kali had already called shotgun, so Jack got into the back behind her. Luckily, Kali wasn't overtall, and there was plenty of room. Behind Reggie he'd have been squished like a grape.

Jack nodded to show he'd heard. He didn't ask any questions, his mind still on Eric. Now that they were on the move, he was second guessing himself. Reggie and Kali could have handled the questioning, but . . . the only way he could be sure was to be there himself. Before this he wouldn't have considered himself a control freak. Maybe it was more that he'd never learned to count on anyone else.

Jack scoured the parking lot as they pulled into Hinkle's motel and spotted his car in front of unit 8.

Reggie was already headed there, so they didn't have to say a word. He parked in the spot right beside Hinkle, and they all got out.

Jack saw the curtain in the window of unit 8 move as they approached the door.

Kali gave it a very definitive knock.

"What do you want?" came the voice from inside.

They all looked at each other. "What, does he think we're selling magazine subscriptions?" Kali asked.

Jack sighed. He was up. "Mr. Hinkle, it's Jack Harkness. I don't know if you remember me. I was one of Liam's friends."

He didn't respond for half a minute. "Jack? You've grown."

"Yeah, five years will do that."

"What do you want?" Hinkle repeated.

"To talk. We're worried about Liam and . . . listen, can we come in? Talking through this door is a pain in the a—butt."

"I'm scheduled to talk to the police shortly. I really don't have time for this."

"Talk to the police about what?" Reggie asked. "Marley's murder?"

Kali and Jack both hit Reggie at once, the former glaring him down like she might incinerate him where he stood if only lasers would shoot out of her eyes. Hinkle's wife . . . or ex-wife . . . was dead, his son was missing, and Reggie was so focused on his mission he couldn't see anything else.

There was no response from the other side of the door. Not for a full minute.

"I think you'd better leave," Hinkle said at last. His voice was ice cold.

"What the hell were you thinking?" Jack asked Reggie under his breath.

"I don't know. I've just waited so long . . ."

"To scare someone off? Good going."

"He got awfully cool, awfully fast," Reggie said defensively.

"Wouldn't you if a bunch of kids showed up and started throwing around the word murder? Especially when you might or might not be in the midst of mourning your ex-wife and kid?"

Reggie hung his head at that.

"I mean it," Hinkle said from inside. "The police say my son might have been stalked. Who's to say it wasn't you. Leave or I'll call the police and let them sort it out."

Suspicion was like an epidemic.

"Come on," Jack said quietly to the others. "I'll try him later on my own. He seems to remember me from when I used to hang with Liam, and I'm not so emotionally invested." He shot Reggie a look. "I might handle things with a bit more finesse."

Kali snorted. Okay, so finesse was not maybe his natural talent, but adaptability certainly was.

Jack pushed them back toward the car, saying over his shoulder. "Okay, Mr. Hinkle, we're leaving. No need to call the police." Let him think they were cowed.

As he waited for Reggie to open the car door and let them in, he scanned the parking lot again.

And froze in place.

Over by the dumpster in the corner of the lot was a figure in a black hoodie and baggy jeans who turned away the second Jack started scanning. Jack had the distinct impression that he'd been watching Hinkle's room. Or maybe watching *them*. Chills shot up his spine.

"Wait," he said very quietly, as Kali held the side door out to him.

He nodded in the direction of the guy in the hoodie. Somehow, from the stance or whatever, he knew it was a guy, even with the baggy, gender-neutral clothing.

"What?" Kali asked, apparently unimpressed. He gave her a quick glance to make sure she was facing the right direction, and when he looked back, the guy was disappearing behind the dumpster.

Jack didn't answer her. There wasn't time. He took off across the lot after the guy in the hoodie. If it was just some guy, no harm, no foul, but if it was the stalker. The killer . . .

Jack was fast, but when he hit the corner of the dumpster and made the turn, he was caught up short. There was no sign of hoodie-guy. None at all. Just beyond there were convenience stores, a gas station, a dollar store, a pawn shop, cars pulling out of the lots, but there was no sign of where he'd gone. Hoodie-guy might be inside any one of the stores or he might be long gone.

He cursed fluently and went back to tell the others.

"So you saw a guy in a hoodie," Kali said. "So what? It could have been anyone out for a walk."

"It wasn't." Jack answered, feeling it in his gut.

There was nothing else to say. He hadn't gotten a decent look. He didn't even know for sure it was a teenager. Best he could say was the guy didn't move like an old man.

"We could go to each of the stores," Reggie said. "Ask after a guy in a hoodie." It was clear that Reggie was humoring him, but Jack wasn't prepared just to let it go. He'd abandoned Eric to talk with Hinkle. With that door slammed in his face, he had to have *something* to show for it.

"It couldn't hurt," Jack answered.

But if anyone had seen a guy in a dark hoodie, they weren't saying. No one had noticed him. No one. Jack knew he hadn't just been a figment of his imagination.

"We could go back to school," Reggie said doubtfully when they seemed to run out of investigative options.

Kali gave him a *get real* look.

"Or we could go to the police station," Jack said. "Maybe find Rayna's friend Officer Stiles. See if she'll tell us anything about last night. Or about Hinkle being back in town."

"Do you think that's likely?" Kali asked.

"Won't know until we try. Besides, we have information to share. Even if the police already know about Hinkle, they don't know about the guy watching him."

"If there was any such guy," Kali said.

Jack shrugged. "Only one way to know for sure. Maybe the police can pull surveillance footage. There are cameras everywhere these days. Maybe one of them picked him up."

Kali gave him a hairy eyeball. After all, hoodie-guy hadn't actually done anything but lurk. It was just Jack's gut . . . But the police might be desperate enough for leads to grasp at straws.

"Can you—?" Jack started to ask Kali, but already she was shaking her head.

"If those cameras were uploading to somewhere, maybe, but they're most likely closed circuit. Maybe I can access traffic cams, but those are all official. If I'm caught . . ."

"Okay, we'll call that Plan B," he said. "First, let's see what we can learn at the station."


Jack always thought he might end up at the police station for one reason or another—for shaking someone down or running off with his brother and getting caught. He never suspected he'd go willingly. He certainly never suspected that having been once he'd return for a repeat performance. But then, he never expected to be in the middle of a murder investigation with his own life in the balance.

The officer behind the desk was the same one who'd stopped them the other day. He took one look at Jack, Kali and Reggie and his brows lowered like storm clouds. "Kincaid's not going to talk to you," he said. "He's in with someone."

"Not a problem," Kali said. "We're here to see Officer Stiles."

"Do you think we just sit around on our thumbs all day?"

"No, I think we have information pertinent to the investigation."

Kali glared the officer down. Jack stood back, amused. The officer might have storm cloud brows, but Kali had the goth glare, along with the piercings and an extra dose of attitude.

Grumbling, the desk officer picked up the phone on the counter. "Stiles? Yeah, some kids here to see you. They say they've got information." He looked at them from beneath his brows. "'What kids?' she says."

"Jack Harkness," Jack said. "Kali . . ."

"Davidson," she supplied, turning her glare on him. Fair enough. They'd been in the trenches together. He should have known.

"And Reggie Driskoll," Reggie said for himself.

The officer repeated the names into the phone and waited for a response. He didn't seem to like it, and hung up the phone with a little extra oomph.

"You wait. She'll come get you."

Kali crossed her arms and leaned up against the counter, prepared to wait.

"Not here," he said, waving her aside so he could help the guy who'd come in behind them.

Kali rolled her eyes and moved fractionally so the guy could get to the counter.

"We could move to the waiting room," Reggie said.

"I don't want anyone to forget about us. I'm not going anywhere."

They didn't have long to wait before Officer Stiles appeared and motioned them in. She didn't look like she'd slept in a couple of days. Her uniform was neat enough, but beyond that it was all drooping eyes and the slight shake of her hands, as if she'd consumed enough caffeine to be vibrating.

She brought them to a desk in the main squad room, which was a warren of desks, computers, ringing phones and other officers. Unlike every cop show ever, Jack didn't see any gangbangers threatening to start a war right there in the station or working girls popping gum and proclaiming their innocence, though there were a few visitor chairs occupied. Hard to tell without overhearing whether they were suspects or witnesses.

There was only one chair at the desk Officer Stiles led them to and both Jack and Reggie motioned for Kali to take it, but she glared at them like they'd somehow suggested she put on an apron and start scrubbing counters. Jeez, try to be polite . . .

Finally, Jack took it himself. Stupid to loom over Stiles. Better to face her eye to eye.

"We know Norman Hinkle's back," he started. She didn't look like she'd have the patience for beating around the bush, not as tired as she was, so he continued, "And we know the police are questioning him."

"How do you know?" she cut in before he could go on.

He resisted glancing at Kali. "I saw him in the grocery store this morning. I followed him back to his hotel."

It was the easiest answer. No reason to bring up any potential computer hacking.

"And then you followed him here?"

"No, he told us he was coming. We tried to talk to him."

"Tried?" she asked.

"Yeah, he was a little defensive."

"Imagine that. Okay, you knew he was in town, and you knew we knew . . . or something like that. So what's this information you supposedly have for me?"

"We weren't the only ones outside his hotel room."

That made her gaze sharpen on him.

"Who else?" she asked.

But Kali had let Jack take lead about as long as she was capable of. "Some guy," she said helpfully, "in a black hoodie. Not too tall, not too short. Maybe five eight-ish."

"Not much of a description," Officer Stiles said, deflating a little. "And what do you mean by 'outside his hotel room'? Was he loitering?"

Kali looked down at Jack, throwing it back to him, giving him enough rope to hang himself. "Not . . . exactly," he said. "I mean, he was lurking in the lot, over by the dumpster. I caught him watching the place, but when I tried to talk to him, he disappeared."

Officer Stiles studied him, and he studied her back, noting the tiny little lines around her eyes and the groves forming alongside her mouth.

"That's it? That's what you've got?"

"He acted suspicious, and he was watching the place. You tell me what reason someone would have to watch a motel room, unless he was stalking someone."

"So some guy in a hoodie who you can't identify looks the wrong way and you want me to do what with the information?"

"Pull surveillance footage, canvas the area . . . something."

Officer Stiles sighed heavily, leaned an elbow on her desk and rubbed at her eyes. "I'm sorry," she said wearily, "I can't help you. Do you know how much trouble I'd get into for profiling a guy in a hoodie for standing around? He didn't do anything wrong. He's not guilty of a crime. I can't waste resources tracking him down."

"What if it's Liam?" Kali said suddenly. "I know you're looking for him, either to protect or question. Probably both."

"Are you saying it was Liam?"

Kali shrugged. "Could be. Height was about right."

Officer Stiles was half convinced, Jack could see, but not quite there yet. "What about that text Rayna got last night, supposedly from Liam, the one that lured her and Evan into that trap? They said they found bedding and blood. Can you tell us—"

Officer Stiles cut him off. "Not Liam's blood," she said, leaning in closely so they wouldn't be overheard.

They all stared at her with identical looks of fascination.

"How do you know?" Reggie asked. "There's no way DNA testing would have come back so soon."

She eyed him, weighing how much to say. But the longer they all leaned in with their heads together, the more suspicious it looked to anyone who might be paying attention. She came to a decision quickly. "Because it wasn't human."

They all leaned away again instinctively, processing that information. "What did the guys say who attacked Rayna and Evan? Did they tell you anything?"

Officer Stiles flicked another quick glance around the station. "Only that Liam was alive the last time they saw him," she said.

Kali gasped in a breath and Jack didn't hear her let it out again.

"Now, you'd better get going. I have paperwork to finish up before I can get home and then I have an appointment with my pillow. I'll walk you out."

None of them protested. She'd given them more than she probably should have, and it had been a stunner. A game changer. They had evidence that Liam was still alive . . . or had been not so long ago.

## INTERLUDE

*It was all coming together now. The players were in place, and he was the only one who could see all the possible moves. They were in check, moving into checkmate. The only question was how many pieces could he sweep from the field on the way to victory?*

# CHAPTER 27

RAYNA

The text arrived while Rayna was staring at her phone rather than working on the class assignments that had been piling up. Mom and Dad had kept her home from school, but not excused her from the work.

> *What's the matter, Meddlers? I left you all the clues—the bodies, the messages, the mementos. If you can't find me now, you never will. I'm growing bored, so I'm taking time off the clock. We're in the end game. No one is safe.*

Rayna's hand started to shake. *No, no, no.* Time could *not* be up. This couldn't be happening.

The number was once again Restricted. And it was a group text. Every one of the Meddlers, new and old, had received the message.

The subtext of the original notes was "I can get to you," as the killer had gone on to prove. This one said "I know you". Maybe even "I'm one of you".

She clicked on the top bar, which gave her a list of everyone included in the memo. No one was left out. Except Grace. She had to shove aside the vision of Grace's face as it had been in that picture, also from Restricted, before the sadness and guilt could swallow her whole. She could break down later. Right now her friends were in danger, and she was determined that no one else was going to die.

Texts from the others came fast and furious.

*Who is this?* Kali asked.

Then Reggie. *Tell us where you are, and we'll bring the fight to YOU. Show yourself, coward.* That was from Jack.

Rayna, meanwhile, was busy forwarding the text to Officer Stiles, the only one she really trusted. She'd no doubt send it to the detectives, but that was okay. As long as Stiles saw it. As long as she was aware.

As soon as she was done, she got onto their other group text. The one without "Restricted".

*We all need to get together and stay that way. There's safety in numbers. He won't come for us all at once.*

*Unless that's exactly what he wants,* Evan texted back, *to gather us all together, block the exits, torch the place like he did the Hinkle house.*

Rayna got the chills. She wasn't sure how much more she could take. One wrong decision, one wrong move, and they could all be dead.

*First thing,* Kali typed, *we sound off. Make sure everyone is okay.*

*Safe,* Rayna texted, though she figured that was clear already.

*Safe,* Jack wrote. *But can't get together. Something's come up at home.*

*With Eric?* Kali wrote back immediately. *Everything okay?*

*Fever is worse,* Jack answered. *Can't leave him.*

*At school.* Charlie wrote. *Stuck in chem class. Save me?*

Not so funny, given the circumstances.

Then they waited. On Reggie. On Maria. On Evan.

*Here,* Evan sent after another long minute of silence. *Dad didn't do it, btw. Says he was there to see Marley, but she didn't answer at his knock. He wasn't the guy she fought with. Sounds like she may have been dead already.*

If true, there were two other men they knew or suspected to have been in Marley's life who could have slipped in and out unseen—Liam Hinkle, her possible accountant, and Dexter Cardiss, her ex and Dalton's father.

*Because, of course, your dad would just tell you if he'd done it,* Kali responded.

Rayna held her breath, anticipating the blow up. This was no time to start infighting.

Evan sent back a rage emoji—face flaming read, eyes squinched, steam pouring out of the ears.

Then nothing.

*Reggie?* Rayna typed. *Maria?*

*Here,* Reggie sent. *Gonna be out of touch. Something I have to do.*

*Don't do anything stupid, man,* Evan said. *Bring back-up. Don't go it alone.*

There was no answer. And still no word from Maria. Rayna's heart started to pound.

*Maria? U OK?* Jack asked. She could almost hear his fear in those few words, maybe because it echoed hers. She was holding her breath and gripping her phone hard enough to break the case, waiting for more.

Nothing.

*Maria?* she sent, as if the third time would be the charm. Maria could be taking a test. Or giving a presentation. Or just have her phone off during school hours.

Rayna was staring at the phone when it pinged again, but even so it made her jump.

*In class. Can't talk.*

Maria! Suddenly all the air whooshed out of Rayna, leaving her breathless.

But what about Reggie?

She didn't want to think it, but that message—the part about clues and closing the case, that sounded like a Meddler. But the part about the end game sounded like a gamer. Was Reggie turning his phone off because he was about to do something reckless and didn't want them to stop him or because he didn't want anyone to be able to track his movements? Or both?

Evan must have had the same idea. She got a private text in, *I know where Reggie's going.*

*To confront Hinkle,* she answered.

*So you got that too? We've got to stop him. I don't think Reggie planted the earring or any of the evidence. He's too upset at the wrongful accusation of his uncle to frame anyone else. Which means that it had to be Liam.*

*He told us so all along,* she said. That text he'd sent to lure

Grace, the one he'd sent to her.

*But we didn't listen. That's the thing about misdirection, it makes you distrust even when someone comes at you straight. That was probably the plan. Liam killed someone else in his place. He took the wrong girl on the wrong day. Rayna, you've been blaming yourself, but that might have been part of his plan—to have us looking one way when the danger was coming from another.*

*And who'd suspect Liam would use his own name to lure people out? It would seem like a smokescreen.*

*Exactly,* Evan typed. *We've got to head Reggie off. If he's going to confront Hinkle and Liam is watching him, it would be the perfect opportunity to take him out.*

*But you can't drive with your arm, and I don't have my license.* Not to mention, her parents would never let her go. They were better off giving everything to the police.

*Kali!*

A minute later, he was back texting again. *She's on her way. I'm going to tell the others. Be there as soon as we can.*

Rayna only hoped it was in time for Reggie.

She hadn't heard back yet from Officer Stiles, but sent her a brief follow-up to let her know that they had planned. She debated calling Detectives Kincaid or Travers, but they'd already shown they had no interest in taking the Meddlers seriously, and she didn't have anything but conjecture to show them. Lots of little bits that added up, but no real evidence. No smoking gun.

They were on their own.

Rayna was trying to figure out how to sneak out without her parents stopping her when her dad knocked on her door. "Ray-ray?"

Her teeth clenched together at the childhood nickname. "Yeah?" she said through them.

"I'm so sorry, honey, but I've gotten called in to work. A boiler . . . well, it pretty well exploded, and the guys aren't getting anywhere with me walking them through the troubleshoot. I'll have to go in. Just for a while."

She nodded. *Was there a chance?*

"Your mom's in a meeting and can't get out for another hour, so . . ." Rayna waited, once again holding her breath. After everything, it seemed impossible that something should finally go her way. "I'll have to take you with me."

Yup, impossible. "But Kali and Evan are on their way. We've decided there's strength in numbers until the police catch the killer. I won't be alone."

"You think two teenagers can protect you better than I can?"

"I think you'll be busy with the boiler and hardly in any position to watch me. Wouldn't you rather I be here with the alarm and with friends? I promise, I'll keep my phone in hand. I've already got 9-1-1 programmed in."

*Please say yes, please say yes,* she chanted in her head.

Dad looked frazzled. The delay of arguing was costing him. An exploded boiler meant flooding, and every second it wasn't under control meant probably thousands in damages.

"Fine," he said. "But you set the alarm right after me, and you text or call me the second they show so I know you're safe."

"Okay."

"And every fifteen minutes after that."

"*Dad!*"

"Don't 'Dad' me. Take it or leave it."

"I'll take it."

"Good." He stepped into the room, kissed her forehead, decided that wasn't enough and motioned her up for a better goodbye hug. Like it was the last time they might see each other. She tried not to feel like someone was walking over her grave.

She walked him to the door and, as promised, set the alarm after him. She counted the seconds until Evan and Kali showed, terrified of being alone.

"So I was thinking," Kali said, as soon as the door closed behind Rayna. "When Reggie and Jack and I were at Hinkle's hotel earlier . . . what if Liam wanted to be seen?"

"Why would he want that?" Rayna asked.

"Why is he doing any of this? All along, I think there's been a method behind his madness. It's pretty easy *not* to draw attention, not to be seen, but Liam, who's pretty unprepossessing usually, easily overlooked, drew Jack's eye, then disappeared suspiciously. It's like he wanted us to see him, to know he'd been there and was watching. Because surely, we'd go back to his last known location. We'd search him out."

"You mean so that we'd go back there looking for him, exactly was we're doing?" Rayna asked.

"That would tie in with that text he sent, '*If you can't find me now, you never will*'," Evan put in.

"But that would mean we're doing exactly what he wants," Rayna said, horrified. "We're walking right into a trap."

"Only we know it. We're prepared. Reggie isn't. He's got tunnel vision. All he can see is his uncle's case and clearing his name."

"Then we'd better hurry!"

"Already on it!" Kali said, and floored the gas pedal. They shot forward like a rocket, barely swerving around the slower car in front in the nick of time.


They pulled into the hotel parking lot and immediately spotted Reggie's car at the far end. Only he wasn't in it. Whatever his plans, they were already in motion. That horrible feeling that had been growing in the pit of Rayna's stomach suddenly sprouted like a beanstalk.

"Damn," Evan said. "He should have listened and brought back-up. He's not totally rational right now."

"What do we do now?" Rayna asked. "You said we were prepared, but how exactly are we prepared to face down a killer?"

"With our blinding wits?" Evan suggested.

"Screw that," Kali said. "I have pepper spray."

"Where did you get that?" Rayna asked.

"Home made. Found the instructions on-line. Easy as pie, just be sure you don't have to rub your eyes or blow your nose in the process. Here."

She handed them both unlabeled spray bottles, the kind used

for perfume or spray-in conditioner. The liquid inside was cloudy. It wouldn't spray very far. Not nearly as far as the pepper spray canisters you could buy off the internet, which meant she'd have to be pretty up close and personal to use it. She didn't want to trust her life to a spray bottle, but what choice did she have. Her idea of a weapon was the Exacto knife she had in her purse, which she'd swiped from her craft room right before Evan and Kali arrived. It had been used for cutting photos for her collage. Now . . . she only hoped she wouldn't have to use it at all.

They scanned the rest of the lot as they got out of the car. Hinkle's car was there too, but there was no sign of Liam. No one hanging around in a hoodie. No one clearly surveilling the place. Not even a single tenant walking too or from their cars into the motel. The parking lot was still and silent, like the streets in an old cowboy movie when everyone knew the gunfight was coming and they had to clear the way or get caught in the crossfire.

Rayna grabbed the knife out of her purse and tucked it carefully into her pocket, blade down. It had a protective cap that fit over it, but she didn't want to fiddle that off in a fight. If she sliced her jeans or herself, so be it. The purse she stuffed under the seat before closing her door. The pepper spray she held in her hand. The others did the same. That was how they approached Hinkle's door.

They sped up as they neared it until they were almost at a full-out run. "I'll knock," Evan said. "Rayna, you watch our flanks. Kali, our back."

She looked back to see Kali bristle at the orders, but she didn't argue. Not now. She had a feeling Evan might be in for it later.

Evan knocked hard, using his knuckles.

"Reggie?" he called. "Are you in there? Mr. Hinkle?"

There was nothing at first. Evan put his ear to the door, but pulled back a moment later, shaking his head to let them know he couldn't hear anything.

"Open up or we call the police," he yelled.

They waited. Rayna's heart was in her throat, and she could practically hear Kali's pounding behind her. They hadn't run that hard, so it had to be fear and anticipation.

Then the door unlatched, and Mr. Hinkle appeared in the doorway. He was almost six feet tall with a retreating hairline, glasses, and a button-up shirt tucked into crisp jeans. He didn't look like her image of a killer, but there was something in his face . . . Something was not quite right.

Evan pushed past him, not giving him the chance to slam the door in their faces. Hinkle protested, but Rayna swung her pepper spray his way, surprising herself that she was perfectly willing to use it if he made the slightest move. She was so keyed up, she was almost afraid she'd depress the sprayer unintentionally. Kali crowded in behind her, leaving the door open for a quick escape.

Only Hinkle didn't let that stand. They all three whirled around as the door slammed shut behind them, and the deadbolt was thrown. They were trapped inside.

With Marley's killer, if they weren't mistaken.

Evan didn't let that phase him. He stepped up, toe to toe with Hinkle and held his own pepper spray high. "Where's Reggie?" he demanded.

Hinkle eyed the sprayer like he had no idea what he was looking at. And maybe he didn't. Then he blinked down at him, his eyes owlish behind his glasses. But she'd seen owls swoop in on prey, and she didn't mistake the look for mild-mannered.

"Reggie?" he asked. But even with that one word, he wasn't convincing.

Then a door slammed open at the other end of the room, and framed in the bathroom doorway was Reggie, bleeding profusely from a head wound, the blood spilling over one eye and dripping down this face, soaking the top of his T-shirt, and he was bowed backward by the torque of a belt tightened around his neck. Holding the end of the belt and just barely visible over his shoulder was Liam. In the flesh. Alive and deadly.

Too far away for their weapons to be any good, even if he didn't have Reggie as a human shield.

"Move for the door or your phones and I finish what I've started," Liam said. He no longer sounded like himself. His tone had gone from his normal *excuse me* to *excuse you* . . . with the understanding that no excuses would be accepted. "Now, throw away your weapons." He tightened up momentarily on the belt around Reggie's neck, and Reggie didn't even have enough air to make a sound.

Rayna made it for him, gasping at the pain on his face.

All three of them threw down their pepper spray. Rayna didn't reach for the knife in her pocket. If she didn't call attention to it, maybe Liam wouldn't notice, and she'd find an opportunity to use it.

Hinkle made a noise as well, and edged around them until he hit the bed, then he sank onto it, his gaze swinging from his son to them. He looked stunned. Had he let Liam in? Reggie? Did he have any idea what he'd set himself up for?

"Why?" he asked, staring at his son standing there with Reggie's life in his hands. "Why?"

Liam's smile was . . . poisonous. Pure evil. He didn't even look like himself anymore. If Rayna had given him much thought before all this, she'd have called him mild-mannered. Quiet. Studious.

Now he looked like what he was . . . a killer.

"You know why, don't you, Dad? Like father, like son." He gave a sudden pointed yank on the belt around Reggie's neck, and Reggie staggered, nearly overbalancing them both. Rayna's hand twitched toward her knife before they recovered, and she prayed she hadn't missed her moment.

"You weren't around to teach me," Liam said, talking to his father, and ignoring the others, at least for now. "But I figured things out on my own, especially when Reggie started investigating that old case. I didn't hang around the Meddlers for very long. Didn't need to once I spotted a few things and started poking around. I found the trinkets you left behind. Well, *Mom* found the earring, but I was the one who knew what it meant."

Hinkle looked like he was going to be sick. "What are you talking about?"

"Marley Thompson, *Dad*. Geez, you'd think you'd remember

the first person you ever killed . . . unless she wasn't your first?"

Hinkle made a pitiful sound and ran his hands down his face, nearly pulling his skin off. He seemed shell-shocked . . . defeated. If he'd killed Marley—and that no longer seemed to be in doubt —Rayna suspected it had been in a moment of passion. Clearly he couldn't face what he'd done. He'd run away to escape his demons, leaving everything behind, including his family. Facing it all down now in the form of his son seemed more than he could take.

Liam made a sound of disgust. "And here I thought you'd be proud of me, Dad, following in your footsteps. Jeezus, man up."

Liam looked around the room and fixed his gaze on Rayna. "We're missing some," he snapped. "Where are the others? You know what they say in Pokemon, 'Gotta catch 'em all'."

He sounded positively deranged.

Rayna caught movement out of the corner of her eye and determinedly didn't glance over at Evan as he edged toward Liam, but it wasn't that big a room, certainly not big enough for a decent distraction, and Liam spotted the movement without her help.

"Anh an ah," he said, yanking at the belt around Reggie's neck again. He'd slacked off a bit to keep him breathing, not ready to lose his hostage, but now . . . Reggie's face was going purple, and he was making a terrible noise as he wheezed in air . . . His eyes were wide and wild with terror. "Another move and your friend dies."

Evan froze. Reggie's frantic sounds stopped, but the terror in his eyes didn't abate.

"If I *don't* make a move we all die," Evan said. "Isn't that your plan? To make good on all your threats."

Liam eyed him. "I don't have anything against you in particular, if that helps. You're just a bonus. I guess you came with the package." He flashed a look at Rayna.

"What did *I* ever do to you?" she asked.

"Nothing," he said, flashing teeth. They were fuzzy and orange, like he hadn't brushed them in a while. "That's just it. I was beneath your notice, even when you bloodied my nose in gym. I tried to get your attention, but . . . Well, I guess I finally accomplished that, didn't I. Wanna date me now?"

He sounded psycho. Hell, he *was* psycho.

"What about Amal?" she asked. "And Grace . . ."

Liam shook his head at her. "You really think I'm going to stand here monologuing all day? Really, if you haven't figured it all out by now, you haven't been paying attention. They betrayed me. Or pissed me off. Doesn't really matter now, does it? Certainly not to them."

"But then, what about Dalton?" Evan asked. "If you were going to take out anyone—" He stopped, suddenly realizing he'd suggested an addition to Liam's hit list.

"Oh, I have something very special in mind for him," Liam said. "Who do you think's going to get the blame? The evidence is already in place. I've gotten so adept at planting it. Now, I'd say we've had just about enough. Answers aren't going to bring your friends back."

"It won't make them any deader," Evan said.

Rayna was stunned. This was no time for jokes, if that's what it was meant to be.

"Too true," Liam said. He pulled a cloth and a lighter from his back pocket, one hand still tightly on the belt around Reggie's neck, and Rayna noticed something she'd been too distracted to notice before . . . or maybe the smell was just stronger now. The smell of kerosene. Maybe not poured *everywhere*—*that* she would have noticed—but on the rag at the very least and maybe . . .

"Now," he said, flicking the lighter on and off to show them what he could do at any moment. That soaked rag was perilously close to the flame. "We have to call our little lost sheep. Jack and Maria need to be here at the very least. They're not escaping this unscathed. Charlie too? Or shall we leave him behind to investigate the fire? He'd appreciate that, don't you think? It's kind of his thing."

He fixed those psycho eyes on Reggie, like he was looking to him to respond. Reggie's eyes were wild. Rayna didn't think he'd even heard the questions, his whole focus on simply surviving.

"Call Jack," he said suddenly to Kali. "It seems like you two have suddenly gotten very buddy-buddy. Tell him you're in danger. You need him," he said the last two words in a sing-song, little girl voice. "He'll come running for you, won't he? The damsel in distress."

"Screw that," she spat. "I'm no damsel, and he's too busy with his brother—"

Reggie made a sudden move, coming crazily alive, desperate to tear the belt away from his neck, kicking and throwing his weight. Liam's attention shot to him, and Evan, who was the closest, dove for him. Rayna grabbed the knife out of her pocket, and rushed for them as well, but it was a bottle neck. They couldn't both get through the door, and Reggie was still in the way. Before they could do anything, Liam regained control, and used the belt like a tether, swinging Reggie's head like a ball into the doorjamb, making a horrible cracking sound. Reggie crumpled like a marionette with his strings cut.

As he fell, Liam yanked at the belt, and it came free covered in Reggie's blood, but Evan was on him, and they fought for the belt. Liam lashed it out of the way just as Evan would have gotten a grip, and swung it like a whip, catching Evan in the face with the buckle, which lashed at his cheek, adding his blood to Reggie's. But before Liam could swing it again, Evan got ahold of it with his one good hand, wrapping it around twice so it couldn't get ripped away.

Rayna held the knife, but couldn't find a moment. Liam and Evan were rolling now, fists and feet going, and she was afraid they'd move at just the wrong moment and she'd get the wrong one, only Evan was one arm down, and it didn't look like he was winning. She had to— She saw her moment when Liam rolled on top, arm pulled back to wale on Evan. She lunged, plunging the knife into his back before his arm came down, but it was a small knife, and while he reared back in pain, he didn't fall to the side, freeing Evan. He only flashed her a murderous look and reached to pull the knife out of his back.

Evan tried to buck him off in his distraction, but he had only limited room to move with Reggie's body filling the floor, and before he could get the leverage he needed, Liam was holding Rayna's knife to his neck.

He stopped moving all together.

Horrified, panicked, Rayna looked back to Kali for help, but she was holding Hinkle down, keeping him out of the fight. Not that he looked much inclined to join.

Rayna's heart stopped. It was game over, then? Just like Liam said? She couldn't see that they had any more moves.

"Now, *call Jack*," Liam said Kali. His hand was rock steady on that knife, and he only glanced at her long enough to see her reach for her phone before turning back to his captive.

Liam had been forced to drop the rag and the lighter in the fight. That was all Rayna could see that they had going for them.

But right now, he held all the weapons, all the advantages, and Evan's life in his hands.

# CHAPTER 28

JACK

Jack paced back and forth in the hospital waiting room. His mother was back there with Eric. His effing useless mother. It should have been him. He knew it. Probably the nurse who'd taken charge of Eric knew it. But Jack wasn't Eric's guardian. He couldn't sign off on anything.

When Kali's call came in, he was half-thrilled. Something, *anything* to keep his mind off things with Eric. He knew his brother would be okay. He had to be. Some antibiotics and hospital-grade analgesic, maybe a sponge-bath to take his temperature down . . .

The tone in Kali's voice, though, put him on instant alert.

"Jack?" she said when he picked up. "How's Eric? Everything okay?"

He heard a voice behind her, sharp, masculine, but he couldn't make out what was said.

Before he could respond, Kali came back, "Nevermind, no time for that. The rest of us are at Hinkle's hotel, and . . ." She took a deep breath in. More of a gasp, really, and then burst out. "It's a trap. Tell the others—"

There was a sharp cry and a clatter as her phone was ripped away or smacked to the floor and a loud cracking sound as if a foot had come down on top of it. And then . . . nothing.

Jack stood stunned for a second, then ran for the emergency room desk. "I came in with Eric Harkness. I need to see him *now*."

The woman tapped at her computer and glanced up from the screen to Jack. "I'm sorry, he's already got someone with him."

Jack made a sound of sheer frustration. "I know, it's my

mother, but something's come up. I have to go, but I can't just leave him."

"I can give him a message," she said.

Damn it! If he left and something happened—to him or to Eric —he'd never get the chance even to say good-bye. But if something happened to the others because he was too slow to act . . .

Every second he hesitated could be someone's last.

"Fine," he said, desperation sharpening his voice. "Tell him I love him and I had to go. Tell him I wouldn't leave now if it weren't life or death. And tell him . . . tell him I'll be back."

He hoped he wasn't making a false promise. The woman behind the counter looked concerned at the message, but Jack didn't give her the chance to ask questions. As soon as he finished, he took off. He'd driven his mother and Eric to the hospital, since she'd been in no shape to drive. He still had the car keys.

He rushed out to the lot, got into the car and took off, headed toward Hinkle's hotel. On the way, he pulled his phone out of his pocket to call Maria. She didn't answer. Damn. School. He checked the dashboard clock. It ought to be letting out any moment now. He left her a message, hoping she would check it, in case she'd gotten a call like he had, only without the warning. She had to know it was a trap.

So she'd stay away just like he was? Hell, with her savior complex, she'd be even more likely to rush in. He had to get there before her. He had to find a way to save the others. He thought about calling the police, but if they came in with sirens and guns blazing . . .

He couldn't risk it. He blew through a stoplight, only realizing when he was halfway through, and forced himself to slow down. If he got stopped and found to be driving without a license, he'd never get to his friends. But he pushed things to the very edge, and blasted through every yellow and just-changing light on the way. By the time he hit the hotel, he could barely contain himself. He threw himself out of the car as he pulled up, and didn't bother turning the car off in case he needed to make a quick getaway . . .

He heard voices as soon as he got up to Hinkle's door. One

voice in particular. "—knew you'd find him," he was saying. "Once I laced the scene with clues—just enough to make him a person of interest, not enough to get him arrested—it was only a matter of time. Reggie was never going to give up. One way or another, I knew we'd smoke out dear old dad."

*Liam.* Jack couldn't process. He experienced a lifetime's worth of emotions in a second. Happiness that Liam wasn't dead, squashed instantly by the stunned disbelief that he was the killer and terror at the thought that Maria and others might be counting on him and he didn't have the wisp of a plan.

There was only one door in, one window. Liam would be watching both. Maybe around back?

Liam had always liked games, from the ones they used to play together to this current craziness where he had everyone dancing to his tune. He tried to think how that knowledge would help him. But Liam held all the cards . . . all the hostages.

He couldn't just give in, give himself up. If he did that, it would be game over. Liam would have what he wanted. He would win. Jack didn't think any of them would survive the victory celebration.

There had to be some way . . .

Surveillance first, but quick, because anything could be happening in there. The motel was single story and long rather than tall or wide, which meant each room probably looked through to the back, if only through a bathroom window, but . . .

He ran around the back of the motel, staying low, beneath window height in case anyone was looking out. What he found was unfortunately exactly what he expected. No back doors. Bathroom windows just wide enough for ventilation in case of steam or . . . Fire. That gave him an idea. He ran down the row of rooms until he hit a pass-through to the front of the motel. Off it were two doorways—one to the front office and one to the coin-operated laundry that was open to residents. He ducked in there, searching and . . . found it. On the wall by the dryers was mounted a bright red fire extinguisher. He grabbed it off the wall and ran back the way he'd come, searching the lot for something he could use to hold down the spray trigger.

Unfortunately, the parking lot, while not pristine, was clean enough. He pounced on the little girl's pink hair band he'd missed in his first scan. It had been lost on the blacktop and, it appeared, run over a time or two until it was nearly flush with the ground.

Jack pulled up short under the bathroom window leading to Hinkle's room. This would be so much better if he wasn't alone. If someone else could hurl the fire extinguisher through the back as a distraction while he blasted in the front, but . . . He hoped someone inside would take advantage of the ruckus he created or that he'd be fast enough to do it himself.

He took a deep breath, pulled the pin on the fire extinguisher and depressed the spray lever, aiming the stream away from him. He quickly lashed the hair band around the lever to keep it in spraying position, then slammed the base of the extinguisher into the bathroom window. It shattered on impact and he pushed the extinguisher through into the room. There was a yelp from inside as the canister landed and went crazy, spraying in all directions and clattering noisily on the tile. Jack had to jump up to look through the shattered window and take in the scene—one body unmoving on the floor, despite the unholy racket, and one guy turning toward the explosion, knife in hand. There was another boy beneath him—Evan, he thought—but he was back on the ground before he could see if anyone was able to take advantage of his distraction. At least now he had an idea of what he faced inside. The flipside was, the extinguisher trick had announced him, taken away the element of surprise. Liam might not have seen *who* exactly had launched it, but he now knew someone was there.

Cursing, he raced for the front of the building again, searching for the tricycle he'd spotted earlier. It looked metal and sturdy. He hoped its appearance wasn't deceiving. He ran up to it, mentally apologizing to whoever it belonged to, and smashed it into the big front window with all his strength. It was tougher than the bathroom window, but not by much. It gave, glass shattering and flying everywhere. There were screams from inside, and then his own as he dove after the tricycle into the room and landed hard on a glass shard the size of a dagger.

RAYNA

All hell broke loose . . .

She screamed instinctively when the crash came through the bathroom and Liam yanked back in shock, momentarily letting up with the knife on Evan's throat. The look in his eyes was positively crazed.

The shock of it got Hinkle up off the bed and flying toward his son. At first, she thought he was going after Liam, that he'd tackle his son and send the knife flying and it would all be over, but instead he dove for the lighter and rag. He came up with both and a strange glint in his eyes. The resemblance to Liam had never been so pronounced.

"Stop," he said to the room at large, holding the lighter and rag together in threat. "I don't give a damn about the rest of you, but I'm getting out of here. I disappeared once, I can do it again."

He moved toward the doorway, everyone else staring, the only sound a metal canister going crazy in the bathroom and spraying froth at Liam and Evan's feet. Reggie still hadn't moved, and Rayna was panicked that he was seriously hurt. She wouldn't think dead.

Her gaze flew to the pepper spray bottles she and Kali had thrown away. If she could dive and get to one on time . . . She didn't see what she had to lose. Liam was never going to let them go.

Before she could go for it, there was a huge blow against the front window and then an explosion of shattered glass, shards flying like shrapnel. She screamed as a shard buried itself in her shoulder. Hinkle howled, others shrieked. Something else came flying through the window and then Jack was rising from the glass fall-out, bleeding from one knee.

He went straight for Hinkle, who was closest. Liam cursed and made a move to pull himself and Evan entirely into the bathroom so he could slam the door. He'd be trapped, but he'd have a hostage. A stand-off with Reggie and Evan's lives in the balance.

She wasn't going to let that happen. Apparently, Kali had the same idea, but Rayna was faster. She grabbed both canisters, tossed one to Kali, and launched herself at the door as it was closing, ramming it open again with her body and taking quick stock. Liam was still on top. She had a clear shot, and she went for it, screaming like a banshee as she sprayed the burning liquid straight in his crazed eyes.

He howled and rolled to the side, off of Evan, who immediately went for the knife Liam hadn't released. But eyes red and watering, already swelling, Liam must still have been able to see movement, because he slashed the knife furiously around himself, and Evan had to pull back or risk losing a finger or getting his wrists slashed. Instead, still on the floor, his scissored his legs, kicking hard and catching Liam in the side. Liam slashed in the direction the kick had come, and Evan's jeans split up the side, but she couldn't see if he was bleeding. There was too much foam.

*Foam!* The extinguisher was winding down now, but it was metal and heavy and would make a helluva weapon.

She couldn't see it directly through all of the mess, but over by the toilet was a spot where the foam still seemed to be churning, pumping out, maybe. She went for it, but the foam had made everything slippery, and jumping over the flailing bodies in her way she came down badly. Her ankle twisted, and she slid, going down with her hands out in front of her to catch herself. There wasn't enough floor left for her to hit it. Instead, one hand went into the toilet while the other slipped off the edge of the tub. She slammed her chin on the seat of the toilet and the pain blinded her momentarily. She didn't wait for her sight to come back to try to extricate herself. She had to get to that extinguisher before Liam got the upper hand with his knife or Hinkle made good his escape. She could only hope Kali and Jack had that handled.

But the extinguisher wasn't where she expected it to be. Her fall had sent it shooting away, sliding across the slick floor. Now it was hidden somewhere under all that foam, and she had no idea where.

A hand landed on hers out of nowhere—a claw, really, ragged nails suddenly digging into her flesh, pinning her in place. She followed the hand all the way to the Liam's raw, angry eyes. He still had her knife, and it was coming straight for her face.

She yanked frantically at the arm that held her pinned, but his claw was like a manacle bolting her in place. She slammed her eyes shut, hoping to protect them at least, bracing for impact . . .

But what came instead was the resounding and unmistakable crack of something hard breaking bone. Her eyes flew open, only to see Liam fall to the ground, lights gone out in his eyes as if a switch had been flipped, and behind him, only half off the floor, was Reggie, holding the extinguisher she'd unintentionally shot his way.

He sank right back to the floor, not looking too good himself, but alive! Wonderfully alive!

Evan jumped on top of Liam, not about to make the horror-movie mistake of assuming a killer was down for the count, and tossed the knife that had finally fallen from his hand into the bath-tub, away from easy reach. Then he kept his seat, pinning Liam's arms to the floor with the press of his knees.

Rayna got shakily to her feet to look back into the other room to see that Kali and Jack had Hinkle pinned as well, one on each arm.

They'd done it. They'd captured two killers.

On their own.

The door to the room suddenly crashed open and bounced against the wall as it was kicked in. An officer stood in its place, her gun out in a two handed grip as she looked around the room for a target. "Freeze," she said indiscriminately.

And then Officer Stiles's eyes grew about three sizes as she took in Norman Hinkle held tightly by two Meddlers and his son just visible through the bathroom door being pinned down by two more, dripping foam.

"Took you long enough," Rayna said.

Officer Stiles gave a laugh that sounded more like a cough

and let up on her two handed grip to go for her radio, which she used to call in the situation before holstering it in favor of her handcuffs.

Neither Mr. Hinkle nor his son were in any position to fight them.

"I was in the middle of something when you called," Stiles said as she slapped the cuffs on Hinkle. "Regardless, of what you all think, they call it 'police work' for a reason. It's a good thing I got your message when I did. Add to that the call dispatch sent out about property destruction at this address, and I figured I'd better come running. Speaking of property damage, I don't suppose you all know anything about that."

"That'd be Jack," Liam spat, glaring daggers at him. "Damn you. Never figured you for a hero."

"Are you making a statement?" Stiles asked. "Because I have to warn you that anything you say can and will be used against you. You have the right to an attorney . . ."

"He's invoking," his father said, glaring at her. At all of them. Like father, like son. Or vice versa.

Stiles glanced back coldly. "You can't invoke for him. Anyway, you're going to need a lawyer of your own."

Reggie started to rise from the floor, tears in his eyes. One bloodshot where a blood vessel must have burst from all the pressure. He tried to say something, probably about Marley's murder, but nothing came out, and from the cringe that crossed his face and the hand instantly raised to his throat, he wouldn't be trying again anytime soon.

"You just lay back down," Stiles ordered. "I've got an ambulance on the way, and you're going to be in it." Then her tone softened. "Anyway, I can guess what you're going to ask. I'm not the one in charge, so I can't promise anything, but with all that's happened, it's a pretty sure bet that we'll be reexamining your uncle's case."

Jack was bleeding. Evan was bleeding. But they'd done it. Help was on the way.

The others—Maria and Charlie—got there first, but Officer

Stiles wouldn't let them into the already-overcrowded hotel room. It was a crime scene. Jack dragged himself out, against her express orders, so that Maria could see he was okay and to fill them in. He was barely through the door when he staggered back under the weight of Maria throwing herself into his arms. For once, she didn't hear any grumbling from him.

Rayna turned back around to check on the others, and found herself wrapped in a hug all her own, pressed against Evan's chest. It was foamy and sweaty and maybe a little bloody, but still unbelievably amazing. For once she didn't let fear rule her. She didn't pull away, but wrapped her arms around him in return. They stayed that way until the ambulance and back up units arrived.

# CHAPTER 29

JACK

Jack left Kali playing video games with Eric and limped back to the porch where Maria sat waiting for him with the frou frou coffee drinks she'd brought. He'd called them that, *frou frou*, the first time he'd seen her with one and ever since she'd brought two. One for him. He'd never admit he was coming to like them.

They'd said good-bye to Amal yesterday, his body finally released to the family. The funeral had been . . . brutal didn't even begin to describe it. Mrs. Mehta had caved in on herself and cried silent tears the whole time. Amal's grandmother's tears were not so silent, and provided accompaniment all through the eulogy. His own eyes had been red and aching from the attempt to keep the tears in and from the number of times he wiped them away before they could fully form.

All the Meddlers had been there, even bruised, bloodied and battle-scarred, especially Reggie, who still had bandages around his head and neck.

He didn't know yet when Grace's funeral would be. He wasn't even sure it would be open to non-family. Her parents had been quiet, hiding from the press and everyone else after releasing one single statement and a photo that . . . no photo could say it all, but this one tried. It was Grace in the school's science lab, colorfully dressed but for a white lab coat. She was holding a test tube in clamps in one hand and flipping a thumbs up with the other. She looked serious and happy all at the same time. So full of life.

He still couldn't believe Liam had gone so far wrong. Was it bad genes? Truly like father, like son? It had come out that

Norman Hinkle hadn't been having an affair with Marley, but he'd wanted to. It was the pain of the rejection, or maybe the harshness of it that had made him snap. And Liam . . . he said he'd targeted Rayna because she'd never paid him any attention, never given him the time of day. Jack could only imagine that he'd been on the list for turning away from Liam when he withdrew from the world. And that Amal was there for whatever he and Liam had been fighting about. He didn't know about Grace or Maria. Maybe they'd ignored Liam too or hurt him in some way.

He supposed they'd find out soon enough. Liam was certainly talking. Now that he had the attention he craved, he was milking it for all he was worth. He wanted everyone to know how he'd pulled their strings, had them dancing to his tune. He wanted to brag about the intricacies of his plan.

*And he would have gotten away with it too, if it hadn't been for us meddling kids*, Jack thought. Liam had never said that, of course, but they were all thinking it. All of the Meddlers, of which, he supposed, he was now one.

"Penny for your thoughts?" Maria said. "No, wait, I bought you coffee. More than a penny, so technically . . ."

Jack realized he'd been staring at his coffee, swirling it around and around. He stopped, set it down and gazed into Maria's eyes. "Just thinking about Liam and . . . everything."

She put a hand over his. "I know. I can't help but think if someone had shown him more attention or . . ."

"No," Jack cut in. Not trying to be harsh, but not willing to let her assume any of the blame either. "Liam was broken. Rejection is a part of life. You don't kill people over it."

"No, you're right," she said.

She was silent for a minute, contemplating her own coffee, and Jack debated what to say next. He wondered whether it was too soon. But then, life was unsure. And unpredictable. He'd always known that, but somehow the message had passed him by.

"At least it brought us all together. At least—" *I have you. And friends.* The whole thing had changed him. He couldn't just withdraw from the world. He couldn't hide his family dysfunction away. Maybe it was time to bring it out into the light and see if there was any help to be had.

"And now you have me," Maria finished for him, reaching out to brush some of his hair back from his face, the better to see him.

## RAYNA

Rayna had put Reggie, Evan and Sierra to work cutting pictures and paper into leaves. She was making a new tree, still a celebration of life, but with darker undertones for the memorial they were holding at school on Friday for Amal and Grace. People had been invited to submit pictures, pieces of poetry, good-bye messages, memories. She was importing them all into a grand collage that would go up at the school.

She was glad Principal Grayson trusted her to do it and had committed to hanging it sight unseen. But she wasn't as concerned about having her work on display as doing justice to the lives they were celebrating.

It was important. It was serious . . . and it was healing. She hadn't been able to save them, but if she could preserve their memories, she'd be doing *something*. Something of significance.

Poor Reggie could still barely talk. His throat had been so damaged by Liam's ligature. But he was getting better. Evan's cuts were healing, and the scar on his cheek from where the belt had lashed him gave him a bit of a piratical look. It made Rayna sad to see it, but it was hard to hold onto that when Evan was talking like a pirate and forming his hand into a hook.

She felt guilty for every laugh he drew out of her. They were rare enough, but even still. She didn't feel a bit guilty for the kisses. He'd earned them and . . . well, hell, it wasn't about earning. It was about irresistibility and inevitability and *it just was*.

"Do you three want to place some of the leaves?" Rayna said. It cost her to ask, so much. She wanted it to be *her* piece, but this wasn't about her. They deserved a hand in it.

Evan, who knew what a perfectionist she was about her art, asked, "Really?" Hand to his chest as though she might have given him a heart attack.

She stuck out her tongue at him. "Yes. I'll direct, of course."

"Of course."

Sierra, Reggie and Evan all approached with leaves. Reggie had chosen a picture of Grace hiding behind a book from the camera person . . . him? Sierra had a larger leaf with words written on it. Rayna had provided a template for those who wanted to include a verse or whatever, but not everyone followed the guidelines. Evan held a photo of Amal at lunch, gesturing wildly as he explained something to the boy next to him, a bit oversized but at least it had been cut to shape.

"Not there!" Rayna said as Evan went to place it too close to another pic of Amal. "How about here, next to the black leaf. I don't want to have too many pictures jumbled up together. We need to space them out with the darker colors and the print."

Evan laughed. "I knew you weren't just going to let us have at it."

"Here?" Reggie asked when placing his. His hand was hovering beside two leaves that collectively formed a short poem, Robert Frost's *Nothing Gold Can Stay*. It put tears in her eyes every time she read it.

"Yeah, there," she said, throat constricting so that she barely got the words out.

Her hands were covered with glue, so she had to wipe her eyes on her forearm.

"Where do you want mine?" Sierra asked.

But the tears had taken over. "Anywhere you want," Rayna said, turning away. "Just—"

Evan came up behind her to hug her to him, and she let herself sob quietly, but just for a minute. And then they were joined by Reggie and Sierra, each one putting their arms around her, all of them sharing in the grief, before Evan shrugged Reggie off. "Okay, enough bromance already. Let's get this done."

The smile hit Rayna's face before she could squelch it, and

she wiped away the last of the tears before turning back to her collage.

"Right there," she said to Sierra, pointing her toward a spot that could use more of the written word. "That'll be perfect."

## THE END

# About the Author

Lucienne Diver spends her days agenting and plotting murder. Luckily, she limits the actual execution to fictional characters . . . so far as you know. She's the author of the popular *Vamped* series of young adult novels (think *Clueless* meets *Buffy the Vampire Slayer*), the *Latter-Day Olympians* contemporary fantasy series of myth, magic and mayhem, and young adult suspense, including FAULTLINES, also from Bella Rosa Books. Her short stories have been included in the STRIP-MAULED and FANGS FOR THE MAMMARIES anthologies edited by Esther Friesner for Baen Books, KICKING IT edited by Faith Hunter and Kalayna Price for Ace, and TRIBULATIONS, a *Rogue Mage* anthology, edited by Faith Hunter for Lore Seekers Press.

She lives in Florida with her husband and daughter, the two sweetest pups in the world, and an overflowing library under the mistaken impression that death is not allowed to take her until she has read ALL THE BOOKS.

www.ingramcontent.com/pod-product-compliance
Lightning Source LLC
Chambersburg PA
CBHW020602260626
47157CB00003B/822